SIX DAYS *in* BOMBAY

Also by Alka Joshi

The Jaipur Trilogy

The Henna Artist
The Secret-Keeper of Jaipur
The Perfumist of Paris

ALKA JOSHI

SIX DAYS *in* BOMBAY

HARPER
FICTION

An Imprint of HarperCollins *Publishers*

First published in the US in 2025 by Mira by arrangement with
Harlequin Books S.A.

First published in India by Harper Fiction 2025
An imprint of HarperCollins *Publishers*
HarperCollins *Publishers* India, Cyber City,
Building 10-A, Gurugram, Haryana – 122002, India
www.harpercollins.co.in

2 4 6 8 10 9 7 5 3 1

P-ISBN: 978-93-6989-890-9
E-ISBN: 978-93-6989-941-8

Printed and bound at
Thomson Press (India) Ltd

MIX
Paper | Supporting responsible forestry
FSC® C010615

This book is produced from independently certified FSC® paper to ensure responsible forest management.

HarperCollins Publishers, Macken House, 39/40 Mayor Street Upper, Dublin 1, D01 C9W8, Ireland

To women everywhere who refuse to be silenced.

You are my tribe.

BOMBAY

MAY 1937

CHAPTER 1

Mira winced as a spasm of pain shot through her. I put my palm on her forehead. Her skin was burning, like a *jalebi* fresh from a pot of boiling oil. I grabbed a cotton towel from a stack by her bedside, wet it in her water glass and pressed it to her forehead. Her brow relaxed. She let out a sigh.

"What about the baby?" she asked, her speech slurred.

I opened my mouth to tell her, then thought better of it. "Let me get the doctor for you, ma'am."

Her eyes shot open, as if she realized what I was going to say. "Oh, no!" Her eyes filled. "We must tell Paolo."

I blinked. According to her chart, her husband's name was Filip. Was it the morphine speaking? "Paolo?" I asked cautiously.

"My love. Taught me how to paint portraits. Until I met him, I could only paint landscapes. After that, it was as if people were the only things I could paint." She spoke breathlessly, as if she were trying to catch the words before they floated away. "And now, Whitney has him copying the masters, which is a pity. What a waste of his talent! People like hanging the fakes on their walls, hoping their guests won't know the difference. Most people wouldn't." She gripped my hand. "I'll have Filip bring my paintings." Her mouth twisted. "Of course, I only have the four left." Her English was inflected with something other than the speech of the *Burra Sahib* or the lilting way we Anglo-Indians spoke. It was softer, the hard sounds squashed down.

She groaned, loudly this time, squeezing my hand so hard it hurt. The morphine was wearing off. I glanced at the wall clock. Two more hours before her next dose.

I eased my hand out of hers, removed the compress from her forehead, now warmed from her skin, and immersed it in the water glass. When I replaced it on her brow, she seemed to relax a little. "You have a lovely smile."

A blush crept up my neck. Once, one of my teachers in third form had said the same thing to me within my mother's hearing. My mother had spat on the ground to ward off evil spirits who didn't approve of vanity. Ever since, I'd been wary of compliments, worried they might cause my mother to fall on her knees and pray to Krishna for my safety.

"Talk to me. Please," the painter pleaded as she clasped my hand once more, wanting me to keep her pain company. I looked at our joined hands, a study in opposites: hers blue-veined and pale, nails bitten to the quick, remnants of paint embedded in the fingerprint swirls, and mine the color of sand, scrubbed clean, slightly chapped at the fingertips. The warmth of her skin, slightly moist from the fever, was strangely comforting, the way my mother's touch was. Mira Novak seemed to crave intimacy as intensely as most patients avoided it; they wanted only to reclaim their body—the one we poked and prodded—as soon as possible, shrugging off the memory of their convalescence.

They had brought Miss Novak to Wadia Hospital around eleven o'clock at night. She was feverish and agitated, cradling her stomach with her arms. The back of her skirt was soaked with blood. Her husband, a pale man with broad shoulders, said she'd been complaining of pain for a few days.

The husband hadn't stayed. He left shortly after bringing her in. When Dr. Holbrook, the house surgeon, finished tending to her—she'd needed a few stitches and quite a bit of morphine—Matron assigned me to nurse her. This was not unusual. Patients who were the least bit foreign were assigned either to me or to Rebecca, the other Anglo-Indian nurse on the night shift, because we spoke fluent English. In the daytime, Matron would assign another Eurasian nurse or take care of the patient herself.

"She may be here awhile," Matron whispered, with a meaningful glance at me.

We're a small hospital, and the patient had been given a private room. It did not escape my notice that she could have been taken to a larger hospital popular with the British but, apparently, there had been need for discretion. Even so, rumors ricocheted around the halls. *This was no simple miscarriage. She had tried to do it herself. Her husband had done it. She had tried to take her own life.* I paid no attention. It was enough to know that a woman needed our help; our job was to heal her.

Even before I read her chart, I knew who she was. Mira Novak. The painter. Famous, even here in Bombay. I'd seen her photo and read about her in the *Bombay Chronicle*. The article said she had studied painting at the Accademia di Belle Arti di Firenza in Italy when she was just fifteen, the youngest student ever admitted. Her Hindu mother, a woman of high caste, had accompanied her daughter from their home in Prague to Florence, and ultimately to Paris, to nurture Mira's talent. Until the age of twenty, Mira had never once stepped foot in India. But when I looked at the images of her paintings in the article, I didn't see Paris or Florence or any of the other faraway places I dreamed about visiting one day. I saw village women in saris, their skin much darker than mine or Mira's. In her paintings, the women sat quietly, somberly, as they painted henna on each other's hands or tended sheep in the hills or pasted cow dung on the walls of their homes. Why was a young woman of privilege obsessed with the ordinary, the poor? I wondered.

She was six years older than I was—twenty-nine by the date

on her chart. To my mind, she was lovely. Smooth, unblemished skin. A brow line that angled toward hollowed cheekbones. Even though her eyes were closed, I could tell they were large, perhaps a little protuberant, but in a way that would be attractive in her face, dominating it, demanding the viewer's gaze. Her nose, which ended in a slightly upturned tip, gave her an imperious look. That must have come from her royal bloodline. She wasn't beautiful. My mother would have said she was striking, that her face had character.

Now she blinked, her eyes round, regarding me curiously, as if we hadn't spoken a few minutes earlier. Her pupils were constricted, and she seemed disoriented.

"Mrs. Novak?" I waited for a flicker of recognition. "You are at Wadia Hospital, ma'am. In Bombay. You were brought in several hours ago." I spoke quietly, in English accented with Hindi.

She frowned. She looked down at her torso, then back up at me. "Not Mrs.," she said, "Miss Novak."

"My apologies, ma'am." I didn't quite understand but I didn't let it show. How could a woman be married and still carry her maiden name? Still, my job was not to question, and after what happened in Calcutta, I was wary of speaking what was on my mind. There, I wasn't the only nurse whose breasts and behind were pinched by male patients, but I was the only one who had complained—often and loudly—which gave the Matron at the Catholic hospital a migraine and the license to banish me from her sight. I was a troublemaker, she said. Why hadn't I just kept my mouth shut like the others?

But I wasn't in Calcutta anymore. I was in Bombay. And I promised my mother things would be different here.

"How are you feeling, ma'am?"

She closed her eyes and laughed lightly. "I've been better, Nurse…" She let it hang, waiting for me to fill in the blank.

"Falstaff, ma'am."

"And your first name?"

Warm honey spread through my limbs. Most patients didn't bother with anything beyond *Nurse* or *Sister.* "It's Sona," I said shyly.

She opened her eyes. "Sona? Like..." She pointed to the tiny gold hoops on my earlobes.

I smiled. "Yes, ma'am. It means gold." I could have told her that my mother had pierced my ears on the third month after my birth. *Auspicious*, the pundit had told her. She'd taken me to a goldsmith—a safer choice than the tailor. The jeweler had threaded a thin black cord through the holes with a gold needle and told her to bring me back in two weeks. If I'd been able to speak at that age, I would have told my mother not to bother with the expense. The tiny gold hoops he inserted when my mother brought me back cost her two months' earnings.

But I said none of this to the new patient. I didn't talk about my life with anyone except Indira. And even with her, I only revealed a little at a time, the way Gandhi spun thread on his *charkha*, adding only as much cotton to the spool as he needed.

Mira cried out, more sharply this time. My body jerked in response. It wouldn't hurt to give her a smaller dose, would it? As soon as I did, Mira's eyes closed. I watched the painter until she was breathing evenly. Then, I left the room to attend to my other charges.

I found Ralph Stoddard in his striped cotton pajamas reading the newspaper by the light of his bedside lamp. He had broken his left leg when he slipped on the floor of his bungalow. His servant had recently finished polishing it, but Dr. Stoddard hadn't noticed. He'd been flicking through his mail, walking toward his study. A retired doctor, he was eighty, if a day. At his age, it was easy to break a bone or two.

"It's three o'clock in the morning, Doctor," I scolded.

He lowered a corner of the paper and regarded me through

the thick lenses of his spectacles, which made him look like an owl. "I've broken my leg, Nurse. Not my ability to tell time." A smile played about his lips—lips so thin they folded into his mouth. "Besides, with that racket—" he pointed with his chin toward his snoring roommate, Mr. Hassan "—who could catch a wink?" He went back to reading the paper. On the front page was more news about the Hindenburg disaster. Casualties continued to be found in Lakehurst, New Jersey, a place so far and exotic to me that I couldn't ever imagine seeing it in person.

"It says here England has started an emergency 999 service." He tapped the paper. "If India had one, I would have used it when I fell like a blasted domino in my house instead of waiting for Ramu to return from the shops." He folded the paper and set it aside. "Fancy a game?" he asked hopefully.

I hesitated. We were short-staffed, and I had many patients to look after. But it had been three hours since my last break, and I could use a breather. Besides, Dr. Stoddard's good humor was hard to resist. He was an insomniac who could always coax me into playing backgammon when I had a little time. At his insistence, his nephew Timothy had brought a game board from home, which Dr. Stoddard now kept on his bedside table.

I asked if we wouldn't wake Mr. Hassan in the other bed. He raised his eyebrows and observed dryly, "Not even the Hindenburg disaster could rouse that man."

When Dr. Stoddard had first asked me if I played, I'd said yes. There was a girl at school in Calcutta who'd tried to teach me. But the bell for the next class always rang before we could finish a game. She was a fast player; it took me forever to catch up.

"Smashing," he'd said, his smile sly. On our first game, I noticed he moved his stone six wedges instead of the five on his dice. I let him. After all, I was there to help him pass the time, not challenge him. After the fifth time he made a fast move, he threw up his hands. "Dammit, woman, why are you letting me cheat?"

Too startled to speak, I stared at him.

He took off his glasses to clean them with the bottom edge of his pajama top. "I cheat. Can't help myself. Need someone to tell me I'm a wanker."

I was appalled. "I don't think I'm allowed to say that, Doctor."

"Who says?"

"Well… Matron would never…"

He leaned across the board and pushed his spectacles farther back on his nose so his eyes were magnified. "She's not here then, is she? Unless she's hiding behind the door."

Automatically, I turned to look at the door to his room. When I turned around again, he had moved all his stones on his side of the board, effectively winning the game.

He gave me a charming smile. "Jolly bad luck for you. Another go, then?"

Tonight, as he set up the board, I turned my wrist to look at my watch. Mrs. Mehta was due for her pill in another half hour.

"Focus, Nurse. Focus," the doctor said.

These days, the game went faster. Ever since I'd taken to calling him on the liberties he took with his stones, he'd stopped cheating. I scrutinized the board with a sharper eye and strategized my moves. Ralph Stoddard had made a competitor out of me.

Ten minutes into the game, I heard my name being called. I looked over my shoulder to see my friend Indira, a stack of folded sheets covering half her face. She worked the same shift I did and we often walked home together, but I hadn't seen her since I clocked in at six this evening.

I excused myself and warned the doctor, "Do not move those stones while I'm gone. I have eyes in the back of my head."

"Cross my heart and hope to die," he said, "like a good Christian." We both knew he was lying; he was an atheist.

I followed Indira down the hall. Perhaps she needed my help changing a bed. But she opened the door to the stockroom and said, "Lock the door."

Puzzled, I did as she said.

Then she turned and lowered the stack of sheets that had obscured her face. There was a cut on her upper lip and a bruise on her cheek.

"Oh, Indira." I rushed to my friend and took the sheets from her, setting them down on the bench in the middle of the room. "Let me see." Gingerly, I touched her cheek where a red spot was starting to bloom. "Sit down," I commanded. Like a child, she did as she was told and started to cry.

The stockroom consisted of a wall of shelves where sheets, towels and pillowcases were stacked. At the far end was a first-aid closet. The nurses' lockers were on the opposite wall. (Doctors had their own changing room.) I loved the clean scent of this room: lavender, linen, rose water, a hint of antiseptic.

I hurried to the first-aid closet and removed the hypochlorite solution, antiseptic ointment and gauze. Back at the bench, I found Indira delicately trying to wipe away her tears, wincing when her hand touched the bruise.

As I cleaned the blood from her lip, I asked, "Balbir?"

She nodded.

I grit my teeth. It wasn't the first time her husband had laid a hand on her. "The cheekbone isn't shattered. Small comfort." I dried the cut with gauze, cleaned it with the antiseptic and applied a little ointment. "Was it the same this time?"

"*Hahn.*" She dropped her voice a few registers, imitating her husband. "'Three girls and no son! What is the matter with you?'" She switched to her normal speech. "As if I could do anything about it!" She was crying in earnest now, not bothering to wipe the tears.

"You'll ruin all my good work, you know," I said gently. I squatted in front of her and took her hands in mine.

She tried for a smile but the cut on her upper lip stopped her. "I know what you're going to say, Sona."

"And what's that?" I released her and bit off a strip of gauze, which I used to pad the swelling below her eyes.

"That having a son is beyond my control. I'm a nurse, Sona! I know that. But he doesn't believe it. You want me to leave him. You've never said it, but I know. And if I leave him, where am I going to go? His mother and father would throw me out of the house and keep the girls." She sniffed. I gave her more gauze to blow her nose. "Can you imagine what their lives would be like? I can't let that happen."

I sighed. Short of treating her wounds, there seemed to be nothing I could do for her. Centuries of tradition had made daughters, wives, mothers dispensable. They either did what their men and their in-laws wanted or they paid an untenable price. To say my mother had been lucky never to have met her English in-laws was laughable. She'd suffered also. When she took up with my father, her family had cut her off as cleanly as an errant thread on a sari.

In my locker, I kept a compact. My mother used cedarwood, sesame seeds and costus root to blend a face powder that made her skin tone lighter. She'd always been proud of my fair skin, which Indians prized for its ability to attract suitable mates, but she still wanted me to use the powder. She also swore by Afghan Snow, a beauty cream endorsed by the king of Afghanistan. I refused to use either, but to appease her I accepted her gifts and kept them in my locker at work. Now, I lightly dusted Indira's cheek and the top of her lip with the face powder.

Indira watched me. "Balbir wasn't always like this. Until our second was born, he would bring me a *laddoo* from the vendor down the street or a sari he'd seen at the bazaar. I loved him then. That was before he started going to Mahalaxmi." With the pressure of so many daughters and the dowries he would have to pay for their weddings, Indira's husband had started trying his luck at the horse track. So far, he'd been losing.

I put my hand on hers. She had happy memories of her husband, and that was good. But those memories paled in comparison to what he'd become.

A knock at the door startled us. Indira and I both stood up. I looked a question at her, and she nodded, straightening her nurse's apron. I unlocked and opened the door.

It was Rebecca, the other half-English nurse who worked at Wadia's. Her eyes narrowed when she saw us. "Don't you two have work to do?" She looked first at me, then at Indira behind me. I shielded Indira from Rebecca's scrutiny.

I gave her my warmest smile. "How are you, Rebecca? Your parents keeping well?" When I first came to Wadia's, I'd assumed she and I, because we shared a common heritage, would become friends. In the end, it was Indira and I who had become close. I wondered if it was because Matron assigned the patients who required the most sensitive handling to me, even though Rebecca had been at the hospital longer. And perhaps the rumors, which might have swayed Matron, were true. Supposedly, Rebecca had become involved with one of the married doctors, who had subsequently transferred to another city. I'd been the subject of rumors long enough—*Sona's father was an escaped convict who had to be sent back to England; he stole from the army before he left; he drugged her mother to bed her*—to know they rubbed your skin raw, making it bleed on the inside. I had no desire to defend my father, but I also didn't want Rebecca to assume I was one of the rumormongers. Sometimes, I brought her slices of toffee butter cake my mother had made or a pink peony from our garden to soften her, ease her into a friendship. So far, it hadn't worked.

Rebecca assumed a strange smile, full of teeth and no feeling. "We're all well, thank you. My sister is pregnant again. And your mother, Sona? How is she keeping? Not too lonely, I hope?"

I flinched. Rebecca still had both her parents. Her English mother had fallen in love with her Indian math teacher while she was at boarding school and married him. Rebecca had two siblings from that marriage—a real family—right here in Bombay. My father had abandoned my mother with two small children. It was something I confided to Rebecca when I first started working at Wadia. Then, she'd seemed friendly enough, gifting me a copy of *Jane Eyre*. Now, she was taking pleasure in reminding me that my mother had been deserted, and I regretted having been so indiscreet.

I felt my face grow warm, even as I answered, "She has her sewing."

Rebecca stepped closer, close enough for me to see the acne scars on her cheeks. "Seamstress for hire," she said, her head tilting in a gesture of concern. "Poor thing." She put a sympathetic arm on my shoulder. It made me shudder, and I stepped back until her arm fell away.

"I need to stop at the pharmacy." I excused myself, skirting around her to leave the stockroom.

Behind me, I heard Rebecca, her voice deceptively warm, say, "Did you fall down again, Indira?"

The hospital pharmacy was a small windowless room lined with shelves containing bottles of pills, herbs and liquids. It was staffed by a short, humorless man named Horace. Word had it that he was an Ayurvedic compounder long before the designation of pharmacist became official. Even without that title, Matron trusted him, having worked with him for twenty years. She also trusted us to sign out only the medication we needed when he left for lunch or for the day. Those of us on the night shift were used to recording which drugs we'd removed on behalf of which patients. I made a note on the clipboard attached to the door of his domain: *Mrs. Mehta* and *Miss Novak*.

My next stop was Mrs. Mehta's room. A woman of forty-five, she was a regular at the hospital. Sometimes complaining of back pain, sometimes indigestion, sometimes migraines that needed immediate attention. I'd learned over time that she had a very trying father-in-law, who lived with the family, and found fault with everything she served for dinner or the way his shirts were ironed or the chai that was served too cold. The only way she found relief was to spend a few days in the hospital.

Her husband, a sweet cherubic man who ran a factory where they made earthen clay pots, was devoted to his wife but frightened of his father, who owned the factory. The Mehta family was well-known in society circles, which included many of Wadia Hospital's patrons, so Matron looked the other way whenever his wife checked in.

As soon as I walked into her room, Mrs. Mehta, who was a light sleeper, raised herself to sitting. "I haven't slept a wink. I've been making chai in my sleep over and over so it will be hot enough for His Highness."

I smiled as I stacked pillows behind her back. "Why not make Bippi do it?" I'd become familiar with the family during Mrs. Mehta's frequent stays and knew quite a lot about her household: her favorite servant's name, her favorite food, her regret at being childless.

She brought the fingertips of one hand together up to her forehead, then let go as if she were sprinkling salt. "His Highness won't accept tea from a servant. It has to be made with my hands, as clumsy as he says they are."

I'd heard this before, of course. "I think they're lovely hands, ma'am."

Her expression brightened. She waved me over. We'd been through this before so I lowered my head without being asked. She placed her palms on my head to bless me. I didn't believe in gods, Indian or Christian, but I appreciated the gesture for the goodwill she wished me. I returned her smile.

I'd brought a pill in a small cup, which I handed to her, along with a glass of water. She took her medicine like a good patient. Matron told me they were sugar pills.

Mrs. Mehta turned eager eyes in my direction. “I hear we have a world-famous patient visiting us.”

That made me laugh. Mrs. Mehta thought of hospital stays as vacation visits, which is what they were to her.

“I know she’s female. And India only has the one female painter everyone knows about.” She looked to me for confirmation.

I pressed my lips to keep from smiling.

“So it must be Mira Novak?”

“You know I can neither confirm nor deny.”

She nodded sagely. *“‘A rogue* chowkidar *can make the village bankrupt.’”*

As troubled as Mrs. Mehta was about her situation at home, she had all the comforts I wished for my mother. A big house. A loving husband. A home full of servants. Enough saris to fill five armoires. Even with her limited resources, my mother had given me so much when she’d had so little. Would I ever be able to provide a life like Mrs. Mehta’s for my mother?

I shook my head. My dreams were cobwebs spun from gold. That’s what my mother would have said.

I stopped at Dr. Stoddard’s room long enough to tell him we’d pick up the game tomorrow, but he pointed to the board. He’d shifted all his stones to one side. I assumed my haughtiest expression and mouthed, “Wanker.”

He laughed. “Dr. Mishra played your side out for me.”

Dr. Mishra appeared from behind the door, a clipboard in his hand. He must have been making notes on Mr. Hassan’s chart. I was surprised to see the Muslim gentleman, now awake, engrossed in *Chokher Bali*, a novel of Tagore’s I’d read in Calcutta.

“I was looking in on Mr. Hassan and was somehow lured into the game,” Dr. Mishra said, his gaze straying to my cap, then my shoes, then the backgammon board on Dr. Stoddard’s table. Was I the only one who made him nervous or was he like this with all the other nurses? He was our house physician, young, unmarried. He'd been recruited from England the previous year. I'd heard he could have continued practicing there but decided to return to India. The nurses—the religious sisters as well as the medically trained nurses like me—were soft on him.

"Keen player Stoddard is. Beat me handily," Dr. Mishra said. The dimple on his chin deepened when he smiled. In a mock whisper, he said, "Quite sure he cheated." His two front teeth overlapped slightly in a way that made him appear humble.

I raised an eyebrow and said, "Popular opinion, that."

Dr. Mishra chuckled, sending his dark curls flying. "'We can't change the direction of the wind, only adjust the sails,' Nurse Falstaff." I wasn't aware he knew my name. The house surgeon and the registrar called all of us *Nurse*, as if we were interchangeable.

"Out, out, the both of you." Stoddard waved his hands, as if he were irritated by our teasing. But he was smiling.

Dr. Mishra turned to say his farewell to Mr. Hassan, who raised his book to wave goodbye. Dr. Mishra gestured with his chin at Dr. Stoddard's leg. "It's healing nicely. We can remove the cast within the week."

Stoddard rubbed his hands together and looked at me, his smile wicked. "Cracking! Looks like you'll have time to perfect your backgammon game."

"And you to perfect yours," I shot back with a smile.

"I'd better get back to my rounds," Dr. Mishra said, walking toward me, looking at my nurse's cap. I was still standing in the doorway. He tried to maneuver around me, smiling shyly at the terrazzo floor. I stepped to one side, only to be in his way again. We must have looked like a couple of awkward dancers. I caught a whiff of cardamom and lime on his lab coat as he finally slid past me.

"Oh, good evening, Nurse Trivedi," I heard him say out in the hallway. Rebecca's last name. So mine wasn't the only name he knew. It made me feel less special somehow.

My shift started at six in the evening and ended at four in the morning. Before I left, I went to Miss Novak's room to give her the morphine she was due. She woke up when she heard me moving about.

"I'm giving you the rest of the dose now before I leave." I rubbed the injection site with a cotton ball and antiseptic solution. She held on to my forearm and closed her eyes.

"Tell me about your father. I've been thinking about mine."

For a moment, I was speechless. I'd never had a patient ask me such a personal question before, and I'd never even talked to anyone about my father except Rebecca, back when we used to share a plate of my mother's bread and butter pudding. I placed the syringe in the enamel pan I'd brought and applied antiseptic where I'd injected the drug.

Mira was waiting patiently. Finally, I mumbled, "Why, ma'am?"

She opened her eyes. "Is he that odious?"

I said nothing.

"Did he hurt you?"

My jaw tightened.

"I see."

We regarded one another. Which of us would blink first? I wondered. Just because she found it easy to talk about intimate parts of her life, didn't mean she could expect me to. And I didn't appreciate being forced to reveal things about my family even my mother and I didn't talk about.

I walked to the foot of the bed and noted the medication on her chart. "Is there anything else you need, ma'am?"

She shook her head and closed her eyes once more. "This isn't over, Nurse Falstaff." Her breathing was now steady.

"Then I'll see you tomorrow evening, Miss Novak."

In the stockroom, I traded my uniform for a jumper and skirt. The uniform would stay in my locker. All the while, I couldn't shake off Mira's question. Back in Calcutta, everyone had known about my father. I'd only been three when he left. But I'd heard the whispers when I accompanied my mother to her clients' houses. He had come from Britain to work with Indian soldiers—many of whom had fought for England in the First World War—when he met my mother. She was a seamstress, and he needed a tear mended in his uniform. They had me, then my brother, and when I was three years old, he returned to England and never came back. I didn't have many memories of him. My mother didn't talk about him, and I never asked. Six months after he left, our family was down to two, my mother and me. My brother died before his second birthday. Why would Mira want me to relive the pain of his abandonment? What was it to her what I knew of my father or what I thought about him?

I was lost in thought when my replacement appeared. Roopa was one of the Indians newly recruited into the English nursing system. She was lively, always ready with a smile. She loved to tease and be teased. She was a favorite of the doctors and orderlies.

"How's the old codger?" she asked as she changed into her uniform. "Still causing trouble?"

I laughed. "Dr. Stoddard is waiting for you to brighten his day."

"Did you win today?"

"Not quite. But I'm up ten *paise*." The old doctor and I had started making bets, albeit small ones, when we played.

She snapped her apron on my arm. "Mind you don't spend it all in one place!" Her laughter followed her out of the stockroom.

With a lighter heart, I went down to the equipment room at the back of the hospital to get my bicycle. Most nights, I walked home with Indira to her neighborhood, and cycled the rest of the way home. At four o'clock in the morning, trams were not an option. My mother worried about my coming home at dawn, but the night shift paid much better than the day shift. And the streets were practically deserted in the early hours. It was quiet, peaceful.

The equipment room had a cement floor and walls painted gray. I found the chemical odors here—so different from the medicinal aromas on the floors above—pleasing somehow. More than once, I'd wondered if I'd have liked to work with my hands, making things instead of tending to people. But my mother had spent every rupee she made on my nurse training, counting on my income to support both of us. When I had received my certificate, I held her hand and pressed my forehead to hers, our private signal that all would be well. What I wouldn't do to ease her worries about our rent, the mutton she insisted on making for me because she was convinced it would bring me strength (even though she never ate meat), the nursing shoes I was required to wear (and the only part of my uniform she couldn't sew)! I wanted to give her the life she should have had instead of the one that had been forced upon her. And nursing was a way to build our savings so that one day I could.

Mohan worked here, cleaning the equipment, oiling the wheels of the gurneys, working the broiler and fixing anything that needed fixing. Tonight, he was repainting a wooden side table, his back to me. I watched him for a while. The smooth, even strokes of his brush soothed me.

I walked to the corner where the bicycles were kept. When he heard me, he looked up, straightened, and offered me a lopsided smile. I'd felt his eyes on me whenever he delivered a piece of equipment or furniture to our floor. He sought me out to say hello and always tried to chat me up. I held back; a woman of twenty-three without a husband (an anomaly in itself) didn't need to invite rumors of assignations that never took place.

However, Mohan was kind. He felt safe. He was a tall man with thick hair that started low on his forehead. His chin was blue-black, eager follicles already on their way to a new beard (although he'd probably shaved before the start of his shift). His shirt was stained with oil, grease and paint solvents—the room's perfume.

Like me, he worked evenings, probably because it paid more. I had always liked the calm of the night, the barely perceptible hum of hallways without visitors, without interruptions. Perhaps he did too.

Mohan wiped his paint-stained hands on a rag, which had seen its share of work over the years. I noticed his fingernails, perpetually outlined in black grease. No matter how many times he washed them, the oil remained a stubborn tenant. Those fingernails were one of the reasons I couldn't imagine Mohan in my bed. The image of his blackened cuticles on my hips sent a shiver through me—and not in the way he might have wished.

I had wheeled my bicycle almost to the doorway when I heard him clear his throat. "There's a showing of *Duniya Na Mane* at the Regal tomorrow afternoon." His smile was hopeful.

My face burned with embarrassment. I'd felt him working up to it yesterday and wheeled away with a quick goodbye, pretending I didn't know what he was about to ask. Now, standing a few feet from him, it was impossible to ignore the unspoken request. I looked down at my handlebars. This was the bicycle that one of my mother's clients had given her instead of paying what she owed for the dress she'd commissioned. My mother deserved more than a used bicycle. More than a two-hundred-square-foot flat so close to Victoria Terminus that the trains threatened to shatter the windows. Mohan wasn't the answer to what I wanted for my mother. And I didn't want to give him hope.

I slid my palms over the smooth steel of the handlebars. "My mother and I are going to the market tomorrow afternoon. She needs new shears." I stole a look at Mohan, whose shoulders now drooped.

His gaze fell on the rag in his hand. "Of course. I understand." He looked up with a brave smile. "We'll go some other time."

I nodded and wheeled the bicycle out the door. Oh, how I hated to let him down when he was such a good man, an honest man. When he married, he would be the kind of husband who would do anything for his wife, his children, his parents. But Mohan would remain a maintenance man. He had no ambitions to be anything else. As far as he was concerned, he'd reached the pinnacle of his career: a secure position with a reputable hospital. A job no one could take away from him. I wanted a larger life. I wasn't quite sure what it looked like or how I would get there, but I knew I wouldn't be working as a nurse forever. No, I had no future with Mohan.

Indira was waiting for me when I came out the door. She was quiet, thoughtful, as we walked toward her home.

The night air was peaceful, free of the low rumble of cars and trams, free of horses *clop-clopping* and the high-pitched hawking of fruit sellers. There was a quarter moon. Several pigeons cooed, milling around a half-eaten roti. We passed a tailor's where two men worked their machines under a dim bulb to meet the insatiable demands of the *Burra Sahib*'s army. The shop next door was also open. A man was weighing grain from a large jute sack into smaller cloth sacks to sell.

"I wish I could be like you, Sona." Indira walked as gracefully in her sari as my mother did. She pulled her cardigan closed and clasped her thin arms around her waist. Early morning was the coolest part of the day even if it was laced with humidity. Later, the temperature would reach ninety degrees in the shade.

"Why do you say that?" I knew of no one who would say they envied me. Not the girls at my government school in Calcutta. Nor my classmates at the convent school where I won a scholarship. Nor my nursing school. Who would want to trade places with a half-caste? Who wants to hear the slurs of *Chee-Chee* and *Blackie-White*? Who wants rocks thrown at them on their way to work? I wanted to trade places with Indira. She was living in a country that accepted her as she was. Generations of her family had lived in India, prayed in Hindu temples. She had the complexion of a roasted almond and dark, dark hair that gleamed in the light. She had family as long as a month and as wide as a year.

"Your mother didn't make you marry at seventeen, Sona. Here

you are at twenty-three, able to go anywhere by yourself. Your neighbors aren't gossiping about where you've been or what your children are up to. You are free."

I scoffed. "Hardly." My mother had been hinting at marriage for several years. So far, there had been no one who had appealed. There was an internist in Calcutta and a teacher I met through one of my nursing classmates, both of whom I found attractive, but one was betrothed, the other married.

Indira asked, "Why do you keep wanting to help me with Balbir? You'll only get yourself in trouble."

I stopped walking to look at my friend. "Remember my first day here at the hospital? You welcomed me with a plant in a small pot. You said chili peppers would sprout and when I harvested and dried them, I was to string them with limes to bring us good luck in our new home. I still have that plant, Indira. And Mum looks forward to making a new garland every year to hang across our threshold. In the meanwhile, she eats the chili peppers raw!" I shook my friend's shoulder gently to coax a smile from her. "Apart from you, no one seemed to understand how hard it was for us to move so far away from our home in Calcutta." My voice caught. "You made me feel we could make Bombay our home. For that, I will always be grateful."

She smiled and patted my shoulder.

Up ahead, a group of young men whispered hotly under a weak streetlamp. The University of Bombay was on our way home; students gathered at this intersection at all hours.

"You have to come, Nikesh!" urged the young man with the wire glasses, so like the ones Mr. Gandhi wore. "Surely you're tired of them strangling our textile industry—the one our ancestors built, yours and mine—for their own profit?"

"What good are protests? The British imprisoned fifty thousand Indians along with Gandhi-ji for protesting the salt tax—"

A bearded student interrupted, "And they only stopped when

the world shamed them into it. But they're back to taxing everything else we make. Where's the progress?"

The glasses-wearer smiled. "It's coming, my friends. And you're all coming to the protest. Now, who's for *chai*?" He held out his thermos.

It was the same everywhere, in Calcutta too. At the *subji-walla*. The *paan-walla*. The rumbling of a patient people who would be patient no more. Oust the English parasites! My father had been one of those parasites, hadn't he? The irony of my existence was not lost on me.

When we'd passed the students, I said, "Indira, if you ever need to stay with us, you know you're more than welcome." Mum and I only had the one charpoy, but I was sure we could manage something.

She shook her head. "And my children? Where would they go? No, Sona. It's kind of you to offer. And I'm grateful for your friendship, but I can't. This life is my fate, Sona. It is the will of *Bhagwan*."

I understood her in the way I understood Indian women who felt the life they were living had been predestined. That there was nothing they could do to change something that needed to run its course. Their children, like Indira's daughters, would follow the same fate. It made me feel helpless—and hopeless for them.

We said our goodbyes at the mouth of her neighborhood. Up ahead, there was a billboard for the popular movie *Jeevan Prabhat*. I knew the plot. A couple is unable to conceive so the husband takes a second wife. Would Balbir be tempted to do the same? I cycled home, saddened by the thought.

I had to be especially quiet when entering our building's courtyard this early in the morning. The landlord's family lived downstairs, and the couple who occupied the flat opposite ours on the open-air landing worked daylight hours and needed their sleep. As I mounted the stairs, I heard the loud snores of my landlords. When I reached the landing, excited moans and sharp cries told me the couple across from us was in the throes of making a family. I stopped for a moment to listen. Their lovemaking aroused a feeling that bloomed from my chest down to where my menses flowed. I'd never been with a man that way. Even the young clerk who had treated me to a movie at the Eros Cinema and tried to sneak a kiss afterward hadn't awakened that desire in me.

As soon as I unlocked the door to our tiny apartment, my mother came forward to greet me. She was always awake when I came home. I'd told her not to wait up—repeatedly—but she wouldn't listen. She told me she napped in the evening, right after I left for work, to catch up on her sleep. I'm not sure I believed her.

Her hand clutched the sleeve of a shirt she must have been sewing. "Everything is good?"

She meant did I still have a job. Keeping my job was mother's greatest concern. In Calcutta, I'd already lost one, and we couldn't afford to lose another. Her business of sewing and altering women's *salwar kameez*, gentlemen's woolen vests and children's school uniforms paid for the food we ate. But it was my income that paid for the rent, dishes, pots, shoes, coats and the medicine for my mother's heart, for which the hospital pharmacist kindly gave me a discount. Given how easy it was to walk away with medications in his absence at the pharmacy, I could have helped myself without noting it on his clipboard, but I'd never been tempted.

I took off my sweater and hung it on the nail behind the door. "Yes, Mum. Everything is fine," I said, imitating the way her head wagged side to side. It always made her laugh, and I liked to see her laugh. Her wrinkles eased; color returned to her cheeks. She searched my face to make sure I was telling her the truth, then patted my arm. She abandoned the half-sewn sleeve and went to the Primus stove to heat rice and *baingan* curry for me and make fresh tea. I sat down on a chair next to the dining table, which also doubled as my mother's sewing table. On the other side was a sewing machine and the twin of the sleeve she'd been clutching when she greeted me.

I put one elbow on the table and surveyed my surroundings. Our flat was just one small room. We shared the privy with the couple on this floor. Against one wall was a narrow bed, which my mother and I shared. A small counter for the Primus stove and preparation of food (although the dining table also served the same function) lined another wall. One bookcase held my nursing books, *Great Expectations*, *Folk Tales of Bengal*, *Emma*, R. K. Narayan's *Swami and Friends*, *Jane Eyre* (the one Rebecca gave me), *Middlemarch*, my mother's sewing magazines, the occasional *LIFE* magazine from the wife next door, and a stack of *Reader's Digest*s. After hearing stories from patients like Mira and Dr. Stoddard and Mrs. Mehta, I would come to this flat, deflated. It smelled of turmeric, sewing machine oil, my mother's sandalwood soap and medicine. Not disagreeable, just familiar. Would the rest of my life be as small, as confined, as this? But as soon as the thought slithered into my head, I was riddled with shame. This had been my mother's life also. How could I belittle what she'd done to feed us and house us and make sure I could have a profession that earned this well? Still, I did wonder: What would my life be like if I could break free of this cage?

I hadn't shared these thoughts with my mother, not wanting to make her feel as forlorn about our future as I did. Instinctively, I knew that were I to go, she would be left behind. I was all she had; my desertion would devastate her. Abandoned by her husband, her baby boy *and* her daughter? I couldn't bear to do that to her.

When she placed the tea and my dinner in front of me, she tucked a stray hair behind my ear, her touch warm against my cool skin. She sat on the other side of the table and picked up her sewing. "Tell me about your day."

She loved hearing stories about my patients. Private hospitals like mine catered to those who had lived in exotic places and came from worlds my mother had never seen. Her clients were local women whose husbands worked as insurance salesmen or clerks in a local bank.

I told her about Mira Novak. She hadn't known about the painter, so I described the paintings I'd seen in the *Bombay Chronicle*. She asked me what Mira looked like, what she and I talked about.

"She asked for my first name, Mum. No one ever does that. Not patients anyway. Even Matron calls me Nurse Falstaff. And she's known me for two years!"

Mum's eyes followed the journey of my spoon to my mouth, as if she were making sure I was really swallowing. I chewed the eggplant curry, which was spiced to my taste; my mother preferred hotter chilies.

"And Dr. Stoddard. How is he? Did you win tonight's game?"

I shook my head and ate another spoonful of cardamom rice. "His new project is to get the 999 emergency number for India. How he would have made it to the telephone with a broken leg is another question."

My mother's laugh was pure happiness. She found him amusing. For some reason, I didn't tell her that Dr. Mishra had finished the backgammon game for me. Or that he had called me by name too. Some things I kept to myself, lovely secrets that were just mine, at least for a little while.

My account of Mrs. Mehta was next, followed by Mr. Hassan with the appendix and a sixteen-year-old boy with tonsils. She seemed satisfied with my school report, as she referred to it.

She took my empty plate to the sink. She would wash the dishes in the morning so as not to disturb our neighbors at night with our flat's noisy pipes. She came back with a red chili from the plant Indira had given me. I watched her take a bite, imagining the searing heat in my gullet. It made my nose itch.

"Sona, there's something I need to talk to you about."

I felt a snag in my chest, like a sweater caught on a nail.

She finished the chili and used a wet cloth to wipe the table clean. "Mohan's father came to see me today."

"Mohan?"

She stopped scrubbing, frowned at me. "You know, the young man who works at your hospital?" She went to hang the towel from the lip of the sink.

"In the equipment room. That Mohan?"

Now she sat down across the table from me, behind her sewing machine, her most prized possession. She picked up the unfinished sleeve and slid it between the presser foot and the throat plate, lowering the back lever to keep the fabric in place. "Yes, Sona, that Mohan. Don't act so surprised. You told me the boy has been mooning at you." She pulled the hand wheel toward her to start sewing two seams together. "His father came to ask for your hand in marriage."

The room spun. So when Mohan asked me to go to the pictures with him, he already thought—or hoped—I was going to be a part of his family. He'd never worked up the courage to ask me out before.

Blood was pounding in my ears, making its way to my brain, where I felt it would explode. I shook my head. "No, Mum. Definitely not."

She blinked. "Why the face, Sona? He's a good man. You've said so yourself. He makes a good salary. He's kind. What more do you want?"

I looked at her, aghast. "What more do I want? The same thing you wanted when you met my father."

Her body stiffened. "What does that mean?"

I sighed. "Mum, I'm tired." We never talked about my father, and I didn't want to start now.

She sat back in her chair, the unfinished sleeve forgotten. "I want to know, Sona." When she was upset about something, she rubbed a spot on her chest, right above her heart. She did so now.

"I don't want to marry Mohan and that's that." I got up from my chair and slid it against the table. "I'm going to get ready for bed." There was so much I could say. That if she hadn't settled for someone her parents picked out for her, why should I? If she wouldn't settle for someone with grease under their fingernails, why should I? If she had had her freedom to choose her husband, why couldn't I? She was a good woman. She didn't deserve my anger. She had loved a man. She'd borne him two children, and he'd left. End of!

I went to fetch my towel and toothbrush and walked into the shared privy on the landing, wondering: Was I more my mother or my father? And if I hated my father, did that mean I hated the parts of me that were him? I studied my reflection in the mirror. My chestnut hair was still pinned up from work. I took the pins out and let it tumble down. Now, for the first time, I noticed my roots sprouted in a straight line across my forehead instead of following the curve of my temples. A gift from my mother. The line of my brows, which slanted downward, gave me a look of perpetual sadness—or was it disappointment? Resignation? Did I inherit that expression from my father? I tried for a different expression, widening my eyes, which raised my brows but made me resemble a startled animal. In my almond-shaped eyes, I saw my mother again. Was the color of my skin somewhere between my father's and my mother's? I would never be mistaken for British, but because of my accent and light skin, I might pass for a Parsi. My lips were neither thin nor plump. Those must be my father's. I tried a smile. It was crooked! Why had no one told me that before? Definitely not my mother's smile.

When I'd cleaned my teeth and washed my face, I went back to our flat. I kissed my mother's cheek, so soft and warm. She was only forty-one years old but looked older. I pressed my forehead to hers. "There will be others, Mum. Mohan isn't the only one." There had never been another proposal before, so the prospect seemed dim, but I was grateful that she didn't bring that up.

She pinched my cheek, the way she used to when I was a little girl and she wanted to hear me giggle. I complied.

Outside our door, there was the clang of milk bottles. It was five o'clock in the morning now. I opened it to see Anish, our *doodh-walla*, setting two bottles on our doorstep.

"*Theek hai*, Anish?"

"*Hahn-ji.* I made the milk especially tasty for you today." He laughed. Anish was a cheerful sort, barely twenty years old, who had inherited this job when his father died.

"Has your sister found work yet?" Without a father, it was impossible for his family to provide the dowry they would need to find a suitable husband for his sister. Anish had told me his fourteen-year-old sister, Anu, had been looking for a job.

His smile was uneven when he said, "*Bhagwan* has been good to us. She found *naukaree* close to here."

"*Accha?* Where?"

He indicated with his chin that it was south of us. He didn't meet my eye when he said it was a *haveli* of women. "There are seven of us at home," he said quietly.

They needed the money. I understood. Anu would be working at a house of courtesans. I had seen the *kotha* on my way to work when the vegetables and fruits were being delivered to their kitchen for the evening's entertainment. The courtesans fed their patrons well and were reputed to have dishes comparable to Bombay's Café Leopold, a favorite of Britishers, Parsis, Muslims and Hindus, many of whom were also regulars at the *kotha.*

What could I say to Anish? On the one hand, his family were sure to be shunned by their relatives and neighbors for having a daughter who sang and danced for men. On the other hand, the courtesans ran a profitable business, which meant Anu could provide for her family more lavishly than they could ever have dreamed. She could fill their bellies with rich curries. I knew courtesans had been part of the royal court before the British Raj began dissolving the Mughal Empire. Now, the women of

Anu's *kotha* owned factories, jewels, buildings. Their children were tutored privately within the house. Anu's chances of an arranged marriage may have suffered, but she would have financial independence that might have eluded her in a traditional union. I wasn't about to judge her choice. She was doing what was best for her family.

I assured Anish, "I'll visit Anu one of these days when I'm headed that way, *accha*?"

His face broke into a smile and the dimple on his left cheek winked at me. He turned and delivered Fatima's milk across the landing before sprinting down the stairs.

Fatima opened her door. I greeted a good morning to her.

She responded with a smile. "How is your job at the hospital? You work so late."

I laughed. "That's because I start so late." I added with a whisper, "You were working late yourself, *ji*."

She giggled, raising her shoulders in a conspiratorial shrug, before picking up the bottles and closing her door. She would be a mother long before her twenty-third birthday.

CHAPTER 2

At the start of my shift the next evening, my first task was to change Mira's sheets. I walked into her room to find Dr. Mishra pressing on her abdomen. Mira's face was pinched. Her breathing was labored.

When the doctor saw me, he said, "Nurse, could you help me for a moment?"

"Of course." I set the sheets down on the only chair in the room.

As soon as Mira saw me, she said, "Sona! Please…" She held out her hand for me to hold. She looked frightened. Her forehead was shiny with sweat. I clasped her hand.

"Just here." He placed my free hand just below Mira's navel. Surprised that he would ask me to do something nurses generally didn't, and even more surprised that he touched my hand, I pressed lightly on Mira's belly.

She let out a yelp that made my stomach cramp. I tried not to grimace. The doctor handed me his stethoscope. His body was so close I could hear him breathe, smell his lime aftershave. I moved the chest piece of the stethoscope in the area where my hand had been, keeping my expression neutral so as not to alarm Mira. I looked at Dr. Mishra as I handed back the stethoscope and tipped my head down slightly. *Yes, I hear it too.* A gurgling that indicated inflammation. He took a deep breath.

"What is it?" she asked now, staring at us.

Dr. Mishra smiled reassuringly. "Probably nothing. When you came to us, you were in the early months of pregnancy, and your body underwent significant trauma with the miscarriage. Dr. Holbrook took care of you in the operating theater. Sometimes, there's residual swelling afterward, which may be the cause of your pain." I noticed that when he talked to patients, he lost much of his shyness.

Mira let out the breath she'd been holding and nodded.

"We should check you out more thoroughly in a few hours when the house surgeon returns." He patted her shoulder. "Rest now." He made notes on her chart, looked vaguely in my direction to thank me and left the room.

"Take a deep breath, Miss Novak. I'm going to turn you on your side now." As I did, she let out a cry. The stitches, no doubt. The surgeon had repaired her from the outside but her insides still needed healing. Delicately, I pulled up her gown and removed the blood-soaked underwear and the wet menstrual cloths, taking care to place them in a container underneath the bed, out of sight. I picked up the rubbing alcohol and a small towel. With a light hand, I wiped her, changed the cloths and dressed her in a fresh gown. I scooted her to the far side of the bed so I could change the sheets on the side closest to me. She grimaced and clutched my hand to stop me.

"My mother was the one who discovered Paolo at the Venice Biennale in 1924," she continued as if we hadn't taken a break from the day before. "She fell so hard for him! Followed him back to Florence, dragging me along with her. When I finally met him, I could see what she saw in him. He's beautiful." She sighed. "Of course, Mama was always falling in love. Which is probably why I can't. She was so messy with it. Tantrums and fainting spells and screaming matches. Father stayed out of her way as much as possible when she was *innamorata*."

I eased my hand from her grip and continued making the

bed. A mother who had love affairs and didn't hide them from her husband? What did he think of her dalliances? Did he have affairs of his own? I'd heard of such marriages among film stars here in Bombay and rumors of unusual arrangements between wealthy couples.

"When I was little," she was now saying, "my father took loads of pictures of me. Dressed me up in costumes. Mama did not like that. When I began painting, she told him to stop and took over. I'd started being noticed, you see. She began showing me off. Like a prize she'd won at the *mela*... I'd craved her attention for so long, but...why did I have to paint for her to see me?"

Tears were rolling down her temples as I helped her lay on her back again. I wiped them for her with a clean cloth. Were those tears of pain or memory?

Mira sniffled. "Father, of course, has his own passions." She changed subjects as often as a woodpecker attacks a coconut palm. "Did you know he's building a synagogue right here in Bombay? There's a lot of money to be raised. He's good at that."

I went to the corner sink in the room to wash my hands and thought back to what I'd read about Jews like her father who had settled in Bombay. India was a refuge for them, safer than it was for the colonized Indians who had lived here for sixty-five millennia.

Mira was saying, "He's awfully busy with the planning. I'm sure he doesn't know I'm in the hospital."

My eyebrows shot up. As busy as he was building his synagogue, couldn't Mira's father find time to visit his only child after she had lost his only grandchild? His absence seemed almost intentional. Cruel, even. A reminder of my father.

I felt the need for fresh air. I opened the window in the room and leaned out. The delicate fragrance of the orchid tree outside her window entered the room, hesitantly at first, then settled in for the night. I listened for the mournful hoots of owls, the skittering night animals hunting for their dinner.

Behind me, Mira said, "It's like music, don't you think? Night music." I made to close the window, hastily, but she stopped me. She held out a hand for me to take. By now, I was getting used to this request from her.

"Eine Kleine Nachtmusik," she said. "A music of courtship. Supposed to be played at night. I imagine the animals being serenaded. The deer in the forest. Moths fluttering around the lights. The field mice." She'd worked her fingers between my own and was swinging our hands lightly as she hummed the piece. Like the animals of the night, I felt as if she was courting me. She began talking about her childhood friend Petra in Prague. "She was my first. We were just schoolgirls trying out something. She fell in love. Followed me around like sheep. It wasn't like that for me. I told you before I can't fall in love. I don't think I'm capable of it."

I tried not to show it, but a Ping-Pong ball was bouncing inside my chest. She had slept with another girl? Did women have sex with other women?

Mira, who'd been watching me, laughed and offered me a wry smile. "You're more Pip than Estella. I like that about you."

I pictured *Great Expectations* on my bookshelf at home. Mira, of course, was Estella. As the more shockable, chaste Pip, I marveled at how Mira could talk so openly about things most of us knew to keep to ourselves? Did she not care what other people thought of her or her family the way I obsessed about what they thought of my English father leaving my family? In that way, I was like most Indians, consumed by the judgment of others, so wary of the repercussions. I'd only known Mira for two days and I knew more about her life than the hundreds of patients I'd served over the years.

"You will love, Sona. Be sure of it." Mira kissed my hand and let go of it. She sighed, lost in the music only she could hear and memories only she was privy to.

Was that a prediction? Or a demand? I clasped my hands together to contain the warmth and the free spirit of Mira Novak a little while longer.

There was a commotion in Mrs. Mehta's room. I'd been looking for Indira, whom I hadn't seen today, when I passed the open door. Mr. Mehta was standing at the end of her bed, his hands clasped in front of his suit coat, a gesture of supplication. "You must come back, Rani. Bippi is threatening to quit. I like her biryani. I don't want her to leave."

Mrs. Mehta's face darkened, not a good sign. She had high blood pressure. "You like her biryani better than mine? Is that what you're telling me?"

Quietly, I stepped into the room and poured her a glass of water from the pitcher at her bedside.

"No, Rani, no!" Mr. Mehta decided to appeal to me. "Nurse Sona, you must know how dire the situation is. I know Rani confides in you. My father can be...demanding. Bippi won't stand for it."

His wife's nostrils flared. "I won't stand for it either. But you never hear me when I say it. Bippi says it and you come running to me."

Her husband looked as if he was on the verge of tears.

The window was ajar. I pushed it open farther and looked out at the night sky. "Is that a lovebird I hear, Mr. Mehta? You're the expert birder. What do you think?" I didn't know one birdsong from another, but I'd heard Mrs. Mehta mention their pet lovebirds.

His curiosity aroused, Mr. Mehta joined me at the window. He turned to his wife, excited. "Rani, come listen! It sounds just like our Dasya and Taara." To me, he said, "Dasya is the blue lovebird. Taara is green."

I helped Mrs. Mehta climb out of bed (although she didn't need it; she just liked the special attention). She came to stand next to her husband and placed her hand on his arm. "Are you feeding them enough? Or do you leave that to that lazy Bippi?"

"How can you even think I would let anyone else feed them? They were my gift to you."

Mrs. Mehta patted his arm and looked at him with such affection that he placed his hand over hers. "They'll be glad to see you," he said.

She walked back to her bed. "Tomorrow. I'll be home tomorrow. Sona, I'm ready for one of my pills now."

In between tending to patients and their dinners, I looked for Indira. I wanted to find out how her bruises were healing and tell her about Mohan's proposal. We chatted at least once during our shifts, sometimes eating our dinner together, but we hadn't crossed paths tonight. I passed Rebecca in the hallway and asked if she'd seen her. The other nurse narrowed her eyes and inspected my uniform. I looked down at my white skirt and apron. Had I spilled something on it? Rubbed against some blood?

"You know, you spend far too much time chatting. With Indira. With patients. With Dr. Mishra. Do you not have enough to do? I could do with fewer patients if you'd like some of mine."

In my convent school in Calcutta, I'd known another girl like Rebecca, who, for reasons I never understood, decided to dislike me. Her name was Charity. She made snide comments within my hearing about my missing father, my scholarship to a school my mother couldn't afford (the other girls came from comfortable circumstances) and my scuffed shoes (they were handed down from another student and, however much I polished them, they remained scuffed). What was it about me that made her hate me so? What had I ever done to Charity to make her treat me that way? At home, my mother would coax the story out of me when I failed to eat my dinner. I thought she would be angry at Charity on my behalf, tell me how unfair the girl was being. Instead, Mum would rock me and said, *Beti, you need courage to get through this life.* She would massage my head with coconut oil and sing to me to soothe my wounded feelings.

But I wasn't ten years old anymore and I wasn't about to run home and cry to my mother. "No one is stopping you from talking to your patients, Rebecca. It doesn't really take up much time, and I'm sure they would appreciate it."

I sidled past her to look in the stockroom. No Indira. I didn't remember her telling me she was taking the day off.

As I was leaving the stockroom, I heard Dr. Mishra cry out, "Morphine!" from Dr. Stoddard's room. Rebecca, who was in the hallway closest to Stoddard's room, hurried inside.

"No, no, no!" I whispered, praying it wasn't the old doctor. I ran in after her to find Dr. Stoddard sitting up in bed, his hair rumpled, looking about to see what was going on. Dr. Mishra was with the other patient, Mr. Hassan, the one whose appendix had been removed.

Rebecca brushed against my shoulder as she rushed out the door. Dr. Mishra looked up as I walked in and said, "It's his heart, Nurse Falstaff. Keep him steady. Talk to him. Nurse Trivedi has gone to the pharmacy to get morphine. He's going to be fine. I have to get Dr. Holbrook." Holbrook was our house surgeon. With that, Dr. Mishra left just as Rebecca, out of breath, brought the enamel pan with the loaded syringe, cotton balls and antiseptic solution.

I grabbed Mr. Hassan's hand. Already my chest was constricting in time with his and I was finding it hard to breathe, but I willed myself to stay calm. "You're going to be fine, Mr. Hassan," I cooed. "Did you hear the doctor just now? Nurse is here with medicine. The doctor is here too." I didn't want him to think Dr. Mishra had abandoned him.

Mr. Hassan was a big man. He was clutching his chest with one hand, his jaw clenched, his eyes squeezed shut, and shaking his head from side to side. Rebecca quickly cleaned the crook of his arm with antiseptic solution. Just as she was about to inject the morphine, Mr. Hassan twisted his body in pain, striking her arm. Rebecca almost lost control of the syringe—it was about to pierce the patient's lung, which would have been fatal. I flung Rebecca's arm away from his chest and held Mr. Hassan down with my elbow to keep him from moving and reopening his appendix scar. Rebecca stood with her mouth open, stunned at what might have happened, unable to move.

"Rebecca!" I said.

She shook herself and injected the syringe into the vein on the inside of his elbow. He calmed instantly. Both Rebecca and I were breathing heavily, but he was drifting off to sleep.

I released my hold on the patient and took a deep breath. I straightened my apron, wrinkled from the fracas. Rebecca was cleaning the site of his injection. Her face was mottled pink, red, pink.

"You didn't have to do that, you know," she said, her voice tight.

I was confused. "Do what?"

"Push me like that. I knew what I was doing."

My mouth fell open. "Rebecca, an injection to his lungs could have killed him," I whispered.

"I was nowhere close to his lungs." She grabbed the enamel pan, her knuckles white on the rim. "When I tell Matron, no doubt she'll take your side in this as she always does. You'd have to murder someone to get on her bad side!" She brushed past the bed so quickly I felt the whoosh of air as she left the room.

I stood still, my heart racing. I'd never had difficulty at Wadia with anyone but Rebecca. I liked our staff. As undermanned as we were, we worked efficiently together, largely because Matron managed us like a military battalion.

"Well, *I* jolly well like you." I turned to see Dr. Stoddard smiling cheerfully at me from his bed. I'd forgotten he was there. "You saved me from the dreaded snores tonight. Think he'll sleep all the way to morning?"

I nodded, still reeling from Rebecca's words. I heard voices in the hallway, which spurred me to action. I pulled Mr. Hassan's chart from the foot of his bed and wrote down what Rebecca and I had administered, how much and who had requested it.

Dr. Mishra walked in with Dr. Holbrook. The surgeon was saying, "Well, you should have asked me first."

Dr. Mishra blinked. "He was having a heart attack. We had to act quickly. And I did come get you as soon as I saw what was happening."

The other doctor said with feigned patience, "Where you come from, they might have called it a heart attack. In English medicine, it could have been an asthma attack or gas pain or an ulcer."

Dr. Mishra stood, incredulous. "I come from the finest medical school in England, Dr. Holbrook. The patient presented the symptoms of a heart attack."

Dr. Holbrook wasn't listening. He examined the patient with his stethoscope, pulled open his eyelids, inspected the site of the surgery for his appendix. "He's fine now, it seems."

"Because we acted in time, sir."

"Yes, well, Mishra. Could have been much worse for you. Lucky break." He clapped his hand on Dr. Mishra's shoulder and left the room. The young doctor's face was dark with anger.

I felt Dr. Mishra's frustration. Dr. Holbrook, with his patrician air, left no room for anyone else to make their case. Matron had told the nursing staff that Holbrook had been in India for thirty years and was used to doing things his own way, even if it wasn't the right way.

The young doctor turned to me, his gaze alighting on my face, my arm and the patient before saying, "Thank you, Nurse Falstaff." I handed him the chart and he signed his name. Then he left.

Dr. Stoddard waved me over and whispered, "Dear girl, that

snorer owes you and your handsome doctor his life, much to my chagrin." He winked merrily.

The heat rising up my neck meant my face would be turning pink soon. "He's not *my* handsome doctor. He's *a* handsome doctor. No, I didn't mean… He's not *not* handsome. Oh, just—" I was flustered in a way that wasn't like me. I rubbed my palms down my apron.

"I see I'm going to have to teach you how to bluff when we start playing gin rummy." He grinned, his crooked teeth on full display.

When I got home, my "report card" was full. There was Mira's talk of Paolo and Mozart, Mr. Hassan's heart attack and Mrs. Mehta's tirade.

There was also, of course, Dr. Mishra. Just thinking of Dr. Stoddard calling him *my handsome doctor* made my face warm. I didn't tell Mum about that. Nor did I tell her how I felt when Dr. Mishra touched my hand. She would jump to conclusions, and I didn't want to encourage her.

It had been an exhausting night, and after dinner, I immediately lay down for a nap. I stroked my cheek with the hand Dr. Mishra had placed on Mira's belly. How cool and dry his touch had been.

Two hours later, when sunlight filled the room, I decided to cycle to Indira's house. I'd asked Matron during my shift if Indira had called. Matron had scowled; she was disappointed in Indira. My friend had not sent a note to say that she had a cold or had been in an accident or was at home with a sick child, and Matron had stayed late, as she often did and was expected to do, to pick up the slack. That wasn't like Indira, who was conscientious to a fault.

By the time I got to Indira's house, my neck was damp and the backs of my knees were sweaty from cycling. Her family lived in a chawl built for mill workers over forty years ago. Age and neglect had blackened the timber and pitted the brick buildings. I stepped over exhausted laborers sleeping on the streets. Posters for the film Mohan had invited me to see, *Duniya Na Mane*, covered the walls of a *paan-walla* next door. This was not the Bombay the English knew. I looked for Indira's building number. On the ground floor was a barbershop. Off to one side was a stairwell that reeked of urine and turmeric, made more pungent by the close quarters. I mounted the stairs to the fourth floor, covering my nose with my hand. I couldn't help but thank our good fortune—Mum's and mine—to have found a cheap room—that we generously called a flat—in a simple two-story house pressed up against the train tracks. At all hours of the day, we heard the melancholy howl, the hissing and puffing, the screeching of trains. After a few months, we became used to the noise but not the quaking of the building as the trains sped past. Still, the only smell we had to endure was the belching of coal smoke, a smell I had learned to tolerate.

I knocked on a door that had once been painted green. It was evident that the next layer down had been blue. Where both colors had worn away was bare wood. The walls were scarred with spit from *paan* eaters who spewed red juice wherever they walked.

A man with plump cheeks and smallpox pits across his nose answered the door but only opened it halfway. A small girl—somewhere between two or three years—clung to his leg. She smiled shyly at me, pulling on her pink skirt. I thought of Rajat and his gummy smile, and I felt a hitch in my heart. What a lovely thing it had been to feel my brother's tiny body pressed against mine in sleep. I missed him terribly after he died, but for Mum's sake, I buried the feeling. It was only when I came face-to-face with little children that memories surfaced—like divers rising from the water, gasping for air—how his laugh had sounded like a hiccup, how he had loved playing with my hair. I swallowed.

Indira's husband wore a white undershirt—or it had been white once upon a time—under a plaid short-sleeve shirt and tan pants. He was in the process of putting on a silver-colored watch, the edges revealing brass links underneath. His frown had chiseled two permanent gouges between his heavy brows. He looked me up and down. My long skirt and shirt must have tipped him off to the half of me that was *Angreji*. In this neighborhood, I would have been better off borrowing my mother's sari.

"*Namaskar.* I'm looking for Indira."

"She is sick."

"Oh. She hadn't called the hospital. We were worried."

"Too sick to call." His black eyes were burrowing holes into mine. My knees trembled. I, who prided myself on my boldness, felt fear, the kind I imagined Indira felt every day. I looked at the little girl. She picked her nose and went inside the house, bored now by the stranger.

"May I see her? I need to know if she'll be coming to help me with the patients later today." It was a tiny lie, but at its heart, it was trying to be true. Indira was assigned to a different roster of patients. My hands had curled into fists, and my fingernails were carving moons on my palms. In my ears was a high-pitched alarm that I knew no one else could hear, like dogs who sense danger before humans do.

"She's sleeping. And I need to leave for work." He managed to slide his body out of the half-open door and shut it behind him. He used his keys to lock the door. Extending his arm to indicate that I should precede him down the stairs, he left me no choice but to leave without having spoken to my friend.

By the time I got back on my bicycle, which an old Muslim man had been guarding for me, my whole body was shaking so much that I had to dismount and walk with the bike until I felt able to steady myself on it.

CHAPTER 3

That evening, Matron found me as I was changing into my uniform. She asked me to come see her when I was done. I assumed it was because she wanted me to cover Indira's patients. Perhaps my friend had called in sick again?

Matron's office looked like a monk's sanctuary. There was a large wooden cross on the wall behind her desk. A smaller one hung next to a Jesus statue on one wall. Every paper on her desk was neatly arranged. There were no stray items or medical apparatus or even a wayward pencil anywhere. I wouldn't have been surprised if the file cabinets had organized themselves. She'd been trained in the Florence Nightingale School and followed its tenets of obedience, discipline and strict adherence to protocols.

She was sitting behind her desk, writing. Matron was a large-boned Englishwoman with ramrod posture and a dark birthmark on one cheek that resembled a cross. When she saw me, she indicated the plain wooden seat in front of her desk. Laying her pen down, she took off her gold-rimmed spectacles. I waited for her to start; it was customary. We both sat for a few moments looking at each other. Her uniform was spotless, crisply ironed. It was this attention to detail and her management of the nursing staff with perfect precision that commanded the respect of the hospital's doctors.

"I've heard troubling news," she said.

My heartbeat quickened. "About Indira? Is she alright, Matron?"

She played with the earpieces of her eyeglasses. "It's about you."

My heartbeat quickened. I sat up straighter in the chair. What had I done? Had I been negligent in my duties with a patient?

"Yesterday, you and Rebecca assisted in a critical situation. With one Mr. Hassan."

I nodded. "Yes, a heart attack."

She tilted her head. "Dr. Holbrook begs to differ with Dr. Mishra on that. In any case, you compromised the health of the patient by jostling Nurse Trivedi's hand, which at the time was holding a syringe loaded with morphine." She folded her hands, one on top of the other, on her desk.

My mouth opened. I clamped it shut. Anger, hot, molten and swift, shot up my spine. This was what Rebecca had threatened. *When I tell Matron no doubt she'll take your side...* Instead of getting credit for a job well done, which I hadn't even sought, I was being held accountable for an imaginary failure. I wanted to shout: *A man's life was saved!* But I forced myself to count to ten, as my mother had taught me. I could not lose another opportunity to set a little aside for a bigger flat for Mum and me. I waited for Matron to continue.

"It is my responsibility at this hospital to ensure the well-being of our patients while they're in my nursing care. Your action yesterday might have resulted in a fatality, which would have meant I'd been derelict in my duties as the guardian of our patients. You are a good nurse. Efficient. Well-liked by the patients. Reliable. What happened?"

My hands had gone cold. I folded them, one on top of the other. I was taking time to gather my thoughts, carefully choosing my words. "It was fortunate, Matron, that Rebecc—Nurse Trivedi and I were able to support one another in a crisis situation." I paused. "She is an excellent nurse. All would have been well had Mr. Hassan not elbowed her while she was administering the injection. The needle was headed for his lungs." I looked down at my hands, as if they could tell me what to say next. "Which would have been disastrous." I met her eye again, imploring her to understand what I wouldn't say out loud. That Rebecca had been about to make a costly mistake, and I stopped it from happening.

Matron frowned. "I see." She unclasped her hands, steepled her fingers. "As to the other point..."

There was *more*?

"It's come to my attention that you've been fraternizing excessively with patients. A little of that is acceptable, but you have responsibilities that would leave you little time for socializing."

My breath caught in my throat. Rebecca again. I wanted to tell Matron that I never spent time chatting if I hadn't already taken care of my work. Was she implying that I'd forgotten someone's medication? Neglected to bathe patients or change their gowns? Forgotten to record their vitals on their charts? I always double-checked my work. I kept my patients' bedding clean, the air in their rooms fresh. While nurses like Rebecca spread gossip like cream butter on toast, I rolled bandages and organized the stockroom supplies. I was never late and never left early. If, after I'd completed my work, I tried to put patients at ease, what was the harm in it? They were with us in distress. Surely, they needed our support in all ways?

I swallowed the words I didn't utter out loud. All I said was, "If I am derelict in my duties, I would welcome the opportunity to be corrected."

She pursed her lip. "The problem is that as a nurse, if you become involved with patients, it affects your work, your judgment. You may be the best of nurses—and I think you are, your patients speak highly of you—but if those you work with mistrust your judgment, there is a problem. A complaint like this one is something I have to pay attention to. I am going to authorize the deduction of two days' pay from your check." She looked away then, as if it was something she was reluctant to do.

Two days' pay? I needed that money. Every rupee counted if I was going to save up enough to give Mum a better place to live. To buy her the clothes in velvet and satin she usually made for others. The heat I felt behind my eyes was a warning of tears to come. Why did this keep happening to me? I wanted to tell Matron, *I hadn't been the troublemaker.* What had I ever done to Rebecca to make her hate me so?

Matron put her spectacles back on her nose. "Do you have any questions?"

I shook my head. The meeting was over.

My talk with Matron had rattled me. I ran to the stockroom where I pushed a fist in my mouth to stifle my scream. I tried not to think of what had happened in Calcutta. Ever since I was old enough to go by myself, I'd been delivering my mother's sewing projects all over the city. Sometimes it was the *chowkidar* who tried it. Sometimes a servant. Sometimes the husband groped me. When it started happening during my nurse training, I'd had enough. My body was my own; why did men think it belonged to them as well? It had been different here in Bombay, at the smaller Wadia Hospital. Perhaps because I was older and didn't look as vulnerable. Now, however, I had a new problem. Rebecca was determined to make my life difficult. And Matron, a stickler for discipline, would be inclined to listen to her.

When I felt calmer, I smoothed my uniform, re-pinned my nurse's cap and went to see Mira. She'd been complaining of pain in her abdomen again and I was told to give her low doses of morphine at shorter intervals. Now, the first thing I noticed was that her color was off. Paler than usual. She had dark circles under those large eyes. As I walked into the room, I saw Dr. Mishra at the sink, washing his hands.

Mira addressed the wall behind me. "Oh, Filip, don't go just yet. You have to meet Sona. Remember? I've been telling you all about her."

I turned around to see a gentleman in an ivory three-piece suit to the left of the door. He practically blended into the wall. He was slightly shorter than Dr. Mishra but more sturdily built. His hair was almost a white-blond, another reason he disappeared into the white wall. I'd been thinking of Mira's husband as a ghost, and here he was in the flesh. He was smoking a pipe. He turned to me and nodded, his expression pleasant but vacant.

Mira extended her hand for me to take. "Filip was a dear to bring me four of my favorite paintings. Well, all my paintings are my favorites, but these are especially important to me. Now, Amit and I were having the most frightful row, Sona." She called Dr. Mishra by his first name?

The young doctor was standing by the bed now. He smiled, the dimple on his chin getting deeper. "Well, really... I would hardly call it a row. A preference perhaps." He looked to Filip for confirmation. Mira's husband nodded with a smile. He didn't seem to mind that Dr. Mishra stood within kissing distance of his wife while he stood at the edge of the room, like a distant relative or a porter.

"Which of the paintings do you prefer, Sona?" Mira lifted her chin toward the wall opposite her bed.

I turned around. Four paintings leaned against the wall. Each was somber in color—cinnamon, caramel, coffee, walnut. They were different in subject matter. I let go of her hand and stepped closer to inspect them. In the one closest to me, five figures sat on the ground, preparing a woman with the fairest complexion for a wedding. The darkest woman among them was fixing her hair. The woman opposite the bride held a container of white powder in the process of making the intended's face even brighter. The bride's hands were painted with henna. Two children, equally as dark as the hairdresser, watched the scene.

My eyes strayed to the second canvas, one with a cinnamon background. Five youths sat in a semicircle with a fifth, the smallest, facing away from them. Each only wore a *dhoti*. A white thread stretched from the left shoulder of the young men across their chest to their right hip. The three oldest boys had gathered their hair in a topknot. I'd seen ascetic Brahmins like these quietly praying for the welfare of others or studying scriptures along the Queen's Necklace, beside the Back Bay. Only the forehead of the middle figure, the fairest, was painted with long *tilaks*. He must have been their teacher.

Behind me, Mira said in a whisper, "Those markings on the forehead fascinate me."

I turned around to see Dr. Mishra, his arms folded across his chest, lean toward her, as if they were alone in a museum discussing an exhibit. "Did you know, Mira, that they represent Lord Narayana and Lakshmi?" He called her by her first name too? When had they become friends? Did Mira hold Dr. Mishra's hand when I wasn't around? A wave of jealousy, something I rarely felt, surprised me. I blushed, ashamed of myself. Why shouldn't they have a right to friendship? I'd seen doctors bond with their patients, so why would this be unusual? Didn't I too favor some patients over others?

I looked for Filip, but he was gone. I remembered the nurses referring to him as the invisible husband, and now I could see why. No one acknowledged his leaving. It was as if he hadn't been there in the first place.

The doctor and Mira continued talking in low voices. I'd seen them like this before as I went about closing the drapes, refreshing her water jug, getting her morphine shot ready. They talked about her art, places she had studied, the paintings he had seen in Madrid or Padua or Amsterdam. They mentioned music from the many countries they had visited—how it differed and how it was similar. They lived in a world so foreign to me, filled with memories they could pluck, like cards from a deck. I felt a twinge of envy. If I'd been born under different circumstances or if my father hadn't deserted us or if he'd taken us to England with him, I too could participate in their conversations, casually dropping the name of the latest opera I'd seen in London or how the river Wein in Vienna glows at sunset or whether I preferred Donatello's *David* to Michelangelo's. We would have made a pretty threesome. All of us in our twenties. The gifted painter, the handsome doctor, the enigmatic nurse. What a fantasist I was!

I forced myself to ignore them and to study the third painting. Three girls, their black hair parted down the middle, heads covered in *dupattas* of various colors, gazed forlornly at the ground. I felt their quiet resignation, their surrender to a fate not of their making. One of them could have been Indira.

The fourth painting was unlike the rest. A dark-haired man in a white shirt, his expression somber, staring at nothing in particular. In his arms were three apples. Even with his long nose and pointed chin, there was something appealing about him. It was a sensuous painting, faintly erotic. The background was subtle shades of ochre.

I scanned the paintings one more time. I turned to face Mira, who was explaining something to the doctor, her hands animated. Should I interrupt them?

Dr. Mishra noticed me first. He looked away and scratched his cheek. Mira's eyes shifted to me. "Well?"

"The first one."

Mira clasped her hands in front of her chest. "*The Acceptance.* This series is my latest. It's that flat dimension of Giotto's—and of course Gauguin's—I was after. There isn't a lot of detail in the figures. See how the bride's hands are red with henna but there is no specific design? I want the observer's imagination to work here. Each observer will create something different." Her face came alive when she spoke of painting, of the nuances that differentiated one painter's style from another's. "People might say—and have said—a child could paint these. But you'd be surprised how difficult it is to paint simply. Just look at Picasso."

Perhaps my jealousy made me bold enough to say, "Which was your favorite, Dr. Mishra?" It wasn't often that I addressed the doctor for anything other than a medical matter. If it surprised him, he didn't show it.

"The three young women. I've seen that look on the faces of girls who deliver babies at too young an age."

The painter put her hand on his arm, smiling up at him. "Exactly."

Dr. Mishra stood straighter. "I don't often get to talk paintings, but I do need to talk medicine now and again." He said to Mira, serious now, "Let Nurse Falstaff know how you're feeling. I've increased your dosage, which should help. I am a little concerned about the lingering pain. Has Dr. Holbrook been to see you?"

Mira shook her head and reached out a hand for him to clasp. "You will come see me before you leave tonight?"

He didn't take her hand but patted her forearm. "I make no promises." He smiled first at her, then at me. He tipped his head slightly, his gray eyes lingering on mine a moment, sending a jolt through me. My legs felt unsteady. My breath sped up. When he'd left the room, I shook my head to cast off the strange feeling.

Mira was looking at me with a crafty smile. "Quite the catch, isn't he?"

"Is he?" I didn't want to pursue this line of conversation. After the proposal from Mohan's father, I was wary of entertaining any entanglements. I took the thermometer from my nurse's apron and unscrewed the cap. She held her mouth open long enough for me to insert it under her tongue. I could feel her watching me as I went about the room, cracking open the window to let out the stale air.

Behind me, Mira said, "100.5. A little high."

I turned and took the thermometer from her. "How is the pain?" I shook the thermometer to clear the reading and noted the temperature on her chart.

"Tolerable as long as I keep my mind off it." She shifted her body, clearly uncomfortable in the bed. I had a feeling she was downplaying her suffering in the doctor's presence.

"Stay please." She kept her voice light, but I heard the plea.

I hesitated. Would Matron be watching my every move now? Would she send Rebecca to spy on me to see if I was fraternizing too much with Mira? I looked at the wall clock and calculated how many patients I needed to check up on in the next hour. I could spend perhaps ten more minutes with Mira.

I pointed to the fourth canvas. "He's different from the rest."

She laughed. It was a husky sound, as if she'd been a smoker all her life. "That is Paolo. He took me to see Giotto's work in Florence—those large murals packed with people in voluminous robes. I loved it. And tried to imitate it." She held an index finger in the air as if she were making a point. "Paolo always said if you could imitate the greats, you could become a great painter. I imitated Giotto's style but instead of religious figures, I painted people on the streets of Florence, lining up to see the inside of the Duomo. Or buying apples at the San Lorenzo Market. Those were some of Jo's—Josephine's—favorites. She sold so many of them. She wanted me to do more like them but set them at the flower market or the Gare de Lyon in Paris." She stopped, as if picturing the paintings. "I was only eighteen you know when I got to Paris. I wanted to stay with Paolo in Florence, but he said I would be throwing a wonderful opportunity away if I didn't go." She sighed. Perhaps she was picturing him. If he looked anything like the painting, I could see why.

"Did you like Paris?" I would have loved to go, but it was an impossible dream.

She spread her arms wide. "Oh, Sona! It was most incredible.

That's where I first saw the Impressionists. I tried my hand at Gauguin's style. I fell in love with Cézanne's apples. And Degas's ballet dancers. It was fabulous when Petra joined me in Paris. She would sit for me. For hours. She was a great model. She's the one with the long hair in *Two Women*. The painting that got me into the Salon." She paused. "She wanted to be a painter too. Maybe because I was one. She wanted to do everything I did. Petra's technique was good, but her work lacked…a focus, a central idea." Mira flushed, looking embarrassed. "I'm afraid I was too harsh with her. Critical. Impatient. In those days, I could be heartless. I told her she should give up painting. That she'd never be any good." She released a wistful sigh. "I can still see her face, the way her eyelids drooped and her mouth went slack. She thought I walked above the clouds, and there I was, squashing her like a flea." She looked down at her hands, playing with the sheet. "I don't know why I did that. And I wished to God I hadn't."

She hadn't been this miserable asking about her baby that first day. In fact, she hadn't mentioned the baby since. I'd never nursed a mother who seemed so indifferent to birth and death. Mira was far more passionate about painting than the child she'd been carrying.

Mira shook her head, as if shaking off her melancholy and plastered a smile on her face. "You liked that one of Po but you didn't say so when Dr. Mishra was here."

My cheeks were on fire. I didn't realize she'd noticed. I said, "Dr. Mishra might think me…"

Mira laughed. "Wanton? Longing for a man? Sona, don't you know it's alright to be all those things and still be who you are? Look at me. I'm all those things—wanton, outspoken, depraved, craving everything and wanting more. I couldn't be an artist if I couldn't show those feelings on canvas. Or in person!"

I found myself wondering what would happen if I told people what I thought? *Mrs. Mehta, tell your father-in-law to stop being such a tosser!* The very idea! But it emboldened me to ask Mira, "Why do you choose to paint such somber women? As if they take no pleasure in their lives. Don't village women experience joy as well?"

Her eyes were dancing when she said, "I would put it to you, dear Sona, that there is joy in the stillness of my paintings. The serenity of the Indian people—so unlike Europeans who seem obsessed with what the future holds—soothes me. Even as the women roll chapattis. Even as the *dhobis* slap wet cloth against the rocks. Even as the henna artist draws on the hands of a betrothed, there is joy. And warmth. And tranquility. Of the likes I haven't found in Europe. I needed to come to India to find it."

She narrowed her eyes and pursed her lips. "You're half Indian like me, aren't you?" It was part answer, part question.

Ah, there it was. The thing that separated me from those who had a right to belong in this country. If they didn't say it to my face, they said it behind my back. They were either curious or disdainful. I let go of her hand and began straightening the sheet on my side of her bed. "My mother is Indian." I didn't tell her I hated my last name. I didn't tell her I hadn't seen my father since the age of three. I didn't tell her I wished him dead. I didn't tell her that if it weren't for him, my mother's life would have been so much better.

She watched me as I tucked the sheet, a little too forcefully, around the bottom corners of the bed. "My mother is from Lucknow. My father is Czech. I've been both Indian and European for so long that I'm not sure which side is more me."

There was a major difference between us, even in our *half-half* heritage, however. She considered her otherness a source of pride. She flaunted it, like a peacock's train. It made her special. It made her an artist. A painter. I, on the other hand, wore my otherness like a scratchy blouse that I couldn't wait to take off at the end of the day.

I looked at my watch, realizing I was late attending to the

pregnant patient who had taken Mrs. Mehta's place now that Mr. Mehta had taken his wife home.

I excused myself, thanking Mira for sharing her work with me. When I'd first met her, I'd thought Mira's ways were too big for the world I inhabited. But like breath, my life seemed to expand whenever I was around her.

I went to the stockroom to drop off the soiled sheets from Mira's bed and get fresh ones for the very pregnant Mrs. Roy. Indira was sitting on the bench in the middle of the room, crying. When she saw me, she turned away. I dumped the sheets in the rolling canvas hamper and went to her. Her hands were cold and her teeth were chattering.

"Balbir said you'd stopped by," she said. "He thought I'd asked you to come. You can't come to the house again, Sona. Ever." Her tears were wetting her uniform. "My girls, they saw everything. They saw their father beat their mother. He told them it was because I was bad. I had done something wrong. I saw the look on their faces. They didn't want to believe him, but with no one to speak up for me, they are bound to. If everyone around you is telling you the sky is red, you're going to start believing it."

I rubbed her hands to warm them. "Oh, Indira! I'm so sorry. I only went because no one at the hospital knew where you were. I thought you'd been in an accident."

"I wish I had been. Then the girls wouldn't have had to watch..."

"Let me see where it hurts."

"No, Sona. You've done enough. You don't seem to understand that your life is always going to be different from mine. You're not really Indian. I am. I promised to be with Balbir for seven lifetimes. Perhaps in the next he'll be kinder to me." She sniffled. "Perhaps he will be one of my daughters instead of my husband. Or he may be my mother. We don't know what fate has in store. You need to stop trying to reverse fate, Sona."

I stared at her. Here I thought I'd been helping Indira when it looked as if I had only hurt her—or encouraged Balbir to do so.

"Promise you won't get involved," she pleaded. "Balbir is an angry man. I don't think it's a good idea for us to walk home together anymore, Sona."

I felt as if she'd punched me in the stomach. I let go of her hands and sat back on my haunches. She was my closest friend, my only true friend in Bombay. Tears pricked my eyes, but I wouldn't let them fall.

Indira let out a moan as she pulled her uniform over her shoulders and buttoned the front, wincing when she had to move her left arm. I could almost feel the welt on her shoulder and the bruises down the back. They were sharp, raw.

The door opened. I'd forgotten to lock it. Rebecca walked in and stopped short, her eyes scanning the room, scanning us. I stood up. Indira rose from the bench, wiping her eyes.

Rebecca pursed her lips, turned her gaze to me. "We have to tell Matron. It's time."

As calmly as I could, I said, "No, we don't. Indira will lose her job."

"This is not your problem," Indira said, looking at me and then at Rebecca. "I am fine."

With an effort, she slowly raised her arms and straightened her nurse's cap. Then, with a nod to us, she left the room.

I started to follow her when Rebecca yanked on my arm. "What you don't understand, Sona, is that we are not supposed to get personal with the sick."

"Indira is one of us. She's not one of the sick."

"Look at her, Sona. She is."

Why was it so hard for Rebecca to just be a friend? But, instead of saying anything, I pulled my apron tighter around my waist. I started to walk out the door.

Rebecca said. "You realize, don't you, that it's easier for us—you and me—to do what you're suggesting than it is for Indira? We are protected. We can do things an Indian woman can't."

I took a deep breath. "I know. But if we don't try to help, what good is our privilege?"

Later that evening, I saw Dr. Mishra and Dr. Holbrook deep in conversation in the hallway. Dr. Mishra was saying, "It's not normal for her to be experiencing this much pain three days after a miscarriage. She would feel sore, yes, but her pain is far greater than normal."

The older doctor frowned and shook his head. "You're still stuck in Indian mumbo jumbo, chap. Those damn hakims and yogis. Medicine is the way to heal this type of issue. I keep telling Matron that too. She's soft on Indian ways. Just look at what she allows that pharmacist chap to do. He distributes herbs for God's sake as well as Western drugs! Listen to me, Mishra. The morphine will make her right as rain in a few days."

"Dr. Holbrook, with all due respect, I need for you to understand that I am practiced in modern medicine. If you'll remember, the hospital board hired me from England after I'd completed my training as an internist. I still feel—"

"Angry with the *Burra Sahib*, are you?" Before Dr. Mishra, who had clenched his jaw, could answer, Holbrook said, "Look here. I've been through this process a thousand times. The mother will take a week to recover and Bob's your uncle."

"Doctor, she's miscarried a child at four months. There was an excessive amount of tissue. What if we didn't get it all?"

Dr. Holbrook checked his watch. "I'm delivering a baby within the hour. Let me explain it to you simply. With miscarriage, the fetus would automatically have disengaged from the uterine lining. What Miss Novak is experiencing is nothing more than constipation. Bound to happen after all that morphine."

He noticed me in the hallway and grinned. "Ah, one of our

model nurses. *Model* being the operative word." He waggled his bushy white eyebrows at me just as Dr. Mishra craned his neck to see who he was talking about. When he saw it was me, he cast his eyes on the terrazzo floor. He seemed embarrassed on the surgeon's behalf.

"Oh, if only I were younger!" Dr. Holbrook was walking backward in the hallway. "Pay more attention to that, Mishra. Leave the surgical medicine to me." He tapped a finger on the side of his bulbous nose and spun around toward the surgery section.

Dr. Mishra hung his head and leaned back against the wall. I knew he had been talking about Mira, trying to save her life. I could also see that she wasn't getting better. The stats I recorded on her chart proved it. Her pain was constant as was her uneven temperature, which was unusual; it should have gone back to normal after surgery.

Men like Holbrook groped and pawed young women like me and laughed about it. They frequently lobbed thinly veiled—and unveiled—insults at Indian doctors and nurses. It must have been so tiring for Dr. Mishra to hear their salty remarks day after day. We had that in common. Different insults with the same power to sting.

I coughed to let him know I was still there if he needed me. The young doctor—what was he? Just three years older than me?—lifted his head and looked in my direction. For a second, his gray eyes seemed to pierce the gloom of the hallway. He pushed himself off the wall. He took a few steps toward me and opened his mouth, as if there was something he wanted to say. Abruptly, he stopped, his restless eyes scanning ground. Then, without a backward glance, he turned and headed the other way.

If he'd taken one more step, I would have met him halfway. It surprised me, that feeling.

I threw the dice and scanned the board. Dr. Stoddard squirmed. "Damned itch. Right where I can't get to it." He was irritable today. He wouldn't be discharged for another several days, and he was getting restless. On the other side of the room, Mr. Hassan lay snoring. He'd been given a sleeping draught after his heart attack episode.

I'd made my rounds changing sheets, distributing bedpans, bathing patients, handing out medicine. I had a quarter of an hour before I needed to check on my charges again. So when Dr. Stoddard asked, I agreed to play one round of backgammon with him, keeping an eye peeled for Rebecca.

While he considered his next move, I thought about how to frame my question.

"Doctor, I'm sure you've seen your share of injuries."

"Umm." He was still preoccupied with the board. Ever since I had shown improvement, he took longer to make his moves.

"Some of those were women I'm sure."

"Of course."

"Were there any injuries inflicted by the men in their lives?"

Dr. Stoddard looked up from the board and pushed his black spectacles up over his nose, resting them on his head. "Now why would you ask that?"

I felt like a traitor talking about Indira like this. She had a right to her privacy like anyone else. "I have a friend. She often has bruises. Her husband beats her because he wants a son. So far, she's only given birth to daughters."

"But, my dear, that's beyond her control."

"Yes, yes. I know that. She knows that. But how can she explain it to her husband so he can understand?"

"Sona!"

I looked at the door. Indira was standing there with an enamel bowl in her hands. Her face was pinched. "How dare you?" She stomped away, as angry as I'd ever seen her.

Dr. Stoddard and I sat for several moments, staring at the doorway, as if she were still standing there.

His tone dry, the doctor said, "I take it that was the battered woman?"

As usual, he was spot on.

My heart was heavy when I entered our flat after my shift. My mother had made *malai kofta* and *masala bhindi* along with chapattis. She told me once that she couldn't abide English food because it was so bland and colorless. She made no mention of what she served my father when he lived with us. He obviously favored bland and colorless or he wouldn't have returned to England.

Mum could see that I wasn't in a mood to talk and she went about quietly fixing me a plate. She'd also made *chaach*, the buttermilk drink with cumin and salt that I loved. She sat across from me, sewing hooks and eyes on a woman's blouse while I ate.

I had apologized to Indira several times for confiding in Dr. Stoddard. She'd softened when I explained that I was trying to find a way for her to talk to her husband without inciting his anger. Still, as we left the hospital, Indira asked me not to walk with her to her street, and I assumed she was still upset with me.

"I'm worried for you now, Sona. I think Balbir will be on the lookout for you." She bit her lip.

I should have been afraid, but I only felt bereft. My only friend at work was rejecting me.

Indira said, "It will be safer for both of us not to be seen together."

Now, I sat in front of my *thali* thinking about my conversation with Indira. My mother's *kofta* was always delicious, but I was finding it hard to swallow.

My mother bit off the thread as she finished fastening a hook. "Fatima is pregnant."

My mood lifted. Our neighbor across the way would make a wonderful mother. She was a happy, healthy young woman with an even temper. I don't think I'd ever heard the couple argue. "How did you find out?"

"I went across the way to give her some of the *kofta*. I added an extra chili because she loves it that hot, but today, as soon as I lifted the lid off the bowl, she threw up over the landing. That's when I told *her* she was pregnant."

I laughed, as my mother had known I would. She knew how to lighten my mood.

"So," she said, pulling another fastener out of her button box. "What happened today?"

First, I told her about Mira. "She's not getting better, Mum. Dr. Mishra thinks so too." At the mention of his name, my mother cast a sharp glance at me. "I saw him arguing with Dr. Holbrook about it. Holbrook thinks it's nothing. He seems to think complications of any kind are the result of indigestion or constipation. The sooner he retires, the better. You should see the way he talks to Dr. Mishra."

"Should I?" she said, her tone shrewd. I ignored it.

I told her about Indira's bruises and how she told me not to walk home with her anymore.

"Leave that girl alone, Sona. It will only bring you trouble."

I got up to put my plate and glass in the sink. "How can you say that, Mum? If it were me who was being beaten by my husband, wouldn't you help me?"

Done with the blouse, she held it up in front of her, looking for imperfections in her work. "Her husband sounds dangerous, *beti*, and I don't want him anywhere near you." After a beat, she said, "Mohan would never do that to you."

I fumed. The voice in my head—the one my mother always told me to listen to—cautioned, *Don't, Sona. Stop!* But today had been a trying day. Men like Dr. Holbrook looking at me as if he could see through my uniform and treating Dr. Mishra as if his Indianness was several levels below Holbrook's Britishness. Indira's husband beating her like a street dog he could kick to the gutter when he felt like it. Rebecca, thinking that her half-English blood was a foolproof shield, protecting her from harm. Matron believing I deserved punishment for something I hadn't done.

I turned and leaned with my back against the counter to face my mother. "Mum, people do things—hurtful things—that never cease to surprise me. And disgust me. They can be charming one minute and betray you in the next. Who's to say Mohan isn't like that? He's kind now. But what if I failed to give him sons instead of daughters? What if he comes to believe that the British behaving badly is down to my English blood?" There they were. The words I'd locked inside me for as long as I could remember. I'd turned the key. Now they tumbled out at breakneck speed. "And what about my father? Charming his way into your life and leaving you with two children and no way to support them? Isn't he the reason we never see your family? Isn't he the reason we live in this cramped room with no air to breathe? The reason we have to watch every rupee we spend. And even then, we don't have enough to buy you new *chappals*. What kind of man does that? I hate him, Mum. I've hated him since I was three. I hated him even more—which I didn't think was possible—after Rajat died. I still miss Rajat, Mum. He was just a baby. He didn't deserve to die." I shook my head at her, breathing hard. "You were fooled into thinking my father was a good man. He wasn't. If he had been, he would be with us here, now, and not in this appalling place with the trains waking us up every hour, the stench of their smoke in our mouths." My heart pounded in my chest so loudly I thought I might pass out. My stomach hurt. I doubled over, my hands on my knees. I wished the last five minutes hadn't happened. I regretted the words as soon as they came out of my mouth. I had no right to hurt my mother like that. Speaking out against my father was like blaming her for being with him in the first place. How was I any better than the people I'd been talking about—people who smiled at you and then stabbed you in the soft spaces? Wasn't that what I'd just done to her?

When I raised my head to look at her, my mother was staring at me, her mouth slack, her forehead creased. I saw her, now, as others saw her. Defeated. Hunched over. Her elbows knobby, her knees bony. Her scalp showing through her thinning hair, the strands now more gray than black. Her fingers, so elegant once, now swollen with arthritis. Soon, she wouldn't be able to thread a needle or sew a hem. *He* had done that to her. She had paid a hard price for loving the father of her children.

"You were only three. I didn't think you remembered him." She began rubbing the spot above her heart. "At least I wanted to believe that. I didn't know all this time…" She looked down at her lap, at the abandoned garment, the silver threads winking under the glare of the single ceiling bulb. She made beautiful clothes for other people, clothes she couldn't afford for either of us. When she looked up at me, her eyes were wet.

"But, Sona… I thought you were happy with our lives. True, we're not as flush as we'd like, but it won't always be like that. That's why I wanted you to become a nurse. You're doing well, and we're saving money." She paused, spit forming at the edges of her lips. "I didn't know you hated being here so much. I didn't know you hated *him* so much."

The only time I'd seen her cry was when Rajat died. Now a tear rolled down the soft pillows under her eyes and into the hollow of her cheek. I rushed to her, kneeled in front of her chair, placing my hands on her knees. "Oh, Mum. I'm sorry. I shouldn't have said those things. I didn't mean them. Truly I didn't. I'm so sorry." I wiped her tears with my palms. "Please forgive me."

There was a catch in her voice as she continued, "You're not wrong. He did betray us. When he left, you were both so young. How could I tell you? Then you got older and, well, it never seemed like the right time. I just thought if you never asked, we could pretend it didn't happen. I didn't want to hurt you, *beti*. I only wanted to protect you." She was crying openly now, the tears wetting my hands. "He promised, Sona. He promised he would stay with us forever. He loved us. He said that over and over. I didn't know he had another family. He never told me. It never occurred to me that he didn't want to marry me because he was already married. In England. He'd been married for five or six years when I met him. If he'd been honest, I never would have taken up with him."

My parents had never married? My father had another family? In England? My chest constricted. *Rajat and I were illegitimate? Legally, I didn't exist?* A headache drummed against my temples. What else didn't I know about the man who had lent me his mouth, the color of his skin?

Mum was crumpling the blouse she'd been working on into a ball. "I was so young, Sona. And so naive. He waited to tell me the day he left. I couldn't believe it. I couldn't believe he was leaving. I couldn't believe he had another family. I couldn't believe he would do that to us. I wanted to gouge his eyes out. I slapped his cheeks, his temples. I beat him with my fists. I kicked his shins, his knees. I threw things at him. Whatever was at hand. A pot. Scissors. Rajat's toys. He let me. I pushed him so hard, his head hit the wall. When he stepped away, there was blood. He looked miserable. But he said nothing. He just left. He left anyway." She hiccupped, trying to catch her breath.

"Mum." I pried the garment from her hands and covered her palms with mine.

She regarded our hands and rubbed my thumb. "For all that, Sona, I loved him. It wasn't all bad. Maybe you can't understand that. Not now anyway. But someday, you will. While he was with us, he was good. He loved you and Rajat. I wouldn't have had the two of you to love if it hadn't been for him. He used to make paper flowers for you, which you would scatter around your bed. He would put Rajat on his shoulders and take both of you to the zoo. You loved the peacocks. When they fanned their trains, Rajat would laugh." She smiled at the memory.

I felt something harden inside, something small and round, like a marble. She was defending him. After all he'd done to her. To us. I released her hands. "Yes, and Rajat would still be alive if he'd been a responsible father."

Worry lines crossed my mother's forehead. "No, Sona. Rajat might have died anyway. His heart was weak when he was born. The doctors said there was nothing they could do about it." She paused, her eyes darting around the table: the wrinkled blouse in her lap, the pinking shears, the pincushion in the shape of a tomato. She wiped her face with the end of her sari and regarded me for a moment. As if she'd made up her mind about something, she nodded. "It's time I showed you, Sona."

"Showed me what?"

Instead of answering, she rose and went to the foot of our charpoy where she kept a metal trunk filled with fabric remnants from her commissions. She used the leftovers for our sheets and pillowcases and my dresses. Once, I asked her if Mrs. Rao, who wanted Mum to account for every inch of cloth used on her garment, wouldn't be upset that Mum was using her fine cotton for our curtains. My mother had tapped the side of her nose. "I have a secret." She pulled a half-finished *kameez* from the stack of clothes she was working on and showed me the seam inside. "Other seamstresses leave extra cloth in the seam so the Mrs. Raos of this world can gain a few kilos. The seam can be let out and no one's the wiser. But our Mrs. Rao is so *patali-dubali* that she couldn't gain an ounce even if she ate a plate of *pakoras* every night. I make it *look* like I've tucked the extra seam allowance in the topstitching. Instead, I save the extra fabric to sew a new *rajai* for our bed every year. It's almost complete!" She grinned, revealing her overbite.

Now she returned to the table and sat in her chair. She was slightly out of breath. Her mouth drooped. Her pallor was gray. In her hand was a stack of letters about six inches high. Envelopes tied together with jute.

Immediately, I rose to help her sit down. Her heart had been giving her trouble, but she had medicine for that. "Did you take your pills today? Let me make you some rose water tea, Mum. I'll put some hibiscus in it as well." I took a step toward the Primus before my mother stopped me.

"I'm fine. Come sit down." She patted the table. I didn't believe her, but I returned to my chair.

She placed the stack on the table.

"These are yours." Slowly, she slid the stack in front of me, her eyes downcast.

I'd never seen them before. I frowned at her.

"Every year since your father left, he has sent money on your birthday—and Rajat's." Her lower lip trembled. She pointed to the envelopes. "There are no written notes. No return address. If there had been, I would have told him about Rajat's passing. There's only British money. The early letters contained a few shillings, then a pound. On your last few birthdays, he sent three pounds a year. I've never touched the money. I saved it for you." She put her hands between her knees, in the well created by her sari. "For your marriage. He owed you that much," she said quietly.

I stared at her. My father had been sending me money for… *twenty years*? "But how did he find out our address in Bombay after we moved from Calcutta?"

"I don't know how he knew. Maybe from one of our old neighbors." My mother looked down at her gnarled hands. "Please forgive me for keeping these from you." Her voice cracked. "I only wanted to do what was best. And…frankly… I didn't want you thinking better of your father for trying to provide for you. I was selfish, I know. I was so furious at him for so long. Just like you are now. But it's time to let your anger go, Sona. As I had to. In the long run, it will do you more harm than good." She wiped her eyes with a scrap of fabric on the sewing machine.

I looked at the stack of envelopes, a small mountain in the middle of our table. "But…shouldn't we use this money for food? Or pay the rent in advance? We could get you new spectacles so you could do your fine hand stitching."

She shook her head. "I've saved enough from your salary and my sewing to do all that. This is your money. Do what you will with it."

I stared at the pile on the table. It was like another presence in the room, pulsing with life, expanding and contracting. I got up from my chair, nearly upending it, and began pacing the room.

So many thoughts were churning, unwinding, then spiraling again. My father remembered my birthday—and Rajat's—every year since he left? Did my father ever write to us? And then, at the last minute, decide not to mail the letter? Did he think it would hurt us to hear from him after so much time had passed? My father had an English wife? What did she look like? Did he have children with her? Boys? Girls? What ages? Did they know about us? What did they say when they found out? Did they ever find out? Did he ever miss us? Did this money make up for all the years of neglect? Would it make me any less angry with him?

What I was looking at was guilt money. He was guilty for lying to us. For abandoning us. Not letting us know if he still loved us. Was my mother inventing memories like the paper flowers and the visits to the zoo? Were they things she wished had happened but didn't?

I didn't want his money—to keep or to use. I didn't even want to touch it.

But when I looked at my mother, the heart medicine she needed, the worn *chappals* she insisted on wearing because she said they were more comfortable than new ones would be, the sari she had worn so often the fabric was transparent in places, I knew we needed more than the money she'd put away.

I let out a long, long breath and stood in front of my mother. She looked up.

I leaned toward her, touched my forehead to hers. Then I pulled my chair up to the table and sat. "Let's count the money," I said.

CHAPTER 4

I was hoping that after his talk with Dr. Mishra, Dr. Holbrook had reconsidered Mira's treatment, but at the end of my shift yesterday, I saw on the chart that he hadn't. The shadows under Mira's eyes had been darker than they'd been the day before. Her skin, paler. Her hair, limp. Her breath, sour. Was no one looking after her? Where was her husband? Why wasn't he demanding better treatment, the way Dr. Mishra was? For that matter, did Filip Bartos ever come and sit with his wife? Yesterday, when he'd left the paintings in her room, was the first time I'd seen him.

Today, as I changed into my uniform for my shift, I was determined; if her husband wasn't going to help her, I was.

I wheeled a gurney into Mira's room. I'd brought two enamel pans filled with warm water, a bottle of sandalwood shampoo, towels and an enamel cup.

But Mira wasn't alone. She was sketching Indira. The moment Indira saw me, she colored and reached for her nurse's cap.

"No, I'm not finished," Mira cried.

Indira said, "Ma'am, Sona is here. That means it's the start of my shift too. I must go." She pinned her cap on her hair.

Mira looked at me helplessly. "I asked Indira to come early today to pose for me. She has such character. Such depth. Take a look." She held up the sketch.

Indira and I moved in close. The charcoal rendering was Indira. The drawing captured her unhappiness, the way she struggled to hide it. The guarded eyes, always at half-mast. The lips that stretched into a flat line, neither turning up nor down at the corners. But Indira's features in the sketch were less defined, blunted even. She could have been any woman. Indira, but not Indira.

Indira looked at the sketch with wonder. She said, "Do I really look like that?" A tear sprung on the inside of each eye. "She looks so helpless. And sad." She glanced at me. "Do I?"

I put my arm around her. "You are you. There's only one of you."

Indira turned to go.

"I have mango lassi in my thermos today, if you'd like some," I said.

She shook her head and left. I turned to Mira and realized she'd been watching us in silence.

I opened the window to let in a light breeze. I smiled at her. "Should we wash our hair today?"

She laughed. "There is no 'we.' It looks as if *you* are washing my hair today."

Embarrassed to have spoken to her as I'd spoken earlier to the young boy scheduled for a tonsillectomy, I apologized and did a mock salute.

"No bother, Sona. I'm always delighted to see you." She waved a hand in front of her face. "Tell me. What are you protecting your friend from?"

I looked at her. "Who? Indira?"

She nodded.

I should have known. As much as Mira liked to talk, she also listened. She heard what wasn't said. She felt what wasn't voiced. It's one of the things I liked about her. "Her home life is not good," I said before turning my attention to the bottle of shampoo and unscrewing the cap.

She raised her eyebrows. "When I first started painting the

women in my work, I saw many with bruises of hard labor or abuse or neglect. I wanted to help, but it wasn't my place. They didn't want me to either. They told me they would be in more trouble at home if I interfered. I couldn't understand it at first, but I finally realized that I could do more good by portraying their lives and their feelings on canvas—for the world to see. That was when the work took over and I ceased to exist. The paintings came alive under my brush. Sona..." She waited until I looked at her. "Let Indira live her life."

Part of me was surprised at her prescience; she was telling me what Indira had, what my mother had. The other part of me bristled at the advice I didn't want to hear.

Mira put her pencils and sketch pad off to one side. "I'm glad you're here. There's something I want to ask you."

What privacy boundary was she going to cross now? I was both wary and curious. "Alright. But first, do you think you could manage to sit in a chair?"

She frowned, then shook her head. I helped her to sit up on the bed instead. She let out a whimper. I glanced at the sheets to see if she was still bleeding. There were a few stains the size of an anna. I would change her sheets after I'd washed her hair. I noticed on her chart that the nurse from the previous shift had given her a dose of morphine not long ago. Perhaps it would take effect soon. I removed the pillows behind her, replacing them with a stack of towels to catch the water. One towel I wrapped around her neck and shoulders.

She asked, "If you had to live your life over again, would you do anything differently?"

Once more, she was probing, disturbing my neat surface of duty and responsibility to delve into the soft, imperfect, messy layer underneath. But instead of rebuffing her attempt to engage me, I found myself admiring how she went about it. Like an arrow heading straight for its target. Not in a malicious way, but because she was genuinely interested.

I said, "Why do you ask?" as I poured warm water over her hair, taking care not to let it drip on her face.

"Because I can talk to you—and Amit—about what matters to me."

I was glad she couldn't see the blush on my cheeks. Why did her close friendship with Dr. Mishra bother me? It was ridiculous. It wasn't as if he and I were… Maybe I was more upset to know that she had anointed him, made him feel privileged to be in her circle, as she had me. She did have that way about her, making people feel special, loved. It was that trait that must have attracted Petra and Paolo—and any number of people she'd met—to her.

I poured some shampoo into my palm and massaged it onto her scalp and into her wavy black hair. It was oily now, but by the time we were done, it would be shiny again. The soothing fragrance of sandalwood filled the room.

"If I had it to do over again," she continued. "I would have been kinder to Jo. Josephine. I've been thinking about her a lot. She didn't deserve what I did to her." Her head dipped slightly. "Jo was—is—an art dealer in Paris—a big name. She sold a lot of my work…" Mira paused. "It was while I was at the Académie there. Jo and her husband, Jean, sort of adopted me. They had me over for dinner, took me to the Louvre—we spent hours and hours there. I sketched while they strolled. They introduced me to the Jeu de Paume, Palais de Chaillot, l'Orangerie, the Impressionists. I fell in love with Gauguin and Cézanne. Jo and Jean were so kind. They listened to my rants about Paolo. And then I did the most horrible thing. It was inexcusable." She paused again. "I betrayed them for no good reason, Sona. I made a play for Jean. Why I did it, I don't know."

Once more, she had shocked me. Had that been her intention? She confessed that she'd betrayed a good friend in the worst possible way. Was she looking for absolution? From me? Who was I to pardon anyone? I waited for her to say more as I rinsed her hair with clean water from the other pan.

"Jean and I had an affair. When Jo found out, she was furious of course. And hurt. Eventually, Jean left her and Jo fired me. I don't blame her, Sona. What I did was awful. She'd done nothing to deserve it—quite the opposite. She made a name for me in the art world. But after what I did, no agent wanted to touch me. I felt awful. I couldn't paint. I had no money. Eventually, I went back home to Prague and flirted with Filip." Guilt had crept into her telling. "My mother was livid. She thought I could do better. A prince or, at the very least, a diplomat." Her smile was wry. "He was neither. Which is probably why I married him. And left for India."

I gathered her hair in a towel and wrung it tightly. I don't know where the words came from, but I knew them to be true. "You weren't in love with Filip."

She craned her neck round to look at me and nodded. "Everyone thought I was brave to defy my mother. Truth was, I didn't want to go to India—where I'd never been—alone. I needed a companion. And Filip was a good companion." She turned back to the front, took a deep breath, then let it out slowly. "I wreak havoc wherever I go, Sona."

I didn't know what to say. This was probably why we weren't supposed to get close to the sick, as Rebecca had warned. I'd been so impressed by Mira, so taken by her worldliness, her sophistication. Now I saw a far more complicated woman, who, as loving as she was to me, had betrayed people who loved her. And she'd done it on purpose. Would she do the same to me one day? She'd known the lines she was crossing and had done it anyway. Only now did she sound remorseful. Normally, I would have tried to replace a patient's darkness with light, left her in good humor. But with Mira I resisted. She'd drawn me in. Allowed me, encouraged me, to get close to her. Hadn't that made me feel important? And then, she'd disappointed me. Was that what my mother felt when she found out the man she adored, the one who had fostered their coupling, was a charlatan?

I gathered my supplies—damp towels, enamel pans, shampoo—and put them on the gurney. When I turned around to tell her I was coming back to change the sheets and help her settle for bed, I saw tears making their way down the sides of her nose onto her lips. Her guilt—albeit belated—thawed a little of my resistance. Wasn't it enough that our bodies, our limbs hurt? Why did we also have to hurt in our heart, the pain tucked so deeply in the soft tissue that we couldn't just pluck it out? I took the handkerchief out of my pocket and wiped her face. Then I turned to go.

She caught my wrist to stop me from leaving. "Thank you."

I nodded. She was thanking me for listening to her without judging her. But in my heart, I had judged. How could I not? I understood what Mira's friend Jo, what her friend Petra, what her lover Paolo must have felt, how Mira had used them. I'd also been on the other side of betrayal. It was ugly, a thing with claws, covered in scales.

It was my father.

Timothy Stoddard was helping his uncle into a wheelchair with a wicker back. The lower part of the chair could be extended ninety degrees to accommodate patients with a broken leg. Dr. Stoddard's cast had been removed earlier that day.

"My dear! Your carriage awaits!" the good doctor said when I entered the room.

Timothy laughed. "She can't very well sit in your lap, Uncle."

The doctor introduced us. Timothy, with his easy smile, was around my age. I put Dr. Stoddard's arm around my shoulder so I could carry half his weight. Timothy steadied him from the other side as we helped him off the bed.

"Where did it come from?" I asked as I held the wheelchair in place and Timothy lowered the doctor into it.

"I still have a few favors I can call in," the doctor said. "I had

Timothy ask Mohan, down in maintenance, to bring it up after the visitors were gone."

He looked at his roommate, Mr. Hassan. "What say you, Fahid? Shall we wheel down to the pawnbroker if you can tear yourself away from that tome?"

Mr. Hassan, whom I was here to check up on, had become used to his roommate's sense of humor. He set down his copy of Tagore's *The Home and the World*. "I'm halfway through, my friend. Can't possibly stop now," he said. For now, his condition was stable. We would keep an eye on his heart while he recuperated from his appendicitis operation. "Bon voyage," he chuckled.

"Get cracking, Timothy!" Dr. Stoddard, tired of his cast, was anxious for the adventure to begin.

Timothy Stoddard's spectacles shielded velvety brown eyes with thick lashes. He grinned at me. "Uncle Ralph has always been a handful. I'm not sure his servant wants him back home."

"I may decide to go elsewhere, laddie. Been thinking of Istanbul," he said. Then he brightened and addressed me, "Why not come with me, my dear? Be good to have a fetching nurse on board the ship. I can teach you that gin rummy game I keep promising."

Timothy, behind him now with his hands on the handles, winked as he passed me. "He cheats, you know."

"I'm well aware, laddie." I smiled.

I followed them to the doorway. Dr. Stoddard exclaimed, "Heave-ho!" Timothy pushed the wheelchair with all his might down the hallway. I clapped softly. It was like a race with only one entrant, and Timothy was making good time. He reached the end of the hallway and turned the wheelchair in my direction. I looked around to make sure no patients were hovering in the hallway. That's when I saw her.

Matron's formidable mien was headed our way, blue eyes blazing.

Using all his might, Timothy was able to bring the wheelchair to a standstill just as it reached her feet. Only then did she notice me. I looked at Dr. Stoddard, then at Timothy. My heart was hammering so loudly in my chest, the noise in my ears was deafening. I would be reprimanded again in the high court of the Matron. My armpits were moist. I braced an arm against the door, afraid for my thudding heart.

Matron folded her arms across her chest. "I take it this is a doctor-approved regulation wheelchair?" We all knew Wadia Hospital did not have wheelchairs at its disposal.

Dr. Stoddard looked up at her with his most charming smile. "Of course, Matron. Would I ride in anything else?"

The doctor and Matron regarded one another in silence. Finally, she turned to me. "Nurse, come see me when you're done here."

Dr. Stoddard said, "She didn't order the wheelchair, Matron, or make me sit in it. She came to look in on Hassan, the old chap." He lowered his voice as if he were sharing a confidence. "Between you and me, Nurse Falstaff is the highlight of his day."

Timothy chimed in, "Nurse Falstaff did try to stop us, but Uncle would have none of it."

The doctor pressed his hands together in supplication. "I'm a brute, Matron. Please, as a favor to me, don't penalize the poor girl."

"Dr. Stoddard," she said, as if she were pointing a finger at him. "What I do or don't do with my nursing staff should be no concern of yours."

"Oh, but it is, dear girl. I'm on the board of the hospital, don't you know? And I say, this girl will not be punished for something I instigated. Right then, Timothy. You may wheel me back to bed." Timothy did as requested, giving me a wink as he went past.

Emboldened now, I looked at Matron. "I need to finish with Mr. Hassan." Without waiting for her approval, I turned on my heel and walked to his bed, busying myself with the blood pressure cuff. I was afraid to look at the doorway. When I finally did, she was no longer there.

Timothy was struggling to get Dr. Stoddard out of the wheelchair. I went to help him. I could tell that while the ride had been exhilarating, it had tired the old doctor. His cheeks and his nose were flushed. Timothy poured a glass of water for him.

"Doctor, I'm curious," I said. "If you're on the hospital board, why didn't you request a private room?"

"Because I like company, my dear. Hassan is great company."

I went back to Mr. Hassan, who seemed not to have seen or heard anything. He calmly put down his novel. I gave him his medicine and a glass of water.

"I'm not sure what to make of a woman who saves my life *and* monitors wheelchair races." The old Muslim grinned, his salt-and-pepper mustache dancing.

I glanced at Dr. Stoddard. His smile was kind when he said, "Heroes should be recognized, my dear. Raise a toast, Fahid."

Mr. Hassan raised his water glass to me. Dr. Stoddard did the same.

The hospital provided food for staff, but the kitchen closed at half past six. The dining room, however, stayed open to accommodate the night shift. My mother packed a tiffin for my dinner every day. Frankly, her food was tastier than anything I could have eaten from the hospital kitchen. I chose to eat my dinner at ten in the evening, which would stay my hunger until dawn, the end of my shift.

I was on my way to the dining room with my tiffin and looking forward to reading my book, *A Room of One's Own*. I'd found it in a secondhand bookshop off the Bhendi Bazaar. I would have preferred eating in the stockroom—it was more private. Matron, however, forbade the smell of curry there, claiming the scent would permeate the sheets and towels.

I had just passed Dr. Mishra's office when I heard him call my name. I backtracked a few steps to find him sitting at his desk. My heart did a little flip and my breath quickened. He started to rise when he saw me and gestured across from him. "Please." His gaze wandered to the fountain pen in his hand, the lampshade on one corner of his desk and then my shoes.

Except for his unruly hair, he was neatly dressed, his shirt and lab coat pressed. His office was a different matter altogether. Prescription pads, medical forms, an inkwell, a letter in progress and a half-full cup of tea cluttered the surface of his desk. A medical journal, open to an article where the corner had been turned down, lay precariously on a haphazard pile of books. I fought the urge to rescue the journal, sensing instinctively that he would not appreciate a reorganization of his particular brand of order. The photo of Gandhi and Nehru, surrounded by leaders of the Indian National Congress, hung on the wall behind Dr. Mishra. The room contained his particular cardamom-lime scent.

I stood, unsure, in the doorway. I wanted desperately to comply with his request—I remembered the feeling of standing close to him, his hand on my hand as we examined Mira—but protocol stopped me. Was it proper to sit with a doctor in his office? Nurses and sisters talked to doctors from office doorways or stood in front of their desks to receive orders or ask a question. Would Matron approve of me sitting *with* Dr. Mishra? I didn't think so. What if she assumed an imagined impropriety? I'd already been in Matron's crosshairs earlier with Dr. Stoddard and his wheelchair; I didn't want two infractions within the space of two hours.

"I must ask you something." His expression was earnest, almost pleading. He combed his fingers through his curls, which did nothing to settle them.

I sat down gingerly, placing the tiffin and book in my lap. My palms were damp. I resisted the urge to rub them on my apron.

His eyes strayed to my tiffin, and he flushed. "Oh, I am sorry! I didn't realize—that's your dinner—I shouldn't have—" His sentences were like the hammering of a flameback woodpecker: *rat-tat-tat*, pause, *rat-tat-tat*.

"Would you care to—" I lifted the lid of the first tiffin. "There's enough. *Chole, karela.*" I opened the second tiffin. "Chutney. Rice." I realized I was blathering. *Stop talking, Sona.*

"Ah. I have tea..." He held up his cup. Sisters regularly came around to deliver tea to the doctors. "Thank you though." With that lanky frame, I wondered if he ever ate.

I felt my neck flush as I secured the lid on the container and waited for his question, listening for footsteps in the hallway.

He folded his hands on his desk. "How do you think Miss Novak is doing?"

Should I be honest? Would I get into trouble with Matron discussing a patient with a doctor? That was definitely not in our remit. On the other hand, Dr. Mishra had specifically asked me, and a patient's health was at stake. After hesitating for a moment, I said, "She's not getting better. I don't see a change in her. The morphine is only hiding her discomfort." I met his eyes to see if I'd overstepped.

But he nodded. "I agree. The morphine isn't the answer. Holbrook thinks it is. I can't seem to change his mind." He rubbed his forehead.

It hadn't occurred to me that even doctors had a Matron of sorts, a higher authority they dare not disobey.

"What would you recommend?" I asked.

"I think there might be residual fetal tissue that has become infected. The only way we'll know is to look inside."

"And Dr. Holbrook doesn't want to operate?"

He shook his head. He picked up the fountain pen and rolled it in his fingers. He was quiet for so long I wondered if he knew I was still there. My stomach rumbled with hunger.

"I came back to India to teach Indian medical students what I'd learned in England," he began. "Here, the British allow only the most elementary curriculum for Indian schools of medicine.

Imagine my surprise when I arrived at Wadia excited to teach and Holbrook assigned me to the night shift when training is all but over for the day. That means fewer Indian doctors at Wadia will get the education they need." He glanced at me to see if I understood. His gray eyes flitted from my face to the pen in his hand to the inkwell. "Independence is inevitable, and things will change. Doctors like Holbrook think it won't happen. That just because the Bombay Gymkhana finally allowed Indians to become members a few years ago, the Brits have made real progress. We all know that's not true." He stopped fidgeting with the pen and looked at me in alarm. "Oh, dear. Perhaps I've offended you. You might be on the side of the Brit— I do apologize."

I took a moment to gather my thoughts. "I'm not on anybody's side, Doctor. All I know is that India is my country too. My father came from England to serve in the British Army. He left me, my brother and my mother behind, which does not make me love him. My parentage is complex." I smiled to let him know I had taken no offense.

"Ah," he said, his fine brows rising.

"So what will you do about Mira—Miss Novak?"

He cleared his throat. "In cases like this, it's often up to the patient to insist the head surgeon find a solution. I've suggested that to her and to her husband. They're the only ones who can get Holbrook to change course." He looked at me hopefully.

"I see." If I understood the meaning behind his words, he was asking me to encourage Mira to champion her own treatment. I wondered why she—and her husband—hadn't already done that. Was it even my place to suggest such a thing? "You'd like me to…"

"Precisely."

I nodded.

"And I'm sorry about… Enjoy your dinner." He pointed to my tiffin. Then he stood and gestured at the door, as if he were a maître d' at a restaurant. I suppressed the urge to tell him which table I wanted.

★ ★ ★

I had very little time to scarf down my meal before resuming my duties. I'd resolved to talk to Mira about her treatment plan, but when I came around to Mira's room with the morphine, I heard voices. Who could be visiting her this late at night? Unsure about whether I should intrude, I stopped just outside the door.

"*Princezno*, you know how your mother is. She's worried sick about you, but she's also hurt. You do nothing but disobey her. Like Filip. Like moving to India. She gets angry. It wreaks havoc with her nerves."

"Papa, you moved to India first. Why is it so wrong for me to?" Mira sounded angry.

"Well..."

"So, she's not coming?" Now her tone was petulant, a disappointed child. That surprised me. Whenever she'd mentioned her mother to me, she'd sounded indifferent, as if they'd been friends who had drifted apart.

"How can she, *broučku*? She's taking the waters in Geneva. Once you're well again, you and I can go visit her." I heard his chair scrape the floor, as if he were inching closer to the bed. "Now, do you want to know about my project? Rabbi Abraham has rounded up three more philanthropists to help pay for the new synagogue. We just need a little more and we'll start building. And this is the best part, Mira."

I could hear the excitement in his voice.

"We are going to ask Ruby Myers to cut the ribbon!"

I heard Mira scoff. "Really, Father! Bollywood royalty? Is this an opening for a synagogue or a burlesque show?" There was a pause. Mira raised her voice. "Sona, is that you at the door?"

I stepped into the room. Mira extended her hand to me. I took it automatically. She looked better than she had earlier. Her eyes were bright. Her color had returned.

"This is my *otec*," she said, pointing her chin at the older gentleman in the room.

Her father rose from his chair to greet me formally, his hat in his hands. He was a beefy man, around sixty, with a prominent nose and rosy cheeks. His beard was close-cropped, neat. His thinning hair was plastered to his head with pomade. He wore a woolen suit with a vest and a gold watch chain like many European gentlemen of his generation. When I was a little girl, accompanying my mother to the homes of wealthy ladies whose measurements she was taking, I saw men like him planted in plump armchairs, reading the newspaper.

Mira beamed at her father. "Papa, this is my favorite nurse, Sona. See how shiny my hair is? She washed it for me." The last word had barely left her mouth when she clenched her jaw, squeezed her eyes shut.

"It's an honor to meet you, Mr. Novak," I said. "I'm sorry to curb your visit, but your daughter needs her rest now."

"Of course, Nurse. I will be on my way." He walked to Mira's bed with his hat in his hands and kissed her forehead. *"Brzo se uzdrav."*

After he left the room, I began to prepare the injection for her, but she stopped me. "I was only pretending. I didn't want him here anymore. All he ever does is make excuses for my mother."

"Oh."

She picked up the sketch pad and charcoal lying next to her. "Papa kept bringing up Filip." She tapped a stick of charcoal on her pad. "We grew up together, Filip and I. He was like an older brother. I half hoped we would grow into passion. But we didn't. Filip let me be. After a while, that was fine." She stopped a moment to look at me, then started drawing again. "Filip seemed to exhibit no particular ambition. No desire to do anything. Whereas I have always had loads of ambition. Mountains of it. My dreams are bigger than this room, Sona. Bigger than this hospital, bigger than all of India. I want so much. All the time." She sighed. "Do you ever feel like that?"

"Yes." I surprised myself. It was the first time I'd said it aloud.

That cheered her up. "I knew it. I wanted to hear you say it." She began sketching in earnest. "For a time, I wondered if Filip was keeping the best parts of himself to himself instead of sharing them with me." She turned those large dark eyes on me. "But what if it wasn't that? What if there was no more to him? What if there was no there there? as Gertrude Stein might say. I'd assumed that the reason he didn't practice medicine was because there was a greater Filip inside. He wanted extraordinary things for himself like I did. That's what I told Mother. She wasn't having any of it. 'Marrying your first cousin! The scandal! Your children will be backward. Why couldn't you have married a baron or a prince?'" Mira stabbed her pad with the charcoal. "I didn't want to marry a baron or a prince. All I wanted was to paint. To be a painter. To be a *great* painter. That's all. Why could she never understand? Why couldn't she see me as I was? Not as she wanted me to be?" Mira threw up her hands, the charcoal stick flying out of her hand, landing on the floor, breaking in two. "And now, when I need her, she won't come because I've disappointed her. I didn't become the person she planned for me to be."

Her cheeks reddened. I felt her frustration. Here she was, so full of feeling, full of wanting, full of the energy she wanted to express through her art. She wanted to be understood by people who should have known better. Who should have cared enough to. I sat on her bed, something I never would have done with another patient, and, for the first time, I reached for her hand, not caring if her blackened fingers dirtied mine. She looked at me, pain flooding those luminescent eyes of hers. Then she released my hand and wrapped her arms around my neck, holding me tight. She wept, huge choking sobs. I stroked her hair. She was so young and so frightened and so alone. How stubborn did her mother have to be to refuse to come to her? How involved in his own life did her father have to be to pay her only one visit? And what about her ghost of a husband? Where was he in all this? He'd brought the paintings she'd asked for. He'd brought the sketchbook and charcoals. But where was his heart? His love?

I rocked her until she quieted. Then I helped her lay down on the pillows.

She declined the injection she was due, saying she didn't need it. Perhaps this was an indication that she was on the mend. At least I wanted to think it. Because I was reluctant to bring up Dr. Mishra's suggestion that she challenge Dr. Holbrook's treatment. It wasn't my place.

As I was leaving her room, I heard hushed voices in the hallway. I recognized Matron's and Dr. Holbrook's. Something about their muted exchange made me hang back in the doorway.

The house surgeon was saying, "…told you before. Horace isn't buying from reputable British sources. Probably Indian. Probably adulterated—"

Matron's deep voice cut in. "Horace wouldn't. He's been running the pharmacy for twenty years."

"And he's your brother-in-law. How will that look if she dies? I'm under enough pressure from Mishra as it is. Fix it, Matron. Or we're both culpable."

Matron mumbled something I didn't catch.

"His system… Clipboard indeed!"

"…always worked before."

"Has it? How do we know… All the deaths… Wish she'd never come here. Doesn't even paint properly. Give me Constable any day. And we don't know, do we, what she might have done to that baby. That type of woman…"

Matron had lowered her voice to a whisper. I couldn't hear what she said.

"Not sure I agree. She's not British. Kipling was right. Savages, every one of them."

I heard Dr. Holbrook's heavy footsteps walking away. Matron remained where she was, looking at the floor, deep in thought. Then she turned in my direction and saw me. Her face lost all color. For the briefest of moments, her eyes were naked with fear. Then she seemed to compose herself, her expression grim. "Are you spying, Nurse?"

"I—I'm on my way to see to the new baby and mother, ma'am." My pulse was racing. I might have just overheard the reason why Mira hadn't improved, why her condition was worse.

"Then you'd better be on your way. The baby is underweight. You need to manage that."

She was talking calmly, as if the conversation I'd overheard had never taken place. Had I imagined it? No, they were definitely talking about Mira! Why hadn't I spoken up for her? Instead, I'd been a coward, complicit in my silence. She deserved better. Should I tell Dr. Mishra what I'd overheard? The line between right and wrong and where my responsibility lay was making my head pound.

It had been a long day. Dr. Stoddard's wheelchair, the request Dr. Mishra made of me, and then the conversation between Dr. Holbrook and Matron—all of it had drained me. I hadn't been able to find Dr. Mishra before my shift ended to tell him what I'd overheard. Maybe I should confide in Indira.

At four in the morning, I found Mohan replacing the wheels on a gurney, which he'd turned upside down. He worked longer hours than I did. I often wondered if he slept in the maintenance room.

Instead of his usual shy but cheerful greeting, he barely looked up when I approached him.

"Have you seen Indira, Mohan?"

He lifted his head and gave me a blank stare. I understood. He was smarting from my response to his marriage proposal. I had to say something or that rejection would become a festering sore. I came close enough to him to see the dark hair in his ears. Ignoring me, he picked up his screwdriver and removed a fastener from the wheel. As usual, the room was crammed with old chairs and tables and broken equipment. Even so, it never felt stuffy until today, given Mohan's mood.

"Mohan, I am not ready to marry anyone. I don't know if I will ever marry. I'm not convinced it's a shift I'd want to sign up for." I was hoping my little joke would help lighten the mood, and I thought I noticed a softening around his eyes. "You're very kind to offer me a life of companionship and security. I want you to know that." I offered him a humble smile. "I'm not sure you're aware what you'd be getting in me. I have strong opinions. I like to do things my way—except when Matron catches me."

That brought a thin smile to his lips. He looked at me then, the corners of his eyes crinkling.

"You deserve better than me. Someone who cooks dinner for you when you come home. And massages your feet after a long day's work. And makes you tea whenever you want it. Knows what you need even before you do. You know that's not me. It never will be. The right girl is waiting for you. You'll find her. She may even come help you here, fixing gurneys and painting tables."

"*Accha, accha!* Stop!" He was laughing. "Indira was here, but she left. Her husband came to get her." Mohan's eyebrows rose to his hairline. "*Maderchod*. The way he handled her. Told her he was going to walk her home from now on."

My ears started ringing. "What did he say exactly?"

Mohan looked away, embarrassed. "'I don't want that *gori randi* anywhere near you.'"

So now I was the *white whore*. It was laughable and cruel at the same time. If Indira's husband only knew I'd never even been with a man.

"Did she seem scared, Mohan?"

He thought about it. "She was startled more than anything. I don't think he's ever come here before. I've certainly never seen him. She started to say he needn't worry, that she'd told you she couldn't walk home with you anymore, but he slapped her.

Then he shook her." Mohan cast his eyes at the gurney, as if he didn't want to meet my eye. "It was hard to see, Sona. After that, she just followed him out the door. Like she was in a trance."

I gritted my teeth. I wanted to scream, *How did men like Balbir get away with it?* Instead, I took a deep breath. "Thanks, Mohan." I walked over to my bike.

"Do you want me to go with you?"

I turned around. The expression on my face must have told him I didn't understand.

"To Indira's?"

He nodded. In that moment, if Mohan had asked me to marry him, I might have said yes. How noble it was of him to want to protect me from the likes of Balbir.

I shook my head. "I'm fine."

No sooner had I cycled two blocks from the hospital than I saw the young Indian students under the streetlamp. They were passing around a pack of Scissors cigarettes. The smoke competed with the strong medicinal scent of the golden shower tree, the flowers of which Mum mixed with rice water as a balm for my sore throat.

"But Gandhi-ji says violence is not the way—"

"How else can we show the bloody Brits we won't be bullied anymore? The elections proved we're ready to govern ourselves and still they ignore us."

"Are you coming to the rally on Friday?"

As I passed them, I turned my head to catch their conversation when my wheels seemed to lock in place. My body jerked forward, almost throwing me off the bike. I looked around for the cause. Indira's husband, Balbir, was gripping my handlebar. He smelled of *paan* and cigarettes. His eyes blazed with anger.

"Stay away from my wife! Indira doesn't need you putting your perverted ideas in her head. Don't come around our house or talk to her at work. You will regret it." He lifted a hand as if he were going to slap me. Fear gripped me, but I willed my body not to flinch. We stared at one another for a long moment.

He leaned close to my ear and whispered, a hint of menace in his voice, "And remember: I can follow you home anytime."

"Even that won't give you the son you're looking for, Balbir," I said quietly.

His mouth sprang open, a look of shock on his face. He wasn't used to women talking back. He loosened his grip on my handlebars.

"Hey, what are you doing?" one of the students shouted. I realized they were talking to Balbir. With a menacing glance at me, he let go of my bicycle and walked quickly away.

The young men were running toward me. "Miss, are you alright?"

I thanked them for their kindness and pedaled away, still shaking. When I got home, as soon as my fingers stopped trembling, I locked up my bicycle. Then I smoothed my skirt and wiped the sweat from my brow before walking up the stairs to our flat.

CHAPTER 5

I went to take Mira's temperature the following evening. She was sitting up against her pillows, alert. There was pink in her cheeks and light in her eyes. I was relieved to see her looking so much better. Perhaps Matron had talked to Horace and the morphine supplier had been changed?

Standing by Mira's bedside was a gentleman in a tailored suit. He was young, around Dr. Mishra's age, and just an inch or two shorter. His face was all angles—a sharp nose, a pointed chin, jutting cheekbones. The hair on his temples was receding, a sure sign he would go bald at an early age. His warm brown eyes, a ready smile, his relaxed stance—all radiated good humor. A man who was used to being liked.

Mira was laughing at something he'd said. "This is why we need you back in Bombay, Dev. To liven things up." She gave him a sideways look. "Liven *me* up." Their laughter hinted at past intimacies. It embarrassed me, and yet, I couldn't look away from him, from them.

He kissed her hand.

Mira noticed me, standing in the doorway. "Sona! Come meet a dear friend of mine." As usual, she held out her hand for me take. "This is Dev Singh, a lovely man when he's not flirting with anyone but me."

Dev was good-natured about the dig. He offered me a cheerful smile, revealing perfectly white teeth.

Mira said, "Sona is the most splendid nurse. Don't you think she's absolutely gorgeous?"

I must have flushed an unattractive shade of pink.

Dev crossed his arms over his chest, as if he were a scientist, studying me in the lab. I didn't have the urge to cover myself, feeling as though I'd walked into the room naked, as I had with Dr. Holbrook. "She does have certain charms. The uniform. The cap. And those white shoes. Absolute stunner."

"Don't be naughty," Mira said.

"And she does have a no-nonsense quality about her." He looked at Mira. "I think she'd tell you when you were out of line. And punish you for it." He made a motion with his hand as if he were slapping an imaginary cheek. But his smile, the way the corners of his eyes crinkled, told me his teasing meant no harm. I didn't want to, but I smiled, enjoying his attention.

"And she'd be right."

We turned to see who'd spoken. Dr. Mishra entered the room.

"Amit!" Dev walked around the bed to shake Dr. Mishra's hand heartily. "I heard you were working at this hospital. How are you, old bean?"

Dr. Mishra smiled at Dev, but his eyes were guarded.

Dev said, "Mrs. Mehta told me you were at this hospital now. The Mehtas have known our family for ages. And she also told me…" He glanced at Mira. "That a certain celebrated painter was in your midst—someone whom I've actually had the pleasure of knowing once or twice."

"Twice, if I remember correctly." Mira laughed, wagging her head in imitation of Indians.

Dev grinned and shook a finger at her.

I felt as if I'd walked in on a private party with the glamorous threesome. I released Mira's hand. "I should go," I said vaguely and took a few steps toward to door.

"Come, come, Nurse Sona," Dev said, ushering me back into the room with a wave of his arm. I could tell he was the kind of man who was used to getting his way. "Can't you see the good Dr. Mishra would prefer you stay?"

Startled, I glanced at Dr. Mishra, who had turned a shade darker. His eyes were fixed on the floor.

Dev continued, "Let me tell you something about this fine fellow."

Dr. Mishra waved his hands in front of him. "There's no need, Dev. Nurse Falstaff, please see to your patients."

"Let her stay. Please," said Mira, who'd been enjoying the banter. "Just for a little while. I want to know more about my doctor too."

Dr. Mishra shrugged. I stayed.

"We were at Oxford together. Amit always had top marks. I could have, of course, but I was busy chasing the pretty ladies." He winked at Mira. "Bloody thing was, he had no one to answer to. No family. Big inheritance. He should have been out there crowing like a rooster. Whereas I—" Dev pointed to himself "—have always had to answer to everyone. My parents. The bride they'd choose for me. Even the driver who brought me here."

Dr. Mishra grinned. "And yet, you still crowed like a rooster."

Dev put a hand to his heart. *"Pure gold is unaffected by a flame."*

I wondered about men—and women—who mixed this easily and intimately with people. I couldn't imagine myself doing it, much less talking to others so glibly. What would it be like to be one of them?

Dev put his hands in his pants pockets. "So, I was just telling Mira here that my parents are having an engagement party for me."

Dr. Mishra's face lit up. "Congratulations, Dev. Is that why you're in Bombay? Your parents have arranged a wedding?"

"To a beautiful woman from Jaipur. Her name is Gayatri Kaur. I've seen her photo, but I haven't met her. I will tonight. She looks formidable, much like our young nurse here."

Something made me bold. I arched an eyebrow. "If I am as formidable as you claim, I would have told you to leave so I could take Miss Novak's temperature."

Dev held his hands up in surrender. "Oh-ho! I stand corrected. Perhaps Nurse Falstaff is the more daunting one." He laughed heartily. It seemed as if nothing could ever roust him from that cheerful disposition. He rubbed his hands together. "So it's all settled. Mishra is coming to the party tomorrow."

"And Sona will accompany him." Mira grinned, looking from me to her doctor.

I almost dropped the thermometer. "What? No—I have to work." I turned to Dr. Mishra. "Don't *you*, Doctor?"

He nodded. "Can't go I'm afraid."

"Look at the two of you. Made for each other." Dev laughed. "Mrs. Mehta promised me she will sort out that scheduling business. She said she owed you, Nurse." He pointed his finger at Dr. Mishra and me. "You are both coming." He turned to Mira. "And you, my dear, will come too. Now that you're feeling better. You know the head of Bombay Talkies will be there."

Mira's eyes widened. "Devika Rani?"

"In the flesh."

The painter clapped her hands. "I'm dying to meet her. Perhaps she'll want to do a film about my women—the women of South India. Oh, wouldn't that be capital?"

Dev looked at Dr. Mishra. "So we're good?"

Dr. Mishra started to object. "I haven't discharged Miss Novak. We need to see—"

"Look behind you," Mira said, pleased. "Filip brought my bag because I'm walking out of here tomorrow. I told him I've never felt better."

We turned around. A brown leather case sat at the foot of the bed. I sighed with relief. Mira was feeling better! She would go back to what she loved best—painting.

The doctor was deep in thought. Perhaps Mira's good turn

had taken him by surprise. Or perhaps he was worried about tomorrow night? Who would take over his shift at the hospital?

Mira clapped her hands. "I can't wait. It's been forever since I've been to a party! Sona, you can help me pick out a dress!"

Dev kissed her hand once again. "It will be a big do. Everyone who is anyone in Bombay will be there. Most of them are my parents' friends, business colleagues, relatives, aunties and so on—so it will be nice to see your familiar faces in the crowd. Until then, Mira-ji, Amit-ji." He patted Amit on the shoulder. "And Nurse Sona." He leaned toward me with a theatrical whisper. "And if this one doesn't claim you, I guarantee there will be others who will. That's what engagement parties are for." He made a rolling gesture with his hand and bowed to the room.

As he left, I felt a current of energy leave with him. What a presence that man had! I looked at Mira, who was glowing. While Dr. Mishra checked her chart, I took the thermometer out of my apron and put it under Mira's tongue.

98.6. Normal.

Mira grinned. "So I'm good to leave, correct?"

Dr. Mishra said, "You could leave tomorrow, but I don't recommend it. You're stable now, but we should have you here for another day or two to be sure. Your body underwent a great ordeal just five days ago."

Mira gave him her most charming smile. "I'll be fine, Doctor. Cross my heart and hope to die."

That was what Dr. Stoddard always said. My heartbeat skipped. In his case, I always took it as a joke between us. Mira's words felt more like a pronouncement.

Dr. Mishra frowned, but Mira could not be persuaded to extend her stay. "And, Sona, come to my apartment tomorrow afternoon. We'll have such fun with the dresses!"

She looked so incredibly happy. How could I say no?

Dr. Mishra left after signing off on Mira's chart and telling her we would all miss her at the hospital. He and I avoided looking at each other for the remainder of the night shift.

Over dinner with my mother, my news was all about Dev Singh. What he looked like, how he was with Mira, how she was with him. "If I hadn't been in the room, Mum, they might have climbed on top of one another," I told her. I'd pretended to be blasé about it, but I'd only ever read about things like that in *Saraswati Magazine*.

"Looks to me like you have a crush on this Mr. Singh."

I laughed. "No, Mum. He's fun to be around, but he's too fast for me. I don't know how this new wife of his is going to handle his flirtations. He was even making eyes at the sink in the room."

My mother cleared the table, laughing.

I turned in my chair to look at her. "Oh, and Mr. Singh has come from Oxford—that's where he and Dr. Mishra went to university—to announce his engagement to a Miss Gayatri Kaur. He said she is very beautiful, but he's only seen a photo of her. It's going to be a big party tonight. Devika Rani will be there, along with other film stars. Mira is going. Dr. Mishra is going. I've been invited too—" I stopped. How selfish of me to go on about a party my mother wouldn't be attending. I shook my head. "But I'm not planning to go, Mum. I don't know any of those people."

"Of course you're going to go! How often do you get invited to these kinds of things? It would be insulting not to go after being asked by the intended groom, Sona. Come, let's see what we can do as far as a dress for you."

I was relieved. She didn't sound peeved in the least. But the thought of going was making my stomach hurt. Meeting new people had never been comfortable for me. At the hospital, my position gave me excellent cover. My patients needed to know someone was in charge, and I could be outgoing in the service of nursing them back to health. They never suspected that I'd rather have been sitting in a corner chair with my nose in a book.

My mother was now rummaging inside her treasure chest. I heard her say, "Ah-ha!" She came back with a emerald silk sari bordered in gold *zari*.

"Mum, where did you get that? It's capital! I've never seen you wear it."

She waited till I'd cleared the table to lay the sari on top. Smoothing her hand over the soft material, she said, "I've never worn it. I thought I would when your father and I married." She sighed. I rubbed her arm and we were quiet for a while.

She unfolded the fabric. "*Accha.* I know you're not keen on wearing a sari, so we're going to turn this into a dress that will make people stop and take notice." She looked at my chest. "We're even going to show some cleavage."

"Mum! What's gotten into you? It's just a party. I can wear any old dress. And that's such an expensive sari. Why would you want to cut it up?"

Her face was stern. "No, you can't wear any old dress, Sona. I won't have my daughter show up at the party of the year looking like a beggar. We're going to do this properly." She held the fabric up to my shoulder, then at my waist. She played at pleating it, gathering the skirt, raising and lowering it against my chest. She didn't use a measuring tape; she knew my measurements by heart since she had always sewn all my clothes. After making a few rough sketches, she reworked the details on one of them. She nodded once, having made up her mind. I watched as she took her large shears to the fabric, slicing the silk.

"Is there anything I can do to help?" I'd never been a talented seamstress. For my mother, I'd hand-stitched the odd hem or purchased the supplies she needed and delivered the finished garments.

She looked at me thoughtfully. "You can pluck some of those flowers from the red silk cotton tree. Those will contrast nicely with your hair."

"I'll do it on the way back from Mira's apartment. Did I tell you she was released today? She's doing so much better. She asked me to help her pick out a dress." I grinned slyly at my mother. "Would you recommend we look for something that shows her cleavage too?"

"Cheeky bugger," my mother said, hiding her smile.

Mira and Filip lived in one of the Art Deco buildings on Marine Drive along the Back Bay. I'd seen these tony flats advertised in the newspaper—along with adverts for steel furniture from the Army & Navy Stores, radios, modern floor tiles. An exhibition of Ideal Homes this year promised the likes of Dev Singh a lifestyle enhanced by aluminum pots and pans, gas refrigerators and sleek toilets.

I pressed the button for Mira's apartment. A buzz and a click later, I was walking up the stairs to the fourth floor. She opened the door in a bathrobe. Her hair was freshly washed and her skin dewy. I was so used to seeing her in a hospital bed that I almost didn't recognize her. She pulled me inside and extended her arms. "What do you think?"

I looked around at the chic sofa and chairs, the steel light fixtures and geometrically patterned tile—so much like the advertising I'd seen. "Like it belongs in *The Thin Man*!" I said. At the Eros Cinema, not far from here, I'd fallen in love with the charming couple Myrna Loy and William Powell, as they drank martinis and solved crimes in New York City. Their flat in the movie could have been the model for Mira's.

Without offering me anything to drink or eat (perhaps that was only an Indian custom?), Mira went to her bedroom and pointed at the bed. There, she'd laid out four dresses. "I'll wear whichever one you choose."

I touched the fabric of the one closest to me. It was a rich hazelnut satin with puffed sleeves and an empire bodice. Next: an ivory silk crepe with a high round neckline and butterfly sleeves that would sway gracefully with the wearer's every move. I couldn't keep from smoothing my palm on the Grecian cowl neckline of the one with a flowing satin skirt. The last dress took my breath away. "This one," I said, lifting it from the bed and holding it against Mira's small frame. It was a shimmery peach satin. The halter top left the back exposed all the way down to the waist where a bias skirt skimmed the hips.

Mira pursed her lips. "You don't think it will make me look too flat? I've lost so much weight in the hospital. Morphine really takes away your appetite."

I smiled. "That's precisely the point. This dress is made for your build the way it is now." I checked my watch. I needed to rush home and get fitted for the dress my mother was sewing for me.

"Pick a dress for yourself. I mean—I don't mean it as charity." Mira gave me an uncertain smile. "Just that it would please me to see you wear it."

Normally, I might have taken exception to such welfare, but I knew Mira meant well, so I smiled. "As far as that goes, my mother has a surprise for me and you."

Mira sat on the satin bench at the foot of her bed and regarded me for a moment. It was as if she were looking right through me. "Sona, your life will be as big as you allow it to be. You will have memories rich and deep enough to fill the hollowness in here." She rubbed a circle on her sternum.

I sucked in a breath. She was doing that thing she did, forcing me open, searching for more. I felt as if I always fell short of her expectations.

"Not all of us are you, ma'am."

She rose from the bench and came to stand in front of me. With the flat of her hand, she rubbed a circle on my sternum and left it there. "I want big things for you, Sona. You do too. It's all in here and out there. Go find it."

I understood that she was encouraging me to explore the world, see things I'd never imagined, as she had. But…she'd had a privileged upbringing. Didn't she stop to wonder how someone like me could do that? Where was I supposed to go? With what money? My father's guilt fund? I could never bring myself to do that. As tempting as it sounded, the practical side of me, the one that didn't want to waste time powdering my face, recoiled. Why give me hope when I had no way to realize it?

I stepped around her. "If I don't leave now, my mother will be cross. Will you be alright?" It occurred to me that I hadn't seen her husband. "Where is Mr. Bartos?"

Her eyes strayed to the dresses on the bed. She began to put the ones she wasn't going to wear back in her mirrored wardrobe. "Out and about. Goodness knows where. He'll be there tonight though. He may have gone to get his shoes polished."

I rushed home on my bicycle, thinking about what the painter had said. Although I'd told my mother I would have been comfortable wearing one of my old dresses, Mira's evening gowns had made me long for something far more glamorous. It was now five in the evening, the time I would normally have left for work. Somehow, with Mrs. Mehta's and Dev Singh's influence, replacements for Dr. Mishra and me had been found for the night shift.

I found Mum at her sewing machine with pins in her mouth and a pencil tucked behind her ear. The table was littered with pieces of the emerald sari and green satin for the petticoat. When I entered, she said, "Dinner is on the counter. First, eat. Then come and try this on so I can baste it."

She was a nimble seamstress and always met her customers' deadlines, but I knew this was a particularly fast turnaround. I had to be at the Singh household in three hours, and I needed to allow at least three-quarters of an hour to get there, first on the double-decker bus, then in a rickshaw. That would be the least expensive way. I was used to riding my bike everywhere in a skirt, but I could hardly do so in a floor-length gown.

I didn't have much of an appetite, so jittery was my stomach. I ate half a roti with some dal and went to the landing to bathe in the bathroom. When I returned, my mother asked me to strip down to my slip. She rose from her chair, dragging pieces of the gown with her. She held up both sides of the bodice and pinned them together to form a center seam between my breasts. I looked down and saw how much of my cleavage was exposed.

"Mum, you know I can't go anywhere looking like that!" I started to pinch the center seam so it would start two inches above my mother's last pin.

She slapped my hand away. "This is my first opportunity to design an evening gown for my daughter. Leave the design to me and we'll argue about it later." She was smiling at her handiwork, which softened my resistance. I hadn't seen her this excited about anything since she'd made my first nurse's uniform—so full of pride she'd been. I kissed her forehead.

From the top of the bodice, two long straps wound over my shoulder and across my back. She'd made them from the *zari* border of her sari. With a stick of white chalk, she made a few marks and then removed the bodice. Next, she brought the long skirt that would attach to the bodice to see how much she needed to hem from the bottom. She planned to finish the hem with the remaining gold border. The skirt was slim-fitting and flared out below my knees. Together with the bodice, the dress created a long elegant column that made me appear taller than I was. We only had the one mirror over the sink so I couldn't see all of me, but my mother's expression was reflection enough.

"All eyes will be on you, my beautiful girl. Now, take that off and let me finish it."

I removed it carefully so as not to undo the pins my mother had inserted.

"Shoes!" I cried. I didn't have the right shoes to wear with this dress.

"Fatima!" my mother said. "Go!"

I dressed hastily and ran across the landing. Fatima, with her rosy cheeks and baby-making energy, answered the door. When she saw who it was, she looked concerned. "Mummi *theek hai*?"

"Yes, Mum is fine." I explained where I was going that evening and that my mother was sewing an evening dress for me but I had no shoes to wear with it.

Fatima grinned. "Come!" she invited me into their apartment, which was more spacious than ours. In one corner was a rosewood almirah. She opened it to reveal a rainbow of *salwar kameez*, many of them with gold and silver threading. Along the bottom of the armoire were a row of shoes, neatly aligned. There was one pair of high heels in black satin.

Fatima said, "My wedding shoes."

I was almost afraid to touch them because they were so sleek. There was not a mark on them. What if I accidently stepped on horse dung while walking or a passing cyclist splashed mud on them? In the streets of Bombay, there were a thousand ways to soil what you were wearing. But Fatima, who seemed to sense my hesitation, said, "Try them on."

I didn't see how I could possibly fit into them. Fatima had smaller feet than I did. They were a little tight, but Fatima told me they would stretch because they were made of fabric. "But, Fatima—" I started to say.

"Sona, look," she said, pointing to her feet, which were already starting to swell because of her pregnancy. "When will I be wearing them?" she laughed.

Her generosity overwhelmed me. I squeezed my eyes shut and opened them again to make sure I wasn't dreaming. I touched her shoulder. "Thank you, Fatima. I promise to take good care of them."

She patted my shoulder. *"Salam alaikum."*

"Alaikum salam."

My mother had done her best. Now she stood back to appraise her results. "Oh, Sona! I think this dress looks better on you than it looked as a sari on me." She took the small mirror off the wall and held it at a distance so I could see the full-length gown. Our room was small, so she had to step out on the landing.

"Farther, Mum. Farther." I could see that if I moved a certain way, half my breast would be exposed. I pinched the two sides of the bodice together.

"Stop that," my mother said as she moved another foot on the landing toward Fatima's door, still holding up the mirror.

"So I could go naked in the streets?"

"Don't you dare try to close that gap tonight. It ruins the design."

Fatima came out of her flat to see what the commotion was about. When she saw me, her eyes went wide. Then she covered her smile with her hand and said something in Urdu. She pointed to my cleavage and clapped, obviously delighted with the dress.

Embarrassed, I walked out on the landing to wrest the mirror from my mother. "See, Mum? People will be staring!"

"For all the right reasons." We turned to see who had spoken. Dr. Mishra was standing in the street just beyond the courtyard. He was wearing a black suit with a mandarin collar, white shirt and tie.

I blushed, feeling foolish in a gown designed to elicit that kind of response.

He looked at Fatima, at my mother, then at the sky above us. "I hope you don't mind. It seemed…a long way to go for a woman alone…especially one who is dressed for a party. I have a tonga waiting for us. Haven't gotten around to buying a car yet."

I could feel my cheeks turning red. I looked at my mother, who seemed as surprised as I was. "H-how did you know where I lived?" I asked.

"Ah. I have access to lots of records. I might even know your birth weight."

I couldn't think of anything to say. My mother went inside our flat and returned with a black shawl. She was grinning, with a sly look directed at me.

"Shall we?" Dr. Mishra indicated the waiting horse carriage up the road.

"Jao," my mother mouthed the word as she lay the shawl around my shoulders.

"Jao," Fatima mouthed, her kohl-lined eyes twinkling.

I went down the stairs and out the front gate.

Dr. Mishra helped me step up into the horse carriage. I cringed, mortified that he'd seen where I lived—the home where we rented a room, with its peeling paint and mildewed walls. He'd seen my street, so narrow that a tonga couldn't get through. He'd seen the trains that barely missed us as they screamed past. What must he think? It was one thing to see me at work with my pressed uniform and tidy hair and another to see me in my squalid surroundings at home.

But if he'd noticed, he didn't show it. He was saying, "Perhaps you've been to a thousand occasions like this one. When the Singhs throw a party, it's a little overwhelming. I thought you could use…some support. I know I could." He attempted a small laugh.

I was still reeling from seeing him in my neighborhood. When I didn't say anything, he stopped talking and looked straight ahead.

I pulled the shawl tighter around my shoulders. When I could find my voice again, I said, "I was surprised to see you."

"Of course, of course. I do apologize. I thought I was helping. Perhaps I overstepped. We work together and perhaps we shouldn't… Please accept my…" He ran a finger around his collar, as if it was choking him. "Would you rather I jump off and you could go the rest of the way in the carriage? I can always grab another one…"

The image of him jumping off the carriage made me laugh. He'd only intended to do a good deed. He'd barely noticed the neighborhood. "Thank you," I said. I turned to meet his eyes, feeling my spirits lift. "Prince Rama."

He smiled. "So now I'm the hero of the *Ramayana*?"

I smiled.

He considered me a moment longer. "Right then," he said, turning his eyes toward the road.

For a while, we were quiet.

"Doctor, I only know what Mr. Singh told me about you. Where were you brought up?"

"Shimla."

I waited. "To wolves?"

"Oh, right. My father was a judge. My parents died in a car accident a long time ago. An auntie raised me."

"No brothers or sisters?"

"None. I learned to play the games my auntie liked to play. Bridge. Pachisi. Gin rummy."

"Dr. Stoddard keeps threatening to teach me gin rummy."

Dr. Mishra tapped my hand with his index finger. "*'Keep your cards close and your money closer.'*" He smiled.

His touch sent such a charge through me that for a moment I couldn't speak.

He turned his head. "Oh, dear, have I overstepped again? Perhaps you're a secret gambler? There, you see? *'When you have an ass for a friend, expect nothing but kicks.'* I must be the ass in that equation."

I chuckled. I hadn't expected him to be funny. He was always so serious at the hospital.

"Tell me more about your friend Dev Singh."

"Dev. Yes. We became acquainted at Bishop Cotton. It's a school near Shimla. I'm two years ahead of him. We saw each other again at Oxford where there were only a handful of Indian students. We became a tight group. Still keep in touch. Dev read history. I studied medicine. He's studying architecture now. And I'm here in Bombay working with some very nice nurses—good nurses." He studied his hands.

It was meant as a compliment and I took it as such.

"You haven't been long in Bombay, have you?" he asked.

"No."

"Have you seen Banganga Tank or the Hanging Gardens?"

I shook my head.

He looked at his watch. "We have some time. Shall we?" He told the tonga driver where to go. "The water tank is an ancient pilgrimage site for Jains. And now devotees of Lord Shiva go there. Me, I like it for its quietly obstinate presence in the middle of all this wealth."

We arrived at a rectangular water reservoir amidst the mansions of Malabar Hill. On either side, a series of steps led into the water. There were *diyas* lit along the edge where worshippers had come to pray. I stole a glance at the doctor. I could have told him then what I heard between Matron and Dr. Holbrook, but he seemed so relaxed. His eyes didn't wander, looking for a place to rest. Maybe I was fretting over nothing. Mira had looked so healthy earlier. Why raise the alarm? I let it go.

The Singhs' three-story mansion was situated at one end of Malabar Hill. Our carriage skirted a manicured lawn with a pond at its center and stopped in front of an impressive stone staircase—wide enough for twenty men to scale. The house was massive, more like a small palace with twenty bedrooms. Men and women in their finery milled about the outdoor veranda while uniformed servants passed around hors d'oeuvres and cocktails. Clay *diyas*, their flickering flames giving off a soft glow, lined the balustrade.

We passed through the veranda into the house where ceramic vases with pink damask roses perfumed the room. Mira stood in the center, surrounded by admirers. She waved us over and introduced us to an art critic, a developer, a musician and a restaurateur. I looked around the room for her husband but didn't see him.

"Filip's sat in the corner there." She pointed to the back of the house. "How do I look, Dr. Mishra?" She twirled around for us.

"Healthy?" he said with a smile that was more of a grimace.

Mira batted him on his chest. "Stop! None of that gloom-and-doom silliness. I'm fine now." She turned to me. "Sona! Take that silly wrap off. Let's see what your mother put together."

I glanced at Dr. Mishra. How could Mira have been so thoughtless? Now the doctor would know my mother sewed my gown. I chastised myself. I was being a snob, not wanting to admit that my mother worked with her hands like a common laborer.

Reluctantly, I unwrapped the shawl, checking the front of my dress to make sure my breasts were not in full view.

"Oh, my! Our Sona has grown up, hasn't she, Amit?"

Dr. Mishra, who had been staring at me, now directed his gaze at his shoes, at the marble floor. "Nice work, Nurse Falstaff."

Mira looked cross. "Amit, you must call her Sona or people will think the two of you have come to rescue someone in an emergency." She glanced at me. "Turn around so I can see the back."

I did as she asked. She gasped. "Exquisite. There's not a woman here who can compete with that. Let's show Dev. He's here somewhere."

As we wound through the crowd—there must have been over two hundred guests—I saw men in maharaja coats, English suits and mandarin jackets like Dr. Mishra's. But it was the women in their jewel-colored saris of silk and satin and chiffon and necklaces of raw diamonds who glittered under the chandeliers. Scattered amidst the guests were Englishwomen, politicians and businessmen in three-piece suits and a handful of Anglo-Indians like me. Western garb may have been more obviously revealing, but the formal blouses of Indian women exposed backs, midriffs and bare arms too—albeit more subtly. Nonetheless, I knew dresses like mine would be subject to critical scrutiny and whispered asides of the Indian women.

"Amit!" We turned to see Dev making his way toward us in his white maharaja coat, the collar and cuffs embroidered in silver thread. He shook hands with Dr. Mishra and kissed Mira on the cheek.

"You've turned out quite nicely—as usual." He winked at Mira. "Ashok Gupta is dying to meet you."

Mira looked impressed. "Another film star? He's here too?"

"He has one of your paintings in his house. Calls you India's conscience. Compares you to Tagore. Says both of you understand the value of women."

"Does he?"

"He says Tagore brought Indian literature into the global sphere and you're doing the same with Indian art."

"So he thinks of me as more Indian than European? Good!" She laughed. "Then I'm dying to meet him too."

Now Dev turned to me. He blinked. "Nurse Sona?" Then he smiled. "I almost didn't recognize you without your cap. Quite a transformation."

I wanted to cross my arms over my chest, which is where his gaze had landed. Instead, I pretended that I wore something this revealing every evening of my life and inclined my head to acknowledge the compliment. I was surprised to feel Dr. Mishra's fingers on my elbow, as if he wanted to steer me away from Dev. But Dev was too quick. He put a warm hand on the bare flesh of my back. My skin recoiled, but he seemed not to notice. He took Mira's elbow. "There are all sorts here tonight. Government officials, newspaper editors, medical administrators, filmmakers. I want to introduce you to a few of them." For Mira, that turned out to be an art historian from Delhi who wanted to write a paper about her. For Dr. Mishra, it was a Parsi gentleman interested in building another private hospital in Bombay. Once he'd engaged them in conversation, Dev led me to the cocktail bar, glad-handing and greeting several guests along the way. At the bar, he asked me what I'd like them to make for me. Other than the odd beer, I'd never touched alcohol.

Sensing my indecision, he asked, "Which sounds better to you? Salty Dog, Sidecar or Death in the Afternoon?"

I laughed. "Are those the names of drinks or sordid novels?"

He grinned. "I think you're more of an old-fashioned sort, aren't you?" He turned to the bartender and ordered a cocktail with bourbon, simple sugar and bitters.

"I'll have one of those too, Dev." It was Dr. Mishra, coming up behind us. "Your father was looking for you."

Dev sucked air through his teeth. He bowed to me, patted Dr. Mishra on the back and went in search of his father.

"What do you think?" Dr. Mishra asked, pointing to my drink.

"Horrible," I laughed. "I think I'd rather have a *nimbu pani*." The bartender, who'd heard me, squeezed limes into a tall glass, added water and sugar and presented it to me with a sprig of mint. I thanked him.

Dr. Mishra slid my old-fashioned toward him and took a sip. He nodded and took another. "Maybe I'm an old-fashioned kind of man."

"You know, Doctor, whenever Mr. Singh is in my vicinity, I feel as if you're trying to rescue me," I said.

"Am I?" He looked into his cocktail glass. "How do you know I'm not protecting *him* from you?"

I arched a brow. "I hadn't realized I was that intimidating."

"Dev called you daunting, remember?" he said dryly.

A trio on the back terrace—sitar, harmonium and tabla—had been playing a song by Kanan Devi, one of my mother's favorite singers. We went there with our drinks to admire the thousand twinkling lamps on the edges of the lawn. Round tables covered in white linen and decorated with gardenia centerpieces dotted the expansive green.

"I told you I'm not selling them!" It was a woman's voice.

The outburst seemed to come from below. Dr. Mishra and I looked down to see Mira and Filip. Mira looked furious, her cheeks an unhealthy red. Filip was smoking his pipe calmly.

"We need the money, *broučku*. The rent is overdue," Filip said.

"And whose fault is that? I'm not the one buying expensive

clothes—" She flicked a wrist at his three-piece suit. "Everything I have is five years old."

"You could buy something nice for yourself." His voice neither rose nor fell.

"With what? I make all the art, and you spend all the money. I—" She gasped.

"Are you alright, Mira?" Now he did sound concerned.

"Yes." She took a deep breath. "I'm fine. I'm working on a plan for the money. Let's just go enjoy the party."

We watched them walk around the perimeter of the stairs and into the far side of the drawing room. They hadn't seen us. Dr. Mishra and I looked at one another. I felt a little guilty and embarrassed at witnessing such a private moment. I wondered if he did too.

The band stopped playing. Someone was tapping a drinking glass. We filed into the drawing room with other guests who'd been on the terrace. There, on a dais, stood Dev and an older gentleman, whom I assumed was his father—so much did they resemble one another. An older woman in fine regalia, whom I guessed to be Dev's mother, stood to the side. Guests on the terraces began to join the crowd inside.

"Friends, thank you for joining us tonight for this most auspicious occasion—at least that's what the astrologer has guaranteed or we may have to ask for our money back…" Dev's father paused for the laughter to die down. He was holding a cocktail glass in one hand. His other hand was firmly on his son's shoulder. "This one has made us proud with his studies at Oxford. Soon he will be one of India's leading architects. A man like that needs a wife by his side who is intelligent, kind, compassionate and supportive. It doesn't hurt if she is beautiful also." His chuckle cued the guests, who complied, the men more so than the women. Dev hid a smile as he lowered his gaze to his embroidered shoes. "Which is why we are honored to add the family of Krishna Kaur and their intelligent, compassionate, beautiful daughter Gayatri to ours for what we know will be a long-lasting and happy marriage."

The musicians started up again, the sitar taking the lead. The gathering made way for a formal procession of the father and mother of the fiancée, their daughter behind them, her head covered by a red-violet *pallu* beaded with tiny seed pearls. I stole a look at Dev, whose lips had parted. He was as curious to lay his eyes on the woman he would marry as the guests were. Everyone had squeezed in closer to catch a glimpse of the soon-to-be Mrs. Singh. Dr. Mishra had been pushed forward as I had, the two of us pressed together in a way that should have made me uncomfortable but did not. He placed a protective palm against my exposed back. His warm touch sent a pleasurable ache between my legs. He must have felt my body relax against his touch because he turned his head to look at me. I returned his gaze. My breath quickened. For a moment, it seemed as if we were alone in this drawing room and he might reach for me. I would have let him. In the end, he cleared his throat and broke off eye contact. He removed his hand from my back. Was that a look of guilt on his face? Did I mistake his gallantry for interest?

With an effort, I turned my attention to the dais where the fiancée's father, dressed as elegantly as the Singh men, was making his remarks about the favorable joining of their two families. Finally, he stood aside to let his daughter, Gayatri, stand face-to-face with Dev. The guests craned their heads for a better look. Slowly, the young woman removed her *pallu*. But instead of casting her eyes downward like a coquette, she tilted her chin up and looked him in the eyes. From the way she carried herself, I could see that pride was her birthright. Here was a woman who thought well of herself. She would be defiant. She would insist on being treated like an equal. They smiled at each other. Was it one of happiness or relief or bravado? Two people who didn't know one another would start a journey of discovering how to be with one another and in what measure they would love and lie.

Dev took her hand in his and turned toward the crowd, who

started clapping. Now I saw the black arches of her eyebrows, the large kohl-lined eyes. Her lips, plump and inviting, her easy sensuality. Her mouth had been painted violet to match her sari. Heavy earrings laden with cut amethysts dangled against a jeweled choker that spanned the top of her neck to her shoulders. She did them justice, as if she were used to wearing such adornments daily. I touched my bare neck, aware that such finery would never be in my future. Even though Gayatri Kaur was on a dais, she lifted her chin, looking down at the crowd. Was it so she could appear more imposing? Or was it because she thought herself better than us?

I heard the guests behind me whisper, "I thought she would be younger."

Another gentleman to my right wondered, "Why did they wait so long to get her married? Is there something wrong with her?" The crowd was dispersing, some heading toward the food and drinks tables, others congratulating the families and greeting the young couple.

A matron ahead of me was saying, "I heard the Singhs' first choice for a wife fell through."

Her companion said, "What I heard was that the Kaurs had to get the older daughter married before they could arrange something for Gayatri. The older one is *pagla*. She fell off a swing when she was little." The woman made a face. "Finally, they found a family who took her off their hands for a substantial dowry. So now it's Gayatri's turn to be married. Although twenty-four is really the limit."

Twenty-four? Gayatri was only a year older than me. If people thought she was too old for marriage, what did they think of me? Did they all talk like this behind my back?

I followed Dr. Mishra to stand in line and give my regards to the families. Mira joined us.

"Isn't Gayatri too beautiful? And so masterful!" Mira imitated a Rani of Jhansi stance, the feisty Maharani who dared to go against the British in the 1857 rebellion.

Mira's enthusiasm and high spirits were evident in the color of her cheeks. "I must ask what Dev's fiancée thinks of the Ajanta Cave sculptures. Her family apparently lives near there." I watched the painter closely for signs of fatigue or waning energy. I'm sure Amit—now I was calling him by his first name in my head!—was doing the same. She had only been released from the hospital this morning and she should have been resting. But other than the gray hollows under her eyes, she seemed fully recovered.

As we approached Gayatri and Dev, who were surrounded by well-wishers, it was obvious that they were very much a modern couple, the kind India adored. Both spoke fluent English, displayed Indian grace and Western manners in equal measure, and talked of books and politics. They seemed at ease with businessmen and academicians alike, discussing India's future. Yes, I thought, they were a good match for each other. Perhaps Gayatri would be the one to curtail Dev's roving eye.

When it was our turn to congratulate the couple, Amit was whisked away by someone, and I was left alone with Gayatri. Her eyes, so large they dominated her face, regarded me with curiosity. For some reason, I blurted, "My mother is Indian." I'd assumed she wanted to know about my coloring, but I realized she was looking at my dress.

"Was it your mother's sari?"

I nodded.

"Remarkable."

I didn't know if I should be flattered or insulted by her comment. She'd already turned to greet another guest. I didn't even get a chance to congratulate her on her engagement.

Dev, who had taken his place next to her again, grinned at me. "Hey, Old Fashioned." He leaned close to my ear. "Your dress is making the old *sahibs* in here very uncomfortable. *Shabash!*"

On the back lawn, bearers were serving plates heaped with meat and vegetable curries or hearty English fare, whichever the guests preferred. They brought rose sherbets, *falooda*, cocktails and limewater as requested. Mira drank every cocktail put in front of her. She kept up a brilliant patter with everyone at our table.

The Indian minister of cultural affairs sat to Mira's right. He was urging her to try her hand at a series of paintings showing the glory of Indian architecture. "Perhaps the palace in Udaipur? Or, since you prefer to paint in South India, what about the Mysore Palace? They're both stunning."

"People are what matter, Minister. I cannot say with buildings what I can say with people as my subjects."

"But what you are saying, Miss Novak, is setting India back in time. These ancient rituals you paint are bound to tell the world that Indians are—are..."

"Backward?" Mira grinned. "How about thinking of my paintings as a way of highlighting all that is good—and true—about India? Traditions that have meaning going back thousands of years. Women who keep those traditions going despite the cost to their health and their hearts." She looked at the minister through narrowed eyes. "Or perhaps it's my style you object to?"

The older man looked uncomfortable. He pulled on his collar.

The matron sitting next to him said, "Rajasthani miniatures are known the world over. That's a beautiful style for you to try, Miss Novak."

"And it's known as a very Indian style, isn't it? But if we limit our idea of Indian art, we limit our experience of India. *She*—India—is so much bigger than our understanding of her. She should determine what represents her. Not us." Mira's eyes were shining as she lifted her wineglass for a sip. The minister wasn't convinced, but I could see the dowager purse her lips thoughtfully.

Mira's husband sat on the other side of her in his white three-piece suit, neither speaking to anyone nor ignoring them. When he wasn't smoking his pipe, he was chewing on the bit, looking at his wife. There was a faint smile playing about his lips, as if he were enjoying the show.

I hadn't much of an appetite, not since the feeling that bloomed within me when Amit placed his hand on my back. Sitting next to him was near impossible. He and I avoided looking at each other. I wasn't sure what to say to him, what to make of what had happened between us. Had I imagined the look he'd given me? Was it merely a spinster's imagination playing up? Just as I was thinking about getting up from the table, Mrs. Mehta accosted me, heavy gold bangles jangling on her wrists. I'd seen her across the room earlier talking to some of her cronies.

She put one hand on the back of my chair and another on the back of Dr. Mishra's. "So, Doctor, did you know our Sona is quite the problem solver?"

Amit's gray eyes turned to mine in question.

I felt the same rush every time he looked at me. I looked away.

Mrs. Mehta grinned. "It has to do with a pair of lovebirds. Perhaps I see another pair in front of me, *hahn-nah*?"

I colored. Amit cleared his throat. Mrs. Mehta patted my shoulder, smiled mysteriously at Amit, and turned her charm on Mira, whom she'd been dying to talk to.

I couldn't take another moment next to him without being able to touch him or say anything meaningful. I rose from my chair. A bearer came up behind me and pulled the chair out in one swift move. Amit looked up at me. "Are you leaving?"

I nodded. I couldn't tell him that he was the cause of my erratic pulse. I needed space away from him, away from the charged excitement of this party, to collect my thoughts.

He pushed his chair back and put his napkin by his plate. "I'll… Let's get you a tonga."

I wanted to tell him I'd take care of it, but I didn't want to call attention to myself so I simply walked up the stairs and onto the terrace. I needed to find my wrap. It was far chillier now that night had fallen. I entered the deserted drawing room and veered left into the hallway. At this point, everyone was on the lawn. There was a cloakroom nearby where wraps had been deposited. I heard Amit's footsteps behind me. I opened the door closest to me. No wraps. I tried the second door. The bathroom. As I walked nearer to the third door, I heard voices, deliberately kept low.

"I thought she was going to be younger."

"What would you do with a younger wife that you can't do with an older one? Both can produce heirs."

I realized I'd happened upon a conversation between Dev and his father. I turned around to retrace my steps but I almost ran into Amit, who was right behind me. He put a finger to my lips to keep me from crying out.

"Besides, *beta*, her family is useful."

"Meaning?"

"Mr. Kaur is an influential magistrate. He will keep your unpleasant...business...out of the courts." There was a pause. Dev mumbled something I didn't catch.

When he spoke again, the elder Singh's voice was stern. "I can't have this happening again, Dev. You will do right by Gayatri. My hands are tied." It sounded like an order.

I felt Amit's hand take mine to lead us back the way we'd come. We ran into a bearer in the drawing room, and Amit asked him to find my wrap. The servant nodded and went down a different hallway.

"We shouldn't have heard that, and we shouldn't have heard Mira and her husband talking either," I said, feeling like an interloper.

"Sona, perhaps I should tell you something...about Dev..."

The servant was back. He handed me my wrap. Amit took it from me and covered my shoulders with it. When I turned to thank him, his face was inches from mine. "Do you know that's the first time you've called me by my first name? Miss Novak and Mr. Singh called me Sona from the first moment I met them. And I've known you a year longer."

He backed up a step. In Bombay, the city of the film industry, you never knew if you were about to star in the next juicy piece of gossip. It was always better to be safe. He'd just crossed the line by calling me Sona, and he was aware of the repercussions. "Come. Let's get our tonga."

"There's no need for you to accompany me."

His head reared back. "In that dress? Have you not noticed the way these men have been ogling you tonight? If I hadn't been by your side, who knows what would have happened?"

That's why he'd been shadowing me all evening? Not because he wanted to be near me but because of my dress? This was too much! The pleasure I'd felt in his company earlier gave way to outrage. I walked quickly to the door and called out to a bearer. "I need a tonga please."

"Of course." The servant went down the front stairs to the road below.

"Sona, please don't be angry. Let me drop you off at your house. I'm not joking. It's not safe at this time of night. There are protests on the streets."

"I leave work at this time every single day. I'm used to the night."

"You cycle home. It's not the same thing."

He knew I cycled home? What was he doing, watching me out his office window?

The bearer came back to the front door. "Memsahib, carriage is here."

Amit got to him before me. He gave the servant a few coins and ushered me down the steps.

"Will you stop being so stubborn and take help when it's offered?"

I slowed down. Wasn't that what I was always telling Indira? I knew she needed help even if she didn't. Was that what Amit was doing? And here I was being stubborn. And petty.

He sensed the change in me as I came to a stop. "Now what?" He rarely sounded exasperated, but he did so now.

"You're right. I need you to take me home."

He closed his eyes. The relief on his face was palpable.

When he helped me onto the rickshaw, I wondered what the people at the party thought when they saw the two of us together. Did they think we were married, bickering as married people do? Or did they assume we were lovers, quarreling, and that all would be well when the spat was over? Like Mrs. Mehta's lovebirds.

It was always difficult to avoid sitting shoulder to shoulder in a tonga unless you were absolutely determined not to. The seat was narrow, and the jostling caused by trotting horses made riders slide toward the middle. I made no attempt to stop the slide toward Amit. Every inch of my skin was aware of Amit's body heat against my thigh, my breast, my shoulder, my cheek. He was trying to protect me from the jarring motion of the carriage by extending his left hand across the back of the tonga. The sleeve of his jacket rubbed against my back, sending goose bumps down my legs. Some urgent need was tempting me to press my body against his. How would I possibly keep from doing that on the forty-five-minute ride to my flat? I clasped my hands together and thought of India's colonial blight, the children of the *kothas*, my mother's eggplant curry. Anything to distract me from laying my hands on him.

I cleared my throat. "Where will Gayatri and Dev settle, do you think?"

Amit was looking straight ahead, as if he were trying to avoid looking at me. "I would have thought Bombay—to live with his family—but I heard someone mention that they would live in Jaipur. Something about Gayatri not wanting to live in a joint family. It's probably just as well."

"Why do you say that?"

"Dev is complicated. It's what I was trying to tell you earlier. He's very hail-fellow-well-met, but he can carry it too far… where women are concerned. I helped him once at Oxford—I'd just started studying medicine. Not yet a full-fledged doctor. There was a young woman he… Anyway, it's a side of him I don't care for." Now he did turn his head to look at me. His lips were a hair's breadth away. "Have I ruined your image of him? Perhaps you—"

I couldn't help myself. I placed my hands on either side of his face and pressed my lips to his. Me, Miss Old Fashioned. I knew you weren't supposed to do that with the tonga driver just six feet away. I knew you weren't supposed to do that with a man who was your superior at work. I knew you weren't supposed to do that sort of thing as a woman—that it was a man's domain. I did it anyway.

But then I felt his lips move against mine. Tenderly. Mine had been an act of frenzy. His was a slow build of desire. I hadn't been dreaming after all. He did at least feel some of what I did.

He pulled away first, taking my hands in his and bringing them down to my lap. He was looking at me as if he were seeing me for the first time. He blew air out of his mouth.

"Dev Singh is not my cup of tea, Doctor," I said.

"That's good to know, Nurse."

He seemed to remember that we were in a public vehicle and reluctantly let go of my hands. Tonga drivers coming from Malabar Hill tended to know all the houses they serviced as well as the owners, the groundskeepers and chauffeurs. If our driver saw us, we'd be giving him plenty to talk about. Slowly, Amit turned to the front and placed his arm behind my back once more. This time, he didn't try to keep from touching me. He moved in closer.

The carriage couldn't make it down our narrow street, so Amit walked me to our front door. He guided me with a hand at my elbow. I wanted so much for him to put his arm around my waist, to slide his hand under my wrap so I could feel his warm palm against my naked back. But it was eleven in the evening, and any scandal—even public displays of affection among married couples—was entertainment for prying eyes. We lived in

India, not Prague or Paris or Florence or any of the places where Mira had lived and loved so freely. Where could Amit and I go (assuming he wanted to)? Not to my flat where my mother was waiting for me. Not to Amit's apartment where word of the indiscretion would travel faster than a monkey can scale a banyan tree. The man who shined shoes at the corner of Amit's apartment building would tell the peanut vendor on the next corner, who would tell his cousin the mechanic, who would tell his wife, the one who cleaned the house of a society matron, and before you knew it, all of Bombay would know Dr. Mishra had had a *female* visitor—or was she a harlot?—late at night. *And did you see the half-naked gown she was wearing?*

So Amit left me at the front door of our building without a word but with a look that told me he wished our evening had ended differently.

CHAPTER 6

The next night, I arrived for my shift in a brilliant mood. Mira was healthy again and back in her modern apartment. And I would get to see Amit, something that made me nervous and excited at the same time.

Last night, as soon as I entered our flat, my mother had peppered me with questions. I described to her in detail what the women at the Singh party were wearing, what people thought of my emerald dress, what Gayatri Kaur looked like, what delicacies were served, a few of the conversations I'd overheard. I left out the ones I wasn't meant to hear. Thankfully, my mother attributed my giddy retelling to the glamour of the event, not to the moment Amit and I had shared, which I would also keep to myself.

Rebecca came into the stockroom as I was changing. "Mira Novak is back." She reached in her locker for her uniform.

"Back?"

"She was brought in again. High fever. I heard she was at some fancy do last night. Probably not the best idea, given how sick she's been." She pinned her hair up and put her cap on her head. "You wouldn't know anything about that, would you?"

I sat heavily on the bench, replaying scenes from the Singh party. Had Mira been hiding her pain?

Rebecca leaned against the closed door of her locker. A smile was playing about her lips. "She's a bit of a princess, isn't she? Always getting what she wants. I wonder if Dr. Holbrook would have allowed her to go home?"

I felt defensive on behalf of Amit. I wanted to tell her I was there when Mira said she was leaving the hospital and there was no arguing with her—which supported Rebecca's claim that she was a princess. That much was true, but there was so much more to Mira than that. I opened my mouth to explain but thought the better of it. Rebecca was goading me. If I responded, I might say something I would later regret.

Rebecca pushed herself off her locker. "She may not make it this time."

My breathing slowed. "What do you mean?"

"Just that. She's really sick. She should never have left the hospital. But you would have known that, being her night nurse." Did I see a glimmer of satisfaction on her face before she left the room?

I tied my apron hastily and pinned my hat on. My heart was beating fast, faster. Mira had seemed so lively at the party last night. How could she have relapsed so quickly?

I rushed to her room. Mira's forehead was lined with sweat. I wiped it down with a cold washcloth. I took her pulse, which was slow. I checked her chart. She'd come in two hours before my shift and was administered morphine for the pain. Dr. Holbrook hadn't seen her, but Amit had, and he'd recommended more morphine in another hour. Mira opened her eyes when I called her name.

"I'm going to take your temperature. Open your mouth," I coaxed.

"Sona," she said. "The paintings."

I looked behind me. They were gone of course. The paintings had been removed yesterday when Mira was discharged. Probably sent back to her apartment.

"Downstairs," she said.

"Downstairs?"

She nodded, just barely moving her head.

There was only one floor below us. The equipment room.

I was still holding the thermometer. "The paintings are in the equipment room?"

She nodded again. She swallowed and then let out a jagged scream. My stomach churned from seeing her in so much pain.

I put the thermometer in my apron pocket and reached for the syringe. I cleaned her skin and plunged the needle into her vein, giving her only half the amount in the vial. The other half would have to wait for another hour. Within seconds, she calmed down.

My breathing was labored. I'd almost felt my heart stop. I went to the room sink and splashed cold water on my face. Right, I told myself, I needed to do something, take action. Mira had sweat so much she would need a change of sheets. I would go to the stockroom to get fresh sheets and towels. But first, I would talk to Matron or Amit or Dr. Holbrook, whomever I saw first, about why she had relapsed.

It happened during the twenty minutes I left her room.

Don't allow yourself to get too close to the sick. Well, it was too late now. Mira was not just another patient to me. I ran to Matron's office. It was empty. Dr. Holbrook was in surgery. I looked for Amit on every floor. Where was he? I hurried to the stockroom to pick up a clean set of sheets and towels and get back to Mira. I was still a few doors away when I saw Rebecca leave Mira's room and proceed down the hall in the opposite direction. I slowed. What was Rebecca doing in Mira's room? Had Mira called out for someone to help while I was gone?

When I entered the room, I could tell something was amiss. Still carrying the sheets, I ran to her bed. Her pallor was a sickly gray and her lips were turning purple. Her breathing was so shallow her chest barely rose. Her skin was clammy. I rang the red bell next to the bed—the one that sounded the general alarm—to summon help while I checked her pulse. Faint. Even so, I asked, "Miss Novak?" She'd been doing so well last night. What had triggered the recurrence? We had all hoped for a full recovery.

Within moments, Matron burst into the room, followed by Amit. I stepped aside to await orders. Mira's chest was no longer moving.

Amit pressed his stethoscope on Mira's chest. He checked inside her mouth, the needle mark on the inside of her elbow where I'd given her the morphine shot. He stretched her upper eyelids to check her pupils. He pumped her chest, then checked her heartbeat with his stethoscope again. He did this multiple times until, with a sigh, he stopped. He glanced at Matron and something passed between them. Matron kissed the cross on the chain she wore around her neck. My hand flew to my mouth to keep from crying out. Amit shot me a look, a silent apology.

Just then, Mira's husband stepped into the room. Filip Bartos stood perfectly still, his eyes scanning the room: Mira, Matron, the doctor, me. He looked alarmed, the strongest expression I'd ever seen in his face.

Amit said, "Mr. Bartos, I'm dreadfully sorry. I know this must be as much a shock for you as it is for us. Yesterday, she seemed to be on the mend." He went to Mira's husband and gently touched his arm. "I tried to get in touch with you several times before she was discharged yesterday. I tried to dissuade her from leaving the hospital. In my opinion, she needed further analysis, but as you know, she was determined to go." He paused, searching the other man's face to see if he'd understood. Filip Bartos merely stared at Mira's lifeless body. Amit dropped his arm. "We knew the morphine was no longer working as well as it should have. Perhaps we missed something. I'm so sorry. She will be missed. *I* will miss her."

I glanced at her chart. Dr. Holbrook had doubled her dosage

since she'd been readmitted to the hospital. Why hadn't he just taken Amit's suggestion about considering alternative possibilities for Mira's treatment?

Filip's face had lost what little color it had. "If Mira wanted to go home, Dr. Mishra, she was going to go home. You don't—didn't—argue with Mira."

Her strong will was one of the things I'd admired about Mira. Was it what had led to her death? I closed my eyes and tried to contain the tears. I'd seen patients die before, and I'd been saddened by their passing, but I'd never been this close to them.

"Let's talk in my office." Amit led the painter's husband by his elbow out of the room. As he passed me, Amit hesitated, as if he wanted to say something. Mr. Bartos's eyes met mine. They were pleading with me, wanting me to do or say something. I could see he was grieving, but I couldn't find the words to help him. Instead, I turned toward the bed. It was Mira and not Mira. It looked like her. But it wasn't her anymore. It was the same way I'd felt about the sketch of Indira that Mira had made.

So many things would change. Our conversations about things Mira knew and I didn't would cease. Her laughter. Her ability to make my day more interesting. How she made me feel like I belonged in her world. I would no longer feast on her stories of the places she'd been, countries she'd lived in, exotic people she'd known. She'd been more than a patient; she'd been my friend. She wasn't just leaving the hospital; she was leaving *me.* I talked to her in my head the way I'd been talking to her just half an hour ago. *Mira. Why did you go? I need you. I have more I want to ask you, more I need to know, more I need to tell you. You made my world come alive. You made me feel. Feel as if I mattered to you, to myself. Please. Don't go!*

But she wasn't listening. She'd already gone.

Matron covered Mira with the top sheet and allowed the attendants to take her away. There was so much blood where the painter had lain. I sat dumbly on a chair, still clutching the stack of clean sheets I'd brought. My brain was working furiously, running through my movements before I left for the stockroom. I'd put the cool washcloth on her forehead. I'd taken her pulse. I'd tried to give her water, but she hadn't wanted any. Before leaving the room, I'd made sure the temperature in the room was to her liking and the window was open to allow fresh air.

In a daze, I glanced at the sheets in my arms, wrinkled now where my fingers were clutching the fabric. I loosened my hold on them. I regarded my fingernails, buffed to a shine. My nursing apron: white as the Himalayan clouds in Mira's paintings. There was no evidence of the painter's distress, her passing. Had it really happened? Was I in a nightmare? I pinched my arm. I looked at the red welt that was beginning to swell. I pinched harder. My eyes filled, and this time, instead of blinking them away, I let them roll down my cheeks.

When Mira talked, I saw the world as if I were in her skin, looking through her eyes. Chartreuse and azure and bloodred and turquoise—I saw the colors of her paintings as she saw them, as energy. That's how she talked about her work. As if by some strange force, her paint and brushes compelled her toward the canvas; she wasn't in control of what or how she painted. Did I understand? she asked. I nodded. Because I *did*. It was like that with me and people I liked. I was drawn to them and reveled in their company, fascinated by their stories. I remembered verbatim all the things they told me, all the things she'd told me. The people she talked about, like her mother, imitating the haughty expression she wore. When she talked about her father, she stroked an imaginary beard, the way she said he did when he was deep in thought. She was a wonderful mimic, and her imitations made me laugh.

Matron was standing in front of my chair. I looked up at her. I could see her mouth moving, but I couldn't hear the words she was saying. She frowned, then shook my arm. I jerked back, the touch startling me, bringing me to the present. She and I were alone in the room.

"There will be questions, Nurse Falstaff. Do you understand?"

I merely stared, my jaw slack.

"Nod if you understand."

Mutely, I nodded.

"We will want to know everything that happened leading up to Miss Novak's death. You may want to write it down. Minute by minute."

"I left the room for twenty minutes," I said helplessly. I extended the folded linen toward her, as an answer. I wanted Matron to tell me it wasn't true. That I was dreaming, as I often did at night, the one where Papa was boarding the train for England, leaving me standing on the platform, alone, clutching the *kathputli* doll he'd given me. He never once looked back.

I retracted my arms, hugged the sheets to my chest. *Why did you go, Mira?*

Matron gently unfolded my arms and lifted the linen from them. "Experience comes with time. Perhaps the dosage was double what she should have received? Or perhaps the time between doses had been too short?"

My heartbeat quickened. I looked up at her, alert now, and shook my head. I wiped my eyes roughly with my palms. "No, Matron. I followed the doctor's directions on the chart precisely. Miss Novak needed a dose before it was time, so I gave her a half dose..." Tears continued to flow onto my nursing apron, much as I willed them not to. I pulled a handkerchief out of my skirt pocket and dried my eyes properly.

"You've been working long shifts seven days a week. That can wreak havoc on a person's ability to think clearly. Perhaps you were overly tired—"

"Ma'am, I don't think— No, I *know* I didn't—" I searched for the right words. "—cause this. I would never have done anything to harm Miss Novak. The long shifts are not tiring for me. I enjoy my work. I enjoy taking care of my patients." I regarded Matron through wet eyelashes, willing her to believe me. I wanted to tell her I wasn't crying because I was sorry I'd made a mistake. I was crying for the loss of a friend.

Matron's eyes went to the enamel pan and syringe that lay on Mira's bedside table. She walked toward it. The vial of morphine lay in the pan.

"You left a vial of morphine and a syringe in the room? What were you thinking? Haven't you been taught never to do that?" Matron's voice brimmed with astonishment.

Puzzled, I joined her at the table. I had removed the pan and the syringe when I left the room. Then I remembered seeing Rebecca leave the room. What had she been doing in here?

My vision blurred. The room tilted. My legs felt unsteady. I turned to Matron. "I don't know how it could have happened. I didn't overdose her and I did not leave anything here."

A chill ran up my spine. Or did I? How could I be sure? Maybe I was in a hurry and forgot to take the paraphernalia back to the pharmacy? I had been overwrought seeing Mira in such a state. Maybe I really did leave it in the room? How could I have been so careless?

She was frowning, her face and brows pinched. She seemed to be angry, disappointed and frightened at the same time. Was she afraid she would be blamed for my carelessness?

"There's no need to make up the bed now. The authorities may want to examine the bed and the syringe and whatever else." She took a moment, looked around the room, her eyes coming to rest on me again.

"You do believe me, Matron?" I tried to keep the desperation out of my voice, but I needed her to know I would never have been so careless as to overdose a patient.

Her eyes strayed from mine. She said, "It won't be just up to me. We'll leave that decision to the board." She stopped just shy of patting my shoulder before withdrawing her hand. The accusation stood between us. "You have other patients to attend to. Go."

Slowly, I rose from the chair, trying to recount every minute detail of the afternoon. Did I make a mistake in her dosage because I was so upset by the turn she'd taken? Was I only imagining that I followed protocol? I'd always been conscientious. I took my responsibilities seriously. The religious sisters at Wadia Hospital were Catholic like Matron, and so were some of the Indian nurses, having been raised in convents, but since I practiced no faith, the other nurses had kept their distance. The only nurse who'd befriended me was Indira. She'd been like a sister to me until her husband drove her away. Mohan told me she'd taken a job at another hospital. She would have understood how I felt. Who would support me now, attest to my competence?

The idea of a new patient in Mira's bed filled me with dread. They would never be as interesting as Mira Novak. How would I compensate for my small life without hearing about her large one? The biggest risk I'd ever taken was kissing Amit, and I was sure it was because Mira had made me bolder, made me feel I could do extraordinary things, things I'd never thought myself capable of. *You will love, Sona*, she'd said.

A worm of doubt snaked its way into my memory. Was it possible that I failed to sterilize the needle? I knew Mira had been poorly so I was saving the leftover morphine for when she needed it next. Did I forget to note it on her chart? The clipboard had been removed so there was no way for me to confirm it. And why would I have left the morphine in the room like that?

What about Dr. Holbrook's claim to Matron that Horace had been ordering substandard drugs for the pharmacy? Had I been giving Mira adulterated morphine? Perhaps the reason she recovered briefly was because Matron had reprimanded Horace after her chat with Holbrook? And if Dr. Holbrook had been right about the pharmacist but neglected to tell Amit what he thought, was he complicit in Mira's death?

My thoughts turned to Rebecca again. Could she have given Mira the extra morphine while I was in the storeroom? But why? To get me in trouble? To spite Mira? After all, Rebecca despised me. She thought I'd deliberately pushed her when we were tending to Mr. Hassan. She complained to Matron about my fraternizing with patients. She always thought Matron favored me and told me as much: *You'd have to murder someone to get on Matron's bad side.* But did she hate me enough to risk a patient's life? Perhaps she only meant to hurt Mira, not cause her death.

Oh, why had I left the room? Would this have happened if I'd stayed where I was? Kept watch over Mira while she slept? But I only left the room to look for the three people who knew more about Mira's care than anyone else. I was trying to help her. That's why I wasn't there when she died.

I went in search of Amit. I knew I should have been attending to my other patients, but my head was filled with the void left by Mira. His office door was open, but he wasn't there. Disappointed, I decided to check in with Ralph Stoddard. He was getting nearer his discharge date, and I would be sorry to see him go.

"Who died?" he said as soon as I entered his room. Mr. Hassan was sleeping peacefully in his bed. His new novel, *Anandamath* by Bankim Chandra Chatterjee, lay by his side.

My eyes became watery, but I wouldn't let the tears fall.

"Oh, dear, oh, dear. Sweet girl." He held out his hands for me to grasp. He looked around his bed for a handkerchief, but I got there first. I rubbed my eyes with my own handkerchief, apologizing for showing such emotion.

"Not at all. Now tell me what's happened."

"Mira—Miss Novak—she…" I couldn't finish the sentence.

"But I saw her just yesterday. Timothy took me in that wheelchair all the way to the discharge station, and she was right as rain. Had a big blond chap with her."

I nodded, struggling to keep my voice normal. "Her husband,

Filip Bartos." I cleared my throat. "Why don't I take your pulse and your temperature?" I did that, while Dr. Stoddard looked kindly upon me.

"We could play a game of backgammon if that would help." Through his horn-rimmed spectacles, I saw the rheumy blue eyes of a man who had seen his share of tragedy. Who was I to bring yet another to his doorstep?

I shook my head. He watched me write his vitals on the chart. "You're being discharged in two days. You must be pleased."

"Yes, but I will miss you, you know."

"And I, you, Dr. Stoddard." I forced myself to give him a smile. My lips barely moved, but it was the best I could do.

After tending to my next two patients, the new mother with the baby boy who lay next to her, and an elderly woman with piles (she took the place of the boy who'd had his tonsils removed), I went once more to Amit's office. Still empty.

The broiler of the mechanical room made its own music—a low hum punctuated with a sharp clang at regular intervals. Mohan was dismantling a crate, the sort medical instruments arrived in.

I coughed politely to let him know I was there. He looked up, straightened and raised his brows. "I heard," was all he said. Word of death traveled quickly in a hospital. Unlike Rebecca, he looked genuinely upset about Mira's death. "How are you?"

I shrugged, afraid I would burst into tears if I said anything. I knew my eyes were red from crying.

Mohan wiped his paint-stained hands on a rag, which had seen its share of work over the years. It was a relief to know that he and I were friends once again. It would have been understandable for him to avoid me, his disappointment over my refusal to become his wife clouding our friendship.

"Did Miss Novak send paintings down here, *bhai*?"

He looked over my left shoulder at a corner of the room.

"Yes. I have them here. I was wondering if someone would be picking them up."

"Before she died..." I had to stop to gather myself. "She told me the paintings were here. I assumed she wanted me to package them to send to her husband."

Mohan walked to where the paintings leaned against the wall. He had taken care to put a piece of wood underneath them to keep paint and grease off them.

"Do you have any large sheets of paper? Brown. Large enough to wrap these?" I knew that all hospital equipment and their parts arrived in this room bound in paper or burlap or some sort of padded cloth. It was Mohan's job to take the items to the right destination. But I assumed he would save the packing materials. In India, nothing was ever wasted. Everything could be repurposed.

He nodded. He walked to the shelves on the opposite wall and bent down to pick up a stack of flattened cardboard as well as some burlap sacks from the lowest shelves. He took these to his enormous worktable, which he cleared.

He and I lifted the four paintings from the floor one by one. We leaned them against the sides of the worktable. I stared at *The Acceptance*, wondering about the women solemnly preparing one among them for marriage. Who were they? Was the bride in the painting enjoying married life? Did she have children now? Who eased her burden after a day's toil, after cooking the evening meal, after feeding the chickens and goats, after tending to her children's wants and her husband's desires?

I started to pack the *Man in Abundance*, the least intense of the paintings. I wondered how Mira chose her subjects, what inspired her to paint Paolo with three apples. I wish I'd asked her what the apples signified.

Mohan picked up the *The Acceptance*. He said, "Sona?"

I looked up. He stood the painting on its side, the back facing me. Tucked into a corner was a little piece of paper, folded over into a square the size of a matchbox.

"Should I take it out?" he asked.

I wasn't sure. Was it meant for me or for Filip or for an art gallerist? I took a sharp breath and plucked it out of the frame. I don't know why but my fingers shook as I unfolded the paper. It was a piece torn from her sketchbook. The slanted handwriting, which I recognized from the titles of her sketches, looked as if it had been scrawled hastily.

Dearest Sona,

I know you will take care of these. As will Jo and Petra and Po.

Yours,

M.

I handed the note to Mohan. His eyebrows rose higher as he read. "Do you think… It seems as if she meant these for you?" He gave the note back to me and surveyed the paintings. "Who are those people she mentioned?"

It took me a moment. "Old friends." Once more, I regarded the canvases. All these paintings? But they were so valuable! I thought back to her last words to me. *The paintings. Downstairs.* Why would she want me to have them? Why not her husband? I read the note again. *As will Jo and Petra and Po.* Were the paintings meant for them? But which ones were for whom? Did she mean for me to send them the paintings? Or deliver them in person? Perhaps there was a message in each frame? I turned the paintings around and ran my fingers on the inside of the frames, feeling for another note. But there was nothing. Except…there were painted letters on the back of *Man in Abundance. "Po."* The canvas with the group of monks listening to their master, *The*

Pledges, was inscribed with a *J. The Waiting* was labeled *P.* The last, *The Acceptance*, was marked *S.*

I stepped back from the worktable, as if the paintings had scalded me. Each had been designated for a different friend. Josephine, Paolo and Petra. But she'd never mentioned a friend whose name started with an *S.* For Sona? Did she mean me? It was one thing to gain Mira's friendship—it had been my privilege—but quite another to receive such largesse. I glanced at Mohan, who was watching me. In exchange for the gift, was I to send the paintings to their intended recipients? How? Aside from the cities where Mira told me they lived, I had no addresses. How would I find them without talking to Filip? I remembered the argument he and Mira had been having under the back terrace of the Singh mansion. She'd told Filip she didn't want to sell these four paintings. She must have known then she wanted to give them to her friends.

I had only met Mira Novak six days ago. Why would she entrust me with such a large, such a personal task?

Mohan asked, "Sona, how will you get them home?" It was as if he had already come to the same conclusion I had without a word exchanged between us.

"Oh." I hadn't thought about that. Each painting was two by three feet. Too large to take on my bicycle.

"I have an idea." Mohan began removing the wooden frames from each canvas. Flattened, the canvases looked vulnerable. He stacked them one upon the other, carefully laying brown paper between them. With the utmost care, he rolled the stack until it resembled a long tube. He tied a rope at each end of the column to keep the canvases from unfurling.

"I'll fasten it to the rack of your bicycle. If men can carry ladders and a family of five on a bicycle, I think you should be able to get these paintings safely home."

I smiled at Mohan. I hoped the woman he did end up marrying would value his small kindnesses. "Thank you, *bhai*."

He wagged his head. As I turned to leave the room, he said simply, "*Bhagwan* will take care of her, Sona."

Once again, I was on the verge of crying for Mira and all I had lost, all her friends had lost, what India had lost. Walking back to the ward, I thought about all those beautiful paintings, the entire body of Mira's work. Her death had put an end to what had been a brilliant career. Mira's talent had been a source of pride for Indians. *One of our own made it despite those who held us back, who belittled every one of our attempts to create, build or improve India for Indians.* I caught myself in my hypocrisy. Here I was aligning myself with the Indian side of me while holding the English side of me accountable. Being an *in-between*, how convenient was it for me to switch allegiance as my mood suited me. I was so deep in thought I almost ran straight into Matron coming the other way.

"Apologies, ma'am."

She regarded me a moment, then consulted her watch fob. "Nurse Falstaff, I don't believe you're at your best right now. Miss Novak's death has probably made it difficult for you to perform your duties effectively. Go home. I will ask the other nurses to take over the rest of your shift. Come see me tomorrow when you arrive for work."

It sounded like a reprimand, less like a sympathetic suggestion. Perhaps her scolding was justified. "Yes, Matron," I said.

I'd been eager to talk to Amit about Mira's death and about how much I'd miss her. But private ambulances had brought two patients involved in an accident. A young Englishman whose scooter had collided with an Indian woman coming out of an alley with her shopping bag. Both were unconscious. Dr. Holbrook and Amit had called in emergency reinforcements from JJ Hospital to help triage the injuries and stave the bleeding on the man's thigh and the woman's stomach. The surgeries would take hours.

I left the hospital at eight o'clock that night. I cycled slowly, trying to delay going home, when I'd have to tell my mother what had happened. My route from Wadia Hospital took me past the High Court of Bombay, where a rally was in progress to protest working conditions of textile workers. A man shouted into a megaphone, "We work fourteen hours a day and still can't feed our families. Men have lost arms, hands, fingers in old machinery that the bloody British won't fix. We are suffocating! We work in rooms without windows, without air..." His voice was drowned out by the rallying cry of the crowd. "Respect our rights!"

I cycled on, passing a Parsi in a suit, a briefcase under his arm. Three Muslim men were chatting in front of a mosque. I stopped to watch a man on the side of the street teaching a crow to remove a *beedi* from his pocket and put it in his mouth. No doubt the trick would earn both man and crow a meal or two. An ice-cream vendor plied his trade from a cart (the night may have cooled somewhat but a day of hard work still warranted a *kulfi*). Next to him, a man sat on a small carpet carving a group of elephants out of ivory.

After a while, even the protesters and street peddlers failed to distract me. I veered away on my bicycle and found myself heading in the opposite direction from home, toward Marine Drive, where Mira had lived. The promenade curved around Back Bay and the beach. I stopped at her building and looked up at the apartment where I'd helped her pick out a dress for the Singh party only last night. It seemed like such a long time ago. I thought I saw a light in her apartment. Perhaps Filip Bartos was there, grieving. He'd looked at me so strangely when Amit led him away from Mira's room earlier this evening.

I spun my bicycle around and headed west toward Victoria Terminus, an intimidating gothic behemoth designed by the British. So depressed was I that I found myself mourning for the tens of thousands of Indians who broke their backs building it with nothing to take home at the end of the day but a handful of coins that barely fed their families.

Three hours later, sweating and out of breath, having cycled through feelings of shame, despair and injustice and trying to outrun them all, I reached the flat my mother and I shared. The shift that should have ended at four in the morning found me home by eleven o'clock. I dreaded mounting the stairs to our landing and telling my mother about Mira's passing. And that I seemed to be the one whom everyone was looking to for answers.

One look at my face and my mother turned, went to the Primus and served me a plate of dal and *makki ki* roti, one of my favorite dishes. She led me to the table, as if I were an invalid, and sat me down. She pulled her chair from the other side of the table and sat next to me. "Tell me."

It was the same when the girls at school bullied me for having a father who didn't love me enough to stay. Or when the Matron of my Calcutta hospital called me a troublemaker. My mother knew when something was bothering me without my having uttered a word.

My throat felt so tight it hurt. I told her about Mira's sudden death. What Matron said. Perhaps I'd been careless with the dosage? Why did I leave the room unguarded when there was a vial of morphine lying about? How could I have left it there?

My mother listened with furrowed brows, the crevices getting deeper the longer I went on. She put a hand on mine. "I am truly sorry about your friend."

"Oh, Mum!" I reached for her, wrapped my arms around her. She knew how much I would miss Mira. For the past six days, I'd shared so much about her. Just the fact that Mum said the word *friend* unleashed something inside I'd been trying to contain. Mira *had* been a friend. She'd let me see a side of her I imagined she shared with very few. Before she came to the hospital, she'd been busy with her painting and exhibiting and wandering in her own thoughts. Being bedridden had forced her to slow down, to reflect on her life and share confidences, regrets and memories about those closest to her. And I'd been there to listen, happily. The six days with her had felt elastic. As if we'd known each other for years.

My mother rocked me, the way she'd done when I was a little girl with a scraped knee, a loose tooth or a doll with a broken arm. I let myself be comforted until my body was empty of misery—for the time being at least. I knew grief came in waves, as it did for the families of patients we'd lost. Perhaps Mira's husband would feel it that way too.

Finally, Mum released me. She rummaged among her fabric scraps on the table and found one to wipe my face. Then she broke off a bite of the cornmeal roti, dipped it in dal and held it to my mouth. "Eat."

I forced down the food. I was an obedient daughter. I'd always obeyed. Somehow, after my father left us, I'd known she needed me to do as she wanted without raising a fuss. She couldn't afford to enroll me in a convent school like the one her middle-class Indian parents had sent her to. Instead, I'd gone to a free government school. At home, she tested me on English, having me read aloud from her sewing books to make my speech sound less Indian and more British. I could pronounce words like welt pockets, palazzo trousers and backstitch before I understood what they meant. Ultimately, my mother's tutoring had won me a scholarship at the private convent school. When she'd wanted me to enroll in a nursing course, I did.

The cornmeal roti was delicious, even though I didn't have an appetite. My mother's cooking was a reflection of how she was feeling. When she was happy, her curries were exquisite. When she was angry or bitter or had been upset by a client, her dishes would be overcooked or too spicy or too sour. Tomorrow's dish would be unbearably spicy.

She prepared another bite for me and held it to my lips. "What about the allegation that you're overworked? Are you?" she asked. The timbre of her voice held the slightest hint of fear.

I waved her hand away. "You're against me too? You think I'm guilty?"

"Not at all." She cupped my chin with her free hand. "I'm on your side, always. I'm asking how you will prepare for the fallout. A decade ago, I would have thought you'd be safe. You're half English. But now...there is such an outcry for the British to leave. Many are afraid; they're going back home." She rubbed the scarred table with her palm. "Now, it's not so easy for Britishers to treat Indians badly or turn their nose up at people they've been ruling for two hundred years. Eurasians are a reminder of past times, not happy ones for Indians who have lived under British control for so long. I sometimes wish that I hadn't insisted on making you so British. Insisting you wear dresses instead of saris. Speaking fluent English instead of fluent Hindi. I just thought that the advantages would outweigh any drawbacks. While that may have been true when I was born, it certainly isn't true now."

She raised her eyes to see if I'd understood the danger. I had. Here in Bombay, we saw the civil disobedience rallies, but in other parts of India I'd heard about riots erupting against oppression, quashed quickly by the colonists. At work, I'd noticed the delay in receiving supplies I'd requested. I'd felt the hostile stare of Indian nurses who were paid less than me; I earned more because of my British blood and because I didn't have reservations about touching patients who were strangers to me the way Indian women were forbidden to. Nearby, Grant College was trying to recruit more Indian women for nursing, but progress had been slow. Patients at Wadia had started to make oblique references to my imminent departure from *their* country. Walking home, I'd heard whispers aimed at me. *Half-half.* It was my country too, I wanted to say. I didn't choose my parentage. India was my home. I was born here. And I wanted to stay.

Was Matron's implication that I had miscalculated the dosage a convenient excuse to get rid of me because my mixed blood made the staff uncomfortable? She was an Englishwoman who would retire to Cornwall where she was from. Amit was Indian. He would stay here, where independence would return the country to Indians like him. I was part Indian, part British, a half-caste. I belonged nowhere.

"I don't know any way to clear the doubt hanging over my head, Mum. All the signs point to an overdose, which only I could have administered. I've gone over every minute, every second of my shift. I don't see how I could have miscalculated the morphine I was supposed to give her." I told her about seeing Rebecca leave the room and the conversation I overheard between Matron and Dr. Holbrook. Might the morphine have been tainted? Throughout, my mother listened attentively.

She tapped my plate. "Eat." She pointed her chin at the roll of paintings I'd brought with me. "What is that?"

I'd been so lost in my grief that I'd merely laid the tube on the edge of the table. I looked at it wearily. "Would you please unroll it, Mum? I need to show you something."

She cleared the table of everything but my plate. Using her shears, she removed the rope fastenings and unfurled the paintings. *The Acceptance* lay on top.

I fished Mira's note from my rucksack and showed it to her.

She read the note, a puzzled look on her face. Then she picked up the first painting and held it in her outstretched arms. One by one, she studied the others. I watched her face closely.

"Mira left you these?" she asked.

"Yes."

"And the people in the note? Jo. Petra. Po. Aren't they the ones you said Mira talked to you about?"

I nodded. "Petra is her girlhood friend from Prague, someone she went to school with until she left for Italy. Po—Paolo—was her painting tutor in Florence. They were together before and after she married Filip. Jo is Josephine. From Paris. Her art dealer. Whom she had a falling-out with."

My mother arched an eyebrow, glancing my way, but said nothing. To her credit, she had passed no judgment on Mira's life. She turned the paintings over. "These letters on the back…"

"I think they signify who each painting is for."

My mother pointed to the lot. "So the one marked *S* is yours?"

"Mira's note was tucked in that frame, and it was addressed to me, so yes, I think so."

Mum picked up *The Acceptance* and studied it. "Do you think you're meant to be the bride getting her henna done?"

I colored. "Really, Mum, I don't know what was on Mira's mind when she wrote that note."

"And you're sure she didn't want to leave these for her husband?"

"The note indicates otherwise."

My mother raised an eyebrow. "It's odd, isn't it?"

I told her about the argument I'd witnessed between Mira and Filip the night of the Singh party.

"Sona, if she wrote this before she died, do you think…she knew she was dying?"

I bit my lip. The thought had occurred to me. But how could Mira have known she would end up in the hospital again, much less lose her life? Or—and I didn't want to think about this—had Mira deliberately taken an overdose? Why? Because she was in so much pain? What other reason would she have had to take her life? She'd been melancholy about Jo and Petra and Po and how she'd treated them. Was she more downhearted than she let on?

My mother began to roll up the paintings. "Would Dr. Mishra know anything about these?"

I frowned. Did Mira tell Amit something she didn't tell me? "I can ask him."

Wrinkles lined her forehead. She rubbed her chest.

"You've taken your medicine?"

"Hahn," she said absently.

I retied the rope around the rolled-up canvases, glancing

every now at then at her worried expression. When we finished, my mother told me to sit down. Then she sat across from me and took my hands in hers. She rubbed my knuckles tenderly. "You may not want to hear this, Sona," she started haltingly. "But the blame will rest on you. Dr. Mishra will not be blamed. Your Matron will not be blamed. Dr. Holbrook will not be blamed. But they will need to hold someone responsible for Mira's death. I worry that as of tomorrow, you will no longer be a nurse at Wadia's."

My mother's image became hazy, as if I were looking at her underwater. I had suspected I might be punished, that my wages might be reduced, but not that I might lose my post. It had taken time to find this position; it would take time to find another. What would I say to another Matron when she asked why I left Wadia's? Would she write to the Matron here to ask what had happened? Or would we have to change cities again? Neither one of us could bear another move. Would Mira's death be the destruction of me? The hair on my arms stood up. If someone else caused Mira's death, were they trying to punish me or her?

My mother was still talking to me. With an effort, I made myself listen.

"You need to clear your name, *beti*," she said. "For your own sake. So this accusation isn't hanging over your head. It's the only way for you to move forward. Maybe one of those people—or all three of them," she gestured to Mira's note. "Maybe they can help you. Maybe they know something about her you don't. Or maybe they know nothing." She pointed her chin at the paintings. "Mira left you a note clearly asking you to deliver these paintings to her friends. She could easily have had them sent. But she didn't. She wanted you to go. Why? There must have been a reason." My mother exhaled slowly. "To find out, you'll need your father's money."

I couldn't believe what my mother was suggesting. "But,

Mum, we'll need the money for rent and food and medicine. Let's use it for that until I find another job."

She shook her head. "No, *beti*. What you need to do first is salvage your reputation so you can continue being a nurse. I'm asking you to do that. You have to go."

I looked at my mother, who rarely asked me for anything but did so many things without my asking. She peeled the skin from grapes because she knew I only liked the sweet pulp inside. She massaged my legs after a long shift at the hospital, but would never let me do the same for her. She sewed, cleaned and pressed my uniforms, always tucking rose petals in the pockets to perfume them. Rarely did she buy anything new for herself. I noticed how the neckline of her blouse and sleeves were fraying. She needed new glasses but refused to spend the money on them even though she had to bend closer and closer to the fabric to see if her seams were straight.

"I can't leave you alone here in Bombay, Mum. Who will take care of you?" I felt something akin to fear. Like the fear I felt after my father left. Who would take care of us?

She squeezed my hands. "Sona, it's not me who needs to be taken care of. I've been caring for you since you were a baby. I will be fine. You need to learn how to take care of yourself. I have kept you soft."

I was taken aback. I thought of myself as strong, capable, able to handle anything that came my way. "You've kept me *soft*?"

"All these years, I've shielded you from those who wanted to hurt you. The market staller who sent you home with bruised fruit. The bus driver who wouldn't let you on his bus. I went back and scolded the fruit seller. And the bus driver. And all the others who hurt you. I should have made you stand up to them yourself. I pushed you toward nursing school so you could support yourself whether I was here or not. I made you more British because I thought it would protect you. I made you so safe that you're afraid to take chances. Think what your life could be if you weren't afraid."

I blurted it out before I could stop myself. "You took a chance on my father and look where it landed you!" My heart was knocking against my ribs. I'd never spoken to my mother like that before.

She released my hands. Was that pity in her eyes? "Oh, Sona. Don't you know that I loved the time I spent with him? I would never take that back. I hated that he lied. I hated that he left but not that he and I came together. And he didn't leave me alone. He left me with you, precious you and Rajat. How could I *not* have taken that chance? This is your life. You should live it the way you want. Go where you want. See the things you cannot even imagine now. Your father's money will make that possible."

I stared at her. My mother thought I lived in fear? Too afraid to step over the line, even to stand up for myself? A memory of me as a thirteen-year-old girl floated into view. I'm standing next to my mother in the headmistress's office. She is telling the older woman that I was cheated out of my number one rank because the teacher gave it to her own daughter, who did not do as well on the test as I had. My mother is speaking softly, but firmly. She is not complaining. She is explaining. The next day, the teacher gave me the rank I should have been given. I had expected my mother to prevail. Because she always had. Why had I never noticed the many ways she had been strong when I couldn't be? She'd needed courage—and more—to overcome my father's betrayal. Without it, how could she have raised a child without family, without money?

I thought about Matron's reprimand when she called me to her office. I hadn't wanted Rebecca to get into trouble over what happened when Mr. Hassan had a heart attack. I should have told Matron what my mother would have. In her own quiet way, she would have explained that without my quick thinking, a patient could have died. And the criticism about being sociable with patients? Why hadn't I told Matron that emotional comfort was part of my remit as a nurse, which I provided by taking my patients' minds off their unease and engaging them in activities they enjoyed. Instead, I had said nothing. *Too soft.*

A knock at the door startled us. We hardly ever had visitors. My mother always saw clients in their homes, taking a small sewing kit of pins, basting chalk, a tape measure. She did her best to refresh our cramped flat by sewing new curtains or crocheting a new tablecloth and quilting a *rajai* every year, but it certainly wouldn't do for her clients to see our humble quarters. Among those were wealthy Indians whose loyalties lay with the British for as long as it served them. Others were Britishers who lived like royalty in India but would have had a stark middle-class existence in England. A few were European gadabouts not bright enough to help with their fathers' estates back home or ones who had transgressed in such a way as to be sent out of sight, out of mind.

I rose to answer the door. It was my landlady, the mother of the brood downstairs. Not for the first time did I notice that she needed to let the seams out on her blouse. Flesh oozed out of her midsection from the bottom of her blouse to the top of her petticoat.

"You have a visitor. A man," she said. She remained standing at our doorstep, eyeing me suspiciously. She pulled her *pallu* tighter around her plump shoulders. "You know I don't approve of guests coming this late to the house."

I glanced at my watch. It was almost midnight. Aside from Amit, who had arrived early in the evening yesterday to take me to the Singh party, Mum and I had never had guests.

"Well, if it's a visitor, I had better go visit," I said, skirting her stout frame. I ran down the steps, leaving her to plod slowly behind me.

Amit Mishra stood at the gate. My heart picked up its pace. The weak bulb cast shadows on his face that made him look ten years older. Or did he look haggard because of the long hours he'd just spent in surgery for the emergency patients? Or because Mira had died on his watch?

"Let me come out to you," I said, opening the gate and joining him in the lane. I led him down the slender path away from the house. When we'd taken a few steps toward the main street, he asked, "How are you?"

"I… It's just so…" I couldn't finish my sentence. I fished my handkerchief from my pocket and blew my nose. "I can't imagine going in tomorrow and not seeing her, you know?"

He lifted his hand toward me, perhaps to comfort me, then dropped it, stuffing both hands in the pockets of his trousers. He hung his head. Mira had been his friend too. It occurred to me that he must have had to suppress his feelings about her death at work. We walked for a while without speaking.

"I know how heartbroken you must be about Mira," he said. "I don't know if this helps, but what happened to Mira can happen to any patient. We see suffering in the course of our day, every day. She told me how you made her suffering bearable. You did so much for her, more than she could have expected. And—I believe—she loved you. One day, we were talking about…oh, I don't know…operas we'd seen in London, how the river Wein in Vienna glows at sunset, how brilliant a cappella sounds in a Prague cathedral—and she said she'd love to take you to all those places. She saw in you someone who was bursting to explore the world but was holding herself back."

Oh, Mira. What made you think more of me than I was capable of? I told you over and over that your world and mine weren't alike.

He pulled his hands from his pockets and stopped walking. I turned to face him. "I'm… I have spoken to Dr. Holbrook and Matron at length. Also, to the hospital board. We discussed the various causes of Mira's sudden death. Holbrook still maintains that she suffered nothing more than gastritis…and that the party at the Singh home more than likely tired her." He hesitated. "But the issue of the syringe left in the room, the missing morphine in the vial…is still a cause of concern. I spoke of your dedication to your work, your patients and your impeccable work record. I said the explanation had to lie outside of your involvement. There are a number of possibilities the hospital will investigate."

A train sped past the chain-link fence. *Chug-chug-chu-chug.* Amit stopped talking. We resumed our stroll.

"Sona, if it makes you feel any better, I've been wondering if *I* made a mistake in her care. Perhaps she didn't tell us about a condition—her heart, a childhood disease, something—that could have caused such a sudden—relapse. If only I could have convinced Dr. Holbrook to do the surgery. I keep thinking why—how—" With a start, I realized he was torturing himself the same way I was. *Could he have prevented the tragedy?*

This would have been the perfect time to tell him what I'd overheard between Matron and Dr. Holbrook. That the older doctor had ignored Mira's pain because he felt she'd not been worthy of his attention. Not British enough. Not chaste enough. Not the kind of painter he approved of. I could have told Amit that Dr. Holbrook suspected Horace in the pharmacy of skimping on quality drugs. How to prove any of that? And what good would it do to tell Amit? He'd only feel worse for not fighting harder for the painter. Besides, nothing would bring Mira back.

Amit stopped mid-stride and turned to me, his brow creased with worry. He touched my arm. I looked at the spot where his fingers lay. "Unfortunately, I won't be at the hospital tomorrow, Sona. My aunt has taken ill in Shimla. I'm about to take a train to Delhi tonight and will go to Shimla from there."

I almost gasped. *Don't leave me with this*, I wanted to say. I crossed my arms over my chest, as if to protect myself. Had my mother been right? With no one to support me when I showed up for work tomorrow, I would be the one held responsible for Mira's death. My eyes pleaded with him. "I've gone over it in my mind so many times. I can't see where I might have gone wrong. I didn't administer that fatal dose, but I can't imagine who did."

He came closer and put his hands on my arms. "I believe you."

I searched his face, desperate for his assurance. His opinion mattered to me, both because he'd been Mira's friend and because I felt he was mine.

He dropped his hands. "If something were to happen... If the hospital... What I mean to say is..." He brushed a hand through his hair. "I spoke to Ralph Stoddard. He may have mentioned to you that he's going to Istanbul. He will need a nurse to accompany him. The post entails full passage and expenses as well as a stipend." He offered a brief smile. "And the company of a lovely old codger. Is that something you might consider if...?"

I felt faint. How could I possibly leave Mum in a city we were both just coming to know? Istanbul was so far away from home. It was the kind of opportunity Mira would have jumped at without knowing where it could lead. The thrill of a new experience would have been enough.

"Think about it," Amit was saying.

I nodded absently and looked at the packed dirt beneath us. We stood without speaking, listening to another train whistle past.

"When will you be back?"

"I don't know. I need see if my aunt will pull through. Of course, I'm hoping for the best. It could be five days. Or three weeks. If you decide not to take Dr. Stoddard's offer, I will help you find another position in Bombay, which would be... preferable for me."

When I met his eyes, I saw the sadness. Mira's death could have been a moment for us to find comfort in one another, but propriety wouldn't allow it. All I could do was nod. I retraced my steps back to my flat, knowing he was watching me until I was safely inside the gate.

As I climbed the steps to our flat, I knew I didn't want to tell my mother that I'd be losing my position even though she was expecting it. I would lie and tell her Dr. Mishra came to tell me my post was safe. Let her have one more night of peace before my inevitable fall.

CHAPTER 7

The next day, I arrived early for my shift to see Matron, dreading the meeting with her. I looked in every room of the hospital on two floors before I spotted her. She was instructing two junior nurses about the Nightingale method of bathing a patient. While she was the same height as the nurses, she had such an imposing presence that she seemed to tower over them. They looked from her to the waiting patient, an elderly woman with frightened eyes.

"Hot water and a towel like this." Matron pointed to the rough washcloth sitting next to the washbasin on the rolling table. "Rub and rub hard. No fancy soap or soft sponges. With those, people tend not to rub as hard and then clean is just a dream." She glanced at the patient, who was now clutching her bedsheet.

Matron turned around to leave the room, saw me waiting by the door and motioned for me to follow her to her office.

She indicated for me to take the seat in front of her desk, then settled in her chair behind it.

She pulled out a drawer to her left and took out some paperwork. "It is my responsibility at Wadia Hospital to ensure the well-being of our patients while they're in my care. I have failed in my duty with regard to Miss Novak. She was an important personage, a national treasure, and her death will be mourned by many.

"I informed the hospital board that I accept that responsibility. Of course, they realize mistakes are made from time to time. They want to make absolutely sure it never happens again. And in order to comply with their request, they're demanding that you be released from your duties effective immediately." Her pale face mottled. Either she was angry at being put in this position or embarrassed to be foisting the blame on me. She looked down at her paperwork as if it contained another part of her script.

I felt numb. My pulse wasn't racing. My breath was even. I glanced at my hands. They were steady. I looked at the floor. White marble with flecks of gray. My scuffed shoes. Amit had prepared me for this. Even so, some part of me had wondered if it had all been an imagining—Amit coming to our flat last night, telling me about the board meeting, telling me about Dr. Stoddard and the Istanbul offer. Now, all I could think was: Would I forever be shunned by every place I worked?

Matron didn't meet my eyes when she said, "Even if you didn't administer the fatal dose, you left a syringe and a bottle of morphine in plain sight in the room. That was a monumental oversight." She touched the cross on her necklace. Was she seeking support from above?

For a moment, I couldn't speak. I *had* left the room longer than was acceptable. The morphine *had* been lying in the open. Twenty minutes would have allowed anyone to walk in and inject a sleeping patient. But did I leave Mira unprotected? Did I do that to her? Other nurses left their rooms all the time to grab something from the stockroom or break for a cuppa. Nothing happened to their patients. I was the unlucky one.

But what about the conversation between Amit and Dr. Holbrook? Holbrook had made a judgment call where Mira's health was concerned.

I cleared my throat. "The six days Miss Novak wasn't responding to treatment..."

She frowned. "What about it?"

Heat crept up my neck. Last night, Mum told me she'd shielded me all my life; she'd stood up for me when I couldn't. She wanted me to be braver, tougher, to take a chance. Well, here was my chance. And even though every sensible part of old Sona was telling me to stop talking, my mouth wasn't listening. I cleared my throat and leveled a hard gaze at the old woman. "Miss Novak was a young woman in pain, looking to us for help. But she was judged to be unworthy of our utmost care." My voice had risen.

The older woman across from me flushed red. "Whatever are you saying, girl? Casting aspersions on our staff won't help your situation. It's insulting and baseless."

"Baseless? You and Dr. Holbrook were talking about her the other day. How Miss Novak wasn't a proper painter. Wasn't British enough. Wasn't a proper woman. She was our patient, Matron!"

"So you *were* spying on us?"

"And to think that she might have been dosed with second-rate medication from the pharmacy—"

"Really, you are too much!" She rose from her chair, staring down at me. "You will clear out your locker at once. And if you're looking for a reference, you won't get one from me."

I stood, without taking my eyes off her. I needed a moment to steady the shaking in my legs. I said, "Miss Novak was a friend. She was kind. She was gracious. She mattered. She mattered to me. She mattered to India. I will miss her terribly."

She looked away, coloring, and touched her cross again.

I made my way to the nurses' changing room in a daze. Had I just stood up for myself? And for Mira? Mira had been nothing but generous with her friendship, making me laugh even as she was in pain, warming me with her words of appreciation, thanking me for taking care of her. She taught me things.

Her stories seemed disordered, flowing this way and that, until they arrived at the point she wanted to make. Once, I'd found her drawing on her sketch pad. Without taking her eyes off her drawing, she said, "It takes three to five years for cardamom plants to produce bright green pods. Those pods look nothing like the shriveled tough-skinned pods we break open to remove the seeds, the ones used to flavor chai or *burfi* or chicken curry. I learned that from a female farmer in Kerala." She paused to see if I was following her before continuing. "Josephine once asked me to produce something posthaste for a client who was eager to purchase one of my paintings. I told her I couldn't do it. She said Picasso paints or sketches hundreds of artworks every year. I told her about the cardamom plants. How long they take to mature. 'I can be both European and Indian, Jo, but not at the same time. Here in India, I'm Indian. I am the cardamom.'" Mira turned her pad around to let me see what she'd been sketching. It was a likeness of me. I took the drawing pad from her and stared at it. It was like looking in the mirror. The features of my face that could either have been Indian or English.

Now Matron's words rang in my head, a cruel merry-go-round of *you left a syringe and a bottle of morphine in plain sight in the room.* How would I ever get past the accusation? Could I live with the knowledge of my failure? *You left the room, you left the room, you left the room.*

Mum's words came back to me too. *The blame will rest on you.*

I opened my locker. A cocoa herringbone skirt my mother had made, a beige blouse inherited from a coworker back in Calcutta, low-heeled brown Bata shoes. A pair of coffee-colored stockings. An extra pinafore. No photos of exotic places. Or beaus. Or friends laughing together. Not much to show for two years at Wadia's. Oh, how I wished Mira were still here! We could laugh about how my pinafore was almost as long as I was tall. I could see her, eyes shining, cheeks flushed. I slipped on my skirt, buttoned my blouse, tugged my woven stockings on, folded my uniform and put it all in my rucksack.

As I shut the door to my locker, Rebecca entered the room.

"So you're leaving us?" She said it as pleasantly as if she were asking me whether I'd noticed the poppies blooming. As if my leaving were a choice. She removed her nurse's cap and unpinned her hair, stuffing hairpins in her pockets, checking her reflection in the wall mirror. She shook her light brown hair loose. It looked pretty like that, down around her shoulders. "Looks like I'll get the rich patients now." She laughed.

From her locker, Rebecca extracted a wide-toothed tortoise-shell comb. As she brushed her hair, I asked, "What were you doing in Miss Novak's room before it happened?"

Her eyebrows shot up. Her look was wary. "What are you talking about?"

"I saw you leaving her room. Right before I went in and saw that she was in critical condition."

She reared her chin and shrugged self-consciously. "Probably thought I heard her calling me. Realized I was wrong." She put her comb back in the locker, avoiding my eyes. She busied herself with her hairpins and her nurse's cap while I looked on, waiting.

I tightened the cord of my rucksack. My throat was dry. My eyes hurt. I had no more fight left in me. What good would it do? My word was no good anymore. "You should wear your hair down more often. It suits you." With that, I left the changing room.

I tried to put off going home for as long as possible. Now I would have to tell my mother it was done. I had lost. Although I had a feeling she already knew.

When I got to our street, Chameli Marg (an ambitious name for a street with no sweet-smelling flowers), a cluster of neighbors were gathered at the entrance to our building. My landlady was holding court. Even from a distance, I could tell by the tenor of her voice that she was angry or aggrieved about something.

As I neared, I heard her say, "…I had to pay for the doctor. Who is going to pay me back?" the landlady was saying, her underarm flesh jiggling with each movement of her hands. When she saw me, she said, "Here is the daughter. Well, Miss Fancy Nurse, you can clear out now. I don't want the *burree aatma* in my house!"

I brushed past her, my heart skipping a beat. I sprinted up the stairs, rucksack flapping against my body. The door to our flat was open. There was no one in the room but my mother, laid out on our bed. Her eyes were closed. She was completely still.

"No, no, please, no!" I prayed out loud. I felt for a pulse on her wrist. There was none. I tried her neck, just under her jaw. Nothing.

"The doctor has come and gone." The landlady was standing at the door. "He said it was a heart attack. No need to take her to the hospital." She spoke as if it were my mother's fault for dying.

"Get out!" I screamed. I flew to the door and slammed it in her face. I turned the lock so she couldn't come in. With my back against the door, I regarded my mother's body on the bed. How could this have happened? She'd had a weak heart but as long as she took her medicine, she was fine. Was it because of Mira's death? She knew I would lose my job over it? I'd seen the resignation and the fear in her face. *Oh, Mum. Did I do this to you?*

From the other side of the door, the landlady shouted, "You need to get that body out of here. I won't have it in my house!"

"Leave her in peace," I whispered into the room. The person who cared for me most in this world was gone. Tears blurred my vision. Who would love me now? Who would ask about my day? Listen to my stories? What would I do without her? I wiped my nose with the back of my hand.

I eased my body away from the door toward the bed I'd shared with my mother for as long as I could remember. I lay down on the bed and nestled my body against hers on the narrow mattress. I whispered in her ear, "Remember when I was old enough to sit on the carousel horse by myself? I must have been four. You said it was time. Time for what? I asked. Time for you to do things by yourself, you said. But I like doing things with you, I said. I know, you said. But you have so many things you will enjoy doing, and I won't always be there to do them with you."

Water ran from the corners of my eyes, down my nose and into my mouth. I tasted salt and sadness and aloneness. "Mum, I'm still not ready to do all those things by myself. I need you. I need you to stay. Can't you stay just a little while longer? Please? Please stay." I wrapped my arm around her waist and held her tight. I sobbed wet, sloppy tears into her shoulder and her flower-print sari, the one I said made her look like a field of lavender when I was nine. I had so much to tell her: being let go at the hospital, Dr. Mishra's promise of an opportunity, how I felt about him—really felt about him—how much I needed her, how much I loved her. None of that made any difference now.

I decided on a burial instead of cremation. I had the feeling that my mother thought herself more Anglo than Indian as she got older, and a funeral would be a better choice. Our neighbors across the hall—Fatima and her husband—and a wealthy matron, a client of my mother's—attended the last rites. The matron wanted me to know how sorry she was and would her dress be ready in time for her daughter's wedding?

I paid a priest from the nearby Christian church to deliver the eulogy, which I wrote for him. And then it was over.

Within one week, I had lost my mother, my friend Mira and my position at the hospital. I was an orphan without a friend.

Once I packed up all the fabric scraps and the few dishes we had, the flat was almost empty. I would give the fabric and my mother's sewing machine to the school next to the Mohatta cloth market, where my mother sometimes tutored novice seamstresses. I had no need for dishes. I gave our bed, table and chairs to the couple who cleaned the building. To my landlady, I gave the Primus stove in return for what she'd paid the doctor. The Primus was worth much more, but I preferred to overpay my debt rather than risk her returning for more.

My last task was to pack our clothes in the battered trunk we'd brought from Calcutta. Then, it had contained our clothes, sheets, towels, and a few pots and pans. I took stock of what was still packed inside. On the top was the evening gown my mother had made for me from the wedding sari she never had the chance to wear. I held the dress up so I could admire her handiwork. A heavy cloth pouch and a photo tumbled out. I picked up the black-and-white photo. Thick paper. Crinkled edges. It was the photo of a man around thirty years of age. White. He was in a military uniform. His hair was parted down the middle.

Him? I dropped the photo as if I'd been scorched.

Gingerly, I squatted on the floor to study the photo without touching it. There were my eyebrows that angled steeply toward my temples. Lips that were neither thin nor full. The hairline that cut straight across the forehead instead of forming an M.

Using my fingernail, I flipped the photo over. *Owen Falstaff, Royal Garrison Artillery.*

I sat back on my haunches. My mother had kept a photo of him all this time. Because she still loved him? After all these years? Even though he had betrayed her? Why didn't she ever show it to me? I squeezed my eyes shut. Now that I had an image of him, could I recall any memories of us together? I waited. Nothing.

I opened my eyes again. Did my mother hide the photo in the green gown deliberately so I would find it after she was gone? But she wouldn't have known when she would die, so that didn't make sense. I contemplated tearing up the photo and throwing it away. He'd been a rotten father and a rotten husband. What did I owe him? Some small part of me though—perhaps the three-year-old me, the girl who must have felt loved before he left—wanted to keep it. In the end, I buried the photo in the suitcase.

I opened the cloth purse. Inside was the English money from my father. "You need to clear your name, *beti*," my mother had said. "And for that, you'll need your father's money."

The only thing I kept of my mother's was that green sari—now the only evening gown I owned. I paid for three red roses, the petals of which I sprinkled among the folds.

She had no jewelry, no gold to call her own, no parents or in-laws who would have gifted it to her upon her marriage.

A week later, I was on the RMS *Viceroy of India* setting sail for Istanbul.

CHAPTER 8

I had reconciled myself to the fact that aside from Dr. Stoddard's offer I had no options. My mother's voice, encouraging me to take chances, to discover new worlds, had taken residence in the back of my mind. I was leaving the comfort of what I knew to explore foreign territory—foreign to me at least. It was frightening and exhilarating at the same time. The opportunity to go as far as Istanbul would take me: half the way to Europe. From there, I could use my father's money to deliver the paintings to Mira's friends in Florence, Prague and Paris. Of course, I would still need to find out where they lived from the clues in Mira's stories.

The day after Amit left for Shimla, I'd received a note from Dr. Stoddard.

My dear Nurse Falstaff:
How delighted I was to learn that you would accompany a fossil like me to Istanbul. If you have never been, it's a delightful place with the most divine baklava and the strongest coffee you've ever tasted. It will be jolly fun. And I'm so looking forward to our backgammon games. Meet me at the gangplank (gallows humor!) next Thursday at 10:00 a.m. I'll be the one with a sour-faced (temporary) nurse in tow.
Yours,
R. S.

I took a tram to the Bombay docks with my battered trunk, which was large enough to carry the roll of paintings plus a few skirts, sweaters and shirts. There were a great many people milling about. Bare-chested Indian men in their *dhotis* carried streamer trunks to the boats. A vendor sliced the tops of his green coconuts with a machete. Workers upended the fruit to pour coconut juice directly into their gullets. A British overseer ordered men to stack cargo onto a waiting bullock cart. A middle-aged Indian woman fried onion bhaji for hungry customers. European women in their ivory dresses, hats and gloves descended from a cerulean-blue Daimler, their driver ferrying trunks to the passenger dock of the steamship. British, French and Dutch families were saying goodbye to their seafaring loved ones.

The RMS *Viceroy of India* was even larger than the Taj Mahal Palace in Bombay. Passengers waved from the four decks to those who had come to see them off. The steamship's hull was a glossy black with a white band while the decks and cabins were the color of Chowpatty Beach. Two enormous black funnels released smoke—or was it steam?

Four days ago, as I was shopping for new shoes for my journey (I had money now to replace my scuffed ones), I went past a travel agency. Posters with images of palm trees urged travelers to go to Calcutta, Allahabad and Mysore. On a whim, I went inside to inquire about the RMS Viceroy. Having never been on a steamship, I wanted to be prepared; I didn't want Dr. Stoddard to think me naive. The agent, a Parsi with horn-rimmed glasses, told me that first-class staterooms—professionally decorated, of course—could be reserved with or without adjoining rooms. There were tennis and badminton courts, a bar and library, a smoking room, a formal dining room and a Pompeian swimming bath. A pool! I'd never been in one!

At the appointed day and time, I waited at the pier where passengers were preparing to board the steamship. When I saw the stolid nurse pushing Dr. Stoddard in the wheelchair his nephew had procured, I came forward. A plaid wool blanket was draped over Dr. Stoddard's legs. He looked up at me through his thick lenses.

He pointed behind him at the nurse. "Nurse Steele. Dependable. Totally devoid of humor, of course. Isn't that right, Steele? I shall miss her." He leaned toward me and whispered, "On the first of never." His eyes danced as if he and I were sharing a private joke.

Nurse Steele maintained such a neutral expression she seemed carved from stone. I nodded at her, professional to professional. *This one is a handful*, she seemed to be signaling.

"Well, then. Shall we, Nurse Falstaff?" he said, smiling up at me.

I took the reins from the older nurse and wheeled Dr. Stoddard toward the gangway.

"I wish to enjoy my voyage to Istanbul. I wanted someone jolly and fetching to accompany me. That's what I told Mishra. Good man. You and I will be together for twelve days on this vessel and we will bloody well have a marvelous time." In his patrician accent, the word sounded more like *maavelous*.

In the wake of my mother's death, I hardly felt as if I'd be a cheerful companion. Would I disappoint the good doctor? It was too late to worry about that now.

The steamship bellowed. We were leaving the Bombay docks. My adventure had begun.

The doctor had a well-appointed first-class stateroom with an interconnecting room for me. I was close enough to hear him if he needed me at night, but my room was private enough to give me space. It was comfortable and far more opulent than the flat Mum and I had shared. The walls were a polished mahogany as was the furniture. I had a bed, a washbasin, a dresser and an armchair. I needed no more.

My job was to get the doctor in and out of bed, help him put on his pajamas, make sure he ate, help him with exercises to heal his leg and prepare him for the day. I wheeled him around the ship for his morning constitutional and his meals. I didn't fuss over him. I knew he would have hated being mothered. If he needed something, he would tell me.

I hadn't counted on seasickness, however. The first few days were the worst. I was pushing the doctor's wheelchair and started to feel nauseous. Automatically, I slowed down. Without acknowledging my discomfort, Dr. Stoddard said, "I'd like to move closer to the railing, Nurse." I heaved into the ocean until I had nothing left. I used my handkerchief to wipe my mouth.

"I'm so sorry, Doctor. I've never been on a boat before."

"Sorry about what? I prefer the view from here." We spoke no more about it. But in the evening, I found a small piece of ginger on a plate by my bedside. I put it in my tea from then on to overcome the nausea.

The doctor napped in the afternoons, which gave my mind free rein. All I could think about was Mum and what a void her passing had left in my life. How she would have loved being on this steamship, meeting passengers from the world over. I carried a small notebook with me around the ship and would settle in a deck chair so I could pour my feelings onto paper.

Dear Mum,

I miss everything about you. I miss your smell—that mixture of rose water, turmeric and cotton that is no one else's. I miss the paper crowns you made for my birthdays, even when I got too old for them. I miss your surprise of a milk toffee—just one—whenever I did well on a test. I miss the tiny jackets you made for my cloth dolls. You attached snaps where the buttons would normally go because you told me they didn't make buttons that small. I used to watch, fascinated, as you bit the thread off with your teeth. I tried to do it too when you weren't looking and ended up pulling out my baby tooth. Remember? You said it would grow back if we put the tooth in a jar and buried it in soil. Day after day, I looked for a new tooth to grow until one day you pointed to my mouth. It's grown in, beti, you said. You knew everything. Everything that mattered to me. Why didn't you tell me there would come a day when I would have to know everything too? But I don't. I don't know what I'm doing. I don't know where I'm going. I don't know where I'll end up. I'm not sure of anything. Why aren't you here to guide me?

Some afternoons, I walked around the ship, wandering from one deck to another, tricking my grief into thinking I'd outgrown it. I came to like the smell of the ocean—a mixture of pickled eggs, shrimp, stale air—and the cool breeze that sprayed my overheated skin. My nurse's uniform elicited more than a few stares and I used it like a shield to prevent personal questions about my life. If a crew member happened to be walking by, I would engage him in conversation to avoid nosy passengers snaring me in theirs. To engineers, I would ask, *How does such a heavy ship stay afloat?* To a petty officer, *How many voyages does the Viceroy make in a year?* After a few days, the passengers who had seen me pushing the doctor's wheelchair stopped seeing me as a curiosity. Once more, I became invisible, which was the way I preferred it. I'd dodged prying questions and sly remarks about my *half-half* looks all my life. There were times I wanted to believe the girls at school really wanted to be my friend, and I would let down my guard. Time after time, I learned that they simply wanted to know the story of my mother and father so they could leverage it for a more privileged status among their friends. I would come home in tears when they avoided me the next day. One look at me and my mother would prepare the *suji ka halwa* I loved, the simple one without raisins or nuts. As I grew older and became more cautious, I sometimes wondered why my mother—and father—had put me in the position of the other. Didn't they realize how hard it would be for me to blend in? The questions I'd be asked? I had trained my eyes to look away whenever Mum told the gossip-eaters that my father had died of a heart attack. I knew my face would give the lie away. It became safer for both of us to stay away from those who fed the rumor mill.

Dr. Stoddard was perfectly pleasant to passengers, smiling and remarking on their health. *Looking fit as a fiddle, young man. Still alive and kicking, Major? Feeling tickety-boo, madam?* Yet, if anyone tried to engage him in conversation, he would invent some activity he needed to join in or a lie-down was in order, don't you think, Nurse? I knew why I was so reticent, but I wondered why he had any reason to be.

He was often invited to share the captain's table, an invitation he rarely accepted, but when he did, he insisted I join him. The other diners sent alarmed glances around the table. As did I. I knew I had no place there, and so did Dr. Stoddard. I had the feeling my ornery charge did it on purpose to irritate them.

We played backgammon together. I now won more games than I lost. Which was probably why he began teaching me gin rummy. He cheated at cards too until I knew enough about the game to see what he was doing. I realized a game wasn't fun for him unless he had a worthy opponent. So I became one. Soon, we were betting sips of port wine, which a steward delivered to his cabin every evening. The winner got to sip; the loser watched longingly. Of course, the winner would get pleasantly tipsy. We also bet teaspoons of caviar, which the doctor ordered from the kitchen. I'd never had caviar or port before. The alcohol went to my head, loosening my tongue and making me laugh more than I ever had. The doctor seemed pleased whenever I scolded him or took pleasure in winning. Of course, there were evenings when the day had been too hard on his bones, his leg, and he only wanted to be put to bed. He was more serious, less flippant on those occasions.

As I tucked the sheets around his bed one evening, he said, "I voted against the board, you know."

I stopped to look at him.

"I know you. So does Mishra. You would sooner cut off your thumb than play loose with a patient's dosage." He removed his glasses and looked down at them, played with the earpieces. "When I was a young doctor in Manchester, I was looking after a wealthy patient whom I diagnosed with tuberculosis. I was so sure I was right. I prescribed rest and mild exercise." He fiddled with his glasses some more. "Turns out he had pneumonia, which we might have treated with arsenic. He still may not have lived, but when he died…guilt followed me everywhere. I thought I could escape it by running to India. And I started over." He put his glasses on again. "Mistakes are made every day in our profession, my dear."

"But that's just it, Doctor. I'm sure I didn't make that mistake. I didn't give Miss Novak more than the prescribed dose. Someone else did. But who? The assumption that I did the unthinkable follows me everywhere." I scratched my forehead. "And where would I go to start over? India is my home."

He nodded. "So how do you intend to salvage your reputation?"

I went to the other room and came back with the stack of paintings and the paper with Mira's handwriting. "Miss Novak left these paintings in my care along with this note."

He read the note. Then he examined the paintings one by one, taking his time. He turned each of them over. Finally, he said, "Wasn't she a brilliant painter? The colors! And the composition is stunning." He considered the note. "The sinitials on the paintings match the names in the note."

"Yes. I believe the *S* stands for me, Sona."

"And who or what are *P*, *Po* and *J*?"

"They're people who mattered to Miss Novak. A lifelong girlfriend. A former painting tutor. Her art dealer." I paused. "I think I'm meant to deliver these paintings to their new owners. And they may tell me things about her I don't yet know or need to know in order to exonerate myself."

He put a gnarled finger across his mouth, deep in thought. "Where are these friends?"

"Petra is in Prague. Josephine is in Paris. And Paolo is in Florence."

"What if what you find isn't what you expected?"

"What do you mean?"

He paused, as if he were organizing his thoughts. "You seem to be enchanted by Miss Novak. You have an impression of her. I hear she was charming. She was bright. She was generous. But you only knew her for six days. The deeper you delve into her past relationships, you may encounter versions of her that surprise you. Versions that may confuse you."

I straightened my spine. "I'm a good judge of character, Doctor. I think I understood her in a way that wouldn't have changed had I known her for six years."

His tone was mild. "It's just that people are not always what they seem, my dear."

His expression carried the weight of eight decades. "Where is your family, Nurse Falstaff?"

"There was only my mother." My eyes stung. "She's gone now."

"And your father?"

I hesitated. Anytime I thought of my father, I felt ashamed or angry or embarrassed. By way of an answer, I went to my cabin and brought the photo of Owen Falstaff with me.

Dr. Stoddard took the photo from me. "I see the resemblance." Then, "What happened to him?"

My face was hot with shame. "He lives in England. With his family." I hadn't realized I was rubbing my hands together, hard, until they started to hurt.

The doctor regarded me for a long moment. "A casualty of the British Raj." He paused. "But that's still not all, is it?"

My eyes begged him not to force it out of me. It was too painful. He would think less of me when he found out. He might leave me at Cairo and send me back to Bombay.

His eyes twinkled. "Unless you've murdered someone, my dear, I think it's safe to tell me. You aren't planning on a second act, are you?"

I choked on a laugh and started coughing.

"I think, my girl, it's time we moved on to the Glenlivet. Port wine is only for backgammon and gin rummy."

Picking up the phone, I asked the steward to bring the scotch. By the time he arrived, I had put the photo back in my trunk. The steward poured our scotch into two lowballs. When he left, Dr. Stoddard ordered me to drink first. I took a sip. I'd never had scotch. The alcohol burned as it slid down my throat but then turned into a warm blanket in my belly.

The doctor watched my reaction and smiled. He lifted his glass. "Go on."

I told him about my father leaving us when I was three. I told him about my brother, Rajat, who died not long after. I told him about my mother having no idea my father was married until the day he left and confessed everything.

"Hmm." We sipped our scotch. "So you're going to Prague, Paris and Florence, correct?" He paused, his expression brightening. "Now how about London?"

"What about it?"

"You're not going to visit your father?"

"Why would I?" My voice carried the resentment of twenty years. I finished my scotch in one gulp.

His gaze went to my empty glass. "That might be the point." He looked at me. "In any case, yours is quite the expensive excursion, dear girl."

"I have some money…from my father." I told him about the annual gift and handed him the pouch of money.

He counted it. Then he gazed at me over his specs. "Not nearly enough, I'm afraid. Unless you plan to outsmart the train conductors."

In less than a minute, my plan had gone from possible to absurd. I felt ridiculous. The night Mum and I had counted the money, it had felt like the kind of windfall Indira's husband was always chasing at the horse races. Why had I ever thought this could work?

The doctor drained his glass. He looked tired. "Let's put me to bed, Nurse Falstaff. We'll have better ideas in the morning. Oh, and drink two glasses of water before you go to sleep tonight, my girl. Trust me."

The next morning, I came to Dr. Stoddard's cabin to help him get ready for the day. When I'd awakened, I felt as if I had cotton balls in my mouth and in my brain. I'd already thrown up twice. My head hurt.

"Feeling a little raw, are we?" His eyes twinkled. He was knitting, a fluffy ball of pale blue yarn spinning on his lap blanket. My jaw dropped—I'd never seen a man knit before. He was neither embarrassed nor startled by my reaction. "It's for my granddaughter."

His fingers deftly moved the stitches from one knitting needle onto another, completing another row. The backside of a sweater was almost done. He must have been knitting all the while we'd been on the ship and never let on. He stuck the needles in the ball of yarn and said, "We're playing tonight. In the Music Room."

I pulled the covers back so he could swing his legs to the side. "You and I?"

"Among others." He leaned on me to help him to the bath. "Wear something fetching."

I cocked my head. "You mean my nurse's uniform with a cap or my nurse's uniform with a cap?"

"Very funny. Now leave me to my bath."

* * *

At nine in the evening, I wheeled Dr. Stoddard toward the Music Room. It was an elegant drawing room with Persian rugs, chairs, even a fireplace. There was a piano next to the fireplace, a harp at the far end of the room and a windup gramophone near the door. As far as I knew, Dr. Stoddard didn't play a musical instrument. So what were we doing here? I asked him.

"Oh, stop fussing, girl!" he said.

I wheeled him into the Music Room. The club chairs, which were clustered around small tables whenever I'd walked by this room, had been rearranged around a mahogany table. At the head sat the captain. The other gentlemen—prosperous-looking men with vests and watch chains and jowls—were ones I'd seen at his dinner table most nights. Each held a hand of cards. Cigar smoke swirled upward toward the ornamental plaster ceiling. A pile of pound notes was scattered in the middle of the table.

"Doctor!" greeted the captain. "Never seen you here before. Welcome, welcome. I believe you know everyone."

Not once did the captain look at me. I was invisible the way the Indian deckhands were invisible, the way the Indian chambermaids were invisible. He'd tolerated my presence at his dinner table, but only because it would have been impolitic not to.

I drew the wheelchair up to the table. Dr. Stoddard patted the club chair next to him. I looked at him in panic. It was one thing to sit at the captain's dinner table but quite another to play cards with men of industry.

Dr. Stoddard addressed the group with a charming smile. "Bloody eyes aren't what they used to be. Nurse here—" he leaned into the table confidentially "—not too clever, mind you, but does her best." He sat back in the wheelchair. "Don't mind, chaps, do you? I'll be her bank. Oh—" he signaled to the server in the room. "A glass of port. There's a good man."

The men eyed one another and mumbled their assent. I was appalled and more than a little hurt at his remark about me not being up to snuff. The last time the doctor and I played I'd won every game. He'd even congratulated me on how quickly and how far I'd come. "Are you sure you haven't picked up my bad habits, Nurse?"

I raised an eyebrow. "You mean cheating? And so obviously, Doctor? Even a child could have sussed you out." I'd become bolder with him ever since I learned he enjoyed the occasional sparring.

The corners of his eyes crinkled when he smiled. "Touché, my girl. Touché." His eyes lingered on mine a second longer, and I felt the gentleness of it—the love a father might give his daughter. Something I'd been missing in my life. I felt heat behind my eyes and looked away.

Now here he was telling everyone they may as well steal money from him as long as I was at the table. I felt my chest constrict in anger even as I kept my expression bland.

The doctor leaned toward me and lowered his voice while the captain dealt a new hand. His blue eyes bore into mine. "Just as I've taught you. There's a good girl."

Dr. Stoddard placed a wager. My fingers trembled. My hands were moist. I rubbed them against my apron, worried the cards would slip out of my hands. I could feel beads of sweat on my brow. The men could see I was nervous. I caught their smug expressions, their sly looks at one another.

The captain threw money in the center of the table. "Won't be long now before we learn what happened to the Hindenburg."

"My wife says her cousin was lucky to have survived." This from a gentleman with a scar on this left cheek. "What a disaster!" He lay a shilling on the table.

"Even King George's coronation couldn't overshadow it." The one with the biggest paunch threw his money into the pile.

"Sorry to have missed the folderol. Seems as if the whole of England turned out for the ceremony," Dr. Stoddard said.

I lost the first hand. And the second. I kept glancing at the doctor to see if he was as nervous as I was. Oh, how I wish he had told me I would be playing in his stead tonight. These men knew what they were doing. They were practiced at winning. I was a novice. Thoughts of how I'd failed Mira, how I'd failed my mother, how I'd failed to keep my post—everything I'd ever done that amounted to failure—consumed me. Sweat ran down the back of my neck.

"Nurse, would you please get me a glass of water?" The doctor's voice broke through my private hysteria.

The captain cocked a finger at the steward. "He'll get it."

The doctor laughed lightly. "Only Nurse Falstaff knows how I like it. Not too cold. Not too warm."

"Of course," I said, rising from the table. I pressed my hand over the wrinkles of my uniform. The men chatted about the recent provincial elections in India and how Nehru would fare as leader of the Indian National Congress while I went to the sideboard to pour water from the pitcher into a glass.

"India will never be able to govern her people without us," the captain said, puffing on his cigar.

Dr. Stoddard looked amused. "Isn't that what India was doing before we came on the scene?"

The captain frowned at him. "Doctor, in case you've forgotten, *'the sun will never set on the British Empire.'* I think every man here knows that." He looked to the others for confirmation. A few nodded. Others pretended to study their cards.

The doctor let out a small laugh. "It would've set a lot sooner if England hadn't used Indian soldiers to get us through our wars." The captain, whose cheeks had turned red, glared at Dr. Stoddard, who smiled at him good-naturedly. "But we're not here for politics. We're here to play cards. Isn't that right, old bean?"

I braced myself against the sideboard. My stomach felt queasy. When I felt able to breathe again, I walked back with the water. I offered the glass to Dr. Stoddard. He placed his hands around mine, startling me.

I looked at him. He held my gaze with his unblinking owl eyes.

"As I taught you," he said softly.

Once again, I felt it. The encouragement of a father teaching his cricket-playing son how to bat. Or coaching his daughter about the perfect tennis serve.

I pulled my chair up to the table. I put the doctor's money in the kitty and concentrated on the game instead of how inadequate I felt. I looked at my cards. I counted which cards were left. I calculated what each player was holding.

I won that hand. And the next. And every subsequent hand after that. The scattered pile of silver and pound notes now sat in a stack in front of me. I was so absorbed in the game that I didn't hear the doctor telling the men he was tired and needed to lie down. I thought I felt, rather than heard, a collective sigh of relief.

Dr. Stoddard began scooping up my winnings onto his lap blanket. That's when I realized the game was over. Or at least my part in it was over.

Dazed, I pulled on his wheelchair and took him out of the smoky room.

"What just happened?" I asked from behind his chair.

"How do you feel?" His voice hid a smile.

"Bloody wonderful, you wanker." He laughed. So did I.

It *was* wonderful watching the egos of those men deflate one by one. At some point during the game, I'd stopped being petrified of losing the doctor's money and started being—what?—reckless? Courageous? Impudent? Who cared? I loved it! Was this the kind of chance my mother wanted me to take? Was this how giddy she'd felt the day she met my father and decided to take the risk? Was this the way Mira felt every single day of her life? She would have thought it weak to be fearful of life, hiding in the shadows as I'd done. If she wanted to paint what no one else was painting, she wouldn't think twice about it. If she wanted to sleep with someone, she didn't need anyone's permission.

The doctor pointed to his lap blanket. "This should get you as far as you need to go, my dear."

I looked at the winnings. It was more money than I'd ever seen! I bit my lip. If only Mum were here to see it! And if she were here, she would tell me it wasn't fair to lay claim to it all. I felt the same way. "It's as much your money as mine, Doctor."

He grinned, wagging a crooked finger at me. "My girl, do not be contrary. You were the champion tonight. Revel in it!"

"Fifty-fifty?"

He shook his head. "Wouldn't dream of it." He paused. "Now about your father..." My heart sped up. Had I said something unseemly after a night of too much port and scotch? I was pushing his chair from behind, and I couldn't see the expression on his face.

"My dear, we Brits have done a lot of damage to your country. I can see you're paying the price." He reached behind the chair to pat my hand. Tears sprang to my eyes.

Dearest Mum,

Dr. Stoddard thinks I should find Father. Well, he didn't say so, but I know that's what he's thinking. But why should I, Mum? He left us in Calcutta with nothing. How could he do that to us?

I'm going to tell you something I saw when I was five that I've never told anybody. That was when we lived in a house with another family and their four children. You and I had a tiny room big enough for a charpoy and a chest of drawers. The family lived in the rest of the house. We kept to ourselves even though their daughter was the same age as me. She spit on me the first time we met (remember you kept asking why I didn't play with her?). One night, I had a bad dream about a dog running after me. I woke up and reached for you. You weren't there, so I got out of bed to look for you. The house was quiet because the family was away at a wedding for a few days. All at once, I realized I could go anywhere in the house I wanted. I went from room to room, bad dream forgotten. I touched the girl's marionette dolls. I moved pieces on the chessboard even though I didn't know how to play. I rifled through their clothing. I was about to step into their kitchen to see if they had any biscuits lying about when I saw you at their dining table. I almost called for you but something told me not to. You were bent from the waist over the table. Your sari was bunched around your hips. I could only see his silhouette, but I knew from his beard that it was the landlord leaning over you, groaning. You weren't making a sound. My heart was pounding so hard I thought you could hear it. I snuck back quietly to our room and pulled the covers over my face. But I could still see it. And I knew it was bad. That's what my father's desertion did to you, to us. It robbed you of your pride and it made me a witness to your shame. If I were to tell the good doctor this, would he still want me to find my father?

The RMS Viceroy was scheduled to make a stop along the Suez Canal so passengers en route to Cairo could disembark. Then the steamship would continue to the Mediterranean Sea and Istanbul.

I missed Amit too. I wrote letters to him every day in my

notebook. I couldn't send them to the hospital. What would the staff think of him, receiving letters from a disgraced, unmarried nurse? I didn't know where he lived either. Sometimes, as I strolled the deck, I pretended we were walking arm in arm, talking, as we'd talked on that tonga ride to Dev Singh's house.

Dear Amit,

I've never seen so much water or so much desert! Calcutta and Bombay and everything in between that Mum and I had ever seen was simply green fields and forests. Along the Suez Canal, there is only one color: sand. Every now and then, we see camel riders, men unloading small cargo ships and ferries, mosques, a little patch of green. Some distance away there are tiny villages and small cities. Along the railing, I often stand behind Dr. Stoddard's wheelchair as he points out the enormous griffon vultures crossing the skies overhead. He tells me that the hot air rising from the desert allows them to fly without moving a muscle.

The doctor has me playing cards with the gamblers, and I fear I'm turning into one myself. He's also got me drinking scotch in the evening. All the things I've been missing out on all these years! Why did no one tell me?

Speaking of things I've been missing out on, do you know what I was imagining the night of the Singh party? I only dared to kiss you, but I would have done so much more had we been alone. I wanted to feel your hands on my body, my hands on yours, the pressure of you against me. I would have liked to—

I felt my cheeks burning as these thoughts raged through my mind. Of course, I couldn't imagine actually saying these things out loud. I wouldn't have had the nerve.

I wish you were here, Amit, and that we were standing on the railing taking in this great big adventure. I'm keeping hopeful thoughts for you and your aunt in Shimla.

Cairo was the destination for many on the ship. Businessmen, traders, tourists and archeologists were taken by buses to Cairo upon disembarking. Several of the men we'd played gin rummy with were climbing into taxicabs waiting at the port. I would have liked to see Cairo, to explore the open-air markets, the busy narrow lanes, drink the thick Egyptian coffee I'd heard the deckhands talking about. But Dr. Stoddard and I were going straight through to Istanbul. I would have to be satisfied with what I could glean of Egypt from the railing of the Viceroy.

As we watched the passengers leaving the port, Dr. Stoddard sucked his teeth. "Do you know…there's a large Dewar's Whisky sign on the rooftop of an apartment building in Cairo. In the square below, Muslim men and women mill about in their long robes. Imagine the contrast." He sighed. "More collateral damage. That's what we English create."

We disembarked at the busy Istanbul port. Dr. Stoddard's son, as wiry as his father, was solicitous to us both but in a hurry to get back to his office. Like his father and his cousin Timothy, he wore glasses too. His tweed suit and white shirt were worse for wear in the Turkish heat.

"Nurse Falstaff, this is my son, Edward. Edward, this is my very capable Nurse Falstaff." He leaned forward toward his son. "She's a card shark. Watch out."

I laughed. Edward smiled, a dimple appearing on his left cheek. He had the same long nose as his father and the high forehead, but the features were softer, blunted. His skin was just a mite darker than mine—I assumed from working under the Turkish sun. I tried not to compare him to Amit, but it was impossible since Amit was so much on my mind. Was Amit's smile more appealing? Was Amit's voice raspier?

"Now, I know you'd like to get back to the office, Edward, but we owe our nurse a little rest and relaxation. After all, she's had to look after me for an age. Poor soul."

My train wouldn't be leaving for Prague for another four hours. Dr. Stoddard had been kind enough to arrange my ticket from the steamship. I couldn't impose on him further. And truth be told, I didn't want to owe him any more than I already did. My trunk was heavy with coins, pound notes and gratitude.

"Doctor, you've already been so generous. I couldn't possibly—"

His son turned his gaze in my direction and lifted a brow. "Brought out the port, did he? And cheated? Had you playing gin rummy?" The laugh lines around his mouth meant he didn't take life as seriously as I did. He winked. "Did the same to me on my maiden voyage."

His father grinned.

Edward took the reins of the wheelchair. "We owe you, Nurse Falstaff. Right then, Father. The office can wait. To the Grand Bazaar it is."

The indoor market smelled like India. There were mounds of spicy turmeric, mustard powder, cumin powder and barrels of pistachios. Many shops sold only essential oils—rose attar, jasmine attar, sandalwood oil, oud. Others sold carpets, fezzes, brass lanterns and furniture. The sharp aroma of leather sandals and shoes permeated the hallways. And the monied smell of glittering gold chains in the jeweler's row was the same as at the Zaveri Bazaar in Bombay. However, Istanbul didn't *feel* like India. Here the female shoppers wore European skirt suits and hats. There was not a *dhoti* in sight. I missed the humble cows and bullock carts of Bombay. I even missed the wily women behind the stalls trying to get me to buy a woven basket I didn't need.

My uniform drew plenty of stares. In Istanbul, I supposed nurses weren't in the habit of shopping at the souks. I felt self-conscious, not knowing where to look. It was similar to the discomfort I felt when Indian rickshaw drivers stared at me on the streets of Bombay. I tried leveling a bold glare in their direction, but usually ended up lowering my eyes in embarrassment.

The doctor stopped to chat with a vendor about his sweet offerings. Cubes of Turkish delights in cheerful shades of rose, lemon, violet. Some were covered in pistachio, others in coconut. "My guilty pleasure," Dr. Stoddard said.

While he quizzed the vendor about the flavor of each one, Edward and I waited in the aisle, watching him indulgently like parents with their child.

"Pater is extremely fond of you, you know. He's written to me at length about how capable you are. How charming. How good-looking. I was almost jealous." I turned to see him smiling at me, his eyes twinkling. "And I must say, he was absolutely off the mark there. I would have called you beautiful."

I couldn't help but blush.

"Tell me. How is Pater doing? I thought he'd be out of the wheelchair by now. Should I be concerned?"

I laughed. "Oh, he doesn't need it anymore. We've got him walking by himself. He just loves the attention. It's a new device, and he means to make the most of it. Your cousin Timothy would take him on joyrides around the hospital."

Edward laughed, a joyous thing that seemed to travel all the way from his lips to his toes. Happiness filled him. I took a second look at him then. His delight was different from Dev Singh's. There was nothing roguish about Edward.

"Timothy isn't my blood cousin. We grew up together. Our mothers were friends. We're more like brothers. He's a few years younger. You should have seen what we got up to when we were younger. Father would take us to Pushkar for the camel fair and pay one of the herders to let us ride the smaller camels. Timmy and I would race each other. We'd be flying across the desert, nary a care about whether we might fall off and hurt ourselves. And Pater would be in bits, watching us bouncing along on those magnificent creatures." The image of that got me laughing as well.

"Did your mother accompany you on those trips?"

Edward's laugh trickled to a small smile. "She died when I was eight."

"Oh, I am sorry, Mr. Stoddard."

"Please. Call me Edward. She was lovely. Father more than made up for it though. He became both father and mother. Taught me about corsages and how to dance properly. I can do both parts, you know. Here, I'll show you."

Before I knew it, he'd placed his arm around my back and lifted one of my arms and we were gliding down the aisle. He was so confident in his steps that he easily steered us around the other shoppers. Vendors came out from their stalls to watch us. I'd never been a graceful dancer, but Edward made me feel as if I were. I caught a reflection of the two of us in a tall mirror outside one of the stalls as he twirled me. *Was that really me?* Mira would have whooped and clapped if she'd been here. Edward wound us back to the Turkish delight stall where Dr. Stoddard was waiting for us in his wheelchair.

"You're a natural," Edward said. He seemed reluctant to let go of my hand. And I found myself not wanting to let go either.

"I was hoping you'd come back sometime today," Dr. Stoddard said. His smile was full of mischief.

Edward bowed to me as if we'd been dancing at a cotillion. As reticent as I'd always been, I couldn't hide my pleasure at being courted like that. I reached up and kissed Edward on the cheek. It was his turn to blush.

"You must try this, my dear. It's like inhaling a rose." The doctor handed me a pink delight, and I took a bite. It was too sweet and sticky for me, but he was right. It was like inhaling a rose.

The doctor and Edward treated me to lunch at a café just outside the bazaar, a place Edward frequented. He ordered for us. Steaming platters of lamb *köfte* arrived, bringing with them the aroma of sautéed garlic, onions, cumin and cinnamon. A salad of tomatoes, cucumbers, olives and green peppers seasoned with lemon and vinegar and a platter of tomato and lentil pilaf accompanied the meal. We ate as Indians, sharing food from the platters. Edward laughed when I swooned after tasting the lamb. Perfectly seasoned, it was a little like Indian *kofta*.

Two men at the next table were playing what looked like backgammon on a rosewood board inlaid with mother-of-pearl.

Edward noticed me watching them. "It's called *tavla*. The player who loses must tuck the board under his arm to show everyone that he's taking it home because he needs the practice."

The doctor leaned toward me. "You, my dear, would never need to take it home." That was high praise coming from him.

Taking a bite of his *köfte*, Edward said to me, "He's never said that to me. You must have won a tidy sum off Pater."

Edward's mahogany eyes lingered on mine a moment longer than necessary, and I had to look away. I'd never been a tease. I wouldn't have known how, not having had much practice. It made me long for a different personality, like Mira's. She and Dev Singh had traded witty quips with ease. I loved Amit's dry humor too but couldn't match it. I'd lived in a world that included my mother, nurses at the hospital and the occasional encounter with neighbors, like Fatima across the landing from our old flat. Sheltered. Wasn't that why my mother had wanted me to go abroad?

I tried hard to think of something to say to Edward. Suddenly, I remembered the sweater the doctor had been knitting. "How old is your daughter?"

Edward frowned. "Daughter? I'm not married."

My cheeks felt warm. I looked at the doctor. "The sweater—you said—was for a granddaughter—"

Dr. Stoddard laughed lightly. From under his lap blanket, he brought out a pale blue mohair sweater. "You must have misheard me, my dear. This is for you. You're going to colder places than you've ever been, and I think you'll need it."

"Oh," was all I could say. He'd been knitting the sweater for me? The only other person who had ever made things for me was my mother. I unfolded it. It was a long-sleeved cardigan with ivory buttons. I ran my hand over the silky mohair.

When I looked at the doctor, he said, "You're welcome."

I was at a loss for words. I rose from my chair to kiss his cheek.

He chuckled. "Goodness. A simple thank you will do."

"Well done, Father," Edward said. "Where's mine?"

"Don't be ridiculous, Edward. Now, tell me…don't you do something with diplomats?"

The waiter brought our Turkish coffees. The coffee was thicker and more bitter than anything I'd ever tasted. I decided one sip was enough.

Edward dropped two sugar cubes in his tiny cup and took a sip. He arched an eyebrow. "You know very well I work for the British Embassy, Pater."

"Ah, yes. Then perhaps you wouldn't mind giving Nurse Falstaff a hand with an inquiry or two she needs for Europe?"

"Where do you go from here?" Edward asked me.

I was caught off guard. I hadn't known where Edward worked, and I hadn't expected the doctor to ask for help on my behalf. I'd given a lot of thought to tracing Mira's journey from Prague to

Paris and Florence, but now that it was before me, I was seized with fear. Perhaps it was the coffee or the idea of going into the unknown, alone. All of a sudden, I wasn't sure I was capable of making this trip by myself. With Dr. Stoddard, I'd been in safe and sure hands; he'd traveled around the world and could guide me around the ship and on to Istanbul. In an hour, I was about to continue the journey by myself on a train to cities I'd only imagined visiting. I could feel my courage dwindling. The lamb I'd just devoured sat heavy in my stomach.

I swallowed the bile in my throat. "Um. Prague. Paris. Florence." I choked on the last word and reached for my water glass. My hand was shaking. The look between the doctor and his son didn't escape my notice.

Edward picked up my coffee cup and emptied it into his own. He poured the dregs left in my cup onto my saucer. "Ahmed will foretell your journey. I'm sure it will be a happy one." He waved to our waiter, whom he knew from previous visits to this café.

Ahmed came to our table with a smile to inspect my saucer. In halting English, he said, "Journey—away, away." His smile disappeared and his dark eyebrows met in the middle of his forehead. "Family. Not good." He looked sideways at Edward to see if he should continue.

The hair on my arms stood up as if it was a cold day even though it was warm outside. My journey was doomed? What had I taken on? Did I really want to do this? But where else could I go? My panic spiraled. I had no home. My mother wasn't waiting for me. I had no nursing post to return to.

The doctor laughed off Ahmed's coffee reading. He patted me on the shoulder and said, "Poppycock! Like those magicians at the Bombay docks. Edward, one man claimed to lift a stone with his eyes! Pure tosh I tell you! Let's get you to your train, shall we, my girl, so you can continue your grand adventure?"

When I relinquished Dr. Stoddard's care to his son at the Sirkeci Terminal, he looked at me through those thick glasses, his owl eyes dancing with mischief. "A little something to remember me by, my dear," he said, putting a smooth piece of glass the size of a three pence coin in my palm. In the center was what looked like a blue eye with a black pupil. "To ward off evil." He shrugged. "I don't believe in fortune-telling, but it never hurts to hedge your bets, does it?" He took my hand in his warm one as if he wanted to lend me his courage. Oh, how I wanted to never let go. How I wanted to cling to his gentle presence and have him reassure me that all would be well always. Wasn't that what fathers did? Fathers who loved you?

Edward paid one of the porters on the Arlberg Orient Express to take my trunk to my compartment. Then he helped me onto the train, which would take me directly to Prague. Before stepping back, he handed me a copy of the Baedeker's guidebook. "Father thought you might need it, so I brought it with me today. Anywhere you go, your first stop should be the British Embassy. Whatever you need, you only have to mention my name at any British Embassy. I'll make sure you get it." His eyes held mine. The lovely tingling I'd felt in my body when he'd twirled me around the Grand Bazaar returned.

The doctor waved from the platform. "Godspeed. And mind the uniform. It's very fetching on you, my girl."

Long after he and Edward left, I found myself blushing.

PRAGUE

CHAPTER 9

With the money I'd earned from the gin rummy games on the Viceroy, I splurged on a sleeper car on the Arlberg Orient Express. Still, I needed to make my funds last, so instead of private accommodation, I was sharing the compartment with another passenger. The uniformed porter with the immaculate white gloves had placed my trunk on the overhead rack.

My fellow passenger was already settled in her seat by the time I arrived at my compartment. She was perhaps ten years older than me. Her pale green skirt suit and matching turban hat with a delicate veil were far more in keeping with the elegance of our car: the gleaming walnut veneer, the velvet curtains, the mohair upholstery.

"That is quite the handsome young man you have," she said, pulling her cigarettes out of her clutch purse and pointing with her free hand toward the window.

"Oh, he—he's not. He's the son of my patient—well, former patient." I was blubbering. The idea of Edward being mine was… preposterous. I heard Mira's voice in my head: *No, it's not, Sona. He could be.*

My fellow passenger laughed lightly and extended her gloved hand. "Agnes Kelmendi."

I wasn't used to shaking hands with women. It flustered me

so much that I forgot to introduce myself. Instead, I did what I usually do with patients—ask questions. Where was she from? What was taking her to Belgrade? Would she go on to Prague from there, as I was doing?

"I'm coming from Albania to work in Belgrade on the new trade fair." She lit her cigarette and shook the match until the flame disappeared. "I'm an interior designer."

Here was another woman like Mira doing things I thought women only did in books or films! "How exciting that sounds. Do you often travel for work?"

She nodded. "Germany. France. My favorite is Italy. The food. Fashion. Art." She took a drag of the cigarette, her face shrouded in smoke. "Have you been?"

I could only shake my head, embarrassed at my lack of sophistication. Would I ever be as comfortable as she seemed to be, traveling alone, undaunted by different customs, different languages?

She reached across and tapped my knee. "You must go."

The porter brought the afternoon tea. I felt a sharp pang when I saw the silver tray with the tea things, petit fours and delicate sandwiches with the crusts trimmed off. For my birthdays, my mother had indulged me with a formal tea. When I was little, the tea had been nothing more than sugar water heated up, tiny cucumber sandwiches and scones with apricot jam. When I reached my teens, Mum began serving real Ceylon tea with sponge cakes and lemon tarts. I'd loved the care my mother took to make the day special. But on the night of my birthdays, on our shared bed, I would hear her trying to muffle her sobs. Without being told, I knew the date was a yearly reminder of what she and my father had brought into being and all that we had missed out on as a family.

Agnes broke into my reverie. She set her teacup down on the little table and waved a hand at my uniform. "Are you going somewhere to take care of another patient?"

"I'm actually on my way to deliver some paintings." I suddenly wanted to show this worldly European woman Mira's work. Surely, she would appreciate the paintings! I took a last bite of my watercress sandwich and pulled my trunk down from the overhead rack. A client of my mother's had given that trunk to her. Battered tweed with two latching clasps and straps. It wasn't heavy, just large and cumbersome. The train lurched slightly, and I lost my balance so that by the time I opened the trunk, my belongings were a tumbled mess. I had kept the brown wrapping paper around the rolled paintings so as not to damage them. I unwound the paper carefully and held up *The Acceptance*. I looked to Agnes for her reaction. But she was looking instead at my luggage. My underthings, blouses, the pouch with my money—everything was in a jumble. My beat up trunk and its disorganized contents on such display was mortifying. I quickly shut the suitcase.

"You see the focus on the young woman being prepared for marriage?" I asked. "What Miss Novak noticed was that while the bride seems accepting of her fate, there is a quiet joy in serenity of the scene."

"Yes, I see," Agnes said. She took the painting from me and studied it. "Lovely brushwork too. You said Mira Novak is her name?"

"Was. Was her name." I looked out the window. "She died recently."

"I'm so sorry," she said, handing me back the painting. "I can see that this painter meant a lot to you." Her voice was sympathetic.

I needed a moment, and I was grateful that she didn't fill the pause with conversation.

The porter came to take the tea things and make our dining car reservations. Agnes asked if eight o'clock would suit me. For a moment, I couldn't speak. I was flattered a woman as cultivated as Agnes would want to dine with me. I nodded.

When the porter left, she said, "Of course, you have something to wear?" She looked pointedly at my uniform.

I looked down at my white uniform with its even whiter apron.

In a softer voice, she said, "You're expected to dine in formal wear."

I suddenly remembered the green gown my mother had made. "Yes! I do have something!" I felt my way to the bottom of the trunk, opening it more discreetly this time.

Agnes parted her pink painted lips and smiled. "That will do nicely indeed."

Cherrywood tables. Tulip-shaped sconces. Plush armchairs. The dining car of the Arlberg Orient Express was far more glamorous than the one on the Viceroy. Agnes was wearing an evening gown the color of an Indian blue robin. Her only jewelry was a wide rhinestone collar. When I walked behind Agnes to our seats, men in their black tie and tuxedos followed us with their eyes. As I had at the Singh party, I felt self-conscious exposing so much of my cleavage, but at the same time, I enjoyed a peculiar thrill from the attention. I thought of Amit and how he'd wanted to protect me from the lusty stares of men. It made me smile.

After a four-course meal of lobster bisque, roasted capon with dauphine potatoes, endive salad and crushed strawberries with cream, I was as full as I'd ever been. By the time we returned, the porter had converted our car into a sleeping compartment. I took the top bunk. I quickly fell into a deep sleep, dreaming of men in black tie selling brass lamps and oud from a stall in the Grand Bazaar.

The next morning, I went to the dining car for a simple breakfast of boiled egg and plain toast with tea. Agnes told me she never ate breakfast and was sipping a cup of coffee when I returned. Again, the porter had transformed our cabin back to sitting quarters—no evidence of the beds they'd been just an hour before. The morning newspaper lay on each of our seats. Agnes was reading hers. I picked up mine.

At last count, the bodies of thirteen passengers and twenty crew mem-

bers had been found at the site of the Hindenberg disaster. The dirigible is dead.

The American film Shall We Dance *with Fred Astaire and Ginger Rogers was a hit at the box office.*

A date had been set for the wedding of the Duke of Windsor and Wallis Simpson.

The Republican Party was losing the Spanish Civil War and Franco was winning.

I stopped reading to gaze out the window at the green hills and small villages rolling by. I tried to picture Mira sitting opposite my seat instead of my Albanian cabinmate, and I felt as intense a longing for her friendship as I had felt for my mother's love.

Mira had often talked about traveling on trains just like this one. She'd described it right down to the mirror above the corner sink. She told me she always left a tiny drawing tucked behind the mirror of every compartment she had slept in. "One time, I drew the face of the porter who was assigned to my compartment. I was tucking it behind the mirror when he caught me doing it. He just winked at me." She'd giggled, and I'd laughed with her. She said she wore the most outrageous outfits to the dining car—peacock feathers in a sequin headband or layers of chiffon so voluminous that diners would have to make room for her along the aisle.

I stood and went to the corner sink. I felt along the edges of the mirror to see if I could feel a gap where something could be hidden. There was no gap. It would have been impossible to slip anything between the mirror and the veneer wall. Puzzling. Perhaps Mira was having me on.

"What are you doing?" Agnes set her paper aside. She was once again in her pale green skirt suit and hat, looking—perfect. Her empty coffee cup lay on the table. She fished around for her cigarettes and lit one.

"Well—" I came to sit down in my seat again "—I think I was told something that turns out not to be true." Now I felt horrible. It was as if I were calling Mira a liar. "But perhaps I simply misunderstood."

Agnes looked thoughtful. She tapped cigarette ash in the glass ashtray that was imbedded into the table. "Things are never as they seem, you know." Odd. It sounded similar to what Dr. Stoddard had said to me. Agnes rolled her cigarette on the ashtray rim. "Take a look at my trunk. What do you see?"

I looked up at the luggage rack and cringed. My tweed trunk, sagging in places, with its tarnished latches, and her smart one—a waxed cotton canvas in warm brown, outlined in leather with brass tacks, and three gold initials: C. R. S.

"It's a beautiful trunk. I'm not sure I could ever afford it."

"Is that what you see?"

I raised my eyebrows. What more was there to see? But I took another look. And then it dawned on me. "The initials are different from yours?"

She released a cloud of nicotine, letting the smoke swirl around her, as if she were a genie from *One Thousand and One Nights*. "If my name were Agnes Kelmendi."

I frowned. "But you told me…"

"Or perhaps Agnes is my name, and I stole that trunk."

"I don't understand," I said.

"Or could I have bought the trunk from someone with the initials C. R. S.? It could also be that I was married to a wretched man with those initials and I claimed the trunk in the divorce." Her white teeth gleamed between pink lips. "Any one of those could be true. How are you to know?"

The train was slowing down. We were nearing Belgrade, where our sleeper car would be uncoupled and added to the train headed for Prague.

"I don't understand," I said. I felt as if I'd missed a part of the conversation and was having a hard time catching up.

"You will." Agnes crushed her cigarette in the ashtray. She pulled on her gloves and gathered her clutch. The porter appeared at our cabin to take her luggage off the train. She cupped my chin in her hand and smiled. She seemed sad. I caught a whiff of her jasmine and sweet cigarette scent when she said, "You're a sweet girl. The world is a big place. You'll learn."

I crossed our threshold and stood in the passageway to watch her walk away, high heels clacking, from the train to the platform, past the other passengers, until she was out of sight. What had she meant?

I was alone in the compartment and found myself missing Agnes's company. Thoughts of what I'd left behind in India flooded my mind. The way the coconut trees swayed in the wind, making the sound of waves lapping against Juhu Beach. A mango so ripe I could squeeze the pulp through a hole at the top and let the sweetness explode in my mouth. Women with bindis on their foreheads, chatting on a doorstep, shelling peas. To stave off the nostalgia, I took out my notebook and wrote to my mother about the doctor, dancing with Edward (which had me tapping my feet), the Turkish delights at the Grand Bazaar, the emerald gown I wore to dinner. I put the notebook away when the porter arrived with afternoon tea.

I took my time over my cream tea, imagining Amit sitting by my side. I told him what I loved about being on the train, how we had to dress for dinner and my fellow passenger Agnes and our strange conversation about her trunk.

When the tray was removed, I spoke to Mira. "Mira," I whispered, "I am here. In Europe. Can you believe it? I can hardly believe it myself. I'll find your friends. I promise."

At some point, I fell asleep and missed dinner altogether. Perhaps the porter didn't want to wake me.

Sometime in the night, I'd pulled on the sweater Dr. Stoddard had made for me because I'd been cold and—although I hated to admit it—because it made me feel less lonely, as if the doctor were by my side. In the morning, I decided to leave it on over my nurse's uniform. It was time to reorganize my trunk before getting off the train. I refolded my blouses and rewrapped Mira's paintings. I realized I would need to change money to tip the porter, pay for a taxi and my lodging. The Baedeker's Edward Stoddard had bought for me in Istanbul told me where to change money in Prague.

I picked up my cloth pouch where I kept my money. With my winnings from the gin rummy games, it had become bulkier and harder to snap closed. Now, it was thinner, lighter.

My hands trembled. I couldn't get my shaking fingers to undo the snap. I took a moment to breathe slowly and calm my pounding heart. I tried the pouch again. This time it snapped open. I shook all the money out on my seat. I began counting. Oh, no! No, no, no, no. It was half of what I'd brought with me. I searched my trunk. Could the snap have opened inside and the money spilled out? I upended the trunk, letting everything I'd just folded and organized tumble onto the seat. I set the paintings aside—thank goodness they were still there! But even as I rummaged through my belongings, I knew the money wouldn't be there. It wasn't. I sank into the seat. Brought my head between my knees. I'd been careless. But...where would I have lost it? The trunk had been with me at all times since I left Istanbul. Except for the times I went to the dining car. That was when the porter entered our compartment to convert it into a sleeper every night. Surely, it couldn't have been him? Porters were beyond reproach. Their integrity and discretion had to be carefully vetted by the train service. If porters stole from passengers, no one would take the train. No, it couldn't have been my porter.

The only other person who had access to my trunk was Agnes. When was she alone with it? Yesterday, she begged off breakfast. I'd gone by myself. But...how could it be her? Surely, she had enough of her own money. What with her smart suit and expensive evening gown and that handsome luggage—something that would have taken a year's salary for me to afford, provided I skipped eating altogether. What was all that about how she'd come by the luggage? That maybe it wasn't hers? Or that she wasn't who she appeared to be? Was she really an interior designer? Was she really going to Belgrade to work on the fair?

The truth hit me like a punch to my stomach. I didn't want to believe it. What a fool I'd been! So naive! Here I was pretending to be an adult when I was no more than a silly girl! All the while, she'd been sitting there with my money, laughing at me.

What could I do now? Tell the porter? What could he do? The train service wasn't going to reimburse me. Tell the police? Belgrade was a big city, and Agnes could have easily disappeared into its bowels. Besides, that was probably not her name. I couldn't go to the British Embassy. They had no responsibility in the matter and were under no obligation to give me my money back.

Slowly, I counted the remaining money. Agnes could have taken all of it, but she hadn't. Had she only taken half because she pitied me? Pitied me for my wide-eyed ignorance? Anger coursed through me. Worse than losing the money was the image of her rifling through my trunk, feeling sorry for my meager belongings. Dr. Stoddard had warned me to be careful. As had Agnes. *The world is a big place. You'll learn.* How embarrassing to be told in advance by a thief that she intended to rob you!

I blinked back my tears. I resisted the urge to quit. What did it matter if I never delivered these paintings? Jo and Paolo and Petra would never know that Mira had left something for them. Nothing said I had to do as Mira instructed. I could run back to Bombay and wait for Amit to find me another job. Then I heard Mira's voice. *How silly of us to have taken our eyes off the money, Sona! So what? It was a major setback, but what was done was done. We're not going to let it ruin our adventure.* She would have laughed it off. The loss was too raw for me to dismiss altogether, but I breathed a little easier. I needed to think about how to proceed. I had enough money to take the trains, but I would have to be careful about how much to spend on food and lodging. I could skip the taxis and take trams instead. Or walk. Miss a few meals.

I braced my arms on my thighs and pulled myself to standing. Mira had written, *I know you will take care of these. As will Jo and Petra and Po*, which meant the paintings needed to be given to their rightful inheritors. I couldn't imagine what else she was trying to say. Here in Prague, I needed to find Petra and deliver Mira's gift to her. I emptied my lungs of stale breath and shrugged off the self-pity.

Before getting off the train, I felt inside the pocket of my uniform for the amulet—the evil eye—Dr. Stoddard had given me. I took it out and left it on the table under the window.

I alighted from the Arlberg Orient Express at Praha hlavní nádraží in Prague. I was tired. My eyes were dry. And I was smarting from my foolishness, trusting a perfect stranger with my belongings and losing my money in the bargain. For the first time, I was far from my mother's touch, far from our flat, far from India. What if I couldn't find my way around Prague? What if I never found Petra? What if I ran out of money? It had been easy enough to win at cards on the Viceroy under Dr. Stoddard's protective guidance, but there was no way I could conjure a card game here where I knew no one. I scolded myself. Was I planning to spend the rest of the journey obsessing about things I couldn't undo? I squared my shoulders and walked toward the station exit.

Outside the station, I stood for a moment, taking in my surroundings. It made me a little dizzy to think how far I'd come. I had toyed with the idea of following in Mira's footsteps, and here I was actually doing it. Was I perhaps standing on the very spot where Mira and her mother had stood, waiting for the chauffer to unload their trunks? This was the station where they would have started their journeys to Florence and Paris. I closed my eyes and took in a lungful, inhaling strong coffee, something akin to vinegar, smoky fumes from the trains, cigarettes and—cabbage? I opened my eyes. There was a man standing a few feet from me playing the accordion, a cigarette dangling from his mouth. He nodded. I nodded back.

I used my schoolgirl French—grateful to have won a place at the convent school in Calcutta—and pointed to the map in my Baedeker's. He indicated which tram to take for the British Embassy. On the tram, I didn't have the proper currency (hellers and koruna), but seeing my nurse's uniform, the conductor forgave my ticket. It was Dr. Stoddard's idea to wear my uniform throughout my journey; I would be visible when it mattered and invisible when it didn't.

Mira had described her birth city perfectly. Preserved bridges, centuries old, gold-tipped spires adorning churches and cathedrals, majestic stone buildings where kings and their ministers had strategized about how to rule Bohemia. Sleek automobiles and trams moved along the same roads as the occasional horse-drawn carriage. Men and women in their tailored coats and Parisian shoes moved with ease around the history that surrounded them.

The British Embassy was as majestic a building as the ones I'd passed through Prague's Old and New Towns. At reception—which was even grander, with enormous oil paintings, silk settees and gilded candle sconces—an Englishwoman with lovely clear skin called upstairs for a Mr. Peabody, a jolly civil servant with eyes that faced in different directions. He came down to the foyer to accompany me upstairs to his office. As we climbed the stairs, he said, "Mr. Stoddard was most insistent we help you with your first visit here." He ushered me into his neat office. "Good chap, Stoddard. Runs that embassy in Istanbul. Rising star."

This was news to me. Edward was so humble that I'd assumed he was merely one of the diplomatic staff.

"Mind you, they all want the Paris post. Currently, however, all eyes are on Spain and Germany. Franco. Hitler. Mussolini. Beastly business. And just north of us, there's unrest with the Sudeten Germans." He folded his hands across his desk. "But you're not here for that, are you? Now then, is it a nursing position you're after?"

"What?" Confused, I frowned. Then I realized he was referring to my pinafore and cap. "No, sir. I need help on two other fronts."

I could tell by the set of his shoulders that my accent had thrown him. Given my last name and ochre eyes, he'd assumed I'd sound properly British. But I'd been raised by English-speaking nuns in India, and while I didn't have the heavily accented English most Indians did, I certainly didn't have the public-school accent he must have been expecting.

A lithe young woman of twenty came in with a tray of tea and biscuits. I realized I was still clutching my trunk, afraid to let it go after the fiasco with my savings. I set it on the floor, against the legs of my chair. I took a steaming cup of tea from the tray and poured a little milk into it. The assistant set Mr. Peabody's cup on his desk, glancing at me quizzically as she left the room. I'm sure she was wondering why Mr. Peabody was talking to a nurse.

"Mr. Peabody, I was in charge of a patient in Bombay who died at the hospital there. Perhaps you've heard of her. Mira Novak. She was a painter." I'd rehearsed this on the train to downplay my alleged involvement in her death.

His eyebrows rose. "I have. From here. Prague. Oh, dear, oh, dear. I am sorry to hear it. Must send condolences." He took a biscuit from the tray. "How can I help?"

"She wanted me to inform her closest friend from Prague. Miss Petra..." I didn't have a last name for her. But if the Novaks were known to Mr. Peabody, he might know their acquaintances. I was hoping they ran in the same social circles. "The Novaks lived next door to her family."

"That might be Miss Hitzig? Of the Hitzig family? If it's the same, we're in luck. Her father is the owner of one of the largest glass companies. Brilliant dinnerware they make. Known all over Europe. Quite forward thinking. Petra Hitzig is the one you're after?"

I didn't know if it was the same Petra, but I knew Mira's family was well-connected, and the Hitzig family sounded like someone they would know. With all the confidence I could muster, I said, "Yes."

Peabody drained his tea and set it aside. "I'll tell Regina to give you their address. Other side of the Charles Bridge, I believe. Family will be devastated. The Novaks left quite a few years ago. Since the first war, Jews have been wary. Understandably. Don't blame the Novaks at all. Hitzig isn't worried. Quite cozy with the Germans he is. Besides, he has a company to run." Peabody clasped his hands on his desk. "Do you need accommodations?"

He changed topics as quickly as Mira used to. It took me a moment to realize he'd asked me a question. "Yes, please."

"I'll have Regina give you a list of those as well. Travel documents tickety-boo?"

"Dr. Stoddard—Mr. Stoddard's father—took care of all that in Bombay." As loathe as I was to admit it, my father's British citizenship—and Dr. Stoddard's connections—had helped me get a British passport.

"Never been there myself. Bombay. Can't take the heat. Break out in hives. Those Indian soldiers. Solid stuff. They'll come in handy should we go to war again. Well, that's me done." He stood and extended his hand. "You're not, you know—but your name—"

I waited for him to finish. I knew he was asking why I looked *in-between*. Now that I'd had practice with the duplicitous Agnes, I felt it was better not to be so forthcoming.

"Not my business. Apologies, miss."

I shook his outstretched hand and thanked him.

"Oh, hang on, Miss Falstaff. There's a letter for you."

My dear Nurse Falstaff,

Did you enjoy that lovely sojourn on the Orient Express? I always say if you're going to travel, do it in style. Food not too bad, is it? I rather favor their Duck a l'Orange.

Now do let me know how you're faring on your own. You know you can always trade that sweater for good money if you run out. Mohair is in style, I hear. My wife used to love my sweaters except she told everyone she knit them herself. Drove me mad, that.

I stay busy with old friends who seem to have ended up in Istanbul as well. We play bridge. Some gin rummy. Bezique. I quite like pinochle myself but Germany has taken all the fun out of it. Of course, I cheat because you're not here to monitor me. Hard to break bad habits when no one is watching you. Quite useful for pocket money though. Edward looks the other way, of course. He sends his love, by the way. I think he was rather taken with you. But I'm an old fool when it comes to love, so ignore me, my dear.

In Prague, try the Beef Tenderloin with Cream Sauce (don't let them skimp on the sauce!). And there's always the Pork Knee if you're feeling adventurous.

I hope to have some good news by the time you get to Paris. Stay well, dear girl.

Yours fondly,
Ralph Stoddard

I had waited until I was back in the embassy's foyer to read the letter. When I finished, my legs were shaking. I slumped in a chair. How could I tell Dr. Stoddard I had managed to lose half my funds on my first train trip in Europe? He would think me careless and, at worst, a fool. Would he shake his head in disappointment? Or would he laugh in his easy, offhand manner? *Nurse Falstaff, I wouldn't have taken you for such an easy mark!*

The female receptionist at the desk was eyeing me. "Bad news?"

I just shook my head and walked out of the building. What would my mother have said about my misfortune? The same thing she would say when I'd come home crying, *The girls at school called me yellow eyes* or *they refused to play with a Blackie-White.* "You'll need to build up your courage to survive them, *beti.*" I should have realized then how much courage it had taken her to manage a life without the man who was supposed to love her forever. How much courage it had taken to raise a reminder of that disappointment on her own.

I took a deep breath. I would write to the doctor but leave out the part about the money. He may have been joking about the sweater, but I would never sell something so precious, made especially for me.

Half an hour later, I arrived on foot at the least expensive hostel on the embassy's list. A frazzled mother balancing a toddler on one hip and a clean set of nappies on the other answered the door. I showed her the note Mr. Peabody had written in Czech for her. She nodded and showed me to my room. It was clean even if the apartment smelled of wet diaper and boiled cabbage. She went to see to her dinner and feed the baby.

I set the trunk on the bed (the springs groaned). To set my mind at ease, I made sure the pouch with my money was still inside. Mr. Peabody had personally exchanged enough pounds to koruny for me to last a few days. I had the Czech bills in my pocket. How would I protect the rest of my savings without taking all the money with me wherever I went?

I unrolled the painting marked for Petra from the trunk and went to find my hostess. She was in the kitchen-cum-dining room, sitting on a chair at the dining table with the child in her lap, spooning what looked like porridge into his mouth. I mimed putting the painting in a bag that could hang over my shoulder. She pointed to a net bag hanging from the doorknob. I shook my head and looked around. I pointed to the canvas bag sitting on the butcher block, which must have been her market carrier.

"Ah," she said. She waved her hand for me to bring it to her. She pulled a loaf of bread out of it and offered the bag to me.

"This is perfect." I grinned. She did too even though I don't think she knew what the words meant. We were making each other understood without sound, and it made me happy.

The five-story apartment building was adjacent to the Vltava River. Like many of the buildings I'd seen in Prague, the Hitzig home and this row of elite residences bore more of a resemblance to British architecture than Indian. Gone were the minarets. Gone were the bulbous domes. Gone was the red sandstone. These buildings were flat-faced, angular, far less decorated than Indian ones, with row upon row of windows. The only embellishments were Greek and Italian statues like the ones from my old schoolbooks. At the top of the Hitzig residence was a colorful fresco of a woman lying on a bed, half-clothed, playing a harp with angels in attendance. Their counterparts in India were statues carved from stone of naked men and women—usually in the process of making love—ornate belts, anklets and bracelets their only clothing. The fresco woman looked as if she were posing. The naked statues did not. I smiled: one point for India.

I steeled myself for what was to come next. Either this would be Mira's Petra or I would have to start my search at the Minerva school they had attended as girls.

When I rang the buzzer to the right of the enormous wooden door, a primly dressed maid, her hair in a bun, answered. Her expression was polite even as I saw a flicker of alarm in her eyes at the sight of my pinafore and cap.

"I'm here to see Miss Hitzig," I said in French, which Mr. Peabody had advised I use with the likes of the Hitzigs. My schoolgirl French would have to do.

She hesitated a fraction of a second before opening the door wider. I entered a marbled foyer. It was cooler inside the building than it was outside. The end of May in Bombay would be sweltering. In Prague, I shivered, glad I'd worn Dr. Stoddard's sweater before leaving my lodging. Straight ahead was the entrance to a small courtyard at the back of the building. To the left was a staircase that encircled the narrow room and seemed to go up and up and up, like that story my mother used to read to me, *Jack and the Beanstalk*. I looked up. High in the center of the ceiling was a leaded glass window. To my right were enormous paintings in gold frames where important-looking white men silently passed judgment on visitors. I could hear the faint sound of music, reminding me of *Eine Kleine Nachtmusik*, the night music Mira had hummed to me.

The maid led me up four flights of stairs. Along the way were more gilt-framed paintings, potted palms and thick rugs under our feet. There was a door at every landing, which I assumed was the entrance to another part of the house. The music got louder the higher we went. Once we were on the top floor, I could see that the stained-glass window on the roof was much larger than it appeared from the ground floor.

The music was coming from the apartment on this floor. The maid made a little moue with her mouth, as if she'd tasted something rancid, and indicated that I would find Miss Petra behind the door. Then she made her way back down the stairs.

I knocked, but the music coming from the flat was so loud I was sure no one inside had heard me. I turned the doorknob, found it unlocked and opened the door slowly.

"Who are you?" Petra demanded. Even though I didn't speak Czech, the tone of her voice told me what she was asking. She was peering at me from behind a large canvas on an easel. She looked exactly as Mira had described her. Red-gold hair falling in waves across her shoulders and down her back. A wide mouth. Freckles across her long nose. The kind of pale complexion that can barely tolerate an hour in the sun. She was so thin I could see her hip bones protruding through her silky hand-embroidered Chinese robe, left open to reveal a slip the color of a peach.

Unlike the cool of the stairwell, Petra's flat was as hot as Bombay. It smelled stale, like the odor of unwashed bodies I knew so well from the hospital. The apartment was one large room that no one had bothered to finish. The walls were redbrick with white mortar. The floorboards were so old that there were now spaces between the wooden planks. Rough wood beams held up the ceiling. It looked like an attic of one of those colonial homes where I'd once attended an unwell servant.

I walked a few paces into the room. *"Vous parlez français?"*

"For God sakes, shut the door!" she said in French.

I hurried to do her bidding. When I turned around, Petra was lighting a match to a cigarette. Through narrowed eyes, she considered her painting, turning her head this way and that. She picked up her brush and dabbed it gingerly on the canvas. Her eyes strayed to me, standing a few feet from her now. She seemed to remember she had a visitor.

"Alors?" she said, taking a drag from her cigarette. For the first time, she regarded me seriously, looking me up and down. She frowned. "Is someone sick?"

I looked down at myself. The uniform again! "No—no. I've come to give you something." I gestured to the canvas bag I was carrying.

"I can barely hear you, you know." Before I could repeat myself, she turned to the bed behind her, a rumpled hillock of white sheets. A few of the pillows were scattered on the floor.

Petra said, *"Káva!"* to the bed. The hillock moved, then stopped.

"Now," she said.

This time, a young man's arm, then a leg, followed by a torso, emerged. He was naked. He stretched and yawned, his stomach muscles contracting. Then he shook his head as if to wake himself and headed to a makeshift kitchen, which consisted of a counter with a two-burner cooktop, a small sink and a wall cabinet.

I'd seen naked men and women in the course of my work, but never outside of it.

Dirty-blond hair hung over his eyes. I watched the muscles of his back move as he lifted the coffee jar, poured the beans into a coffee grinder. Then he reached for the tap to fill the most unusual coffee maker I'd ever seen—a stainless steel globe with a green plastic handle. He filled the funnel with ground coffee, plugged in the cord. His buttock muscles tensed as he walked to the radio near the bed and turned the knob. Suddenly, silence. I followed his walk back to bed.

Petra said, "Pretty, isn't he?" She smiled through a smoky exhale. I blushed, embarrassed to be caught staring. I turned to Petra, who had returned to her canvas. "It's about Miss Novak. Your old schoolmate."

She blinked. "Mira?"

I loosened my grip on the canvas bag. "I'm sorry I bring sad news. Miss Novak was recently treated at the Wadia Hospital in Bombay, where I work. She died three weeks ago—quite suddenly." I watched her reaction. At the hospital, some people had fainted on the spot when I told them a patient had died.

Petra's mouth was somewhere between a grimace and a smile. "Mira? *My* Mira? But she can't be more than twenty-nine? Same age as me. She's too young. Are you sure you have the right Mira?"

"You've known each other since you were little girls. You went to Minerva Gymnasium together? She called you *ovce*?"

Petra's brush dripped yellow paint onto the floor. She looked down at the splat, which was rapidly creating a star pattern on the wood. Only then did I notice paint splotches scattered all over the floorboards. I doubt the maid ever came in here. Perhaps she wasn't allowed.

Petra's hand shook as she set the paintbrush on her palette. She pulled her robe closed and crossed her arms over her chest as if she were suddenly cold. She seemed to be in shock. I waited for her questions.

"How? And how do you know?" she finally said.

"My name is Sona Falstaff. I was the night nurse in charge of her care in Bombay. She was admitted for a miscarriage. She underwent minor surgery and appeared to be recovering, but after six days…nothing could be done." I didn't want to tell her about the morphine, the accusation leveled against me, the gossip circulating in the halls about a possible abortion or the aspersions cast on Mira's flamboyant lifestyle.

Her forehead creased. "She was pregnant?"

I nodded.

"But she never cared for babies. Told me she'd rather die than break open her body that way." Her cigarette had burned down enough to scorch her finger. She dropped the stub on the floor and blew on her finger to cool it. I realized that the blackened spots on the old hardwood weren't paint; she was in the habit of dropping cigarettes wherever she seemed to be standing.

"So what happened?" She was rocking back and forth on her heels, her arms clasped around her thin frame. I saw the glint of tears in her eyes.

I chose my words carefully. "Everything was done that could be done. I know no more."

"Then what are you doing here?" Her tone was hostile. She wiped at her eyes with the flat of her hand.

I'd seen it before. The transition from shock to anger. I knew it wasn't personal, so I never took it that way.

"I wondered if you'd talk to me about her. I only knew her for six days. You knew her from girlhood."

"But I hadn't seen her in—oh—six years. When she married

Filip. No, wait. I saw her two years ago when she came to exhibit her work at the National Gallery. They organized a retrospective in her honor." Petra pushed her hair back behind her ears. "She left Prague when she was fifteen to go to Florence. A few years later, her father moved the family to India."

"So I heard."

Petra opened her mouth, then looked over at the bed, where her male companion seemed to have fallen asleep again. She turned to her canvas with a critical eye. She'd been painting him, lying in bed, his leg uncovered, his head turned away from the viewer. She raised her voice to address him. "Looks like I'm out of charcoal paint, Henrich. I need to go out and get more." She sat on the bed and started pulling on short boots over her bare feet.

The boy—I saw now that he couldn't have been more than sixteen or seventeen—raised his head, pointed to the coffeepot and said something in Czech. He sounded irritated. I was sure it had something to do with the fact that the coffee was ready and she was the one who had made him get out of bed for it.

Petra blew him a kiss and walked briskly to the door. She was still in her slip and Chinese robe.

I stood dumbly in the middle of her flat, canvas bag over my shoulder, while she opened the door and went through it. What had just happened? Was I meant to follow her?

She'd almost shut the door behind her when she stopped herself, stuck her head through the opening and gestured with her chin that I should follow.

Out in the street, Petra walked quickly, her robe fluttering around her. I had to jog to catch up. Most people we saw on the street were wearing suit jackets or light coats. I was comfortable in my mohair sweater over my uniform. Petra seemed neither to feel the cold out here or the stifling heat of her apartment.

Two middle-aged women with shopping bags were coming toward us, their hands encased in gloves. Each wore a jacket and skirt tailored for their figures. They looked disapprovingly at Petra's far more casual attire, but she seemed not to notice.

She kept her voice low as she said, "It's difficult now. You don't know who's listening. Which side they're on. It's best to keep personal business to yourself." We turned left at the corner and kept walking along the Vltava. "There's talk of another war. We don't want Hitler anywhere near here but with talk of a Munich Agreement, it's a possibility. Henrich—" she pointed back at her building "—is German-Czech. But we don't talk about which side he's on. I don't want to know." She crossed her arms over her flat chest. "Peace is fragile."

We had walked two long blocks from her building when she entered what looked like a coffeehouse with the sign *Kavarna Slavia.* Across the street was a massive renaissance building four or five stories high. It looked as grand as the Royal Opera House in Bombay. Petra saw me looking and said, "The National Theater."

The café walls were lined in rich red-dark mahogany. The white marble floor and the tall windows overlooking the street brought in more than enough light for a cheerful effect. The smell of coffee and pastries reminded me that I hadn't eaten since my cream tea on the train the previous day.

It was three o'clock in the afternoon. The café was a cacophony of people chatting, glasses clinking, a man playing jazz on the piano. Every now and then staccato laughter burst through the din. Petra said hello to a great many people. There were older men in close-cropped beards who wore elaborate costumes, like the Shakespeare plays I had been to in India. Petra kissed their cheeks. She didn't introduce me. Several young women and men called out to her to join them. She smiled and waved them off, settling for a small round table with two chairs. As soon as we sat down, she pulled a silver case out of her robe and lit a cigarette.

"Was it Filip's?"

For a moment, I was confused by her question. "Oh, you mean the baby?" Before I could answer, she asked another.

"Was it painful for her?"

I hesitated. It was against code to discuss a patient's medical details. "She was suffering," I said simply. Given the heavy dose of morphine I had to administer every four hours, it was hard to tell how much pain she was in when so much would have been dulled by the medication.

There was a glass ashtray on every table, and the room was thick with smoke. Petra twirled her cigarette on the rim of the ashtray. She seemed somber now, less brusque. Her eyelashes were wet. I sensed that underneath her bold manner was a woman not fully in control of her feelings. I looked away, my eye resting on a painting of a gentleman in conversation with what looked like a female genie. Or was it a ghost?

"The green fairy," Petra said. I turned to see her pointing to the painting. "He's drinking absinthe. Makes you see things that aren't there."

A waiter in a white shirt, black vest and black pleated trousers carrying a small round tray approached our table. He greeted Petra with a smile, and they exchanged pleasantries in Czech. She said something and I caught the word *kafe*. I hoped she wasn't ordering coffee for me. I was used to tea heavily tempered with milk. Two days ago when I'd been served Turkish coffee, my stomach had protested.

Petra took a deep drag of her cigarette. "Where was Filip all this time?"

"Her husband brought her to the hospital. I saw him two times after that. He might have visited on other occasions, but I didn't see him. I do the night shift."

She blew smoke from the side of her mouth. "Did her father come to see her at the hospital? Did her mother?"

"Her father came. Her mother couldn't make it." I decided it was better to be vague than misrepresent the situation.

Petra scoffed. "Mira's mother didn't like her husband paying attention to his own daughter. It's why she was always taking Mira off to Paris and Florence and Rome. And when the three of them were together, Mrs. Novak pretended to be weak and helpless so her husband would be forced to think only about his wife. But even in death?" She shook her head, blew smoke from her mouth. "On the first day of school, all Czech children bring a small bouquet of flowers for the teacher. Mira's mother would forget to prepare one. Mira was embarrassed to come to class empty-handed, so she found ways to miss the first day of school. One time, I made my mother send me with two bouquets so I could give one to Mira, but she was too proud to take it." Petra wiped her eyes with the back of her hand.

I remember the painter telling me she'd been raised by governesses, which meant she wouldn't have had as much contact with her mother as I had had with mine. So perhaps a motherless existence was normal in the world she and Petra had been born into. Still, Mira had cried when she learned her mother wouldn't come to sit at her bedside. From everything Mira had told me and what Petra was telling me now, Mira's mother didn't deserve her daughter's affection. She must have made the painter think she was unlovable. It angered me. Wasn't that how my father made me feel when he couldn't love me enough to stay in India?

"The irony is that her father was too busy to pay either of them any mind," Petra was saying. "He'd become obsessed with building that synagogue in Bombay. He felt at home in India. Her parents have a house in Bombay, but they're usually somewhere else. On a tiger shoot or visiting a physic garden or taking the waters somewhere."

Petra's eyes had welled up. She sniffed. I reached in my pocket for a handkerchief, but an old gentleman got there before me. He was one of the people Petra had nodded hello to when we entered the café. He'd been sitting alone at a corner table. He was a dapper sort: flower in his buttonhole, handkerchief in his breast pocket. His suit was a little loose on him, as if he had shrunken inside it, but made of quality material. Having a seamstress for a mother had taught me the difference between choice and cheap fabrics.

The gentleman had his hat in his hand. Petra looked up at him and touched his arm. She spoke in Czech. He patted her shoulder, leaving his hand there for a long moment. Then, he offered me a smile before placing the hat on his head. He walked to the café entrance a little shakily.

Petra watched him go. "My grandfather—my *dědeček*. He lives in the apartment below mine. My parents have the first floor. It's been our family home for two hundred years." She gathered her copper-colored hair from the back of her head and pulled it down her left shoulder. "I think he likes me more than my parents do. He comes to this café even though it's a place for artists and writers and actors. Tradition forced him to run the glassworks factory like his father before him and like my father now, but I think my *dědeček* would have loved being a playwright."

The waiter delivered a coffee to Petra and a hot chocolate with a large mound of whipped cream and a sliver-thin wafer for me. He set a bowl of sugar cubes, a small jug of milk and two pastries on the small marble table. After giving us our cloth napkins and utensils, he left quietly. I was touched that Petra thought to order something other than coffee for me. She smiled when she saw me examining my drink. I was wondering whether to spoon the cream into my mouth first or try to drink the hot chocolate through it.

"Mira loved the hot chocolate here." Petra poured milk in her coffee and stirred.

I took a bite of the crumbly pastry, surprised at the creamy center. I was used to my mother's bread pudding and Indian *katli* and *burfi*, which were dense, heavier sweets. The Czech pastry hit my empty stomach with such a rush that I had to stop chewing for a few seconds. "You said the Novaks left Prague—what—ten years ago?"

Petra took a sip of her coffee. "Mira's father—like mine—is Jewish. He didn't feel safe after the big war. Being so close to Germany rattled him—he rattled easily. No country in Europe felt safe. And since his wife was Indian…" She lifted her shoulder in an elegant shrug and lit another cigarette. "Her mother took it hard. She didn't want to go back to India. Loved the European lifestyle. French couture. Italian cuisine. The freedom. She used Mira's painting as an excuse to travel all over Europe."

I wiped crumbs from my lips with the cloth napkin. "Did Miss Novak enjoy that?"

"Oh, she welcomed the absences from school. For Mira, painting was the only education she needed. She much preferred painting all day in a studio to sitting in class with a chemistry book. Art was her air. Do you know what I mean? It allowed her to breathe."

Petra had barely touched her pastry. Now she broke off a flaky bit and chewed it.

"I remember one time our history teacher told us to write an essay about what influence the Habsburg dynasty had on Europe. Mira brought in a large painting three times the size of this coffee table. She'd painted an abstract piece with all these wild colors. The teacher said, 'What's this?' 'Inbreeding,' she said." Petra laughed. It was a hoarse sound, a smoker's laugh. "The teacher didn't know what to make of it. But Mira was completely serious. In her mind, she had done the assignment."

When Petra laughed, I could imagine her with Mira, two young girls doubled over, giggling. I wished I'd been a part of their friendship, their shared experiences.

Mira's friend rotated her cup on her saucer. Smoke from her cigarette swirled up to the ceiling. I noticed she'd drained her coffee while my hot chocolate sat, cooling. I'd eaten all the whipped cream. I took a sip.

"She was a real talent, Mira was. I have skill. But I have to work hard at it. Mira only had to be shown a certain style and she picked it up right away. Realism. Cubism. Impressionism. Post-Impressionism. Surrealism. So easily." She stubbed out her cigarette in the ashtray. "Like the style just crawled up her arm into the fingers holding her brush."

Was it resentment or admiration I heard in Petra's voice?

She studied me with her green-brown eyes, a hint of wariness in them. "Why have you come all this way to tell me? Couldn't you have written?"

"I didn't have your address. Or your last name. Mira had given me hints. She told me you'd been at Minerva together. I would have gone there to find you if the British Embassy hadn't been able to help me. Luckily, your family is well-known here."

A young man with a goatee and round tortoiseshell glasses set his satchel down on the table next to us. He greeted Petra in Czech. She didn't seem pleased to see him. Her response included a lilt of her chin to indicate me. Was she saying I was a friend? Did she say anything to him about Mira's death?

In French, she said, "This is Pavel. He teaches history at Charles University."

Pavel smiled. He was one of those who smiles easily and often—like Edward Stoddard. He shook my hand. "Bonjour." His hand was slightly sweaty. "I'm an associate professor. Not full professor yet." His deference was charming. He gestured for the waiter to take his order. To me, he said, "Where are you from?"

"India. Bombay."

The young man grinned. "But that's fantastic. You've come all this way to see Petra? How do you know each other?"

Petra cut him off in Czech and stood up, gathering her silver cigarette case. I stood up too, not knowing what I was meant to do.

Pavel said to me, "Are you coming to Petra's exhibit tonight? It's going to be a big splash."

"She's not interested." Petra's reply was curt.

"But I am," I said. "Perhaps there will be others there who knew Miss Novak."

"Mira?" Pavel's face lit up. "We all know Mira. She's so famous now. And we're all famous by extension. Isn't that so, Petra?"

Petra narrowed her eyes and pursed her lips. Just then, another one of Petra's friends came in. She kissed the woman on her cheek and turned to me. "Well, thanks for coming." She was dismissing me?

Pavel said to Petra, "That's it? This woman has come all the way from India—" He turned to me. "We all know about Monsieur Gandhi. We admire what he's doing. India deserves her freedom." He turned to Petra again. "And you're leaving her here?"

I looked from Petra to Pavel and back again, as if I were watching a badminton game.

The other young woman, who had gone up to the bar to order her coffee, now returned, looking from Petra's darkened face to Pavel's confused one. "What's going on?" She eased herself onto a chair at Pavel's table and opened a fresh pack of cigarettes.

Pavel spoke rapidly in Czech. Petra rolled her eyes and walked to the door. I stood, watching her leave the café, wondering what had just happened.

Now Pavel switched to French. "She speaks French, Martina. She knows Mira."

Martina expressed the same enthusiasm Pavel had upon hearing Mira's name. She said, "You know Mira? She's brilliant. I always wanted to paint like her, but my talent lies more in photography. I like taking pictures of people."

I didn't want to dampen their spirits, but I did want to explain why I was in Prague. I told them what had happened to Mira. Pavel's face was halfway to a smile before he realized I was serious. He reached for Martina's cigarette carton and matches. Martina's face was frozen, aghast.

"Comment?" they both said at once and then looked at each

other. "Wasn't it just two years ago she was here for that retrospective? She's too young. And healthy."

I hadn't been invited to sit at their table, but I pulled up a chair anyway. The waiter appeared with their orders and left as quietly as he had come.

Pavel cleared his throat. "We all went to the same schools. Did things together. But Mira and Petra—" He stole a look at his companion. "They were very close. Petra worshipped the ground Mira walked on. And more than that. She had a thing for Mira. Mira just laughed it off, but for Petra it was a big deal. Then Paolo came along." He smiled and so did Martina.

My ears were ringing. This was Mira's Paolo.

With a raspy chuckle, Martina brought the fingers of one hand together and said in an exaggerated Italian accent, "Pa-o-lo!" She continued in French, "Mira couldn't stop talking about him. She must have been—oh—fifteen? When she went to Florence to study with him—"

Pavel almost choked while taking a sip of his coffee. "Her mother went to Florence to study Paolo and dragged Mira along. Her mother was crazy about him." He and Martina shared a laugh.

This was not news to me. Mira had told me of her mother's infatuation with Paolo. Was that why Mira had made a play for him as well? To get back at her mother for her inattention, her jealousies?

The café had maintained a steady stream of customers going in and out, friends greeting friends. Sitting with Pavel and Martina, I could almost pretend this was how I lived my life. As if I spent afternoons gabbing with friends, drinking hot chocolate, munching on pastries. Gossiping about people we had in common. My actual existence seemed so staid. Home. Hospital. Home. Market. Home. Without my job and without my mother, was that even my life anymore?

The waiter came around and Pavel ordered in Czech. Martina said something to him, pointing to his stomach. Pavel gave her a sideways look as if to say, *Leave me alone about my eating.*

"Did Miss Novak enjoy studying with Paolo?" I asked.

They laughed again, Martina leaning against Pavel. "She enjoyed *studying* Paolo." Her laugh turned into a cough. I recognized the signs of a chain-smoker.

When she recovered, Martina cleared her throat and said, "She could talk of nothing else. She was completely—" She asked Pavel something in Czech.

He said, "Smitten."

"Smitten!" Martina said, holding her cigarette aloft.

"Did he love her back?" It was bold of me to ask, but I wanted to know. Mira hadn't given me a clue either way. She'd only talked about how she would always love Paolo whether they were together or not.

Martina made a face. She turned to Pavel. "As much as he loved anybody, I suppose. We never met him. Only heard about him."

Pavel sat back in his chair and shrugged.

"What about her husband, Filip?" I asked.

They looked at each other. Martina smoked. Pavel drank his coffee. Finally, Pavel said, "Filip was safe. He didn't demand anything from her. Mira was daring. Adventurous. Her parents wanted her to marry and stop creating scandal with men and women. She was very free. So Filip stepped in. I don't know if she asked him to do that or if it was a gallant gesture on his part. They got married, but Mira still had her affairs. Filip looked the other way and that seemed to suit them both."

"He wasn't jealous?"

"Filip?" Martina shook her head. "I don't believe so." She looked at Pavel. "He's what? Ten years older than us?" She turned to me. "We all know him, but not well. I don't think it's possible to know him. He's very quiet. He's always there, hovering in the background. I always wondered what Mira saw in him."

I thought about how Filip was an invisible ghost at the hospital. There but not there. Mira had said she'd never been in love with him, that she'd never properly been in love with anyone.

"He was her first cousin, you know," Pavel said.

"So she said," I said. "Were they planning on having children?" I had to ask because of Mira's cryptic remark about the baby being Paolo's.

"Mira?" Martina smiled. "Not in the least. She never wanted children. I've known her since she was this high." Martina indicated the level of the bistro table. "Not once did she ever say any different."

Unless they asked, I wasn't about to tell them Mira had arrived at the hospital presenting a miscarriage. But I felt an aching sadness. For Mira. For the loss of her talent. For the cavalier way news of her death was being received by the two people in front of me.

I excused myself and started to get up. That was when I realized I still had the canvas bag my hostess had loaned me. I'd forgotten to give *The Waiting* to Petra.

"There will be more friends of Mira's at the exhibition tonight. Petra's big show. Why don't you come?" Pavel wrote the address on the napkin. "Where are you staying?"

I gave him the address and he told me which tram to take to the gallery.

I decided to walk to my lodgings. It seemed as if I'd been sitting for days. And as long as I was in Prague, I wanted to take in as much of this world as I could. After all, I might never pass this way again. Meandering through New Town, I caught a whiff of sizzling meat and freshly baked bread, scented soaps and dusty stone. I sidestepped trams and horse droppings. Down the wide boulevard facing Wenceslas Square, I admired elegant women's couture through shop windows. A woman walked out of the Bata shoe store with her children carrying several shopping bags. At a leather goods shop, I decided to buy a belt with a small purse in which to carry my money. Back on the boulevard, a barbershop poster promoted the benefits of well-groomed beards. I stopped to look at an ad in a pharmacy window, which promised a lush cleavage and the secrets of looking younger. I smiled at these claims—outrageous, so similar to Bombay adverts, yet still appealing.

Finally, I made my way to Old Town Square. My Baedeker's encouraged a stop at the Astronomical Clock, a favorite tourist spot. It told Old Bohemian time, Babylonian time, German time and Sidereal time, not to mention the journey of the sun and moon across the constellations. Everywhere I went, I wondered if Mira had stood in that same spot, what she'd been doing there, what she'd been thinking and whom she'd been with. If I closed my eyes and pictured her face, imagining her singular linseed smell, I could almost feel her next to me.

Finally, I arrived at my lodging. I wanted to bathe and change out of my uniform. I had just enough time to dash off a quick response to Dr. Stoddard before going to the exhibition hall.

Dear Dr. Stoddard,

I never thought I would miss our steamship casino. You've turned me into a gambler. Next time we meet you'll have to teach me a new game, preferably one where you have a chance of winning against me. (This is where you groan at my arrogance.)

I arrived in Prague safely and am now settled in a lovely apartment overlooking the Vltava River. The food is every bit as delicious as you predicted, especially the Beef Tenderloin with Cream Sauce. I didn't let them skimp on the sauce!

The city is so beautiful and so different from Istanbul or Bombay or Calcutta. Everywhere I look, there are church spires and cobblestone streets and a golden fog that envelops everything. It makes me think of Mister Rochester at Thornfield Hall and how Jane Eyre felt seeing his house for the first time. (Pay no mind. I'm being a silly schoolgirl with her schoolgirl fantasies.)

Thanks to you (and Edward), the embassy helped me find Petra, Mira's girlhood friend. She was so forthcoming about Mira's life here. It seemed idyllic. Petra introduced me to other friends of Mira's, who were able to enlighten me further. Tonight, they've invited me to an exhibition Petra has organized of her own work. So I must dash.

Lovely to hear from you.

Yours humbly,
Sona Falstaff

I hated lying to him. But if I were to tell him the truth—there had been no beef tenderloin, Petra had not been particularly friendly—he might worry. His health was fragile; I couldn't do that to him. Still, I wished I could confide in someone about my dwindling funds. Keeping it to myself was giving me a bellyache, which was why I had to—very reluctantly—turn down the meal my hostess offered. I smiled at her, gesturing with my watch that I needed to leave.

It was a fine May night, mild, requiring nothing but a sweater. I took the tram to the Manes Exhibition Hall, a functional monochromatic building so unlike the Gothic or Renaissance or Art Nouveau architecture of the city. Manes was partly on the waterfront and partly on the Vltava. Jazz, the kind heard at the British clubs in Bombay, blared from the open windows and doors. There seemed to be no one at the entrance taking tickets or monitoring the event. I walked into a brightly lit space with high ceilings. It was so crowded that the waiters had to hold trays of canapés above their heads to snake through the exhibition space. The Czechs looked British but they dressed better, like the French. The young women wore impossibly long chiffon scarves around their necks, the ends of which reached their behinds. They wore shapeless sheaths cut from expensive silks or pleated trousers with satin tops. A few men had goatees like Pavel. Others had long hair to their ears or shoulders. Many wore colorful suspenders as an accessory. I felt underdressed in my sweater, homemade tweed skirt and cotton blouse, but no one took notice of me. I was invisible once again, and that suited me just fine.

I caught snatches of French conversation as I walked through the maze, looking for Petra and Pavel.

"More villas are going up at Baba Colony. They're so modern..."

"I can't say I've read it, but everyone is talking about it. Before her book came out, were you aware that Gertrude Stein...?"

"I heard they're cracking down on the plays at the Liberated Theater..."

"Swing is never going to be the rage that jazz is..."

"I know! Czechoslovakia's first airport. My father has already reserved a seat..."

When the crowd parted enough for me to catch a glimpse of Petra's exhibit, I gasped. There was a painting of Mira reading. Mira bathing. Mira looking out a window.

A tap on my shoulder made me jump.

"You made it," Pavel said. "Come. I'll introduce you. You've met Martina." The woman from the café smiled at me and raised her cocktail glass. Next was a man in a beret and an impressive satin cape. His name was Emil. Then came Gerta, whose blond ringlets bounced every time she moved. Everyone had a glass of something in their hands—champagne, red wine, scotch, absinthe. Emil plucked a glass with orange liquid from a passing waiter's tray and handed it to me.

I thanked him and took a sip. It was sweet and strong. I tried not to make a face and resolved to put it down somewhere the first chance I got. Scanning the paintings around the room, I said, "It's all…"

Pavel said, "About Mira?"

I nodded.

"I told you Petra was obsessed with Mira. Couldn't get over the fact that Mira had other lovers. Petra had been half-hoping Mira would be here tonight. She'd invited her. A reconciliation of sorts."

"Had they fallen out?"

Gerta laughed. "Mira was tired of the adulation. People do get tired of being on a pedestal you know. Of course, I wouldn't know…not yet anyway." She laughed good-naturedly. "You realize that with Mira's death, Petra's paintings have just shot up in value?"

It bothered me when anyone talked of profiting from death. I waved the glass in my hand. "Petra never mentioned that she was putting an exhibit together about her paintings of Mira. When I arrived at her apartment this morning, she was painting—"

Martina raised a tweezed eyebrow. "A young boy? Beautiful, brown-blond hair?"

I nodded.

"Henrich. All the painters use him. Mainly speaks German. Answers to *káva*." Pavel's group laughed.

"What do you think?" Pavel and I were both startled by Petra's voice. She was wearing the same silk gown as she had this morning (didn't she have any other clothes?) but now her hair was in braids. She had a satin pink boa wrapped around her neck and glitter on her eyelids. She looked quite ethereal.

"I call it my farewell to Mira."

I frowned. "But surely you couldn't have known about—about her passing before today?"

Petra looked as if I'd struck her. Her face was ashen. She turned away, parting the crowd, which quickly closed the gap. I lost track of her. Had she known of Mira's death before I arrived? How? It had been three weeks since her passing. I hadn't seen any notices in the paper about the death of the renowned painter. So how did Petra find out? Did she produce these canvases because she knew Mira had died? If she knew, why did she act so surprised when I told her?

The cocktail had given me a headache. I left shortly afterward, saying my goodbyes to Pavel and his group. I knew I wouldn't be able to give Mira's painting to Petra this evening. I would have to manage it tomorrow before leaving for Paris.

My hostess sent me off the next morning with strong coffee and homemade apple rolls. The coffee was bitter until I added a little sugar and a lot of milk. Perhaps someday I would get used to this taste that Europeans seemed to prefer. In halting French, she asked me about my next destination, I told her I was going to Paris to speak to Mira's art dealer.

"Be well." She smiled. Her baby smiled too, showing me his first two teeth.

Trunk in hand once more and the leather belt around my waist (I hoped it looked more like a fashion accessory than an eyesore), I walked to Petra's apartment. I wanted to give her time to recover from the art reception the night before, so I loitered around New Town for an hour. Given the way everyone had been drinking last night, I had a feeling the reception had lasted until the early morning hours. The same maid let me into the Hitzig residence. I walked to the top floor and knocked.

When Petra didn't respond, I tried the handle as I had the day before. It was unlocked—again. Petra was sprawled on her bed, the sheets covering only half her body. I crossed the room to the bed and held my hand under her nose to make sure she was breathing. Her mascara had run down her eyes, giving her a ghoulish appearance. The hair on one side of her head was matted and her sheath from the day before was stained with vomit. She had a bruise on one arm.

I set down my trunk and went into her makeshift kitchen to boil water. A search of the cabinets revealed a bag of coffee and an open packet of biscuits. The only cups were in the sink, waiting to be washed. I plunged them under hot water (there didn't seem to be any soap). When the coffee was ready, I poured it in one cup and put cold water in the other. I brought both to her with the packet of biscuits.

"Petra?"

She stirred.

"Drink the water first, then the coffee. I have something for you. From Miss Novak."

She opened her eyes, gummy with mascara and eyeliner. When she saw me, she groaned. "You're the nosy one." She closed her eyes again.

I'd been called worse by patients. With stubborn ones, you have to have a stern hand (but a kind one, per the nursing handbook). I pulled her up by her hands, which were sticky. She pushed me away and sat up, bunching the pillows against her back. She reached for the coffee first, but I held it away from her and handed her the water.

She drank greedily and held her hand out for the coffee.

"Mira cared for you, Petra," I said. "I could tell by the way she talked about you."

I had her attention now. Petra shot a look at me, her eyes large in her elfin face. "Really?"

"She told me she wouldn't have survived school without you. The two of you saw every Voskovec and Werich movie that came to the cinema and laughed until you fell out of your chairs. You both cried at the showing of *The Bartered Bride* and cursed the scheming matchmaker. You ice-skated every winter hand in hand. You skipped classes to sketch together at the park above the train station."

Petra wiped her nose on the sheet covering her. Her cheeks were wet with tears, but she was smiling. "She was so much fun! Always up for an adventure. She led; I followed. That's why she called me *ovce*. Sheep. I didn't mind. She meant it as an endearment. She was a good mimic and could imitate everyone in class—our teachers, the tutors, the gym instructors. We had this chemistry teacher with only three fingers on his left hand. It fascinated us." She hiccupped and giggled. "We spent hours imagining what could have happened to him. Was he born that way? Did he have his fingers cut off just like that fable of *The Girl Without Hands*? Did he pass out in a winter storm and get frostbite? In class, he would hold up all eight of his fingers and say something like, 'I want you to memorize ten elements for tomorrow.' We knew he did it on purpose to shock us.

"One day, Mira—" Petra began to laugh hard. She had to start again several times before she could finish. "One day, Mira folded two fingers of her left hand into her palm and taped them down. She did the same to me. All day, we went around saying, 'There are ten rules I want you to follow,' and held up all eight fingers. He caught us, you know, in the hallway. We felt awful, but he just laughed and said he could have us do an experiment that could make it happen. He became our favorite teacher that year."

Petra looked down at her ruined dress and plucked at a wrinkle. "I've missed her. Every single day since she left Prague. I spent some time with her in Paris when she studied there, and we had such fun. I can't believe she's gone." She chewed on a fingernail. She looked so small and fragile. I could picture the little girl she once was, in pigtails, waiting for her friend Mira after class so they could go off on another adventure. Mira told me she'd outgrown her friendship with Petra, but clearly Petra hadn't outgrown her fondness for Mira. She would never again share those escapades with her girlhood friend.

"Mira left a painting for you." I pulled *The Waiting* from my trunk.

She set the coffee cup down on the floorboards and took it from me with both hands. She ran her finger over the layers of dried paint. For several minutes, she said nothing. "Do you know why she chose this one? It's one of her most famous. She would never sell it."

"No. She left instructions for me to give it to you. There is another painting for Paolo, whom you've heard of. And one for Josephine, whom you must have met in Paris when you were there with Mira..."

I turned the painting over to show her the *P* on the back of the canvas. "She left this too." I showed her the note Mira left with the paintings.

Petra skimmed her fingers over the handwriting. "That's definitely Mira's scrawl." She looked at *The Waiting.* "This reminds me of the young girls we once were." She pointed to the subjects. "I know these girls are Indian, but in their faces, I see our young selves just before we changed. A time when we trusted our fathers and mothers because we didn't know them well enough. When finding the feather of a songbird was the most important thing in the world before boys came along. When we were made aware of our femaleness that would come to overpower any other part of us." She caressed the painting once again with her fingers. "But why did she give it to you? Had you known each other in Bombay before she came to the hospital?"

I sat on the bed next to her. The nurse in me had to ignore the soiled bedding and pretend the yellow smudges on the pillows were makeup. "No, I'd only known her for six days while I was her night nurse. But we talked a lot during that time. She told me something about you that I think she wanted to say to you directly."

Petra cocked her head, like a bird listening for a call.

I was careful with my words. I wanted to make sure I conveyed Mira's thoughts accurately. "She was happy you came to Paris. She thought you made a great model. You sat for her for the painting that won her a place in the Paris Salon. But when you showed an interest in becoming a painter, she said she was not very kind. She told you that you would never be any good, that you should give it up before you disappointed yourself." I paused. "Miss Hitzig, she truly regretted saying those things." I paused. "She said, 'I don't know why I did that.'"

A tear fell from Petra's cheek onto the sheet. "Oh, how I hated her when she was cruel. She often was, you know. But it was true. My father paid for a place for me at the art institute here. I could never had gotten in on my own. I really wasn't good. But I wondered if I would have been better if she had just encouraged me a little. I worshipped her." She looked up at me. "I'm a better painter now than I was then. Still, Mira did hurt me. A lot."

I felt like apologizing to her even though I hadn't been part of their circle. "I knew her for such a short time. But I wish I'd known her longer. She told the most wonderful stories about you, about Paolo and Josephine."

"She was like that. It was her gift. I always hated when a new girl arrived at school and Mira would become fast friends with her. They would do everything together for the first week, and then Mira would drop her just like that." Petra snapped her fingers. "Then she would come back to me." She smiled. "Sometimes she did it only because she wanted something from me. Usually it was money."

I cocked my head, puzzled.

"Her parents wouldn't support her unless she sold a painting, but she couldn't paint that fast so she was always short of money." She shrugged. "And I was always lending it to her. Of course, I knew she'd never pay me back. I understood. Filip never earned anything."

That image unsettled me. Was Mira only interested in people as long as she was getting something from them? Did she show interest in me because she needed me to do her bidding? Like delivering these paintings? But that was absurd because she couldn't have known she was going to die. Perhaps the woman Petra knew had been savage and selfish but she had changed with time? Or were there two sides to Mira and she chose which side to show to whom. Which was the real Mira Novak?

I sucked in a breath. "There's something I haven't told you. Miss Novak died from a morphine overdose. It's not clear who administered it. Sometimes I've wondered if she took it herself, but that seems preposterous." I glanced at Petra to see how this remark had landed. She was playing with the bedsheet, frowning. "Still, if there's anything you know about her that might help…" I didn't finish because I didn't quite know what to ask.

Petra was thoughtful. Then, she said, "As her nurse, wouldn't you have been responsible for administering the morphine?"

I looked down at the sheets. "It's complicated. I know I didn't give her the overdose but I don't know who did."

"She wrote that note to you while she was in the hospital, right? Why would she have done that unless…?" Her eyes filled again.

She left the sentence hanging in the air. I sat with that a moment. It was hard to imagine any of us knew when or how we were going to die. "Last night, you said you called your exhibition your farewell to Miss Novak. What did you mean?"

She sighed. "I thought that the paintings would allow me a release. Like I had finally gotten over her. A goodbye of sorts. I know what they all say about me. And I wanted for it to be over. But it only made me miss her more."

I rose from the bed, taking her coffee cup with me to the kitchen. I scrubbed the cup and dried it.

"You know what's strange?" she asked.

I turned to her and rested my weight against the counter.

"What Pavel says is true. My grandfather won't be the only one buying my paintings anymore. With Mira's death, they will sell easily. And I'll have plenty of my own money, separate from my father. Do you think I should sell them?"

She sounded like a child asking if she could have another ice cream. I didn't know what to tell her. I shrugged and tried my most sympathetic smile.

"Well, at least I'll keep this one. *The Waiting.* It's beautiful."

We were quiet for some time.

She finally said, "Mira and I hadn't talked since her last visit to Prague. I'm pretty sure she and Paolo stayed in touch though. Talk to him. He'll know more."

"I'm hoping he might. I'll see him in Florence." I paused. "Would you have an address for him?"

She shook her head and said in a small voice. "We're not friends."

I took Mira's note from her and put it in my waist belt.

Petra hiccupped. I gave her another glass of water. She took a large gulp. Her large eyes, so naked with feeling, studied me. "I hope you find peace, Miss Falstaff."

It startled me. A sentiment like that coming from a woman I'd dismissed as a child. Was I seeking peace? I thought I was searching for Mira's sake. Was Petra implying I was searching for mine? Maybe there was more to Petra than I'd given her credit for.

I picked up my trunk. It was time for me to leave for Paris.

PARIS

CHAPTER 10

I was lonely. The visit to Petra's had left me depressed, and I'd come away a little less enchanted with Mira. I missed my mother, who would have made her *suji ka halwa* and recited a lovely Tagore poem to soothe me. I missed Amit. I resisted the urge to ask Dr. Stoddard about him. I was sure he would guess how I felt about Amit, and I wanted to keep those feelings to myself. I missed the old doctor, too. And Edward. It made me smile every time I thought of our dance in the Grand Bazaar. I found myself wanting to be with someone to whom I mattered. I also missed India; I longed for the familiarity of her aromas, her heartbeat, her people.

After disembarking at the Gare de l'Est in Paris, I headed to the *hôtel particulier* where a brass plate informed me that I was at Her Britannic Majestic Embassy. Edward Stoddard's advice to go to the British Embassy in every city I visited had been helpful so far. Where the one in Prague had been impressive, the one in Paris was dazzling. Like a palace from a fairy tale. Crystal chandeliers. Walls lined with tall mirrors and gilded columns. Under my feet, a plush carpet patterned in crimson and gold. Through the floor-to-ceiling windows on the back wall, my eye was drawn to a green lawn, exquisitely manicured.

When I announced myself to the receptionist, he handed me

an embossed envelope. It was addressed to me in Dr. Stoddard's cramped handwriting. I'd never been so happy to receive a letter in my life.

My dear girl,

I'm delighted you made the most of your visit to Prague. Hope you're unraveling the mystery of that most mysterious painter. No need to be under any obligation to us. Edward only did what he would ordinarily do. We are here to assist you in any way we can.

Now, I have a matter to posit to you.

It's understandable that you may not wish to visit your father, but if you leave this life without having said your piece to him, you will not be at peace yourself. I know he hurt you and your mother, but don't let him hurt you anymore.

I've been wanting to tell you something ever since I met you. Not even Edward knows of it. But it might help you understand something about your father.

I left a fiancée behind in England when I came to India. I had every intention of sending for her and marrying her after I'd got myself settled in Bombay. But then I met Deva. Never known anyone like her. She had an inner calm that I found soothing. I'd been feeling so low about losing my patient back in England because of my carelessness. Mistakes are made, but I never thought I'd be the one to make one. The man who died in my care was my fiancée's brother. She was heartbroken. I couldn't forgive myself. I had to get as far away as possible to escape my feelings of failure. I had hurt her. She'd forgiven me, never blamed me for her brother's death. Never changed her mind about marrying me. But I wanted to outrun my guilt. So I came to India. And fell in love with Deva. Did I do it to keep from returning to England, the scene of my colossal failing? Or did I want to start a life with an extraordinary woman?

I married Deva. We were happy together. Edward is the result of that union and the most magnificent accomplishment of my life. When he was eight, Deva was killed by a streetcar.

People looked at Deva and me in the way they probably looked at your father and mother. As if we'd broken some law. We were an abomination in their eyes. It didn't used to be that way. There was a time when the British government encouraged marriages like ours—like your mother and father's—to create liaisons and ease tensions between themselves and Indians. But the ill will could never be eased, not as long as the British were in power. Mixed marriages were the casualties.

There was such a cloud of disapproval around us that Deva and I didn't often mix. There were others like us, but no one wanted to be part of a club of outcasts. When I first met you, I knew you were one of us. And you confirmed it.

I thought often about how callous I'd been toward my fiancée, breaking off our engagement in a letter. Too much of a coward to see her in person. I never went back to England. My family weren't keen on connecting with me. Hers either. They were all ashamed of me. I was ashamed of myself too. I'd run from England. Then I'd run from my obligation to Elizabeth.

All this to say, my biggest regret in life is to never have faced Elizabeth and apologized to her for my callousness. I can't help but feel that your father wants—needs—to tell you that as well, that he's sorry for his desertion. And if the mountain won't come to Mohammed. . . Promise me you'll think about it.

All my love and admiration,
Ralph Stoddard

I stood with the letter in my hands a long time. All around me, serious men in dark wool suits, British colonels and majors, secretaries in pencil skirts and sweater twinsets bustled about the reception area, walking purposefully from one direction to another. And still, I stood without moving.

Dr. Stoddard had been married to an Indian woman? We'd had twelve days on the steamship together. Why hadn't he told me then? I'd shared feelings with him—being rejected by the hospital, being rejected by my father—that I hadn't shared with anyone but my mother. He had listened. He'd looked at me as a parent might—with acceptance, without judgment. But he had done exactly what my father had: abandoned someone who had placed her faith in him, as my mother had done with my father. I'd hated my father for it. Had I been a fool once again, placing my faith in the doctor? How could he so easily have won my affection, which I usually doled out in small measure—and snatched it away so brutally?

Another stunner: Edward was a *half-half* like me? I'd mistaken his darker skin for time in the sun when it was actually his birthright. Had he grown under the shadow of disgrace as I had? Been subjected to the same hurtful slurs? Had he cried in his mother's arms as I had? Yet, I hadn't seen in him the hard kernel of resentment I carried. Was that because unlike mine, his father had stayed, brought him up even after his wife died? Edward worked for the British Embassy, not the Indian Embassy. Which meant he had British citizenship through his father, a father who acknowledged parentage. Edward had true privilege.

Someone touched my elbow. It was an older woman with short blond hair and a button nose. In her younger days, she would have been quite handsome. There were soft pillows under her eyes.

She had a soft, soothing voice. "I'm afraid if you stand here much longer, you might get run over. Is it bad news?" She glanced at the letter in my hand.

I realized she thought I'd received word of a death. To show her it wasn't that, I smiled. "Nothing like that. But a shock just the same."

"Then you must come to the lounge and we'll get you a cup of tea. Alright?"

I picked up my trunk and let myself be led to an elegantly appointed room. A steward came forward. "How may I assist, Madam Phipps?"

"Tea for the lady please." When the steward left, she turned to me. "Anything else I could get you? Have you come for a travel document?"

"No, ma'am. I came for help with lodging. For two or three nights."

Her eyes went to my trunk. "Of course. You are from—no, let me guess—your accent—India?"

"Bombay." I held the letter aloft. "I was instructed to come. Dr. Stoddard and his son, Edward Stoddard, suggested—"

She brightened. "Eddy? Yes, of course. He told you to come here?"

I nodded.

Madam Phipps grinned. "Then let's see whom we can get to help you."

"Are you also with the embassy?"

She laughed charmingly. "I guess you could say that. I'm the ambassador's wife."

In the end, Mrs. Phipps gave me the name of an old friend, a Madame Renaud, who lived alone and liked company. I counted the money I had left. It was just enough to get me to Florence. But here in Paris, which I'd always heard was an expensive city, I would have to be very careful and hope my lodging wouldn't cost too much. If worse came to worst, I could always spend the night at the train station.

I checked the address for Madame Renaud. The white apartment building came to a point where Boulevard Raspail intersected with Rue Bréa. Filigree balconies framed the windows. On the ground floor was a café, one with bicycles parked on the cobblestone sidewalk. I almost walked away. Surely, this lodging was far above my budget. The ambassador's wife hadn't discussed terms with me, and I'd been too cowed to ask.

Madame Renaud was a graceful woman whose home might have been majestic in another era. She lived in one of three apartments on the fourth floor. The sofa cushions sagged but were covered in a beautiful rose-colored mohair. Over time, thousands of footsteps had worn a path on the Persian carpet. The floor-to-ceiling velvet drapes looked like they needed a good cleaning. I wondered if the Great Depression had anything to do with the state of her home. In precise French, Madame Renaud told me to take the first room to the left of the front door.

All day long, I'd been carrying my trunk and my arm ached. As if I'd said it out loud, my hostess said, "You must be tired. Get settled and then we'll have dinner."

Dinner was cod lightly sautéed with mushrooms and onions. Warm bread and a green bean salad accompanied the meal. She poured red wine in our glasses. The table was set with fine china and silver utensils. I unfolded the damask napkin in my lap, wondering whether she ate this formally every day. She was perhaps sixty years old with thinning gray hair pulled up and tied in a knot on the back of her head. Her black dress was a good cut made from heavyweight wool jersey. She wore small pearl earrings and a thick chain around her neck that held her eyeglasses.

She picked up her wineglass. "Frances—Madame Phipps—tells me you know Edward Stoddard."

"Yes, madame." I took a mouthful of the fish. It was delicately spiced with salt and butter. It was delicious. I hadn't eaten since I got off the train, and I was ravenous. "I know him through his father, Dr. Stoddard."

"Ah, I have not had the pleasure of meeting his father. I've sat next to Edward at the Phipps house for dinner. He is quite charming."

I flushed, hoping she didn't notice. Why did it matter whether she thought he was charming?

She buttered her bread. "How do you find Paris, Mademoiselle Falstaff?"

"It's just as beautiful and seductive as Hemingway described it. Or Zola. Or Guy de Maupassant."

"You're a reader, mademoiselle?"

"I'm afraid so. I've never had many friends." That I would reveal something so personal about myself—an unflattering portrayal at that—surprised me.

But Madame Renaud only laughed. She held up her glass for a toast. I clinked mine to hers. "That makes two of us." She took a sip. "I suspect you are not here for a sightseeing tour."

"No. I'm here to deliver the news that someone has died."

She put her fork down. "*Mon Dieu.* Frances said you had come from Bombay."

I chewed on a green bean. "I needed to give the news in person. And hand over a painting as well."

"A painting? That sounds interesting. Would I know the artist?"

"Her name was Mira Novak. In recent years, she mainly painted scenes of Indian women and men in the rural areas."

"I have heard of her. I think there was an exhibit of her work here some time back. May I see the painting?"

I left the table to look through my trunk. I unwrapped *The Pledges* and brought it to the table. She wiped her mouth on the cloth napkin and extended her arms to take the painting from me.

She felt for her glasses and put them on. She took her time studying the painting. "Quite good. The composition is striking. As is her subject matter. My husband and I went to India in '22. Such a beautiful and unknowable country. We encountered spiritual people like these. Praying for the lives of others all day long." She removed her glasses, letting them hang on her chain. She handed the painting back to me with a shaky hand. "Such a warm people, the Indians are. They invited us into their homes and fed us when they barely knew us." She took a sip of her wine. "My husband would have enjoyed meeting you, mademoiselle. He died last year." Her lips trembled, a prelude to tears, but she held them back. She took another mouthful of wine instead.

I reached for her hand. The skin was papery but warm. She clasped mine. Every time I experienced death in the course of my nursing career, the tear in my heart grew just a little wider.

We continued eating our dinner. She moved to take our plates, but when I rose from my seat to help her, she said, "Sit, sit. I cannot bear to have people in my kitchen."

She returned with two plates of what looked like custard. She'd added three blueberries on the top of each. It looked too perfect to eat. "Panna cotta," she announced. "It's Italian. But no one is perfect," she chuckled.

I took my first bite. It was like *rasmalai* but lighter, more delicate. I couldn't enjoy it as I normally would have, however. I was so anxious about my diminishing resources. I set my spoon down.

"Madame…if it's not too impertinent…may I know how much you require for my stay?" I flushed to the roots of my hair, sensing this was a vulgar question, but one I needed to ask.

Her lips curved in a smile. "It is most impertinent. Friends of Frances are friends of mine. And I do not ask friends to pay for their stay, mademoiselle."

I released the breath I was holding.

Before turning off my bedside lamp that night, I read Dr. Stoddard's letter again. I wanted to see if my thoughts were any clearer. On the one hand, the doctor was my friend, helping me from thousands of miles away. On the other, he was the enemy, a deserter, as my father had been. How could I reconcile the two? Was Dr. Stoddard telling me that the reasons for my father's bad behavior were more complex than I realized? That I must forgive my father the way the doctor wished to be forgiven? I willed my thoughts to settle, but they refused. My sleep was fitful. My dreams, dark.

"Josephine?" The man scratched his cheek. "You mean Josephine Benoit? She'll be at the *Marché* today."

I'd come looking for Josephine in the Seventh Arrondissement, which is where Madame Renaud said art galleries were located. On a city map, she showed me how Paris was shaped like a nautilus and divided into sections called arrondissements. After trying several streets along the Seine, I found Josephine Benoit's name on a glass door. Through the display windows, I spied two paintings that could have been Mira's. But the door was locked.

Monsieur Maillot, whose name was on the gallery door adjacent to Josephine's, was a beefy man in an expensive suit. Around ten stone. He showed all the signs of an overexercised heart. Flushed cheeks. Perspiration across the forehead although it was a fine day. The roll of his neck bulging from his starched shirt collar. My nurse's training wanted to tell him to cut down on meat and walk after dinner.

"Which *marché*, monsieur?" I asked.

He looked me up and down. I might have thought he was assessing my fashion sense just as the women of Paris had when they saw me approaching, but the instinct to shield my body from him told me otherwise.

"Le Marché aux Puces." He pointed vaguely toward the north of Paris, his eyes on my breasts.

I didn't want to be there any longer than I had to be, and I was anxious to leave. "Will I be able to find her there easily? There must be a hundred stalls." I'd read about the large market in Baedeker's.

He looked at me more closely, as if noticing me for the first time. "Are you related?"

I didn't know what he meant. "Pardon?"

"You're Miss Benoit's cousin from Martinique?"

"Uh, no. I'm from India."

His forehead creased. "India? Miss Benoit represents an artist from India, doesn't she?"

He must have been referring to Mira, but I didn't want to talk about her with anyone but Josephine. I pretended not to hear.

Monsieur Maillot's cheeks resembled balloons as he blew air through his mouth. "The *Marché* is large. Gets larger every day. There you must be careful what you buy, eh? There are some..." He rolled his hand in the air. I caught his meaning. That was what people always said about our Bombay markets.

His phone rang. He backtracked to his desk as he talked to me. "Ask for Louis Le Grand. He'll know where to find her." I heard his *"Allô"* as I closed the door behind me.

Walking to the flea market would take me an hour. But because I was saving money on lodging, I decided to take the metro. The flea market turned out to be a warren of stalls along narrow passageways with a variety of items for sale, not unlike Bombay's Hutatma Chowk. Instead of betel juice stains on the walls and the aroma of incense, fennel seeds and honest sweat, the French flea market smelled of plaster, stale cigarette smoke, leather and something metallic, like brass. To my left was a man selling used china and porcelain. The stall to my right featured a wrought iron chair, delicate in comparison to the sturdy teak chairs in old Bombay houses. At other stalls, used household wares and framed paintings were displayed on makeshift walls, vintage tables or hanging from the ceiling. I saw birdcages, antique books, enamel cookware, heavy mahogany furniture (much like the sideboards in St. Joseph's visitors lounge). After a half hour, I'd turned down so many alleys that

I felt as if I had walked in a circle. How would I ever find Josephine in this maze?

Every few stalls, I would ask if the shopkeeper could point me to Louis Le Grand. A few shrugged their shoulders. Others ignored me completely. I tried not to disturb those who were in the throes of a negotiation, but I couldn't help but overhear, fascinated that vendors here used the same tactics that Bombay vendors did. *Madame will not find anything finer than this lace. Even in the Netherlands they are begging for anything this delicate. I have customers as far as China who would pay four times what I'm charging, but they cannot travel so easily here as madame can.*

Finally, a gentleman I'd spoken to a few stalls back whistled. I turned around, as did several other customers and shopkeepers. He gestured to me to come closer. When I did, he leaned in and pointed to a store at the end of the lane. I thanked him and hurried along.

This stall was different. Instead of a canvas covering, there was a glass door at the entrance. It looked like one of the more prosperous shops. I stepped inside. On every wall, and even on the ceiling, were paintings. Some framed, most not. In the center of the store was a desk with even more canvases piled on it. In front of the desk, her back to me, stood a very tall woman in an elegant navy skirt suit. She wore a mustard cloche on her blue-black hair, which was styled in waves, as I'd seen on other European women. She was examining a canvas in her gloved hands.

The man I assumed was Louis wore a striped cotton shirt, sleeves pulled up to his elbows, and black pants with suspenders. His arms were crossed over his chest. "I talked to her just last week. She doesn't want to take anything less." His crowded teeth were like the slats of a fence that were about to collapse.

The woman murmured, "The painting is not good enough for my clients."

The shopkeeper pointed his palms to the ground. "Madame, she has the hashish. It has taken her like a lover. If it's good enough for Hugo and Baudelaire… That's what she says. *Et alors*, she needs the money."

"That may be, but my client won't pay as much as the artist wants."

"Which client is that?"

I could tell by the way she tightened her shoulders that the woman was annoyed by this question. "Monsieur Le Grand, I never reveal the names of my clients," she said as if she were scolding an unruly child. She lowered the canvas, set it on the desk.

Louis waved his hands about. "I know, I know. *Désolé.*" But he seemed more exasperated than sorry.

"We will pay half of what you're asking."

Louis ran a hand across his mouth and shrugged. "Leave it then." He seemed to notice me for the first time. He lifted his chin at the painting under my arm and asked. "Mademoiselle?"

I'd been so absorbed in their conversation that I jumped. That was when the woman turned around. She was the color of coffee with just a dab of milk. Her eyes were the same color as her skin. She might have been South Indian. In fact, it was how Mira had described her. Josephine was wearing cream gloves. A strand of pearls glowed against her dark skin. The only thing that gave away her age were the creases around the corners of her mouth. She might have been forty or fifty—it was hard to tell. Maroon lipstick lined her thin mouth.

I must have been staring because Louis asked again, "*Puis-je vous aider?*"

I'd forgotten to greet the proprietor with the bonjour Ralph Stoddard had told me was customary. I nodded to Louis. "Bonjour." Then I took a few steps toward the woman. "Madame Benoit?"

A frown creased her forehead.

"You knew Mira Novak?"

She blinked. "I *know* Mira," she said cautiously.

"I'm afraid I have some sad news." Noticing Louis, whose eyebrows had risen in surprise, I said, "Perhaps we could talk privately?"

But Louis was quick. He was grinning now, his overbite on full display. "There you are, Madame Benoit. Mira Novak's work will fetch a pretty penny on the art market now. You have a few yourself, don't you? Your future is looking very bright indeed." He picked up the small canvas from his desk. "Shall I wrap this for you? Full price?"

Josephine, whose high heels brought her eye level with Louis, stared him down as if she were a foot taller. Her jaw tensed. She reached into her purse and placed a wad of French francs on his desk.

Louis clasped his hands and moved them up and down. "*Merci*, madame." He began wrapping the small painting in brown paper, inserting cardboard on both sides of the canvas to protect it.

As soon as he handed it to Josephine, she turned and click-clacked her heels out of the room. She was walking so fast I had to run to catch up to her.

Once we'd passed a few stalls, she tucked the painting under her arm and stopped to light a thin cigar with a gold lighter. She snapped it shut and took a deep drag. When I'd caught up with her, she said. "You cost me a negotiation." She didn't look angry, but her voice was tight.

I was a little out of breath. Sweat had made my underarms damp. The temperature was sixty degrees, twenty degrees cooler than Bombay. I should have been cold. "I'm sorry, madame. But I've come a long way to talk to you. From Bombay, in fact."

Her eyes shifted from the cigar to my mouth. It was as if she were deaf and trying to read my lips. "And you are…?"

"I was Miss Novak's nurse. She took ill in Bombay. I'm afraid she did not live more than six days at the hospital."

We were stopped in front of a group listening to a jazz band. The guitarists were improvising, each playing a solo. I had had to speak loudly to be heard over them. Several people looked over at us.

She stood perfectly still, oblivious to the customers who had to go around her. Her eyes were fixed on the ground. It was littered with bits of food from hurried lunches, cigarette butts and sales chits. I gave her time to digest the news. She didn't appear upset, just shocked. Everyone grieved differently.

"Miss Benoit?"

So deep in thought was she that she didn't hear me call her name. I tugged the burning cigar from between her gloved fingers and threw it on the ground, squashing it with my shoe. Gently, I pried the wrapped canvas she'd just bought from under her arm; it was in danger of falling to the ground. Taking care of the needs of others was as natural—and automatic—to me as breathing.

After several minutes, Josephine straightened her spine and considered me. She seemed to have made up her mind about something.

Finally, she looked up at me. "Mira's gone?"

I nodded.

"Good." Her tone was businesslike. She took sunglasses out of her purse and put them on. If she'd appeared remote before, she was more so now. Were the sunglasses part of her daily ensemble or were they meant to conceal emotions visible on her face? She checked her watch. "I'm late for an appointment." She went around me to leave the flea market.

"But, Miss Benoit, I've come a long way."

She wheeled around to face me. "Are you deaf? I don't care." The spit landed on my face. Without another word, she turned on her heel and quickly wound her way through the busy market.

I was still holding the painting she had bought. "No, wait, Miss Benoit!" I shouted. "I have your—" She only walked faster. But I didn't want to be accused of stealing her purchase. If French society was anything like the British Raj, I would automatically be branded a criminal. Age-old bigotry would be my judge and jury. I fought my way through the throngs, keeping my eye on the mustard cloche ahead. I was used to the Bombay bazaars where patrons allowed the current of the crowd to guide them instead of carving their own path through the whirlpool. Here in Paris, I needed to elbow my way through the mob to catch up to Mira's friend.

She was headed for the metro, the same one I had taken to get to the *Marché*. I followed, clutching two paintings now, one of them Mira's *The Pledges*. Josephine entered a first-class car. I hesitated for only a second; I had a ticket for second class, but the doors between the first-class and crowded second-class carriages were locked. I knew that if she disembarked, I would lose track of her.

The first-class compartment was empty except for two businessmen and a heavyset woman surrounded by shopping bags. Josephine looked at me, astonished, when I sat down next to her. This close, I could smell her fragrance—a hint of citrus with musk, peppercorn and the cheroot she'd been smoking. It was subtle but enough to mark her as a powerful woman.

"I don't want to know." Abruptly, she rose and took another seat.

"But..." I followed her and offered the painting she had purchased from Louis. She looked at the parcel. Her mouth opened and then closed. She grabbed the painting without a thank-you.

Hers was not a reaction I'd expected, especially when Petra's had been the opposite. She had grieved the way I'd thought she would. Mira had told me once that Petra could never pretend. Her emotions came hot and fast. Josephine was completely different. What confused me was that she was Mira's art dealer. Shouldn't she at least want the details of her death? Mourn for her friend and client? Show an iota of feeling? Surely, she needed to know who would handle any paintings left in the estate.

My hands curled into fists. I wasn't used to showing my anger, but I felt it bubble to the surface. I'd come thousands of miles to tell this woman about Mira only to be rebuffed in such an ill manner. Josephine seemed angry—not pained—by the news. I could, of course, simply thrust *The Pledges* at her and leave it at that. My duty would be done. But Josephine's reaction was baffling. Maybe it had something to do with Mira's betrayal of Josephine and her husband.

I made an attempt to sit next to her. She held up a palm. "Don't." It was a command. "She obviously got to you. The way she got to everybody. Fine. You've said what you've come to say. Now go." She turned toward the window.

I found another seat and kept my eye on her. I needed to give her Mira's painting. I just needed to find the right time.

I followed her from the underground to the Vavin exit, adjusting my eyes to the sunlight. On all four corners of the intersection, patrons dotted the terraces of cafés on Boulevard du Montparnasse. To my left was a graceful café called Le Dôme.

Josephine crossed the street. I followed. Josephine wove around the tables of another large café on the corner: La Rotonde. Down the street were two other sparsely populated coffeehouses, La Coupole and Le Select. At La Rotonde, everyone seemed to know Josephine. On the terrace, patrons waved to her from various tables. The waiters kissed both her cheeks. I hung back. She seemed not to know I was there. She stopped in front of a table where three men sat smoking and chatting. All three stood to kiss her.

Josephine asked the one with the high forehead, "Picasso's not with you today, Marcel?"

Marcel smiled. His eyes were narrow and his nose sharp, but the symmetry of his features made him handsome. "He's at the studio with Dora. Working furiously on his painting for the Expo."

Another man at the table, his eyes deep-set and brows in a permanent frown, said, "That's an angry painting. He's furious with Franco and Germany for bombing Guernica."

The man with the coarse face and pug nose of a boxer looked at him. "Miró is angry too, Manny. If you were a Spaniard, wouldn't you be?" He took a sip of his beer, leaving a line of foam on his mustache.

Josephine smiled. "I hear anger only makes the two of them paint faster."

The men laughed.

From another table, a mild-mannered man in a suit and bow tie piped up. "Picasso's lucky they gave him a studio to paint in. They didn't do that for everybody." He had papers in front of him, which he was marking with his pencil.

Marcel said, "Louis, you stay out of this. Stick to your own propaganda." It was a friendly thrust.

Except for the dapper one called Louis, the others had the look of my patients after three days in the hospital. Their hair unkempt. Their skin a little sallow. Their shirts rumpled. On the train, I'd heard one tourist tell another that the Montparnasse area, where we were now, was a refuge for poets, writers and painters. The men talking to Josephine were probably taking a break from their art.

The boxer lit one of his Pélican cigarettes. He blew smoke through his nostrils. "What about you, Jo? Will you return to Martinique? There's talk—"

Josephine shook her head. "There's always talk, Fernand. If it comes to that, then yes, my sister and I will go back. I'm trying to get her to be a little less political in her essays."

"She is a bit of a champagne socialist," Marcel said with a sly grin.

Josephine smiled. "Don't tell her that. She would be shocked." She stole a look inside the café. "Have any of you seen Berthe? I looked for her at the *Marché* but I couldn't find her."

"One of your lost causes, Jo," said Manny. He winked at me. "Is this another one?"

I was mortified to have the men turn their attention on me.

I tried to look away but Josephine saw me. Her face froze. She turned back to the men and spoke sternly, "No, Manny. She's not. If you see Berthe, tell her I'm inside. She's a talented painter… when she's working. Better yet, say nothing. Or she'll run the other way."

The men chuckled. I was envious of how easily Josephine chatted with the men outside. How deftly she thwarted their attempts to engage her in topics she didn't want to participate in.

She walked the few feet toward me, her back to the men. "Stop following me. Don't you have a shred of dignity?" she hissed.

I flexed my jaw. I'd had enough of bullies in my life. I'd lost my job. I'd lost my home. My family. I'd traveled far. I wasn't going to let this woman treat me as if I were nothing. My pulse was racing, and I was furious, but I managed to control my voice. "I have to give you something from Mira and I'm not leaving until you let me hand it to you."

"Whatever it is, I don't want it."

"Why not?"

She pressed her lips together as if she were trying to keep from saying something she'd regret. Josephine struck me as the type of woman who didn't like scenes, and I was forcing one upon her. She shook her head as if she couldn't be bothered to answer, turned around and entered the café.

Inside, La Rotonde was all red velvet booths and warm wood paneling and white tablecloths and bright yellow lamps with fringed shades—a little like the shades in Bombay's Chinese district. Sophisticated and humble at the same time, La Rotonde looked like the kind of place that I imagined Bombay's fashionable set frequented, listening to jazz and drinking cocktails every evening. The aroma of coffee and alcohol mingled in the air.

On the walls, someone had tacked hundreds of pencil drawings and cartoons—there was even a small sculpture of a cat, stretching.

Josephine took a booth at the back with a clear view of the front door. I sat at a table nearby but behind a pillar, out of her line of sight. Like Kavarna Slavia in Prague, the waiter who approached her table wore black pants and a white shirt with a black bow tie. The ensemble was overlaid with the largest white apron I'd ever seen.

"Bonjour, Henri."

"Bonjour, mademoiselle. *Vous voulez...*"

Josephine ordered something I didn't catch.

When he came to ask for my order, I asked for the same thing she'd ordered.

"Campari," he said. *"Bien."*

He was about to leave when I asked, "Why do they leave their drawings here, the artists?" I asked.

The waiter followed my gaze. "Patrons who can't afford to pay, do. When they come back with the money, we give their artwork back to them. In the case of some painters—like Picasso—the owner would rather have the art than the money," he said dryly. "Dealers like Josephine—" he indicated her with a discreet tilt of his head "—often see sketches here from the artists they represent, but they choose to leave them up. It's good publicity."

"Jo! *Désolée, désolée!*" a plump woman in a loose dress, frizzy hair tumbling out of a floppy hat, ran up to Josephine. Her cheeks were flat. Her jowls had fallen into her neck. She might have been thirty or forty or fifty. It was hard to tell.

She kissed the art dealer on both cheeks. Josephine accepted the greeting, turning her cheek this way and that, but didn't smile.

"Berthe."

"Thank you so much for rescuing my painting. You know how cheap Louis is, Jo!"

I understood then that Berthe was the painter whose work Josephine had bought at the flea market.

"Have you eaten today?" Josephine asked Berthe after she sat down. Josephine called for Henri to bring an omelet with salad.

"And some of those cornichons too," Berthe added, looking at Josephine with a sheepish smile.

"Here," Josephine said, as she pushed her glass of Campari toward the woman. She spoke gently, far from the stern voice she'd used when I first approached her. "Berthe, I've told you about giving your work away. You are too good. Your work is too precious."

"Yes, but I needed my medicine. And Ricard needs it." She looked down at her fingernails, bitten to the quick. She balled her hands into fists, I assumed, to keep from biting them again.

Josephine took Berthe's pink hands in her own mahogany ones. Berthe had a fair complexion with freckles covering her face, her arms and her hands. "You don't need it, Berthe. And you don't need Ricard to keep you from painting. He makes your life so much harder—"

"But I do need it, Jo! And I need Ricard." Berthe had tears in her eyes now. "If I stop the medicine, I can't paint."

"Do you really know that or are you just afraid that it might be true?"

The omelet arrived and Berthe attacked it with the fervor of the half-starved. In between bites, she said, "I know it. The one time I stopped, I had such a headache I couldn't concentrate. Ricard had to get me some just so the pain would go away." She turned large pale blue eyes on Josephine, who sighed.

"Alright. If you won't stop, at least find me next time and let me sell the work for you so you can eat. I can get you more money than Louis Le Grande can. I want you to at least eat and stay strong."

Berthe smiled, revealing two missing teeth along her lower gums. "You're so good to me, Jo. Pardon me for forgetting." She eyed the wrapped painting sitting on the table. "Can I have the money now?"

"I have to sell it first."

"What if you advance the money to me now?"

"Will you give it to Ricard?"

"He takes care of me, Jo. You know that."

"Then the answer is no."

"What if I don't give it to him?"

"Then you'd be lying, and the answer would still be no."

"He's my whole life."

"Painting is your whole life. You've worked so hard for it."

Berthe swept her plate clean with a piece of bread. "Alright then. Can I have a Pernod?"

Josephine nodded and signaled to the waiter, then dug another cheroot out of the packet in her clutch.

Berthe reminded me of patients who felt sorry for themselves. They protested loudly as if they were the injured party when they had caused their own problems to begin with. Like Mr. Mittal who hadn't followed instructions about how to clean and dress his wound and had returned with a more severe infection only to blame us for not treating it properly.

Outside, we heard voices chanting, faint at first, then getting louder. Like the protests of the textile workers back in Bombay.

Patrons left their seats to look out the café entrance; Josephine and Berthe stayed put. I got to the front door in time to watch a procession parading down Boulevard Raspail with placards that read *Les Riches Doivent Payer!*

A well-heeled customer consulted his gold pocket watch and said to the woman he was with, "They don't realize the danger they're in. Another war is coming; you can be sure of it. It will take a lot more than these protests to stop it."

"They have every right to protest." This was a younger man in a white shirt, the first four buttons undone, and an open vest. "Look at how many are without work. Four years ago, these cafés were bursting with patrons. Now look. Only every fourth table is taken."

My stomach roiled. I wondered if coming to Europe had been such a good idea when there seemed to be so much unrest brewing under the surface in Prague, and now in Paris. I'd heard the conversations everywhere I went: there might be another bloody war like the one the world had just endured. The battle between the Nazis, the Fascists, and the rest of Europe and the Americas. As they had done in the last war, the British would send the Indian Army to fight on their behalf. A tiny country like Britain couldn't wage war otherwise. Indian soldiers would lose lives senselessly in a war they neither instigated nor profited from. I could picture the casualties, the mutilations and the deaths overwhelming the hospitals back home. My legs started to shake at the image, and I had to hold on to a café table to steady myself.

I was a little weak-kneed when I settled in my seat again. The waiter brought me a glass filled with red liquid. When he saw me eyeing it suspiciously, he said, "You've never had a Campari before?"

I shook my head, feeling foolish. Would I never be as worldly as Mira or Josephine or Petra? Who did I think I was, sitting at a café in Paris, pretending to be an adult?

"It might be a little bitter for your taste. But it's good to drink before dinner." He grinned, revealing a gap between his two front teeth. On someone else, it might not have been charming, but on him it was.

Gingerly, I tried a sip. It was sweet, light and, as he'd said, a little bitter. But I liked it. I drank the whole thing in one gulp. Given what I'd just seen outside, I needed the relief it brought. I asked for another. I was beginning to enjoy myself, thinking, *Look at me now, Mum. I'm taking risks. Doing things I've never done. Only, I wish you were doing them with me.*

Josephine and Berthe were arguing about a commission Berthe still needed to paint.

After my third Campari, I needed to use the WC. I asked the waiter where it was, and he pointed to the stairs. I wound my way behind Josephine's booth a little unsteadily. It felt good, like my limbs were so loose my body could fold into itself. The image made me smile. I held on to the banister as I made my way down the stairs. When I opened the door to the WC, someone pushed me from behind so hard I fell against the sink, hitting my head on the mirror above. A man was pressing against my body. I smelled beer and the woody scent of a cigarette. The rim of the sink was putting so much pressure on my stomach, bile rose to my throat. I felt clumsy hands pushing my skirt up around my hips. It had happened so fast I hadn't thought to scream. Then I realized I couldn't. He had his meaty hand clamped around my mouth and nose. I couldn't breathe. I gnawed at his hand until I found skin I could bite. He screamed, *"Guenon!"* I tried to use my right hand to punch him in the ribs. But his body was too close and my fist landed on his back without impact. He caught my arm and bent it upward. The pain brought tears to my eyes. I bit him harder. All at once, I felt his body lift off my back. I fell forward and braced my arms on either side of the sink. I rested my head against the mirror, breathing hard.

"Ça va?"

I turned to see Josephine. Behind her, a man stumbled out the door, holding on to his hand, and headed for the stairs. Josephine's back was to the overhead light. I couldn't see her expression. Three glasses of Campari shot up my gullet and I turned to the sink in time to vomit. I didn't realize I was crying. Snot was running down my nose. The blue sweater the doctor had knit for me was soaked. Was it water or vomit?

"I don't know what I'm doing," I cried, feeling humiliated. "Why am I here? In Paris?"

"Wash your face."

I turned on the tap and splashed water on my face. There was a small towel on a wall hook, which a hundred hands had wiped. Josephine reached around me to give me her handkerchief. I wiped my face.

She gripped my arm and led me out of the WC.

I stopped. "I have to pee." I was five years old again, needing my mother to hold my hand.

She said, "Go."

Before I came back out, she handed me her suit coat and told me to take my stained sweater and blouse off.

She walked me to her booth and helped me sit down. Berthe had disappeared. She'd taken the wrapped painting with her.

"Merde!" Josephine let out a sigh of frustration. She shook her head. She called the waiter over. I was too tired to understand their rapid French.

When he left, she gave me her glass of water. I drained it in one swallow. "You have to take it easy with the Campari." She asked Henri for another glass of water.

I should have known better. Hadn't I made a fool of myself on the Viceroy in front of Dr. Stoddard with a few too many glasses of port? I felt so idiotic I couldn't look at her. "Where did he go?"

"He ran." She lit a cheroot with her gold lighter and blew out smoke. "I haven't seen him here before. There was a time when I knew almost everyone here. But so many—painters like Gris, Matisse—and writers—Hemingway, Fitzgerald—they've left Paris. The cafés used to be so crowded the tables spilled out onto the streets. Now, it feels more like a ghost town." She tapped her slim cigar on the ashtray.

"The ones who are left are the surrealists. Like the men outside. The one with the battered nose is Fernand Léger." She exhaled smoke through the side of her mouth to direct it away from me. "Next to him, Marcel DuChamp. The third is Man Ray. They call him Manny. The one at the other table is Louis Aragon. More of a writer and a collector of art. Each of them is a genius in his own way. Then there's Picasso—he's still here. He's a little of everything: a surrealist, a cubist, a futurist, a pioneer."

Henri returned with a clean tablecloth, the same as the ones that were draped over each table. Josephine instructed me to wrap my damp clothing in it.

"I'm sorry," was all I could say.

Josephine regarded me through the smoke. "What's your name?"

"Sona Falstaff."

"Falstaff as in Shakespeare?"

I cocked my head, stumped. It felt as if water was sloshing to one side in my brain. I'd never given any thought to my father's surname.

"You shouldn't be here. You're too young to be by yourself."

It was what I'd been feeling but hearing her say it was embarrassing. "I'm twenty-three." I could hear my voice, sounding all of twelve years old.

Henri brought another glass of water and Jo pushed it toward me. "My point."

I took a sip. Then another. "Miss Novak told me you only represent female artists."

She inspected her cheroot and dropped more ashes into the ashtray. "I'm not ready to talk about her. But if you're asking why I don't have male artists in my stable, I would ask you, don't you think men have had enough of a head start?" She pulled the ashtray closer to her, let me consider her remark.

"They're special, artists are. Like children. Very talented children. But they need love. They need to be told they are doing work that people need to see. That they are important."

"You sound like a mother." I didn't know if Josephine was married or had children.

"I suppose I am a mother of sorts. To Berthe, whom you met. Chana Orloff. Sonia Delaunay. Germaine Richier. More importantly, I'm their guardian. I protect them from bad news. I bring opportunities to them. I hold on to their money for them when I know they can't do it for themselves."

"You love them?"

She plucked a piece of tobacco from her tongue. "I do. If I could do what they do, I would. But you see, I don't have the talent. I know how to massage it, but I don't have it." She signaled for two cups of coffee. "I'll tell you this though. I would rather spend time with any of my artists—even those who drink too much or gamble—than the people who come to my sister's Friday evening salons. They talk a good game about equality, and how everyone must have the same earning power and so on. But in the end, they're just talking to their boeuf bourguignon and champagne. The artists? They're doing something. They're saying something important in the process."

Henri brought the coffees. He talked to her in French so rapidly that I couldn't catch it with my rudimentary skill. Josephine answered him just as rapidly. He laughed and went to take an order at another table.

She smiled at me. "He asked if you were related to me."

For the second time today, my skin color had been called out. "Your gallery neighbor, Monsieur Maillot, asked me that too."

"You're an attractive woman. The French love the exotic. The mysterious. Josephine Baker. Kiki de Montparnasse. Fujita, that artist from Japan, because he has a quirky look. The French eat it up."

I wondered what my mother would think of being called exotic. In a land of Indians, she had hardly stood out. Here in Paris, would she spit at the ground, warning the evil spirits away, or would she be pleasantly surprised, taking in the compliment? I found myself chuckling.

Josephine grinned at my reaction, her even teeth on display. She crushed her dwindling cheroot in the ashtray and drained her coffee.

She began gathering her pack of smokes, her gloves and her clutch. "How many days will you stay in Paris?"

I thought about it, about my remaining funds. "I will probably leave the day after tomorrow."

"Where are you staying?"

I told her.

She regarded me with somber eyes, pupils dark like the bottom of a well. "I'm probably going to regret this." She sighed. "Meet me at the Musée d'Art Moderne tomorrow at eleven o'clock. It's far enough from the Expo that you won't be swallowed by the crowd. And do be careful. People are crafty. If they can, they will take advantage of you." She slid out of the booth.

Her remark reminded me, as I'm sure she intended it to, of what had happened in the bathroom earlier. My eyes watered. It felt like I was being reprimanded. Or was Jo mothering me the way she mothered her clients, the way my mother had, protecting me, making sure I was safe? When would I no longer need that protection? Had Josephine ever needed it? She seemed like someone who catapulted from childhood to adulthood, skipping the insecurity in between. Maybe I was teetering on that edge. On one side, a woman who sheltered behind the front lines, and on the other side, one who marched into battle. Josephine was in the second camp. So was Mira. Which side would I end up on?

The next day, I stood with my back to the Musée d'Art Moderne, watching people enter the Expo grounds. A shuttle carrying a dozen passengers wove its way through the masses. Visitors were taking a break along the stone walls of the Seine, watching the boats float along the river. Others consulted their maps and pointed to the pavilions on the other side of the Seine they wanted to visit.

"Not as many people as they expected," Josephine said, approaching me. She was wearing another well-cut skirt suit in maroon wool with a matching tilt hat. She took me by the arm and guided me toward the Avenue du Président Wilson. After yesterday, when she'd been so brusque, her casual touch—as if we'd known each for ages, as if we were friends—surprised me.

"The Expo was supposed to be an opportunity for Paris to get back on its feet," she said. "But there's so much uncertainty in the air about war that many who had planned on coming didn't." We stopped at the Place du Trocadéro.

Josephine said, "They asked for seven hundred murals to be created by artists around the world. I thought it would be a great opportunity for Mira. I knew she would have been accepted because of what she painted. South Indian women." She uncoupled our arms and began walking toward the Trocadéro Fountains. "Mira refused. She said the fight for power between the Soviets and Nazi Germany would upstage everything else. Now look at the two largest pavilions flanking the entrance. See their flags?" She was pointing to the tallest structures on either side of the Pont d'léna.

"Those two countries are declaring their fight for world domination. If Germany wins, and Mira was convinced they would, she feared for the future of the Jews. She said she would never participate in anything that hated half of her without just cause." Jo looked at me. "She was always so sure of herself, her convictions. I respected her for that. It frustrated me and made me proud of her at the same time. Unlike Berthe, who cannot stand up for herself. Poor thing. She'll always let people use her."

As Jo talked, I studied her. Yesterday, she didn't even want to talk about Mira. After what Mira had told me, I could understand Jo's anger. But here she was, telling me what she admired about the painter.

The art dealer skirted the fountains and walked toward the Pont d'léna. The Eiffel Tower loomed on the other side of the Seine. Up close, the tower was massive. We were quiet as we crossed the bridge. Josephine stopped to lean on the stone wall and watch the boats below as so many others were doing.

"So. You were fascinated by Mira." She regarded me, assessing me. I felt my neck flush. Was it so obvious?

"Her stories took me outside of myself, outside of India. She'd be talking about an art exhibition she's seen in Vienna one minute and Mozart's symphony the next. Things I'd not been exposed to."

Josephine laughed lightly. *"Eine Kleine Nachtmusik?"*

"Yes. What's so amusing?"

"It was part of her seduction routine. She took your hand in hers like this, right?" Josephine held my hand the way Mira had, hers so dark against mine.

My mouth fell open. Were none of the moments with Mira, moments where I'd felt special, privileged to be in her company, exclusive to me?

"When Mira wanted you to love her, she had a repertoire she employed. Mozart was one of them. But it wasn't real, Miss Falstaff. She did it because you were there. If you hadn't been there, she would have done the same thing to someone else who was."

She must have done the same thing with Amit, I thought. I looked away, trying to hide my disappointment.

She patted my hand in sympathy. Then, with ever so slight a change in the pitch of her voice, she said, "I was married to a lovely man when I scouted Mira Novak at the *école*. I saw Mira's enormous talent, what she was capable of, right away. No one had to teach her how to paint well. She'd always had it. She just needed someone to shape it. Jean and I were both charmed by her. She was eighteen then and a little lost. Mad about her Italian tutor Paolo. She'd left Florence because he wouldn't commit to her." Josephine's attention wandered off, and I sensed she was recalling a memory.

She blinked and continued, "We also saw her loneliness, which we mistook for vulnerability. I told you how artists need to be protected. People like me make sure they're protected from greedy collectors. Mira was fierce, but in the way a young girl dresses in the clothes of an older woman to keep fear at bay. Like a child, she was always testing the limits of what others would put up with from her. She slept with anyone and everyone. No one was off-limits. To prove she could."

Jo looked into the murky waters of the Seine below. "She got involved in marches for equality—like the one you saw yesterday at La Rotonde. She thought that just because she was half Indian it gave her the right to defend every injustice the world has ever known. She was a wild bird looking to land somewhere. Prague was her city of birth, but it wasn't her home. She studied in Paris and loved it here, but she couldn't make herself heard amidst the chest-beating men ten years older and twenty kilos heavier than she was. She studied in Florence and spent all her time mooning over Paolo. None of that was good for her painting."

Josephine reached for her cheroots. She removed one but didn't light it. "I was the one who recommended she try painting in India. Perhaps because she was still infatuated with Paolo. Perhaps because I knew that the half of her that was Indian hadn't yet seen the light of day. It needed to grow inside her. And look what happened." She smiled wide, a mother proud of her chick. "Her art took on new meaning. She wasn't desperate to prove anything. She was excited to *show* something. She could fight injustice without having to march for it. She showed women at work, the kind of grinding labor they neither chose nor wanted. That is—*was*—" she paused, her mouth getting used to the word "—her genius."

Jo's account was similar to what Mira had told me from her hospital bed. Why she painted what she did. How she came to discover the essence of herself in India. But one thing differed. Mira had made it seem as if she'd been in control of the relationship with Paolo, and Josephine was saying otherwise. From the time Jo met her to the time Mira arrived at our hospital, ten years had passed. Why would Mira say the baby she lost at Wadia's was Paolo's?

"Tell me about Paolo," I said.

Jo made a face. She lit her cheroot. "He was her tutor." She exhaled a plume of smoke toward the sky. "Mira was fifteen when she met him in Florence. What was he doing getting involved with a student half his age? He was beautiful, I'll give him that. Mira loved painting him. But he disgusted me. Did you know he was also sleeping with her mother? That really played with Mira's head. It tortured her. *He* tortured her. What kind of monster does that?" She shook her head.

Josephine went on, "It makes me angry to think how much more she could have accomplished without being distracted by him. His interference cost her. In the end, the tryst with him left her so unhappy. You have no idea how often Jean and I went to her lodgings to find her in bed. For days. I would have to coax her into better humor. Bring food to her. She loved those little macrons from Ladurée. I would buy them in every color. She would stuff herself and be happy for a minute. I would settle her in bed and brush her hair until she fell asleep." Josephine smiled indulgently.

"As I said, for all her remarkable looks, her talent, her forceful nature, she was still a girl. I don't think her mother or father taught her to be anything but that. When Mira was at her lowest, I wrote to her mother, who was touring the Physic Garden in Chelsea. She told me Mira was just moody. She would get over it. I wrote to her father, who was trekking through the Alps with his Himalayan Club. He never answered. Mira had no one and nowhere to go. She needed a place where she could feel secure. And paint without interruptions. I gave her money to go to India where I knew she'd blossom. Instead, you know what she did?" Josephine pointed at me with her cheroot.

I looked down at my hands.

Josephine turned her eyes on me, the pupils darker than before. "She slept with my husband. Ruined my marriage."

"So she said."

Josephine turned around and leaned against the wall on her elbows. "Poor Jean. He didn't know what he was getting into.

She was just playing. Testing, testing, testing, as she always did. How far could she go before someone stopped her?" She tapped ash from her cheroot into the Seine. "Did she tell you she took my money? She'd borrowed against a future commission, one of my biggest deals. Well, it would have been one of my biggest deals if she hadn't reneged and left for Prague with no intention of completing the work."

That I hadn't known. Mira had told me she was broke when she went to Prague. "This may be small comfort, madame, but I believe she wanted you to know how much she regretted what she did. She wished she could undo it. One of the last things she said to me was that you and your husband had been so good to her. That you had made a name for her in the art world."

Jo threw the cheroot into the river. "Did she tell you I fired her?"

I nodded. "How many years has it been since you represented Mira?"

"Nine."

I thought about the timeframe. "After she had left for India?"

"Like a fool, I hung on. Because she told me what she told you. How sorry she was. How she regretted betraying me like that. She cried. I took her back. When you're young and beautiful and charming, you can get away with so much."

Josephine was watching my reaction with a faint smile on her lips. "She left that part out, didn't she? She was like that. She lied or left parts of the story out when it suited her. I have a name in the art world. Artists want to be associated with me. She wanted that association, wanted people to think well of her. And you, Miss Falstaff, played right into it. We all did."

I shook my head, trying to understand Mira the chameleon. "Have you had any contact with her since?"

"She asked me to be her dealer again."

"When?"

"A year ago. She said she didn't think her dealer at the time was doing justice to her work. She needed more money."

"What did you say?"

"The first time, I hung up. She called again. I said I would do it if she would paint that mural for the Expo. She declined. I understood. I wished her luck. She called a third time, telling me how much she needed me. I didn't even wait for her to finish her sentence. I hung up. She broke my heart once. I wasn't going to let her do it again."

Josephine readjusted her shoulders. "Now, I need to visit a couple of pavilions. You're welcome to do the same. But not with me."

I couldn't let her leave. I still had more questions. "She came to the hospital after a miscarriage."

Josephine's eyebrows shot up. "Miscarriage? Mira never wanted children."

"That's what her friend Petra said."

Recognition flared in her eyes. "The friend from Prague. Whom she grew up with. I believe she sat for *Two Women*."

"She did. She couldn't believe Miss Novak changed her mind about children. Neither could her other old friends in Prague."

Josephine shrugged. "I find it hard to believe too."

"Would you have any idea—any idea at all—why she would have changed her mind? Do you know if a pregnancy would have put her in danger?"

Her forehead puckered. "Isn't that a question for her doctors?"

"Yes, but I thought you might know something—anything—that might help."

She looked at her shoes, shiny black leather with a block heel. "What does her husband say? Someone told me she'd married a friend from Prague." She looked at her watch. "If there's nothing else…"

"There is. Mira wanted me to give you this." I pulled the

rolled up *The Pledges* from under my arm and handed it to her along with the suit jacket she'd loaned me the day before.

She studied the painting thoughtfully. If she was surprised to see it, she didn't let on. Maybe that deadpan expression was her trump card when she was negotiating, as she'd been doing with Louis Le Grand at the *Marché*.

"It's hard to turn away from it, isn't it? The colors of India, of warm earth and sun. This is exactly what I wanted her to paint. It's quite good." She asked, "Did she want me to sell it for her?"

"All I know is that she wanted you to have it. What you do with it is up to you." I turned the canvas over. "See your initial on the back?" I pulled Mira's note from my skirt pocket and showed it to her.

With a frown, Jo looked at the painting again. "She wanted me to have this one in particular?" Her eyes focused on the central figure, the sage with the double tikka. After a few minutes, she smiled. With wonder, Josephine said, "Our Mira finally understood. I told her once that my role was threefold: teacher, protector, promoter. I am the teacher here, aren't I?"

"Perhaps the painting was her way of acknowledging that," I said. "And as an apology for what she did all those years ago."

The art dealer looked at me askance. "Perhaps."

I left Josephine there, on the bridge, searching for clues in Mira's gift.

I wandered around the Expo for an hour before returning to Madame Renaud's. She came to meet me in the hallway, pulling on her gloves. She adjusted her hat in the wall mirror. There was an excitement about her, as if she were in possession of a secret and was dying to tell someone.

"There's a gentleman waiting for you in the café downstairs. Handsome. Lovely manners. Quite charming."

"For me? A gentleman?" I knew no one in Paris aside from the ambassador's wife, Madame Renaud and Josephine.

She inserted a pearl pin through the hat and dabbed her lips where she'd applied a light pink lipstick. "I must go to my friend Solange's for dinner. I'm assuming you'll be alright on your own." Her eyes were full of mirth. "Or not on your own."

I was puzzled by her comment. She patted me on the arm and opened the door. "Oh, I hope you'll invite him upstairs for... Well, I'll be home late...much later." She gave me a knowing smile and shut the door. I heard her heels echo on the stairs.

I was hot and a little tired from walking around the Expo. I washed my face and drank some water before going downstairs to the café on the ground floor. Outside, there was only one customer sitting at a café table.

It was Amit Mishra.

He rose from the chair when he saw me. He took a few steps toward me, then stopped. I stood still, not sure what to do. We seemed to be frozen in place, an invisible wall keeping us apart. And then...a voice, Mira's voice, whispered, *Sona, your life will be as big as you allow it to be.* I rubbed my sternum where her fingers had once drawn a circle. *I want big things for you, Sona,* she'd said. *You do too. It's all in here and out there. Go find it.*

I ran to him.

I put my arms around his neck, not caring who was watching or what they thought. I was in Paris, not Bombay. Here, I could do what I wanted, be what I wanted. And this was what I wanted. He wrapped his arms around me and squeezed. He released me long enough to place his lips on mine, not the fleeting kiss I'd given him the night of the Singh party, but a proper kiss. One that made the ache between my legs unbearable. I grabbed his hand and pulled him toward the entrance of Madame Renaud's building. Before we went inside, I pulled him back, cradled his face in my hands and kissed him again. I wanted his very breath to become mine. All the way up the stairwell, we stopped to caress and hug and press our mouths together. Only now did I understand why Madame Renaud had left in such a hurry. She wanted to give us the luxury of time. Once inside the apartment, I shrugged Amit's jacket off. He unbuttoned my blouse and unhooked my bra. He gathered my breast in one hand and sucked hard on my nipple. I groaned with pleasure, loudly. I unbuttoned his shirt, unzipped his pants, caressed his erection. The litter of clothes grew as we made our way to the bedroom. When we were skin to delicious skin, I clasped my arms around his neck and wrapped my legs around his torso. He licked his fingers and teased me where I was wet. When I begged him to enter me, the first thrust was painful, but the one after that and the one after that was glorious. Oh, how delicious it felt—as if he and I had been doing this with each other all our lives. He lowered me, still clinging to him, onto the bed. When our coupling left us breathing so hard I felt my lungs would rupture, it was much, much better than anything I'd imagined.

Mira had told me that life was for the taking. All I had to do was claim it.

I had.

"Surely, you didn't just follow me here to Paris?" I asked when my breathing returned to normal.

Amit pushed himself up on one elbow to look at me properly. He traced the underside of my breast and circled my nipple. I closed my eyes. "I was in Shimla longer than I expected. When my aunt recovered, I hurried back to Bombay and found you'd gone. But there was a letter from Dr. Stoddard telling me you'd taken him up on his offer, which, given what the board decided, made me glad. He wrote that Mira had sent you on a mission to Europe—and you'd probably be in Paris right about now." He laid a warm hand on my arm. "I heard about your mother. I'm so sorry, Sona."

I sighed and turned on my side to face him. "She surprised me, Amit. She said I lived too small a life. That I needed to leave her, that I should go see the world. I'd always thought I stayed because I needed to take care of her. I think it was more that

I was hiding. My mother wasn't the only one who saw that. I think Mira did too."

He moved his hand to my hip and stroked my leg. "She did. She told me once that she meant to take you out of yourself."

I thought of Mira in her hospital bed. "I miss her. Her stories. Her laugh." I traced his eyebrow with my finger. "What happened to your position at Wadia's?"

He took my hand and kissed my palm, making my groin tingle. I draped my leg over his thigh. "I made up my mind to resign when I was in Shimla. Then I received a most interesting offer. From one of the men I met at Dev's party. He invited me to a gathering with a man called Ambedkar." Amit's face was alight with excitement. "Have you heard of him?"

I nodded. "In the *Bombay Chronicle*."

Amit sat up to face me, gesturing enthusiastically with his arms, the way the college students did when they spoke of Indian independence. "Ambedkar's a Dalit. Whip smart. Because of his low caste, he might never have had the opportunity to become a lawyer were it not for support of the Maharaja of Baroda. Ambedkar may even end up writing India's constitution when we get independence. He's all for getting rid of the caste system."

I loved how animated Amit became, how passionate.

"I got so fired up at the gathering I asked how I could help. Well, the gentlemen I met at Dev's is putting together a global hygiene consortium to help poorer communities—many of whom come from lower castes. He asked me to join them. We're in Paris meeting for the first time. We're organizing and formulating a plan. It's important work, and it affords me a lot more respect than men like Holbrook will ever give me."

I tapped him on the nose. "You look like a boy on his first visit to a sweet shop."

He grinned. "And I want every *jalebi* I see! England has left us so poverty-stricken. But their departure gives us opportunity. Just think, Sona! We can design better health practices. Build roads and railways. Strengthen our economy instead of theirs. I want to help with that."

His enthusiasm made me feel it was possible, that it would happen as he said. I pulled him down to lie next to me again.

"It'll take time, Sona, but if we start now, we'll be ready."

I ran a finger along his earlobe. "How did you find me? Here, at Madame Renaud's?"

He placed his hand on my back, drawing my body to meet his. "You think you're the only one with connections to the wife of the ambassador?" He reached for my mouth again, making me forget what I was about to say.

My fingers brushed my lips where Amit's mouth had been. I smoothed the sheets, still warm from our bodies. I lay on my back, going over every lovely moment with him, sometimes smiling, sometimes sighing. Tomorrow, Amit would take the Night Ferry to London and the morning flight to Bombay the following day. I would be moving on to Florence. I marveled at my new life. How had I gone from a woman who took no chances to one who traipsed around the world, sleeping with men she wasn't married to?

By the time Madame Renaud returned, everything in the apartment was in order. As she took off her hat, she said, smiling, "Did you have a nice time, *chérie*?"

I kissed her powdered cheek. "You are a romantic, madame."

"So are you, mademoiselle." She laughed.

The next morning, Amit and I met at the Louvre. I told him I wanted to see the paintings Mira had talked about. In Cézanne's *Apples and Oranges* I saw the vibrant yellows and rusts of Mira's *Man in Abundance*. The look on the faces of *The Waiting* bore an uncanny resemblance to the subject of Manet's *A Bar at the Folies-Bergère*. Mira had captured the somber atmosphere of Gauguin's *When Will You Marry?* in her *The Acceptance*. As

I stood in front of these paintings, so full of color, I could feel Mira by my side, whispering in my ear what she most admired about them.

Afterward, we walked hand in hand to the Tuileries, looking down the elegant pathway to the Place de la Concorde. To our left, old men played boule, clapping when one of them bested the ball of another. To our right, men and women sat on lawn chairs listening to a violin concerto. Children chased each other among the horse chestnut trees. Amit stopped walking and turned to me. With a finger on my chin, he tilted my face up and leaned in to kiss me.

We peeked in the Jeu de Paume, a former tennis court that recently had been turned into an art museum with Picassos and Matisses and the female artists Josephine represented. In front of a colorful Léger, I smiled, remembering the painter with the battered nose at La Rotonde.

By the time we reached the Musée de l'Orangerie, where Monet's *Water Lilies* awaited us, we were famished. On Rue Saint-Honoré, we found a bistro with a table so small our knees touched. Amit ran his hand along the length of my thigh, sending lovely tremors up my spine. The waiter placed a potage of potato and an *omelette aux fines herbes* with *haricots verts* in front of me. I missed the strong spices of India, but I began to love the subtle seasoning of French food. The white wine, cool and crisp, went to my head. Amit was telling me he'd like to show me Notre Dame and Sainte-Chapelle, that he'd loved coming to Paris while he was studying in England, but all I could think about was that he would be leaving tonight. My body wanted as much of him as I could get. I pressed my lips together, trying to suppress my craving, wondering what Mira would say about my brazen desires.

Picking up his glass, he smiled back, puzzled. "What?"

"How far is your hotel?" I asked.

Amit raised his brows. He paid the bill and took my hand,

practically lifting me off my chair. We ran along the Seine, crossing the Pont Neuf to the left bank and arrived at his hotel. The receptionist glanced at me as Amit picked up his key. Had we been in India, he would have asked if we were married and told half a dozen relatives what we'd been up to the moment we left the foyer. This gentleman merely smiled and wished us *bonne journée.*

Amit had barely closed the door to his room when I placed a palm on his neck and brought him down on the bed with me.

I can't believe it's me either, Mira.

He pulled a few strands of hair from my face and tucked them behind my ear. "You have a freckle on your earlobe. I noticed it the first time we met."

"You did?" I lay on my stomach, my arms folded under my chin.

"I'd always wanted to see it close-up."

I chuckled. "Is it everything you imagined?"

"More."

I was sleepy and closed my eyes.

"Sona, my work will take me all over Asia during the coming year. Maybe longer." He paused. "I would love for you to come with me."

I opened my eyes and stared at him. That was impossible. Unmarried men and women didn't travel together.

"But we'd be traveling to areas that are primitive, unsanitary. I can't—it would be selfish of me—to ask you to take that risk."

I was wide-awake now, my heart unsteady. "Are you asking me to marry you?"

"I wish I could. But there's no way—not now. I would never put you in danger."

I glanced at the sheets, at Amit's naked chest, at the light filtering through the curtains. Did I want to marry Amit? I'd been so preoccupied with desire that I hadn't considered marriage. But he wasn't proposing, was he? He was giving me reasons why he couldn't. Besides, he was Indian, fighting for a free India. A casteless India. I was half Indian, half enemy. What would that coupling look like in the eyes of those who considered the English their oppressors? Gandhi. Bose. Sardar Patel. Bhagat Singh. Even women like Begum Hazrat Mahal. None of them were *half-half.*

Amit was still talking. "I can't ask you to wait." It sounded less like a statement, more like a question. He blinked, waiting for me to respond.

I wasn't about to repeat my mother's life. Sleeping with the enemy. Wasn't that what her family had thought? Wasn't that what everyone would think about us, Amit and me? What they had thought of Dr. Stoddard and his wife? Amit's work was meant to bring the world's attention to a serious problem. It was meant to be public. That meant *we* would be public. The two of us would be on display. People would judge not just his work but the choices he made in his private life. The results of his labor would be tarnished. *Blackie-White. Chee-Chee.* I didn't want to be responsible for ruining the good he could do for his country. My country too, although my claim felt tenuous.

There was so much I could say and so much I didn't want to. I turned my head to the other side of my pillow, away from him.

FLORENCE

CHAPTER 11

I arrived at Florence's Santa Maria Novella train station on a Monday. I'd slept the whole way from Paris. The conversation with Amit had left me drained. I hadn't been able to come up with the right response—if there was one. What if I'd said I would wait for him to complete his mission? Who knew how long it would take? How would India react to one of their own consorting with the other side?

I used to be able to do double shifts at the hospital without tiring. Now, I was as exhausted as I'd ever been, sitting on a train for thirteen hours. I'd saved money staying at Madame Renaud's but I still had to be careful. Skipping the expense of a sleeping compartment, I slept sitting up the entire trip to Florence. My neck was stiff. My legs felt like rubber. I had a headache.

As I stepped onto the train station platform, I was surprised by its pristine simplicity. Unlike the train stations in Prague and Paris, the architecture of SMN bordered on severe. The gleaming travertine floor with alternating bands of red and white marble looked as if no one had ever walked on it. Men and women passed through unadorned entrances and exits. Even the signage—*Uscita*, *Tabacchi*, *Giornali*—was a simple typeface. The New India Assurance Building in Bombay was similarly plain, built as it was from reinforced concrete, but at least it boasted bas relief sculptures of sari-clad women and turbaned men. The Florence train station was so spare it felt as if someone had forgotten to complete it.

A young boy in knickers called out headlines from the newspaper he was waving about. I slowed to look at the paper, *Corriere della Sera*. From the photo and a few words similar enough to French, I gathered that a woman had been fatally stabbed on a train and that she was involved with the resistance movement. Underground uprisings seemed to be everywhere—in Bombay, Prague, Paris and now Florence. Could Agnes have been a spy or a collaborator? I wouldn't be here long enough to find out. Once I found Paolo, I was going back to Bombay.

My stomach gurgled. I'd only had a cup of tea and toast on the train. The British Embassy was twenty-five minutes away by foot, but I couldn't muster the energy to walk there. I wanted simply to find a cheap pensione where I could drop off my trunk and then find someplace to eat.

Across the street from the station, the entire wall of a building was covered with a poster: *Credere, Obedire, Combattere*. In the center was a middle-aged man in a military uniform and shiny black boots, his mouth open as if he were making a speech, one arm extended. I recognized Mussolini from the newspapers. In Paris, café patrons had talked about him. *Did you hear he wants to join forces with Hitler?* The bottom of the poster read *Federazione dei Fasci di Combattimeno*. It didn't take a knowledge of Italian to understand the Fascist doctrine. As I had in the parts of Europe I'd seen so far, I felt a watchfulness among the people. As if everyone were looking over their shoulder for the enemy.

I waited for a tram and a horse carriage to pass before crossing the street. If I followed the Baedeker map along Via degli Avelli, I would be in a big piazza flanked by Santa Maria Novella church. It was a popular tourist area, so I hoped I could find a cheap hotel nearby.

In a narrow alley to my left, I spotted a pensione sign. I looked up at the narrow building. The contrast between the austere train station I'd just left and the Renaissance building in front of me was jarring. I followed the arrow to the top of the stairs, lugging my trunk, which seemed to get heavier with each city. The building smelled musty, like a chest that hadn't been opened in decades. At the top was a pitted wooden desk, empty except for a large ledger and what appeared to be a photo album (I could see a few photos peeking out that hadn't been glued yet). As if by magic, an old woman in a loose black dress emerged from a curtain behind the desk. She was wiping her hands on the apron tied at her waist.

"*Buongiorno*, signora," she said. Her eyes darted swiftly to my ring finger. She corrected herself. "Signorina."

One of the advantages of being a nurse in a hospital were the different nationalities we encountered. I'd been able to pick up a few pleasantries in several languages: *good day*, *hello*, *yes*, *no*, *excuse me*, *please*.

"Buongiorno. On parle français?"

She gave me a small smile and shrugged. Her eyes were the color of acorns. The wrinkles fanning from them were those of a woman who had lived a long life.

I held up one finger and made a gesture to indicate I was sleeping in a bed. She laughed, revealing a missing tooth along her upper gum. From what I could gather, she then asked me how many nights I intended to stay. I wondered how many days it would take to find Paolo. I had no idea, but I held up three fingers.

The woman nodded. She opened the ledger and turned it around to face me. In the list of names down the first column, I saw ones that appeared to be French, Spanish, Dutch and English. I was used to presenting my passport and visas everywhere by now, and I fished in my bag for them.

When she noticed my address, she asked, *"Dall'India?"*

I was writing my name in the ledger. *"Si."* I looked up and smiled at her.

"Péro…" She flipped a few pages in the ledger and pointed to a name: *Raji Murty.* Then she mimed putting on a sari by turning around and around and flinging a phantom *pallu* over her left shoulder. When she'd stopped, she pointed to my skirt. I burst into laughter when I realized she was asking me why I wasn't in a sari, like her former guest. The eyes of the old woman crinkled in amusement.

It was too difficult to explain why I had a British passport instead of an Indian one. I simply shrugged. She shrugged in return, then gave me a key and pointed down the hall and then up.

I pointed to my stomach and mimed eating food.

"Ah," she said. She pulled aside the curtain behind her to reveal a tiny dining room. There were three tables, one of which was occupied by a woman my age. She was eating.

The old woman rattled off something in Italian. The woman at the table looked up and saw me. She said in English, "Lunch is included. She's inviting you to sit at a table." She was an American.

I walked into the room to shake the diner's hand and introduce myself. Her handshake was limp. "Taylor," she said. She was eating what looked to be creamy rice. My mouth watered.

"I'll just get settled in and join you later." It was hard for me to contain my excitement at meeting a fellow traveler with whom I could speak English. Trying to communicate in languages other than my own was exhausting. I hurried along to the next floor and to my room. I knew it would be monastic, and the room did not disappoint. There was a cross on one wall with a single bed underneath it. The quilt was old but clean. There was a wooden chair against a table. What touched me was the single daisy that had been placed in a tiny vase on the table. It was something my mother would do—and had done on countless occasions. Like the time I'd passed my entrance to nursing school or when I'd sewn my first dress or when I won a medal in sixth form for the hundred-meter race. I was suddenly consumed by homesickness. For my mother. For her flowers. Her kindness.

"Hello, Mum," I whispered.

When I returned to the dining room, Taylor had disappeared, and the Signora was waiting to serve me a big bowl of bean soup with potatoes and tomatoes, greens of some sort, country bread and a generous helping of garlic cloves. My hostess grated a wedge of what looked like dry cheese into my bowl. The soup wasn't dal, but it was hearty and satisfying.

Dessert was an apple. The signora sat at the table across from me and sliced an apple. She offered me a slice, before taking one for herself. The apple was remarkably sweet, the kind we sometimes got in Bombay from the Himalayas. We ate in companionable silence.

The only lead I had for Paolo was that he had taught Mira at the Accademia di Belle Arti di Firenze, which was located on Via Ricasoli. With my Baedeker's in hand, I ventured out on foot. The air was warm, almost eighty degrees, weather I was used to in Bombay, and I was grateful for my half-sleeve linen shirt. Cyclists, horse-drawn carriages, automobiles and pedestrians vied for purchase on the cobblestone roads. Everywhere I turned, there was a poster with Mussolini's image. As much as I tried to ignore them, the words *credere*, *obediere*, *combattere* turned into an unsolicited mantra with each step I took.

I passed several bakeries, a butcher shop where a skinned pig hung from the ceiling and a café where the patrons stood at a bar sipping cappuccinos.

After a time, I stopped in front of an Italianate building (at least that's what my tenth form teacher Mrs. Norton, who was married to an architect, would have called it). The facade was a beautifully proportioned arcade. Two female students with satchels hanging from their shoulders and canvases under their arms entered the building through enormous wooden doors. I followed them, finding myself in a foyer of sorts.

To my left was a wide, quite beautiful, stone stairway leading to the upper floors. Directly in front of me was a rectangular courtyard, flanked by classrooms where students were painting or drawing or sculpting. To my right was an open window beyond which was a counter. A woman sat behind the counter with her back to me talking to a younger, quite pregnant woman who was sitting at a large table. The table was laid out with two plates of what looked like pillows of dough topped with a red sauce and a basket of bread. Steam rose from the plates. The two women were talking animatedly in Italian and I managed to catch the words for soup, olive oil and salt. An argument about cooking?

"*Buongiorno*, signora," I said, imitating my pensione landlady.

The woman turned around in her chair to face me. She looked to be about fifty. Her eyes were watery, but she wasn't crying. Her mouth was pursed but not in a flirtatious way; she seemed to have been born with that expression. She was wearing eyeglasses low on her nose. Now she lowered her chin so she could see me above the rim of the glasses. *"Si?"*

"Do you speak French or English, *per favore*?"

There was a pause, and I feared I might have insulted her somehow. After a few seconds, she said in French, "Madame, we have students from all over the world. We can speak in English if you wish."

I smiled. "Thank you. I'm looking for an instructor named Paolo."

"There is no one here by that name, *signora*."

"Perhaps he taught here a while ago?" I calculated swiftly. "Around 1924 or '25?"

She pushed the glasses up her nose, as if she were closing a door.

"Please, *signora*. I have traveled all the way from India to find him."

Something in her relented. Her forehead relaxed.

"Do you have a surname?"

I hesitated. What kind of fool arrives in a city without the full name of the person they're looking for? Why hadn't Mira made this easier? "He would have taught a young artist by the name of Mira Novak."

She said nothing, but I could tell by the lift of her eyebrows that something had registered.

The pregnant woman at the table snapped her fingers. In broken English, she said, "She speaks of that lothario! Paolo..." She batted the back of one hand against the other, as if she were willing her memory to cooperate. "Paolo, Paolo...beautiful face... Paolo Puccini!" She smiled triumphantly.

The woman at the counter shot furious Italian at her friend. Something about why she was interfering. Why wasn't she at home serving her husband? Her lunch companion wasn't offended. Instead, she laughed. If I understood her correctly, she said, "Why do you think I'm not there?"

The administrator turned to me again with a frown. "My niece! Coming to office so pregnant. Always eating. She is eating for three, we are told." She sighed. "But she is right. Unfortunately—or fortunately, Mr. Puccini no longer works here." She took off her glasses and splayed her hands.

"Do you know where I could find him?"

Once again, the pregnant woman spoke. I caught "Borgo San Frediano" in the long string of Italian words between the women.

My watery-eyed friend shrugged her shoulders and straightened some papers on the counter.

I waited. Finally, she said, "We have a very strict policy, you understand. Paolo became friendly with female students." She dropped her chin and lowered her voice. "Although the *ragazze* also were a little too friendly with him. In Paolo's case, it was Miss Novak—and *la mama*." She looked at me with resignation. "*Che fiasco!* This we could not tolerate."

The younger woman at the table whispered loudly, "The mama was *innamorata* with Paolo." She shook her head.

The older woman was watching my reaction. Seeing none, she said, "*Va bene*. You can find him..."

She turned to consult her friend, who repeated, "Borgo San Frediano."

The pregnant niece rubbed her enormous belly. "Everyone falls in love with Paolo. You did too, didn't you, Zia Maria?" she teased. I nodded to the women and turned to go.

I had barely walked two steps away from the window before the older woman began scolding her niece, something about how she should stay out of other people's business. The younger woman's laughter ricocheted around the stone walls of the school.

Borgo San Frediano was on the other side of the Arno. Tourists tended to stay on the Duomo side of the river so they could visit the cathedral, or the Uffizi Gallery. I had to cross the river to the south side by way of the Ponte Vecchio where I heard English being spoken everywhere. As I walked across the bridge, I found myself envying the English and American women, their flowing silk dresses and skirt suits, their wedge heels—which seemed to be all the rage here. I felt conspicuous in my nurse's uniform and sensible shoes. The *Inglese*, as they were called, were asking to see the heavy gold bracelets and necklaces on display at the shops along the bridge. And shopkeepers were only too happy to usher them into their stores—an espresso and almond biscotti at the ready. I wondered what it would be like to be as free with money as these women were.

I skirted around the shoppers and stepped up my pace.

Paolo's street turned out to be only two blocks long. I walked up and down the street hoping to find—what?—a sign for a painter? Or a painting tutor? I still didn't know Paolo's exact address. I would have to knock on doors. My heart thudded in my chest. I was confident within the walls of a hospital, but outside of it, my courage often faltered. I took a deep breath and knocked on the door to my right. No answer. I knocked on the next door. And the next. If someone answered, I asked, "Paolo Puccini?" After several shakes of the head, a man with a broom answered his door and pointed to the building opposite.

I knocked on the door he indicated. No answer. I turned to the man with the broom, who nodded and gestured with his hand that I should knock harder. I did.

"E adesso?"

The bellow had come from above. I staggered back several steps to look up at the second floor. The man with a paintbrush in his hand and an appropriately paint-stained white shirt must be Paolo. The pregnant woman at the Accademia had not been wrong; he was striking. Dark curls framed his face. His complexion was that of a betel nut—smooth, earthy brown. He wore his shirt open at the throat and his sleeves rolled up his forearms. He was the man in Mira's painting of the *Man in Abundance.*

"*Mi scusi*, signor." It was all I could manage before I relapsed into English. "I'm looking for Paolo Puccini, the painter."

"Why?" he asked in accented English.

I didn't want to shout Mira's name on the street or cause people to pull the curtains open on their windows. I looked around to see if the man with the broom was still watching. He was.

From above, I heard Paolo firing rapid Italian at the man, who tapped his chin with the back of his hand and disappeared into his building.

I sighed. "It would be easier if you could let me in or you could come down to talk to me."

"Do you want to commission a painting?"

"What? No."

"Well, I'm painting now."

"But I have something for you. It's important that I give it to you."

He examined me more closely. He hesitated. "Do you know Caffè Doney?"

"No."

He disappeared inside the room. When he came back to the window, he had a piece of paper in his hand. He blew on it before letting it float down to the ground in front of me.

"That's the address. I'll finish up here. Meet me at four o'clock there."

He disappeared inside the room again.

I picked up the paper. On it was scrawled, in black paint that was still wet, *No. 81 Via de' Tornabuoni*.

I had just enough time before meeting Paolo to go to the British Embassy, which, according to Baedeker's, was only a few blocks away. My pulse quickened; perhaps there would be a letter from Amit. I'd told him the British Embassy was the place he could reach me. Or perhaps there would be a message from Dr. Stoddard. I had not answered his last letter because I wasn't sure how to respond. His revelation—how he had deserted his fiancée—had changed something between us, at least in my mind. I had found him wanting, as I had found my father. Yes, there was the other half of him I loved, the half who had looked after me on the Viceroy, shown me unimaginable kindness. He'd taken such delight in teaching me gin rummy. Introduced me to port and caviar. Taught me to trust my instincts when it came to card games. He'd brought out a daring in me I hadn't known I possessed. And he'd connected Amit to me in Paris. How could I find half of someone agreeable and spurn the other half?

But…didn't I feel the same way about my mother sometimes? Loved the half of her who made me *nimbu pani* when I was sick? And secretly despised the part of her so blinded by love that she had made my existence shameful? I didn't want to love and hate in equal measure. I didn't want to be consumed by these ugly thoughts.

I didn't realize I'd been standing at the door to the British Embassy with my fists at my sides, my gaze fixed on the cobblestones below.

A woman was talking to me. I looked up. She was holding the door open, asking if I was coming in as well. I followed her inside.

A letter from Edward Stoddard was waiting for me. I read it as I walked back down the stairs.

Dear Miss Falstaff,

This envelope contains two letters. One from my father, who speaks of you often and always in affectionate terms. And this one, from me.

I hope you don't think me too forward to write to you directly for I feel as if I know you as well as Father does. He has told me about your mother in India and your father in England. Please don't be cross with him for that. I practically forced it out of him after I pestered him for details about you. (And now I hope you're not cross with me.)

When you return to Bombay, I hope you will do us the honor of gracing us with your company. As it happens, I have recently been posted to the British Embassy in Bombay and will be leaving within a fortnight. Father will accompany me. A blessing, since I have wanted to look after him. He has always been such a loving force in my life. After my mother died, despite his long hours at the hospital, he redoubled his efforts to spend time with me. We fished weekends with the Koli seafolk along the Bombay coast. We spent hours designing and building fighter kites to be entered into festivals. He arranged for the daughter of his closest friend to put a rakhi on my wrist because I didn't have sisters to wish me health and happiness. Nothing will give me more pleasure than showing him the kindness he has always shown me.

If at any point you require assistance, know that I am here to help. My offer (our offer?) of hosting you in Bombay at our humble abode will stand until you tell us otherwise.

Your friend,
Edward Stoddard

I walked out of the building and across the road to the stone wall beyond which the Arno flowed gently. I looked at the gray water below. My reflection was in shadow, but I knew my cheeks were flushed. First Amit and now Edward? What would my mother say about this turn of events? She, who wanted the best for me but felt Mohan was the best on offer. *I wish you were along on this ride, Mum. It's been full of lovely surprises!*

I looked inside the envelope and extracted the other letter.

My dear girl,

By the time you read this, you'll be in Florence. Promise me you'll take a gander at the Uffizi, especially the secret passageway leading all the way to the Pitti Palace. So many stories, so many assigna-

tions that corridor could tell! I've always thought it would be lovely to have secret corridors in hospitals where we could take refuge from needy patients or mourn a favorite patient who had just passed. Tell me you don't favor the idea even a little bit.

I didn't hear from you after my last letter. I realized you might bear a grudge (or, in my more hopeful moments, only a tiny grievance) at my callous desertion of Elizabeth, my fiancé. I assure you that my only intention in divulging such a private matter was to show you that my cowardice might be equal to that of your father's when it comes to making amends.

You have tremendous courage, my dear. You've held your own where many fatherless children haven't. You've undertaken an impossible task by the painter you so admire. You've ventured forth on your own. Many women—Indian or European—would never consider doing that. I have no doubt you will accomplish your goal. You are that determined (and that foolhardy if you'll pardon the old man in me). It's because of your pluck that I know you will be able to face your foe.

Did I tell you I looked for Elizabeth a few years ago? Age makes one reconsider one's decisions and atone for transgressions. I found she had never married. My fault, I suppose. I kept meaning to write a letter, apologizing for my unforgivable behavior, but I never did. Would it only have served me, released me from my guilt, or would it have helped her to know that I still thought about what I'd done all these years later? I suppose I'll never know since I was too much of a coward to send that letter.

Now it's your turn, dear Sona. I don't encourage you to see your father because it will help him feel better, but because it will help you feel better. Your resentment has no place to go until you talk to him.

Did you know military uniforms have buttons with a regiment number? Your father is wearing such a uniform in the photo you showed me. Edward did some digging and found the last known address of Owen Falstaff. I know you'll think me a nuisance for pushing the issue, but humor an old man, will you?

Give it another think. I hope you will. If you are in need of that address and/or of funds, please write to Edward. He would rather love to hear from you. He's talked of you often since you left. Godspeed.
In love and friendship,
R. S.

I folded the letters and stuffed them back in the envelope. The bells of the Duomo began ringing, reminding me that if I were to make it to the Caffè Doney to meet Paolo by four o'clock, I had to hurry. Crossing the Ponte Santa Trinita, I walked past an impressive brick building with a crenellated top. A small bronze plate beside the entrance read *Officina di Salvatore Ferragamo*. Ah, the shoe designer mentioned in Baedeker's. A small square in front of the building led to Via de' Tornabuoni.

The buildings on both sides of the street were a far cry from Paolo's humble—slightly run-down—studio. Standing solidly side by side were the palaces of the wealthy, palaces built five hundred years ago during the European Renaissance, according to the guidebook. On the ground floor were boutiques (there were men standing just inside the entrances to hold the doors open for clients) and cafés. The upper floors, with their long drapery, appeared to be residences. I passed a couturier where an elegant woman was pointing to a photo in a magazine. A few of my mother's clients—Englishwomen—had sometimes asked her to copy a dress featured in *Marie-Claire* or *Vogue*. As I passed the shoe store, I heard a customer say in English, "Oh, what Mr. Ferragamo could do if he weren't confined to those ugly Italian materials!" In the shop across the street, a saleswoman was showing fine lace to two women. Straight ahead was an enormous poster for an exhibition of Giotto, the painter whom Mira had drawn inspiration from.

Finally, I arrived at the Gran Caffè Doney, which Baedeker's touted as a favorite of expats, many of whom owned residences along this street. The café was so crowded that it was impossible to move around the tables and chairs without dislodging a lady's hat.

Inside, I looked for Paolo. He wasn't at any of the tables. While I waited next to the counter, I considered the pastries in the glass case, which lacked the hot oranges, pistachio greens and marigold yellows of Indian *mittai.* Here, there were jellies, petit fours, biscuits, all manner of biscotti and something labeled tiramisu, a word I tried out loud—quietly, of course. A generous coating of chocolate powder atop several layers of custard and wafer-thin pastry. My mouth watered.

I pried my eyes from the pastry bar and looked around again. A couple was leaving, and I made my way to the empty table with a view to the street. To my left was an old gentleman in a lightweight suit reading a paper. *Osservatore Romano.* There was a tiny coffee cup on his table. The waiter, in his black-and-white uniform, approached him, bent toward his ear and spoke in a low voice. The man looked up at the waiter. I could catch the gist of what he said. *I will read what I want… I'm not scared…don't need Fascists.* The waiter cleared his throat and went to stand behind the pastry counter.

I waited an hour for Paolo, nursing a cappuccino, which I decided I liked better than the other coffees I'd tried in Europe.

"Signorina?"

I looked up. If I hadn't been sitting, I might have swayed. Up close, Paolo was even more beautiful. A few errant curls from his dark hair fell across his forehead. And those sculpted lips! The bottom lip was a plump pillow with an indentation down the middle. His mouth was framed by a mustache and goatee.

On another man, it might have looked gauche, but he looked like a modern day Ali Baba. A straight nose, perfectly symmetrical. Eyes that made him seem at once sleepy and alert. Had he looked the same ten years ago, when Mira first met him?

"You have something for me?" He held a lit cigarette between his thumb and index finger.

I tried to stand up, but the area was too crowded, and I ended up in mid-bow, feeling foolish. "I'm…Sona Falstaff."

He nodded and sat down. He signaled to the waiter for two coffees.

"I nursed Miss Novak."

"Mira?" His voice went up an octave. "Is she alright? We haven't heard from her in weeks and we've been worried." He grasped my hands and leaned forward until our heads were almost touching. "Tell me she and the baby are okay."

He knew Mira had been pregnant? He suddenly seemed so overwrought that I felt the café was the wrong place to be having this discussion. Paolo must have seen the shock on my face. He ground his cigarette in the ashtray. "You'd better come up." He left a few coins on the table.

We walked less than twenty paces before arriving at the entry to a circular courtyard. Two cars were parked in front of the palazzo's doors, an Alfa Romeo and a Mercedes-Benz. Framing those doors were frescos of maidens watering flowers. Around us, ivy climbed the walls. There were four wooden mailboxes. Four apartments then.

Paolo held the lift door open and gestured for me to enter before him. We took an elevator up four flights.

"My wife will not appreciate your being here."

After all the stories of his womanizing, I was surprised to learn he had a wife. I frowned, wondering what I'd done to offend a woman I'd never met.

"Oh, it's not you. It has to do with any woman I look at. But she is at the cinema, so…"

The lift opened onto a grand apartment. He gestured to the white velvet sofa where I took a seat. There were two pale blue armchairs opposite. The coffee table was framed in tubular chrome, defying the old-world character of the room: tall ceilings and windows, plastered walls, elaborate moldings. I wondered who played the grand piano in the corner. Hanging from the ceiling in the middle of the room was a crystal chandelier.

Paolo was still standing. "Now tell me about Mira."

I thought I should get to it, like ripping off a bandage, quickly. "I'm sorry to bring you such sad news, Mr. Puccini. Miss Novak passed away several weeks ago."

Paolo stared at me. A crease formed between his brows. "What? How?"

"She was admitted to the hospital for a miscarriage."

He put a hand over his mouth. His eyes were wet. He made a sign of the cross. "The baby... How did it happen? How does a woman die of a miscarriage in 1937?"

The door to the lift opened. The woman who entered the apartment was in a simple black dress that hugged her curves. This must be Paolo's wife. She must have been a good ten years older than him. I'd seen it the other way around, with men decades older than their wives, but never with the man so much younger. If Paolo was in his forties, his wife must be in her fifties. Although she had kept her figure, her jawline was starting to soften and her ankles had thickened. She kept her eyebrows thin and her lips painted red.

Paolo was still standing in the middle of the living room, mute.

The woman took off her black slouch hat and considered her appearance in the baroque mirror above the sideboard. "Well, that was hideous. The film was nothing but propaganda." Her flat nasal tones, which I recognized as American from patients I'd met in India, was a stark contrast to Paolo's more melodic speech.

She removed her gloves one finger at a time and laid them on the sideboard. "This one was about food if you can believe it!" She mimicked an Italian voiceover. "Mussolini thinks that using poetry and music to awaken the flavors of food is the ticket." She laughed and slipped out of her high heels. "I was sure that Florence Foster Jenkins was going to invite us all back to her place to listen to her awful singing. I was lucky to get away!"

Finally, she turned toward the living room and noticed me. "Oh," she said, with a questioning glance at Paolo. Her voice was tight. "Who is this?" Her eyes darted from me to her husband.

Paolo seemed dazed. "This is the woman who took care of Mira. Miss Falstaff, this is my wife, Whitney."

Whitney frowned. "Took care of her…how?"

Paolo ran a thumbnail across his forehead and inspected the floor. "When Mira was in the hospital."

His wife narrowed her eyes. "Mira was in the hospital?"

I stood up calmly. I was familiar with her type, the kind of woman who could easily spiral into hysteria. "I was her nurse, ma'am. At Wadia Hospital in Bombay."

Whitney, who still hadn't moved from the sideboard, said, "Why?"

I was confused. "I work there, ma'am."

"No, you goose. Why was Mira there?"

I looked at Paolo. It was his duty to tell his wife. But he couldn't seem to take his eyes off the floor.

"Is someone going to tell me what's happened?" Whitney then looked at her husband. "Oh, my god. Has something happened to the baby? Paolo! Is the baby alright?"

I looked from one to the other. Mira had said something about Paolo after learning she'd lost the baby. How did Whitney figure into it? I was in the middle of something I didn't understand and didn't want to understand. My neck was getting hot, and I hoped they hadn't noticed the pink mottling around my throat.

Whitney stood with her mouth agape. She turned to her husband. "So there is to be no baby?"

Paolo looked at his wife, incredulous. "There is no more Mira. Mira's been stripped of her life. Think about that." Anger turned his skin darker.

His wife raised her tweezed eyebrows, incredulous. "But we were supposed to have a baby. We were supposed to get the baby. That was the bargain."

"But Mira—"

Whitney walked toward him. She pointed a pink fingernail at her chest. "I don't care about Mira. I never have. If we don't have a baby, we don't get this." She spread her arms wide. "We don't get the apartment. We don't get the monthly allowance. We don't get anything but what you make from your…paintings… such as they are."

Paolo's eyebrows drew together. "What does that mean?"

His wife waved her hand dismissively. "Oh, for God's sake, Paolo. You're copying old masters."

Paolo's nostrils flared. "Isn't that what you told me to do?"

"Because your other paintings don't sell, *caro*! I thought you were going to be one of those successful painters like de Chirico." She put a hand to her forehead. Paolo's jaw tensed. He opened his mouth to say something just as Whitney seemed to realize I was still in the room. She turned to face me. "Is there anything more you have to tell us?"

I thought of the painting in my bag, but I didn't think it wise to give it to him in front of his wife. "No. I should—I should go." I started to walk toward the front door. "Perhaps, Mr. Puccini, you could walk me out. It's getting dark."

"Of course." Was that relief I saw on his face? He would rather deal with his wife later, which I understood. We left before she could object.

In the elevator, Paolo reached for the packet of cigarettes in his shirt pocket. He tapped one out of the pack—it was labeled Nazionali—and reached for his vesta case for matches. "We even have to smoke Italian cigarettes because of him," he muttered. "They taste like cow piss."

I assumed he was talking about Mussolini.

When we crossed the courtyard to the street entrance, Paolo said. "Whitney's father owns this palazzo. He's American. Shipping magnate. He bought this building cheap from an Italian family who lost everything in the stock market crash. Then he divided the residence into four apartments, one of which we live in. He's never taken to me. Probably because I'm not the kind of person he wanted for his daughter." Paolo sighed. "He will let us stay in our apartment and Whitney will inherit the entire building upon his death but only if we give him a grandchild. Whitney and I can't have children. Which is why Mira was helping us out."

Under the streetlight, he watched me while I thought about what he'd said. So Mira was having a baby for the Puccinis? I supposed there were all sorts of arrangements for couples who wanted to adopt. This one shocked me, not only because I hadn't come across it before but because this one involved Mira, a woman who, by all accounts, hadn't wanted children.

When I could find my voice, I asked, "But how?"

"What do you mean?"

"Well, wouldn't her husband want to claim the baby? I mean he would think it was his, wouldn't he?"

Paolo sighed. He looked crestfallen.

"Look, can you meet me tomorrow? I will explain everything. Now is not the time. Whitney will think what she usually thinks if I spend too much time with another woman. I must go to her."

"Of course."

He rubbed his chin. "Mira and I used to meet at Cascine Park. It's—it's along the Arno…"

"I can find it." I could tell he was finding it hard to concentrate.

"There's a statue there of an Indian prince. I can meet you… at ten. That's when I'm supposed to be at my studio, working."

So his wife would suspect nothing. "I'll see you then." I didn't want to imagine the heated discussion that would follow upon Paolo's return to his apartment.

The next morning, I found the statue at Cascine Park on the other side of the Arno. The park ran over three miles along the length of the river. I walked through forests of maple trees, oaks, elms and pines. It was peaceful here, a few Florentines strolling among the meadows, talking quietly.

Paolo was late so I read the inscription on the statue, which stated that the Indian Prince Rajaram II was taken ill during his European tour and died in Florence. He was cremated, his ashes spread in the Arno, against the wishes of the Catholic Church, which did not want the remains of a heathen—even a royal one—polluting the river.

"Now you can see why Mira liked it here." I turned to find him pointing at the prince's effigy. "It reminded her of India, this statue. She admired the defiance of convention, which, if you know—knew—Mira, was what made her special. She didn't care for rules."

He was right. Mira would have appreciated the nod to disobedience just as she appreciated the way Indians were defying the British in their own quiet way. I regarded him as he surveyed the Arno. Paolo had understood Mira.

He was dressed in another white shirt splotched with paint, sleeves rolled up to his elbows (or was it the same shirt from the day before?). I tried not to stare at the dark hair on his forearms, so much like Amit's. I had the ridiculous urge to smooth the strands across his skin. A man and a woman passed us. Both turned around to smile at him. He even attracted the attention of men.

We walked along the gardens. "This is where Mira and I came

to sketch and paint. The only place her mother wouldn't intrude." He paused. "I cared about her deeply, you understand?"

That surprised me. Mira's friends had only spoken of her love of Paolo, not his feelings for her.

He stopped to face me. "I have no money of my own. I couldn't be with a woman who needed me to support her." His eyes implored me to understand.

"But Mira came from wealth," I said.

"Her parents were wealthy, but her mother cut Mira off as soon as she and I..."

Ah, the strange triangle between Mira, her mother and Paolo.

Paolo looked away. He pulled on his face with the flat of his palm. "It was complicated. Her mother was very persistent. She wanted an exclusive relationship—just her and me—which I did not. At the time." He glanced at me quickly to see if I'd caught the implication. I had. His habitual pattern was to fall in bed with one woman after another. When he met the one who could support him—Whitney—he married her. But I could see why his wife was still wary. With a gorgeous husband like him, she would have to keep an eye out for predators.

I was carrying the rolled-up painting of *Man in Abundance*. "Mira left this for you."

He took it from me. "I always liked this one. It was one of the first things I taught her, this brushwork of Cézanne's. When she learned it, she asked me to sit for her." His smile carried memories.

"Do you think your wife will let you hang it?"

He grinned. "I think this one will go in my studio."

"Mira also left paintings for Josephine Benoit in Paris, and for Petra Hitzig in Prague. Do any of those names sound familiar?"

"Yes, of course. She talked about them."

"I understand you two were in touch even after she married Filip Bartos?"

"Anytime she came to Italy, we saw each other. Mira was Mira.

She was fun. She was lively. I don't think she and Filip were suited to one another as a couple. She'd wanted to provoke her mother, as she always did, by marrying someone her mother didn't approve of. Mira was bored of Filip within a year of marriage."

We walked along the ornate stone fence surrounding the monument of the prince. Irises of every color bloomed around us. Daises and lilies and hyacinths lined the paths. I caught a whiff of sweet peas. On the other side of the river, Florence gave off an ochre glow. It was that light that reminded me of India. Or maybe it was the pace of the people. They seemed in less of a hurry, ready to make time for a friend or to merely watch people from a park bench.

I stopped to admire the peacock finials and bas-reliefs on the roof over the statue. It was the heat of his body more than his breath that told me Paolo had come to stand behind me. I turned around. He was so close our arms touched. Was I, in this moment, trying to live Mira's life? If Paolo weren't married, would I have made a play for him?

"If I'd ever fallen in love with a woman, it would have been her." He looked wistful. "And even now, I still hear her. Feel her. Smell her. She was so full of life. She wanted to experience it all. But she also wanted to experience it with everyone she came into contact with." He plucked a daisy and pulled at its petals. "You may think me a Romeo, but Mira was herself a Juliet. She experimented with everyone. To see what it was like." He laughed lightly.

I nodded. "By all accounts—Petra's, Josephine's—you were the one she cared about most. You were different." I paused. "You were a prize. She captured you when other women couldn't." I worried I was speaking too freely, but I couldn't stop. "Perhaps you were too much alike? Both of you so sure of how easily you could seduce. The power must have been intoxicating."

Paolo looked amused. "It was certainly exciting for her to come between her mother and me. Veena and I met at an art exhibition in Venice. She pursued me." He threw the now dismantled daisy on the ground. "Mira always wanted her mother's attention—any way she could get it. She saw that coming between us would get her noticed. It did. Her mother was furious and went back to Prague. Mira stayed, but she lost her inheritance."

He studied me for a moment. "Did she tell you about the first time she got pregnant?" Did I imagine the look of guilt on his face?

"The first time?"

"She ran to Prague and to Filip. He was her savior. If she got into trouble, he rescued her. Filip had a medical degree by then, but he never practiced. I've been wondering if that first operation—it was done at home, not in a hospital—had something to do with her miscarriage."

Mira had had an abortion years before the miscarriage? The news would have shocked me a month earlier, but now I considered it as a nurse. I'd seen the dangers of performing such a procedure at home when the women presented themselves at the hospital. Lack of sterilization, improper tools—any number of things could compromise the procedure. Poor Mira.

We began walking again, the pea gravel under our feet crunching with each step. I said, "I was put in charge of her for the evening shift. Her husband brought her in. Naturally, I assumed the baby was his."

"Well, Miss Falstaff, this may be difficult to understand, but I do want a baby with Whitney, and when she couldn't conceive, we decided together that I should approach Mira. She was only too happy to comply—we were paying her handsomely—but she said we must keep it from Filip for as long as possible. She wanted time to break it to him gently."

"By breaking it to him gently, do you mean…"

"Yes."

"That you were impregnating her?"

"Yes."

"And your wife agreed to that?"

He hesitated. "Not at first. But we had few options." He paused. "Mira and I spent a week in a hotel in Milan—away from Florence—"

"And your wife."

"*Certo.* Mira returned to India and we waited. A month later, she called with the news. Whitney and I were ecstatic. The pregnancy was progressing nicely. Mira was healthy. And the baby would look like me. If his skin was a little more olive, that would be fine. I am Italian after all. It would have been perfect." He sighed. "How exactly did Mira die?"

I hedged. "An overdose of morphine."

Paolo looked alarmed. "How?"

Oh, what was the use in keeping the truth at bay? "There was a vial of morphine left in the room. I was blamed for the oversight, but, Mr. Puccini, I swear to you I did not cause her death." I willed him to believe me.

His eyebrows knitted together. "So then, what could have happened?"

I debated whether I should share my suspicions. "I can speculate, but none of it is verifiable."

He pinched his nose. "Wait. How did she end up in the hospital in the first place? Mira was having my baby. I'd like to know. I'm going to have to explain it to Whitney anyway, and I may as well have all the facts."

I chose my words carefully. "Well, I'm not sure I know much more. Her husband said she'd been complaining of abdominal pain and a severe headache for a few days. She started bleeding but waited hours before she asked to be taken to the hospital. When she arrived, it was obvious she'd had a miscarriage, and she was in a lot of distress."

His forehead was lined with worry. "Did she suffer terribly?"

I hesitated. "She remained in considerable pain even after she lost the baby."

Paolo thought for a moment. He said, "Neither Mira nor Filip wanted children. She always said she wasn't going to have any."

"What changed her mind? Why did she say yes to you and your wife?"

Paolo rubbed his neck with his palm. "Well, the money we were giving her would have allowed her to paint for a whole year without selling one painting. Her paintings sold but there was never enough money once her parents cut her off. Filip didn't work, but he liked good clothes and wine and nice places to live."

Was Mira the kind of person to whom this would have seemed a reasonable bargain? If she were with me now, I would ask her if having a baby for her former lover's wife was worth the money? What about her dignity? Her pride? Or was I judging her too harshly as I'd done with Dr. Stoddard? As I'd done with her when she confided her regrets. She and Paolo and Petra and Josephine lived in a world so different from my own. With a different morality. How could I impose my beliefs on them?

Talking to her friends made me question how well I really knew Mira. There seemed to be many different Miras. I had known several versions of her. Mira the painter. Mira the patient. Mira the lover. As I had with Dr. Stoddard, I questioned whether we could know anyone completely. *Things are never as they seem*, Agnes had said. I kept having to learn that lesson again and again.

We walked from one end of Florence to the other; the city was surprisingly compact. Paolo revealed small details about Mira, laughing at her observations about the Italians. He took me to the Uffizi Gallery, where he insisted the best art in the world was displayed. Michelangelo, Botticelli, Giotto, da Vinci. With a wink to the guard, Paolo led me to the Vasari Corridor, the secret passageway the Medici family used to go to the Pitti Palace unobserved. Dr. Stoddard had urged me to see it. Paolo said it was Mira's favorite place for a hurried tryst, right between the Rembrandt and Velazquez. The soft pillows of his lips parted in a smile that was both joyful and sad. He was going to miss her.

She had loved him, and he had loved her, of that I was sure now. But love didn't mean a lifetime of togetherness, did it?

When I returned to my lodgings—so much more humble than Madame Renaud's—my hostess patted me on the shoulder. She seemed to sense I was troubled. And tired. She stretched an arm toward the curtain. I went through it and sat at the small scarred table. She brought a bowl of pasta and a hunk of dense bread. The pasta smelled heavenly. It was smothered in a light cream sauce with what I thought were mushrooms. She pointed to the pasta and said, *"Tartufi."*

"Tartufi?" I said.

"*Si*, *si*, signorina. *Tartufi*." She pointed again. She imitated pigs snorting, digging in the earth. I had no idea what she was trying to tell me, but her explanation made me laugh, which made her laugh too. Something in my chest loosened, and I felt good for the first time that day.

As I lay in my bed that night, I talked to my mother. *I did it, Mum. I did what Mira asked of me. I traveled thousands of miles to places I've never been, ate food I've never heard of, walked through cities and gardens and down alleys I wouldn't have ventured to find the three people she cared about most. At times, I was frightened out of my mind. At times, I was lonely. There were surprises, some of which delighted me (Edward, Amit), some of which scarred me (Agnes, the man in La Rotonde). It was like the Ferris wheel you took me on when I was six. The higher we went, the more the fear—and the thrill—gripped me. At the top, you pointed to the buildings and parks and lakes I'd only ever seen on a map. And when we got to the bottom, I wanted more than anything to go back up again. Well, I want to do that when I get back to Bombay. This time, I won't keep to myself. I'll let people see who I am, make an effort to learn who they are. I'll do things I haven't done before. Things you and I could have been doing all along. Like picnicking along the Queen's Necklace. Taking in an afternoon matinee at the Regal. Flying kites at Chowpatty Beach. I'm thinking of finding a private position, taking care of someone like Dr. Stoddard. I'm sure Edward, who is the kindest of men (you would love him, Mum!), will help me with that. And there's Amit. I'm sorry I kept my feelings for him from you. I just wanted some time alone with them. But I think you guessed them anyway. There wasn't much I could hide from you.*

I found myself smiling, picturing my mother as she listened to my plans.

Then, an image of Dr. Stoddard came unbidden. *Go see your father.*

But that was an impossible request! Why should I go see him? To me, he would always be a deserter and a philanderer. Ralph Stoddard thought my father hadn't had the courage to face me. Would going to England confirm that? What about his English family? How would they react when I showed up, claiming him as my father? Would they be shocked? Angry? Would they throw me out of their house, call me a liar or money-grubber or fantasist?

And if I didn't confront my father, would I be a coward too? Here I was in Europe, half a day from him, and I finally had the chance to tell him what I thought of him. Was I scared to do so? Or was I worried that when I came face-to-face with him, I would lose my resolve to pummel his chest and throw myself in his arms instead? I wanted to go on hating him. It was the one sure, steady thing in my life. I didn't want to let go of it. But who knew when I might return to Europe once I was back in Bombay? This was my chance. Should I take it?

Tomorrow, I planned to leave for India via Algiers by train and then by ship. I'd been to a travel agency. The woman there had helped me determine the least expensive route. I had just enough money left to pay for it. But something made me hesitate.

To go or not to go. It was the most important decision I'd had to make in my young life.

LONDON

CHAPTER 12

Owen Falstaff's house sat in a row of identical two-story houses, neat and compact, each with a glossy black front door, a brass door knocker and a gleaming black iron fence. They stood shoulder to shoulder like matchsticks in a matchbook. There were three steps from the sidewalk to the front door, sixteen from the sidewalk across the street, where I was standing. Yet, I couldn't seem to make the journey.

Before leaving Florence, I had sent a telegraph to Edward at the Bombay Embassy to ask for my father's address. He'd sent me the reply immediately, asking if I was in need of funds. I had bristled at the suggestion. I wasn't a charity case. I'd been frugal. I'd worked out with the woman at the travel agency that I could make it to England with the money I'd set aside for the trip back to Bombay. After that, my future was vague. I didn't have enough to get back home. I didn't know how I would manage, but I would figure that out as I went. I'd managed so far, hadn't I?

I may have hated my father, but I'd been curious about London as long as I could remember. Some things were the same as Bombay. Double-decker buses. Trams. Cyclists weaving in and out of traffic. Policemen in helmets and white gloves directing traffic in the middle of the street. Ice-cream vendors pushing their carts. Buildings with pediments, gothic turrets and columns similar to Victoria Terminus. But the skies were overcast, gray, and the absence of color made London grim. Instead of women in lime-green saris bent over long-whiskered *jharus*, here men in hats and jackets swept the streets. In London people didn't meander. They walked with purpose, as if they were each on a mission of great importance. No time to exchange pleasantries.

I wondered how long I'd been staring at my father's house. There was an intimidating quality, a blinding whiteness, to the Falstaff house that differed from the warmth and welcome of Indian homes—even the estate of the Singhs. A simple movement of my left foot, then right, then left would put me at the small landing in front of the door. I'd rehearsed the motion in my head. I watched a phantom version of myself mounting those steps, putting my hand on the knocker, lifting the ring and striking the brass plate. *Knock, knock, knock.*

From the corner of my eye, I spied a movement of the curtains in the window to my right. Without thinking, I turned in the opposite direction and walked as fast as I could to the end of the block. Out of breath, I stopped, bent forward and vomited into the gutter. My nose was running. I removed a handkerchief from my pocket and wiped my mouth and nose. Why couldn't I make myself knock on that door? I'd been so brave, braver than I could have imagined, to leave my home, my mother, my country. I'd crossed boundary after boundary to end up here, at the home of my father. And now I couldn't summon an iota of courage to come face-to-face with him?

The voice in my head said, *You've come this far. Go back and finish what you came to do. Stop being a milksop!*

I swallowed, cleared my throat. I turned around, startled by a small boy in muddy wool knickers who was staring at me. He carried a soccer ball in his arms. Had he seen me hurl my morning tea into the sewer grate? Shame made me avert my eyes.

This time, I crossed to the other side of the narrow street

and walked back to the house. 1059 Pinkney Lane. *I can do this. I deserve to do this. I've come so far. What will I say when I finally see my father after twenty years? Will I spit in his face? Will I slap his cheek? Will I cry and tell him how much I missed him and wanted him to come back home to us, to me?*

The front door of 1059 Pinkney Lane opened. I froze. A woman stood at the door, regarding me. She wore a navy dress patterned with white flowers and cinched at the waist with a white belt. Her high-heeled shoes matched her dress.

"Won't you come inside?" she said timidly.

I opened my mouth, then closed it shut. Was she talking to me? I felt as if I'd been caught doing something I shouldn't have. Like when Matron scolded a nurse for sneaking a cigarette on her break.

The woman at the door had kind eyes. She said, "Please."

I made myself walk toward her. Left leg up the first stair. Then the right. Then the left. Now I was standing three feet from her. My father's first wife.

Up close, I could see the wrinkles around the corners of her mouth and the grooves lining her forehead. Her cheeks and the tip of her nose were pink. She looked to be in her late forties, although I knew from my nursing experience that the fair skin of Englishwomen aged faster than that of Indian women.

For a moment, we stood, regarding one another. Her eyes studied my face. Perhaps she was looking for signs of her husband in my features. I didn't know. I thought I saw the slightest nod of her head, but I might have been imagining it.

She opened the door wider and smoothed her dress with her free hand. "I've made tea." She said it as if we had an arranged meeting.

Directly in front of me was a set of stairs that I assumed went to the second floor. To my right was a small drawing room. A sofa and two armchairs flanked a stone hearth. She closed the front door and indicated with a gesture that I might take a seat. Then she ducked her chin and excused herself to get the tea.

On the fireplace mantel were photographs in silver frames. One was of a man in a British army uniform, his beret at an angle over his right ear. He sported a small mustache. His high forehead and the hollows of his cheeks were so much like my own. It was a formal photo, the kind the military took. It must have been taken years after the one my mother kept, when he was a younger version of the man on the mantel. I could see the toll the years had taken on him.

I moved to the next photo. The same man, a little younger, stretched out on a sandy beach on his side, one arm supporting his head. He was wearing a T-shirt and knickers, smiling at the little girl in front of him. Her back was to the camera. She couldn't have been more than three years old, the same age I was when he left India. I could have been that girl. I felt a longing for him so intense my chest hurt. The girl had a bonnet on her head. A shirtless boy of five or six, his head resting on the man's legs, squinted at the photographer, whom I imagined was the woman who greeted me at the door. A clock on the mantel trilled the half hour.

"Brighton Beach."

I whirled around. She was setting the tea tray on the sofa table. "The children loved it there." She tucked her dress under her before sitting down. "So did Owen," she said as she poured a cup of tea for me. She held the cup and saucer up for me to take from her hands.

Was I dreaming all this? This woman, her invitation to take tea, the clock. It seemed like something I'd conjured.

I took the offering and perched on the edge of an armchair.

"I was afraid you would come someday." Her eyes avoided mine as she poured a cup for herself. "And half hoped you wouldn't." When she looked at me again, her eyes were shining with tears. "I didn't know about you and your mother." She looked away again. "Well, that's not entirely true. I knew there was something. His letters gradually grew more distant after he'd been in India awhile. I had to do something to bring him home again. I made up an excuse. I told him our son was out of control and needed his father. If Owen didn't come home, we'd have to send Alistair to military school. So Owen came home. To his family." She took a sip of her tea.

His family? What about my family? How dare he leave us with nothing when he seemed to be doing quite well here in London. The house, the neighborhood, the wedding ring his wife wore. For Rajat's birthday and mine, he could only spare a pittance? My cup rattled on the saucer. My hands were shaking with rage.

"He was different when he came back. Distant. He was happy to see the kids right enough. But with me… Well. We changed houses. Thought a new environment would help. Eventually, we got back to things. The kids' schooling. Lucy's dance classes. Alistair's cricket."

She set her cup on the tea table and smoothed her dress with her palms.

"Then one day, I found the drafts from the bank. And a photo of two children. A baby and a girl of about two, whom I imagine was you. At first, I was in denial. Then, I was consumed with hate. For him. For your mother. I burned his clothes, his books, all his military papers. I saved nothing for my children. How could he have deceived not only me but his children? Why couldn't he love them enough to stop himself from…"

I couldn't bear to hear her go on any longer. My tea had gone cold. I stood up and set the cup on the table. My hands curled into fists. "Where is he?"

She looked at the photo of him on the mantel, the older Owen. "He died seven years ago. Cancer."

The *dhobis* in India slap wet clothes on rocks—*thwak!*—to loosen the dirt on them. That's the sound I heard in my head when my father's wife told me he was dead. Died the year of my sixteenth birthday. All those years of hating him. And for what? I wasn't going to be able to call him a coward. Nor would I ever get an apology. "But I've been receiving letters from him for twenty years."

She touched the collar of her dress. "When I found the drafts and realized he had been sending you money, I was furious. That was money my children could have used."

My father's wife dabbed her lips with a napkin. "Then I held you in my hands. The photo. It must have cost Owen a lot of money to pay for it. On the back were your names. Sona. Rajat. You existed. I couldn't hide from you any longer. No baby deserves to be deserted. I thought about all the years you two had missed out on a father. I told myself your mother had probably found someone else and married. Perhaps you did have a father after all. But the more I thought about it, I knew that was another lie I was telling myself."

Her eyes filled. Her voice trembled. "I thought about my own children. How they would feel if they'd grown up without Owen. Even if we'd divorced and I'd remarried, they would have known their father deserted them. They're older than you. They would have remembered. And perhaps hated him and longed for him at the same time." She played with the wedding ring on her finger. "I think I finally understood how you must have felt." She directed a wet gaze at me. "You're here now because you wanted to tell him what a heel he was. And also to see if he still cared about you. That's what I wanted when he came home from India. To know if he still cared about us." Her tears were creating a wet blotch on her dress.

Her gaze went to the framed photos on the mantel. "He should never have taken on another family. Of course, he knew that. It's the sensible thing, the right thing. But that wouldn't be fair to you, would it? You exist because of him. You are a part of him." She was quiet. She fished out a handkerchief and wiped her eyes and nose.

I did understand. But that sludge of resentment sat heavy in my stomach. Now, not only did I hate him, I hated her. She kept him from us, my mother and me and my brother. She *knew* we existed—or at least some version of us—and she made him choose. As if it was a choice. They were his first family. He was only on loan to us.

In Dr. Stoddard's case, there had been no first family in England to claim him when he fell in love with Deva. Breaking off with his fiancée had been as easy as a handwritten letter. The obligation to return home hadn't taken precedence. Was that how my father had made his decision? The first family, the one he'd committed to long before he met my mother, was the one he had a greater obligation to be with. In some way, he was honoring a long-standing code, same as he would have honored a military code. Did that make it easier for me to understand his leaving?

"If my father is dead, then who has been sending those letters?" Surely, it couldn't have been my mother, trying to spare my feelings? Mum's look of shame when she admitted keeping the letters from me suggested otherwise. She believed my father had sent them.

"I have." She wiped her eyes again. Her mascara left a smudge under each eyelid. "The last few years, I realized you might need more. You were probably going to school or studying for a profession and would need it."

I swallowed. I may have been angry with my father, but his wife had tried to atone for his mistake. She had no obligation to. Should I be grateful to her? Thank her? But did a few pounds a year make up for her deception in all this? The fact that she had lied to get her husband back? For her, it hadn't been atonement but guilt. No, I would not thank her.

"My brother was a year and a half younger than me. He died

after your husband left." I wanted to see her reaction, for her to feel the pain I felt whenever I thought of Rajat.

"Oh," she said, the tears coming faster now. "I'm so sorry."

I turned to the photos on the mantel. A young man wearing a dark robe and a mortarboard had his arm around a young woman. Both were grinning at the camera. I could see the resemblance in their faces. It was like looking in my mirror.

"That's Alistair's graduation from Imperial College. Lucy was eighteen at the time. Of course, that was a few years ago. Alistair is twenty-eight now. Lucy is a year younger. She has a daughter. My granddaughter."

I heard her voice behind me, but it sounded far away. All I could think was that these were my father's children. Which meant they were my siblings. *I had siblings.* I had a half brother and a half sister. And I was their half sister. I almost laughed. Would everything be a *half-half* in my world for the rest of my life?

Her hand on my shoulder made me jump.

"I—I'm sorry." She pulled her hand away. "I wondered if you might want to meet them someday. They have an aunt and an uncle but all their grandparents are gone. No cousins. It might be good to…"

Meet my half-siblings? Was that something I wanted to do? "Do they know about me?"

She walked back to the sofa and sat, her hands in a prayer pose, her fingers on her lips. "I told them when I found those things about you and your mother after Owen died."

"How did they react?" I almost didn't want to know. What if they hated me on principle? Someone with whom they had had to share their father's affections. I'd been rejected by him. Could I stand to have another rejection in my life?

She sighed. "It took them some time. Alistair was angry. Lucy was confused. But that was seven years ago. I think it would be different now. You were an idea then. You're real now."

Had this been a wasted trip? I didn't know yet. I hadn't had the chance to throw my pain in my father's face. Which had been the whole point of this journey, hadn't it?

I realized I knew nothing about my father's wife except her role in dividing our families. "What's your name?"

She smiled for the first time. "It's Marion, Sona. My name is Marion."

"I'll let you know, Marion."

I walked out.

The Falstaff home was at the north end of Chelsea. I walked from there to St. James's Park. I needed to think. What would be the harm in meeting a brother and sister who had been there all along? Would meeting them mean I'd forgiven my father, forgiven them for keeping him from me?

I wove my way through tourists eager to catch the changing of the guards at Buckingham Palace. I barely noticed where I was, so engrossed was I in my thoughts. I'd be lying if I said I didn't have a certain curiosity about Alistair and Lucy. Had they inherited mannerisms from their father that I'd inherited too? Was it in our gestures? Was it in our speech? What about our differences? Our English, for one. Their accent would be different from mine. Our clothes? They would certainly be better turned out than me. Would that separate us, divide us so that we couldn't be part of the same family?

I wound around Piccadilly Circus, watching the swirl of cars, trucks and double-decker buses, Wrigleys Gum, Schweppes Tonic Water, Ryman's Insurance advertisements on their sides. A glowing Guinness Is Good For You sign loomed over the circle. Leaflets announcing the coronation of George VI and Elizabeth pressed up against the edges of the sidewalks, wrapped themselves around the streetlights. They littered the steps of the Statue of Eros.

Staying in London to meet my half-siblings would require

a few days at a hostel, which meant spending more money. I didn't even know where Alistair and Lucy lived. Would meeting them mean a trip outside of London? Marion said she had a granddaughter. So that meant I had a niece? I'd always wanted an extended family, the kind Rebecca and Indira had. Could I handle coming out of the cocoon my mother and I had built for ourselves and allow more family into my life?

I wandered to Trafalgar Square. Two policemen escorted a drunken protester away from traffic. I knew I'd reached Covent Garden when I started seeing marquees for shows: *The Tales of Hoffmann*, Puccini's *Turandot*. On impulse, I bought a ticket for the afternoon performance of *Tristan Und Isolde*. I didn't have the right clothes nor the money to buy them. I'd never even been to an opera before, but I knew it was the kind of thing my mother or Mira or Amit would have wanted to see. Besides, it would take my mind off the endless merry-go-round of questions crowding my brain.

By the time I left the theater, I'd made up my mind.

I found the General Post Office and sent a telegraph to Dr. Stoddard via Edward.

It's your turn, I wrote.

In St. James's Park, the scorching heat had men fanning their hats in front of their faces and women waving their skirts around their knees. From my bench, I heard men and women around me complain about the record-breaking temperatures. "It's barely June!" I smiled, wondering what they would make of Bombay temperatures—and the crushing humidity. Bees shopped hyacinths for the sweetest nectar. Bluebells crowded under the trees, giving off a fresh green scent. I let my head settle on the back of the bench, my face turned toward the sun, and listened to children imploring their parents for an ice lolly. "Mummy, I'm melting!"

I smelled Dr. Stoddard's lavender-oakmoss-vanilla shaving

cream as he approached my bench. My eyes still closed, I asked. "How did it go?"

"About as well as you would imagine. No, worse."

I opened my eyes and squinted up at him.

Ralph Stoddard sat down heavily, leaning on his cane to steady himself. He looked as tired as I'd ever seen him. There were gray bags under his eyes. Liver spots on his forehead. Red splotches on his cheeks from the sun. His lean frame seemed to have no fat left on it at all. He rubbed his leg, the one he'd broken. "She said she'd often wondered what she'd say if I ever came back." He turned his head to regard me. "She said what hurt her the most was that I'd married a black woman and had a black child."

The doctor paused. He knew I'd been called Blackie-White just as his son had. And most Britishers would have referred to his Indian wife as black. It was another way of dividing people, separating those who belonged from those who didn't.

"What did you say?"

"I bid her a good day."

I blinked. "And?"

"And I came here." He removed his hat to wave a fly away from my shoulder. "Who is the patron saint of lost causes, my dear?"

I frowned, thinking. "Saint Jude, I think?"

"We must go pay him a visit when we return to Bombay."

That coaxed a smile from me. Dr. Stoddard had taken a flight from Istanbul as soon as he received my telegram. Edward was leaving for his new post in Bombay, and if I hadn't caught his father in time, he'd be on the same flight.

"I had a postcard from Mishra a few weeks ago. From Paris." He was looking at three young women in sleeveless blouses walking past and laughing at something one of them had said. "Wondered if you ran into him."

I avoided his eyes. "Paris is a big city."

The doctor took a moment. He nodded. "Quite so."

"Do you feel better? About Elizabeth?"

"Let's see… I feel better about leaving her all those years ago. But I do not feel better about her," he said dryly. Then he used his cane to stand upright and offered me his arm. "Shall we go home, my dear?"

BOMBAY

CHAPTER 13

Bombay
June 1937

Filip Bartos was handsome in the way men are when they wear the right clothes and Brylcreem their hair. But the man who answered the door was different from the Filip Bartos I had seen twice at Wadia Hospital and at the Singh party. This one looked like a man haunted. The hollows under his eyes told me he hadn't been sleeping well. He'd been clean-shaven when I'd last seen him at the hospital after Mira's death. Now he was scratching three days of stubble on his chin.

When he saw me at his threshold, recognition flickered in his eyes.

"You're the nurse."

"Sona Falstaff."

His smile was faint. "Mira liked you. She felt she could talk to you about anything."

I couldn't speak for a moment. "May I come in, Mr. Bartos?"

"Of course, of course! Apologies!" He moved out of the way quickly, as if he had awoken from a trance. He wore a shirt that had probably been white a week ago. His eyes were bloodshot and his hair needed a good washing.

* * *

Six weeks had passed since Mira's death. Yet, the apartment was still mourning her. There were coffee cups on tables and chairs—some empty, some half-full, the coffee long gone cold. Men's shirts, trousers and socks lay on the floor or on the sofa. The air was stale, the heat in the room oppressive. Outside, it was a sweltering ninety degrees, the humidity high enough to water houseplants. The collar of my blouse was already damp. I fought the urge to open the windows and start the fan; it wasn't my house.

I sat at the edge of an armchair. Not for the first time did I ask myself what I hoped to achieve. Was I here to have him relieve me of the weight I'd been carrying around since Mira's death? How much of what I'd learned about her in the past several weeks should I share with her husband?

Filip's cheeks were hollow, which concerned the nurse in me. "Have you eaten lately, Mr. Bartos?"

He waved an open arm about the living room. "Yes. Don't worry." He took a seat on the sofa. "I'm sorry I have run out of coffee."

"Please don't trouble yourself."

We sat for a few minutes in silence. I waited. Eventually, he asked, "How may I assist?"

I touched my hat, a maroon beret, which matched my summer dress. I'd bought it upon my return to Bombay. "I'm here because of Miss Novak." I paused. "I didn't have a chance to tell you how sorry I am. I couldn't face you after..." I swallowed, my mouth suddenly dry. "I miss her terribly. I think about her all the time, as I imagine you do. You may know that after she died, the Matron of Wadia's let me go. The board seemed to think I'd overdosed your wife with morphine. But I want you to know I hadn't anything to do with that. I would never ever have hurt Miss Novak." I realized I was leaning toward him from across the coffee table, trying to reach him through his haze of misery.

He stared at me blankly.

I continued, "For the few days I knew her, she and I talked as if we'd known each other forever. Like we were sisters. She was so worldly, something I was in awe of—and envious of. I loved the way she seemed to move through life." I stopped. "I need you to believe that harming Mira was not something I was capable of, even by accident." I'd intended to sound confident, self-assured. Instead, I sounded desperate.

Filip sat up straighter. "I do believe you. You're not at fault. I am."

I blinked. "What?"

"I administered Mira's extra dose."

"Of morphine?" My hand went to my chest. My heart began hammering my ribs. All this time I'd avoided him because I was convinced he assumed I was guilty!

He nodded. "She begged me to give her more. She was in so much pain. I couldn't bear it."

My breathing became shallow. He was confessing to a crime. My voice was a whisper. "You caused her to die?"

He sighed. "No, not intentionally. It's— I didn't know—" He stood.

He started pacing with his hands clamped on top of his head. He turned to look at me. "I didn't know she was pregnant, Miss Falstaff. I couldn't see... Anyway, she didn't want me to know. I didn't know until the miscarriage. If I'd known, I wouldn't have—let her—get pregnant."

No one I'd met in Europe, including her best friend Petra, would dare tell Mira what to do.

"She had been with many men and women, Miss Falstaff. I hope that doesn't come as a shock."

"It doesn't."

"It's an arrangement and it works—worked—for us. I was

very fond of her and she of me." He paused. "She knew I would be there for her no matter what. But there is one person whom she kept going back to. He's an old tutor of hers in Florence. Paolo. Perhaps she talked of him. She was his pupil...in many ways. Her painting improved under his tutelage. But when she began an affair with him right under her mother's nose, it created no end of misery. Paolo was trouble. He encouraged it. He drove a wedge between Mira and her mother. He lied to Mira over and over. He was going to take care of her forever. He loved her so much that he would move anywhere with her. He didn't. She stopped painting altogether. She couldn't function. Then she got pregnant. He didn't want anything to do with it. She came to me and asked me to take care of her. I did." He looked at me and shrugged. "I have a medical degree. But there was a complication."

My mind was reeling. Paolo talked about the first time Mira was pregnant, but he never mentioned it was his baby. Filip was saying it was. Paolo didn't tell me that he'd promised Mira a life with him when he'd clearly had no intention of doing do. Mira had lied. Paolo had lied. Filip had lied by omission.

"She promised she would be more careful. Earlier this year, when she went to Milan for a week and told me it was to see an exhibition, I believed her. She didn't tell me she was going there to see Paolo. She knew I wouldn't approve. It was when we came to the hospital and she was bleeding that she told me. I was taken aback. I wanted to shout at her, ask her what she was thinking. After what happened the first time, it was dangerous for her to get pregnant. She said she was doing it for the money they were going to give her. She would never have become pregnant otherwise. We had money issues ever since her break with Josephine, but we always managed."

Another thing Mira never talked about with me: money. She told me stories of which painting had gone to which buyer, sometimes imitating their big bellies or their affected pince-nez.

It wasn't until Amit and I overheard her at the Singhs' party that I realized she was struggling. Both Petra and Jo told me they had loaned her money they never expected to get back.

Filip sat, resting his elbows on his thighs, staring at the rug under his feet. "When you started taking care of her at the hospital and she miscarried, she should have started to recover quickly. She was on morphine for the pain—which helped. But gradually, her pain came back. I suspected she was underplaying the pain because she wanted to be home and get back to her painting. I told Dr. Holbrook, but he said she might be suffering from gastritis or referral pain. He put her on more morphine.

"That last day, after you left the room and I came to visit her, she was having difficulty breathing. She said she was going to die. I told her that was ridiculous. She was in a hospital and the doctors were taking care of her. For a while, her breathing returned to normal, and she relaxed. But then she had a painful spasm in her abdomen and begged for more morphine.

"At first, I resisted. But seeing her in so much pain was unbearable for me. So I took the empty syringe by her bedside and injected her with more morphine." He looked at me helplessly. "I didn't know you'd just given her a dose before leaving the room." Tears clumped his lashes. He hung his head and let them spill onto the carpet.

"Did I—did I leave the morphine in plain sight?" I had to know. I'd been so sure I hadn't.

"No." He glanced at me, coloring. "I'd heard nurses joking about your pharmacy. The man in charge wasn't there, so I helped myself. I'm—I'm sorry."

I sat, stupefied. Mira had died because of an oversight and not one of my own making. I should have been relieved. Instead, I felt hollow. And I felt sorry for Filip Bartos, who would carry his guilt with him for the rest of his life. I knew that I wouldn't tell Amit or Matron about what Filip had just told me. I knew Mira would not have wanted it. He was her savior, as Paolo had put it. Josephine, Petra and Paolo only knew what she chose to tell them. And I only knew what she chose to tell me. With Petra, she'd made me think they had a deep friendship when Mira had rejected her at every turn. Mira made Josephine sound like her devoted art dealer when Jo had fired her years ago. She glorified Paolo when he'd disappointed her in every way possible. Filip was one person she'd never made up a story about. He was her security. She depended on him.

Somehow, even after all I'd learned about her in Europe—the betrayals, the slights, the lies, the abuses—I could only see Mira as the girl who loved art and books and music and painted things greater than herself, than all of us. She was not as sure of herself as I'd thought, as I'd wanted to think. I needed a heroine, and she became mine. In reality, she was starved for a mother to love her, for someone to say they cared about her, not just her talent. Filip filled the hole in her life she was so desperate to hide from everyone. He saw her, all of her. And he hadn't flinched.

Across from me, Filip wiped his eyes on his sleeve.

I took a deep breath. "Did you know she sent me to Europe to deliver paintings to Paolo and Petra and to Josephine Benoit, her art dealer?"

He shook his head. "No, but I know why. You put her on a pedestal, she said. She encouraged it, that much is true. But deep down, she wished you would open your eyes. To know that everything was not how it seemed, that people weren't who they said they were. She knew you'd lived a sheltered life, Miss Falstaff. She also knew you needed to leave that shelter. This was her way of helping you."

I was so surprised that I couldn't speak for a moment. "When did she tell you all this?"

"After her second day at the hospital." He rubbed his hands together. "I know how it seemed, Miss Falstaff. I'm a man who keeps to himself. Mira needed someone to talk to, someone she could trust. You were that someone."

What a surprise to learn that Mira had talked to him about me. I cleared my throat. "I've brought the painting she gave to me. I don't feel right keeping it." I handed him *The Acceptance.* I'd had it framed.

He barely glanced at the painting before handing it back to me. "Mira wanted you to have it, Miss Falstaff. I hope it brings you happy memories of her."

Mira had even told Filip about the painting. She trusted him with everything. All this time, I'd assumed she and he lived separate lives.

I stood. He did too. I shook his hand, the way Agnes had shaken mine on the Arlberg Orient Express.

His grip was firm, dry.

I left. I never saw Filip Bartos again.

CHAPTER 14

Bombay
1956

I watch my daughter's arms undulate like the wings of a swan. She is one of twelve dancers, women and men, who are part of the Uday Shankar Dance Troupe. The Royal Opera House is full and, thankfully, air-conditioned. Indira has loved dance since she was three years old, often making up her own routines for songs she heard on the radio. She's going on tour with them to Europe and then on to America. I would have preferred her to study for a degree but being selected for an esteemed dance company is a remarkable achievement. Who knows? She may return to college at a later date. Or maybe never.

Still, I'm nervous about her going, a girl of eighteen. Then I remind myself, didn't I travel through Europe—alone—at twenty-three? I'd had no idea what I was doing, which was probably a blessing. At least Indira will be traveling with a group. But I worry. What if someone steals her money as Agnes stole mine? What if she falls for someone like Mira fell for Paolo? What if she's attacked by a stranger as I was in Paris? Fear for her makes my palms sweat. I force myself to concentrate on the stage.

The performance is somewhere between ballet and classical

Bharatanatyam. There are twelve dancers, six of them women of various ages. I hope the older ones will look out for Indira. I remember the kindness of Madame Renaud, the French ambassador's wife, even Pavel and Martina in Prague, and of course Dr. Stoddard. Each gave me the courage to move on to the next stage of my journey.

Edward puts his hand on my arm, letting me know it's intermission. I'd been deaf to the clapping. All these years later, I love these simple gestures of his. I cover his hand with mine and smile at him. He's going out to the lobby to stretch his limbs. He was the biggest chance I took. Not the steamship voyage to Istanbul. Not the train trips around Europe. Not the haphazard way I went about looking for Mira's friends, wandering alone through the streets, not sure what I would find. Not the trip to my father's house in London.

And not Amit. I learned he never made it back to Bombay. His employer sent him to Burma to conduct hygiene studies among cholera patients. He wrote to me through the British Embassy in Bombay to tell me he missed me terribly and would be there for at least two years, building a team to do the work. By then, Indira was already growing inside me, and I didn't want to force Amit to marry me—as I'm sure he would have offered to do. I'd already decided the day we parted in Paris that our union would do more harm to his work than it would help him. But the care we had taken that night in Paris to avoid conception had failed. Three months later, when I realized I was pregnant, I hadn't despaired. He'd given me Indira.

Amit's work would take him from Burma to Bengal to Nepal to Afghanistan to Geneva to London. Perhaps one day he would settle in India again. Perhaps one day I would tell him about Indira. Or keep her to myself.

Leading up to Independence Day, so many Anglo-Indians like me left India. Had they decided their identity lay with the other or did their English families claim them? By the time I returned from Europe, I was excited to claim India as mine. I wanted to join the marches, wave placards, shout from the rooftops that India deserved her freedom. I would roll the bandages, organize the work, bring cheer to those on the front lines. Edward understood. He and I were more alike than Amit and I were. For us, there had always been a choice. And we'd chosen India.

When Dr. Stoddard arrived in London, I was down to my last pound. He came with me to meet Lucy and Alistair, my half-siblings. I don't know if I could have done that without him. He bought our plane tickets to Bombay. It was my first time on a plane, and I held on to his hand during the entire journey. It was something I'd always imagined I'd do with my father—hold on to his hand on the Ferris wheel or on the walks to school. All my life I'd been looking for my father to hold my hand only to find that the hand belonged to Ralph Stoddard.

Edward was waiting for us at the Bombay airport when we arrived. I was surprised at my reaction, how excited I was to see him. I remembered Agnes telling me, *That's quite the handsome young man you have.* I'd said he wasn't mine, but what would happen if he were, I wondered. Goose bumps traveled down my arms. Within a month, he'd proposed. If he ever wondered why Indira came early, he never brought it up.

Mira sent me on that journey to take chances. It's what my mother wanted for me too. And it's what I want for my daughter. How my mother would have loved her granddaughter! Indira is fearless. She believes she is capable of conquering the world. She charges into the unknown, places I was too scared to go at her age. When she falls, she gets back up and tries again or moves on.

I had considered naming my daughter Mira. But the painter had already lived a life full of music and art and love and play and outrage and laughter and wins small and large. Indira, Balbir's wife, hadn't. I wanted to give Indira the life she didn't and couldn't have. So I named my daughter after my old friend. I never saw Indira after her last day at Wadia's, but when I look at my daughter—brave and daring and spirited—I imagine my friend smiling at her.

Until I took that trip to Europe, I hadn't given my mother credit for being the risk-taker she was. She gave up her own family for a man whom she loved desperately. She'd taken a leap, and when he couldn't fulfill his promises, she hadn't regretted the chancing. I haven't forgiven him yet, but I keep trying.

Twice, we've visited Alistair and Lucy in England. We send letters back and forth and share photos. Lucy's family visited us in India about five years ago, and we traveled with them to the Ajanta Caves, New Delhi and Shimla, places where Mira loved to paint. Indira is a few years younger than Lucy's daughter, Ellie. They write to each other, and they're looking forward to seeing each other when Indira's dance troupe performs in London.

It's such a comfort to me that my daughter had a chance to know her grandfather, Ralph (I could never get used to calling him that, so I just addressed him as Doctor, which Edward and Indira teased me about no end). He took my girl to the Hanging Gardens to catch fireflies, read to her from *Tales of Krishna*, showed her his photo albums to tell her about her grandmother, Deva. Indira only knew Ralph Stoddard for the first five years of her life, but I know he'll be in her memories always, as he is in mine.

The lights are flickering in the theater, which means intermission is over. Edward takes his seat next to mine, puts his hand on my knee and smiles fondly at me.

He's been much happier since leaving the British Embassy. When it seemed the British were making a hash of the handover to India, he was disheartened and confused. Here he was, half British and half Indian, like me. He felt, as I did, that he could do more good helping Indians rebuild a country that had been left depleted and wanting. He found work with an organization that was moving India's dependency on British goods to those produced in India. Sometimes, when I catch him in profile, I see his father and I can't help but smile. When I need counsel over a troubling matter, I talk to Ralph Stoddard in my head. He always reassures me my choices are the best choices.

We clap when the curtain lifts and the dancers take their places on the stage. It occurs to me that Mira's painting *The Acceptance* is also like a stage set, with the lead in front and the minor players in the background. It hangs in our bedroom.

I kept in touch with Pavel, Petra's friend. He's now the director of the History Department at Charles University. He wrote to tell me the Hitzig family was sent to a camp called Terezin in 1942, despite Mr. Hitzig's belief that his business dealings with the Germans would save his family from death. Mr. Hitzig couldn't or didn't want to understand that his people, who employed thousands of Czechs in their businesses and contributed so much to the arts, could be considered an inferior race. Terezin became home to a hundred and forty thousand Jews. Pavel found out through a number of sources that while Petra was there she began encouraging the children to draw. She scrounged and begged for pencils, paper, chalk, cardboard—anything the children could use to draw a happy return home, a favorite birthday, what Heaven was like, a fantasy garden they would like to create. Only a small number of those children escaped the gas chamber, but for all of them, Petra provided paradise through imagination for a short time. Eventually, she, along with her family, were sent to Auschwitz. I think of her often, much to my surprise. She was fragile but sweet, and when the time came, she was brave.

I sent a postcard to Josephine Benoit's gallery a few months after I returned home. In the short time I spent with her, I came to believe she cared for her artists more than she cared for money. The postcard was returned with a *no addressee known stamp*. I assumed she and her sister had returned to Martinique safely before the start of the Second World War. But when I heard four years ago on All India Radio that Mira Novak's work was being installed permanently at the National Gallery in New Delhi, I knew Jo had had something to do with it. I took Indira to see the exhibit and told her about my friend, the painter. I told her about Mira's belief in her art, in India, in her conviction that only by seeing the world do we learn to see ourselves. Indira had taken my hand and squeezed. When we got home, she told Edward and me that her life and dance were one, that Mira's story had decided it. I'd wrapped my arms around her, around Indira.

Edward learned through his connections that Whitney had divorced Paolo in Florence. She'd married a wealthy American, a widower with two children, and finally persuaded her father to settle his fortune on her. I imagine Paolo continued to duplicate master paintings for commissions, pieces that would hang in the homes of the nouveau riche, the wives of whom he would most likely bed.

At night, I sometimes look up at *The Acceptance* and think of her.

"Hello, Mira," I whisper.

* * * * *

Acknowledgments

Usually, I start out by thanking my publishing team. This time, I'd like to acknowledge the thousands of readers who graciously write to me or comment on social media how the novels helped them through a difficult time in their life or gave them a more complete understanding of the country of my birth. I'd like to recognize the more than nine hundred book clubs and libraries that have kindly invited me to talk about my ten-year writing journey; the hundreds of podcasters, bloggers and journalists who rightly want to debunk the idea of overnight success (my debut, *The Henna Artist*, took ten years); and the many colleges, alumni associations and women's organizations that know there is no age limit for creative output. Without these champions and their ongoing loyalty, my writing career would not exist. I am humbly indebted to them.

Now for the folks you may never meet, the ones who work so hard behind the scenes to place books in your hands—books that arouse curiosity, broaden understanding, introduce new worlds and generate heart-pounding excitement. If you do meet them, you'll see the fire in their eyes that says, "You've gotta read this!" There's my insightful agent, Margaret Sutherland Brown, of Folio Literary Management and senior editor April Osborn at MIRA. Harlequin/HarperCollins' Loriana Sacilotto,

Margaret Marbury O'Neill, Heather Connor, Nicole Brebner, Laura Gianino, Ashley McDonald and Lindsey Reeder all have a hand in making my books shine.

For *Six Days in Bombay*, I traveled to the cities I wrote about—Istanbul, Prague, Florence, Paris, London and Bombay (I still call it Bombay as I did growing up in Rajasthan; it wasn't renamed Mumbai until 1995.). In each city, I relied on the expertise of historians, artists, teachers, archivists and librarians to understand the climate of 1937, the interwar period when resistance movements were bubbling under the surface throughout Europe and India.

Dr. Martina Klicperová, research scholar at the Czech Academy of Sciences, took me on a walking tour of Prague, pointing out political and cultural landmarks important to the understanding of the interwar period. She also reviewed my final draft for accuracy. Igor Lukes, professor of history and international relations at Boston University, shared relevant information and introduced me to Martina, who in turn introduced me to the learned nonagenarian Ivo Feierabend, professor emeritus at San Diego State University. Vadam Rhoads was a fascinating tour guide of Prague's 1930s Art Deco architecture. Each expert contributed to my knowledge of the political and economic concerns of Czechs in 1937.

In Florence, Dr. Ermelinda Campani, director of Stanford University's Bing Overseas Studies Program in Florence (which I attended in 1978), explained the reasons for Mussolini's popularity in the '30s, adding relevant anecdotes from her own family. Art historian Samuele Magri, whose extensive knowledge extends to 1930s couture, architecture and culture, treated me to an enlightening walking tour of Florence. Who knew that Ferragamo's famous wedge heel was a consequence of Mussolini's invasion of Ethiopia and the subsequent sanctions imposed by the League of Nations? Samuele, that's who! My father's extensive contacts led to a chain of Italian pundits: Dr. Gettu, Dr.

Coppala, Dr. Collepardi, Professor Rod Jones, Saverio Spadea and Federica Giacobbe. I'm grateful to them all.

Professor of history at Santa Clara University Dr. Naomi Andrews told me about the progressive Naral sisters from Martinique who held political and cultural salons in 1930s Paris. The character of Josephine is inspired by them. Photographer and friend Meredith Mullins kindly connected me to the generous Adrian Leeds in Paris, whose assistant Patty Sadauskas put me in touch with her archivist friend Claire Khe. Claire made the 1937 Parisian art scene come alive. She sent me information about the world of Man Ray, André Breton, Fernand Léger, and other surrealist and cubist painters as well as photos of 1930s Montparnasse, period magazines and Paris's robust café scene. I had the good fortune of sharing an author talk with the delightful Cara Black for Adrian's expat book club in Paris. @bookswithishika hosted me at Penelope Fletcher's Red Wheelbarrow Bookstore. Zara Faridany of the Wellesley Club of Paris (which has adopted me) hosted me at her stunning apartment along with Sally Katz, Pamela Boulet, Ellen Maycock, Margaret Peyrard, Kathleen de Carbuccia and Molly Cyr, my new besties.

I spent several days in London's Chelsea neighborhood, St. James's Park and Piccadilly Circus to walk in Sona's footsteps. Luckily, a plethora of literature, video footage, magazines and movies about 1937 England helped supplement my notes of the period.

In 2019, I went to Istanbul and Bombay. I wandered the alleys of the Grand Bazaar, sampling the flavor of the city and its Turkish fare. I'm from northern India and had never been to the south until five years ago. I fell in love with Bombay, which was a much smaller city in 1937, more manageable and accessible, making it possible for our protagonist, Sona, to walk the streets at night without fear. Numerous literature regarding mounting protests, rallies and riots by Indians against their British oppressors informed my account of 1930s Bombay.

While in Europe, I had the pleasure of meeting some of my foreign publishers, who hosted me with fanfare. Julia LeLoup, Claire Deslandes, Etienne Chauvard, Marine Charoy, Margaux Mallet, Camille Corso are my superteam at Éditions Bragelonne. They couldn't wait to share their gorgeous cover for my third novel, *The Perfumist of Paris*, which they were about to release. At the Turin International Book Fair, Daniela Pagani and Sabine Schultz showed me how much love my Italian publisher, Neri Pozza, gives my books. Serena Stent, Darren Shoffren, Kate Harvie and publicist Debbie Elliott took me to an incredible lunch overlooking the Thames, courtesy of Harper360, my UK publisher. In Barcelona, I met the charming Mathilde Sommeregger, Susana Herman and Silvia Bastos of Editrends/Ediciones Maeva, my Spanish publisher.

Bonuses in Barcelona included lunch at the home of author Ana Briongos and her husband, Tony, and meeting author (and now friend) Donna Freitas, who read an early version of this novel and gave me brilliant notes.

My brother Madhup Joshi improved this novel immensely by giving me a great idea that propelled the story forward when I was stuck. My brother Piyush hosted me on my 2019 trip to Istanbul and Bombay. Thank you, brothers! My father reads all my novels and is always ready, willing and able to find pertinent experts. Love you, Dad! My Indian posse, my neighbors Gratia and AJ, and my assistant, Sara Oliver, provided emotional support when I was lost. Finally, my love, Bradley Owens, who gave me the nudge to become a full-time writer, gets enormous credit for this novel, my previous novels and any future novels I'll write.

Author's Note

The concept of identity fascinates me. I came with my family to the United States from India when I was nine. Until then, I had known only Indian people, Indian food and Indian customs. The moment I stepped on American soil, I was enchanted. America was new, exciting. I quickly picked up American English (so different from the British English I'd been taught by the Catholic nuns in India), American dress and American culture. It didn't take me long to identify as American instead of Indian. But my otherness followed me everywhere. My favorite food was Indian. I loved Indian jewelry and my mother's silk saris. And I bristled when anyone criticized India. So which was I: American or Indian? And which country did I owe my loyalty to? Could I be split on that score and still be patriotic to both?

In this novel, my protagonist also struggles with her identity: Sona is Anglo-Indian, the product of an English father and a Hindu mother. Such a union was more acceptable, encouraged even, when the British first came to India without wives and needed companionship. However, by the late nineteenth century, exclusive British communities had been established, and Eurasian children came to be seen as neither fully English nor fully Indian. They were resented or prized or manipulated to benefit the British Raj.

As one of those in-betweens, Sona is torn. She sympathizes with India's fight for independence from the British. At the same time, she takes advantage of her British blood—better pay, better education, better job. But in 1937, the setting of the novel, political tensions are high and the tide is turning against the British. Sona, like some other Anglo-Indians, is beginning to be seen as the other, the enemy. Which identity will she choose? Which one is she allowed to claim as hers?

In 2019, I traveled to India and visited the National Gallery of Modern Art in Delhi to see the work of Amrita Sher-Gil, a painter who never seemed to grapple with her identity. Her mother was Hungarian Jewish and her father was an Indian aristocrat. Amrita was a prodigy, indulged by her wealthy parents. She studied and painted for several formative years in Paris, becoming the youngest member admitted to the prestigious Paris Salon in 1933. Ultimately, she felt the pull of her father's birth country and went to paint in India. She applied the avant-garde techniques she'd learned in Europe to her paintings of Indian village life. These she thought might have been her best work. We'll never know how far her talent could have taken her because she died quite suddenly in 1941. She was twenty-eight.

What made Amrita different from Sona and me? I wondered. How was she able to move so easily in both cultures? I've taken liberties in exploring the answer to those questions by loosely basing the character of Mira Novak on Amrita. The fictional Mira has a Czech father and an Indian mother. Like Amrita, she's a painter. She's flamboyant, sexually fluid, political, outspoken, talented and utterly charming.

In many respects, Amrita Sher-Gil's life closely resembles the inimitable Frida Kahlo's. Kahlo's parentage was also *half-half*, a Mexican mother and a German father, and she was free-spirited and fierce. Yet, while Amrita is recognized in today's elite art world, she is not a household name like Frida Kahlo. Had Amrita lived longer, she might have gained recognition not simply as an Indian painter or a female painter but as a global phenomenon.

Amrita Sher-Gil is my inspiration for this novel, and it's important to me that she and her work are not forgotten. It's my way of reclaiming the Indian part of my identity.

It's also important to me that the work of women—whether it's in the world of art, science, music, math or education—be acknowledged as avidly, as intensely, as passionately and as widely as the work of men.

About the Author

Born in India and raised in the US since she was nine, ALKA JOSHI has a BA from Stanford University and an MFA from California College of Arts. Joshi's debut novel, *The Henna Artist*, immediately became a New York Times bestseller, a Reese Witherspoon Book Club pick, was long-listed for the Center for Fiction First Novel Prize and is in development as a TV series. In 2023, Joshi was selected for the Forbes 50 Over 50 List, celebrating women who are shattering age and gender norms across all sectors of the American economy and culture. *Six Days in Bombay* is her fourth novel.

ALSO BY ALKA JOSHI

The Jaipur Trilogy

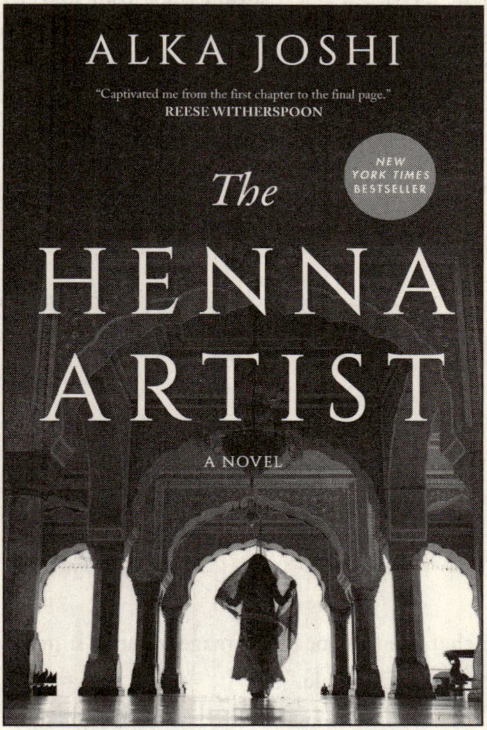

Praise for *The Henna Artist*

"Eloquent and moving… Joshi masterfully balances a yearning for self-discovery with the need for familial love."

—*Publishers Weekly*

"Rich in detail and bright with tastes and textures, *The Henna Artist* is a fabulous glimpse into Indian culture of the 1950s."

—*BookPage*, starred review

"Reading *The Henna Artist* is like travelling in a car that is going at just the right speed. At times, author Alka Joshi stops to point out sights and scenes on the way. At other times, she revs up the story and you find yourself on a thrilling ride to an unknown destination."

—*The Week*

"Lakshmi Shastri… empowers me."

—Freida Pinto, Actor

"Joshi has constructed a bewitching glimpse into the past with a tough heroine well worth cheering on."

—*Booklist*

"An entertaining debut about an important theme—balancing family with personal ambition—that allows readers to escape into a fantasy teeming with sensory pleasure."

—*San Francisco Chronicle*

"Vibrant characters, evocative imagery, and sumptuous prose create an unforgettable tale."

—*Christian Science Monitor*

"Romantic, old-time Rajasthan leaps to life… I can hardly wait for Alka Joshi's next masterpiece."

—Sujata Massey, internationally bestselling author of *The Widows of Malabar Hill*

"Fantastic, so evocative and beautiful and full of life and light… and deeply satisfying in its storytelling."

—Leah Franqui, author of *America for Beginners*

"Read this book slowly and savor it: Every page is rich with intricate pleasures for both the mind and the heart."

—Anita Amirrezvani, author of *The Blood of Flowers*

"Bold, ambitious, beautifully written… The broad cast of characters will etch themselves into your psyche."

—Tom Barbash, author of *Stay Up with Me*

Praise for *The Secret-Keeper of Jaipur*

"Alka Joshi is a master storyteller."

—Christy Lefteri, author, *The Beekeeper of Aleppo* and *Songbirds*

"An applause-worthy encore."

—*Booklist*

"An engaging and powerful story."

—Pam Jenoff, author, *The Lost Girls of Paris*

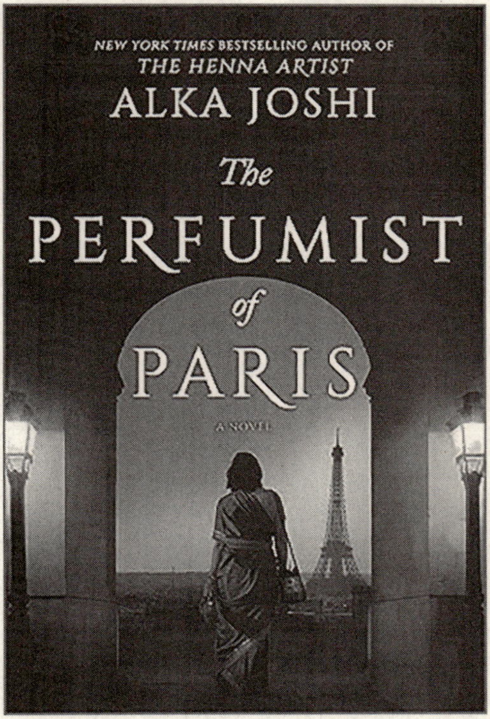

Praise for *The Perfumist of Paris*

"[A] sensory reading experience… Complex, intelligent, and emotionally charged."

—Sarah Penner, *New York Times* bestselling author of *The Lost Apothecary*

"An absolutely luscious and unforgettable read."

—Meg Waite Clayton, *New York Times* bestselling author of *The Postmistress of Paris*

HarperCollins *Publishers* India

At HarperCollins India, we believe in telling the best stories and finding the widest readership for our books in every format possible. We started publishing in 1992; a great deal has changed since then, but what has remained constant is the passion with which our authors write their books, the love with which readers receive them, and the sheer joy and excitement that we as publishers feel in being a part of the publishing process.

Over the years, we've had the pleasure of publishing some of the finest writing from the subcontinent and around the world, including several award-winning titles and some of the biggest bestsellers in India's publishing history. But nothing has meant more to us than the fact that millions of people have read the books we published, and that somewhere, a book of ours might have made a difference.

As we look to the future, we go back to that one word—a word which has been a driving force for us all these years.

Read.

Harper Collins · 4th · HARPER FICTION · HARPER NON-FICTION · HARPER BUSINESS · HCCB HARPERCOLLINS CHILDREN'S BOOKS

HARPER DESIGN · Harper Sport · HARPER PERENNIAL · HARPER VANTAGE · हार्पर हिन्दी · BOOKTOPUS